Big Night Out

Welcome to your Big Night Out – and the drinks are on us. Inside you'll find cocktail recipes to get you in the party mood, song lists to create the perfect atmosphere, short stories to transport you on a night out to remember . . . and, just to make sure you *do* remember, there are even hangover cures for when the party ends.

And while you're painting the town red, you'll also be raising money for the charity War Child, which helps children around the world whose lives have been torn apart by war. As if you needed any more encouragement to have a night on the tiles with the rich and famous . . .

Praise for the UK edition of *Big Night Out*:

'A star-studded collection of stories and tips donated by writers and celebs to help raise money for the War Child charity. If you only pack one book this summer, make sure it's this. Five stars.' – *Company*

'The essential night-to-remember guide . . . grab your girlfriends and have a ball.' – *Cosmopolitan*

'*Big Night Out* is the perfect dip in, dip out, holiday read. It's brimming with fab short stories . . . ' – *New Woman*

Big Night Out

Edited by
Jessica Adams,
Maggie Alderson,
Nick Earls &
Imogen Edwards-Jones

PENGUIN BOOKS

Further information about this book may be found at www.girlsnightin.org

Penguin Books

Published by the Penguin Group
Penguin Books Australia Ltd
250 Camberwell Road
Camberwell, Victoria 3124, Australia
Penguin Books Ltd
80 Strand, London WC2R 0RL, England
Penguin Putnam Inc.
375 Hudson Street, New York, New York 10014, USA
Penguin Books, a division of Pearson Canada
10 Alcorn Avenue, Toronto, Ontario, Canada, M4V 3B2
Penguin Books (N.Z.) Ltd
Cnr Rosedale and Airborne Roads, Albany, Auckland, New Zealand
Penguin Books (South Africa) (Pty) Ltd
24 Sturdee Avenue, Rosebank, Johannesburg 2196, South Africa
Penguin Books India (P) Ltd
11, Community Centre, Panchsheel Park, New Delhi 110 017, India

First published by Penguin Books Australia 2002

1 3 5 7 9 10 8 6 4 2

Cover and text design by Nikki Townsend, Penguin Design Studio
Typeset in ITC Galliard by Post Pre-press Group, Brisbane, Queensland
Printed and bound in Australia by McPherson's Printing Group,
Maryborough, Victoria

National Library of Australia
Cataloguing-in-Publication data:

Big night out.

ISBN 0 14 300023 3.

1. Short stories, English. 2. Short stories, Australian.
I. Adams, Jessica. (Series: Girls' night in, 3).

823.0108

www.penguin.com.au

Contents

Additional illustrations by Anna Johnson

Neil Morrissey &
Hugo Speer

Foreword

This is the third in a series of fabulous books that have included original stories by pretty much anyone worth reading. But it's not just a good read – the royalties for this book will go to the charity War Child to assist children in war zones around the world.

The atrocities of September 11th were a terrible reminder, if any were needed, of the divided and violent world we live in. They have ushered in an era of unprecedented global instability in which the work of organisations such as War Child could not be more vital.

Conflict is born out of the hatred of adults, but it is invariably children who suffer most. Be it those killed, maimed or orphaned in America or Afghanistan, or the millions who continue to suffer across the world, if we adults do not take an active responsibility for children's wellbeing, the future will offer no more hope than the present.

With the help of initiatives such as *Big Night Out*, War

Child will continue to work towards a more peaceful world. We will intervene in emergency situations wherever appropriate and effective. In the longer term we continue to focus on education and communications, in the firm belief that ignorance is the lifeblood of conflict.

You have in front of you a fine collection of stories, and in buying this book you have contributed to a great cause, because children are the future.

Neil Morrissey, Trustee

Hugo Speer, Patron

Stella McCartney

Introduction

Royalties from every copy of *Big Night Out* go towards War Child's valuable work throughout the world. Part of that work includes providing communication and education projects for children. Education is essential but often inaccessible to children in many places in the world. War Child provides children with safe-play areas and wind-up, battery-free radios, by which they can receive educational programs to continue their schooling wherever they are. The radio also provides health information and news and entertainment, giving children a vital contact with the world outside their immediate surroundings.

So thank you for buying this book – you've just helped these children, and do have a great night out on me.

Stella McCartney

From the Editors

Jessica Adams

Big Night Out is the third book in a series created especially for War Child. It all started over a bottle of wine (or three) and a few notes on the back of a beer mat, and I don't remember the rest, but anyway . . . By the end of 2002, the total money raised from these three books will be over $1.5 million dollars. *Girls' Night In* and *Girls' Night In – Gentlemen By Invitation* were huge bestsellers, and we hope *Big Night Out* will follow suit. It would certainly be a nice reward for me, Maggie Alderson, Imogen Edwards-Jones and Nick Earls, who seem to have spent large chunks of the last twelve months emailing the living hell out of each other. I have great memories of Maggie in her dressing gown in Notting Hill one morning, fast-talking to Kate Moss's agent. I also remember Imogen sitting on comedian Steve Coogan's knee, willing him to give us his favourite Big Night Out songs (he did). Nick Earls fulfilled one of my teenage fantasies by producing a fabulous piece from Go Between Grant McLennan. And as usual, Penguin Australia has made the whole thing look sensational. I should also like to thank Chris Manby and Fiona Walker for starting the whole thing off (twice) and the original *Girls' Night In* girls who came back to help for the third time running. Kathy Lette seems to have been helping us forever. So too do Marian Keyes and Jane Owen, Melody Osunaya and Freya North. Our web site guru James Williams has been indispensable to the success of the books, and we can't thank him enough. At Anglers Lane, I would also like to thank Nessa O'Neill who represents all the things I like about War Child – the dedication, the energy and the craic.

Nick Earls

Well, Jessica got me into this, and once you're in, you're in. Oh, then there was that rather convincing trip to Kosovo in October 2001 to see how some of the money had been spent . . . War Child is the kind of organisation that makes you sleep less so that you can do more. With so much of the money raised spent in the field, and spent carefully to deliver the best possible return, it's the kind of organisation that makes even rather self-focused people (okay, that might be me) want to put time and energy into helping out. I have great admiration for Jessica, Chris and Fiona for getting this started, and I've really appreciated the chance to become part of the team for *Big Night Out*. And also part of the team at the brand new War Child Australia – it's been exciting getting all that started too, and the support from everyone involved has been invaluable in putting together the Australian end of *Big Night Out* – as has the support of Fiona Inglis and all at Curtis Brown Sydney, and publishers, agents and booksellers worldwide. The huge amounts of money raised so far could not have been raised without the enthusiasm of all of these people. It's made a big difference, and we're very grateful. The sale of a few books buys a sack of wheat, a few thousand buys an entire playground. Among other projects, the first two books built dozens of playgrounds in places that had recently been war zones and, as I've had the chance to see in Kosovo, those playgrounds have gone on to become important parts of their communities, and significant in fostering optimism for the future. Let's not stop selling these books until every child in the world is secure, and fed, and has safe access to a good set of monkey bars.

Maggie Alderson

I have been speechless with admiration ever since Jessica told me about the first *Girls' Night In* project and it has been an incredible privilege to be a co-editor on the third book. What an amazing bunch of people are involved with these projects – as contributors, on the editorial side and on the ground with War Child. It brought a major lump to my throat to watch the first news reports of the bombing of Afghan villages and to know that War Child was already on the way there, baking bread for civilians who no longer had homes – not just faceless 'aid workers', but people I had actually met and spent time with as a result of this project. Thanks to all who have made the *Big Night Out* dream a reality: Julie Gibbs, Nikki Townsend and our Australian editors Sophie Ambrose and Saskia Adams – and all at Penguin Australia, for doing everything with grace and style. Jonathan 'J-Lo' Lloyd, Carol Jackson and Tara Wynne at Curtis Brown UK, for reading the small print. All our contributors for their time and inspiration. And to all the PAs, publicists and pals of the famous, whom we have mercilessly harassed in the name of War Child – it's appreciated.

Imogen Edwards-Jones

What a team, what a project, what a fabulous book. Nick Sayers, Lynne Drew, Georgina Hawtrey-Woore and Maxine Hitchcock at HarperCollins deserve particularly large drinks and tasty bar snacks for their continued commitment to this project on its third outing. Their calm in the face of approaching deadlines is laudable, as is their ability to wade through endless emails, and reams of paper when it came to reading and checking all these fine stories and *Big Night Out* serving suggestions. The publicity department deserves a sturdy jug of something strong for all their help with publicising this book. Their enthusiasm and energy for the project has been unsurpassed and their bright ideas amazing. I'd particularly like to thank Fiona McIntosh and Sara Wikner for all their hard work in making this project such a success. But the largest, most deliciously alcoholic round of all probably goes to the lovely Karen Moline, the handsome Perry L. Van Der Meer and the goddess that is Candace Bushnell. For not only have they helped with this fantastic collection for War Child, but they are about to put together one of their own. So thank you. Oh, and my agent – the vaguely attractive Simon Trewin – hasn't been bad either, he's landed us a few award-winning fish on the way. Thanks!

And thanks to . . .

Sophie Cunningham, Stephanie Cabot, Eugenie Furniss, Mary-Anne Harrington, Deborah Schneider, Joely Tonna, Marshall Cullen, War Child Canada, Harriet Evans, Lindsey Jordan, Josephine Fairley, James Topham, Dominic Norman-Taylor, Century, Matthew Wherry, Conville and Walsh, Karin Catt, David 'Davo' Evans, Simon G. Brown, David Smiedt etc., etc.

FOR MORE INFORMATION ON *BIG NIGHT OUT; GIRLS' NIGHT IN;* AND *GIRLS' NIGHT IN, GENTLEMEN BY INVITATION*, PLEASE VISIT WWW.GIRLSNIGHTIN.ORG

War Child Australia is now official! Following the overwhelming success of the *Girls' Night In* series, War Child has set up an office here to make it easier for Australians to be part of its work in providing immediate, effective and practical aid to children affected by war. War Child Australia intends to keep its admin costs to a bare minimum, and to direct as much money as it can towards projects assisting children in places affected by war, such as Rwanda, the Balkans, East Timor and Afghanistan.

If you'd like to help, one excellent way would be to send us a donation (as a cheque or money order payable to War Child Australia) to:

War Child Australia
PO Box 461
TOOWONG QLD 4066

If you'd like to find out more about War Child Australia or to donate online to War Child (through its UK office) please go to www.girlsnightin.org and follow the links.

Thank you!

BiG NiGHT Out

Kaz Cooke

Kate Moss's

Best Ever Good-time Party Dress

'It's a long pale-blue bias-cut dress that John Galliano gave me for my twenty-first birthday. I still wear it and I always have a good time in it. If I was going to wear it tonight I would put it with a pair of strappy silver shoes and my blue Fortuny coat.'

Julian Clary's
All-time Favourite Cocktail
for a Big Night Out

Snowball

Vodka
Advocaat
A twist of lime
Lemonade . . . and a cherry

(I'm a bit hazy on quantities)

Joan Collins's

Never-fail Party Beauty Tips

1. Take a Power Nap: even if it's only ten minutes of closing your eyes you'll feel refreshed and ready for the fray.
2. While lying down, place either cold tea bags or cucumber slices on closed eyes. This reduces puffiness and swelling.
3. Have two outfits to choose from. There's nothing more annoying than if the zipper breaks or the dress makes you look fat. Try the clothes on the day before to make sure.
4. Eat something before you go to the party, then liquor won't hit you so fast. A banana or a few crackers are good.
5. Wear red lipstick – it's the most glamorous cosmetic ever. The great glamour movie stars of the 30s, 40s and 50s all had glowing lips. Think Rita Hayworth, Lana Turner, Hedy Lamarr or Ava Gardner – none of that washed-out look for them!

Marian Keyes

Wishing Carefully

Be careful what you wish for, they say. So when Siobhan came back from Australia with an Aboriginal dreaming bowl and invited us all to place a wish in it, I'm ashamed to say I wished for a fairytale romance. It wasn't the kind of thing I would normally do but I was a bit wounded at the time. Even while I was folding up the note to put in the bowl, I hated Mark for turning me into the sort of person who made such pathetic wishes.

Naturally enough, I told everyone that I'd wished for peace in the Middle East. The only person I told the truth to was Siobhan – who confessed that she already knew, that after everyone had left she'd unfolded the notes and read them all. She was quick to reassure me that I wasn't alone; the person who'd claimed he'd wished for his mother's arthritis to improve had in fact wished for a silver SL320 Merc with many optional extras, including heated leather seats and a CD player.

'It's just a bit of fun,' Siobhan said, but I was keen to

have faith in the future, and hoped it would come true. In a way it did.

Would you believe it, less than a week later I met a man. Not just any man, but a fireman. The job alone was sexy, and he was gorgeous – arms the size of my thighs, huge barrel chest all the better to crush me against. The only thing was . . . he was shorter than I expected firemen to be – but never mind, I was off tall men.

And he was a kind and caring person; only a kind and caring person would put their life at risk entering burning buildings to rescue sleeping children and climbing up trees to bring home beloved cats.

We hit it off, he asked me out, Siobhan smiled proudly from the sidelines as if it was all her doing and suddenly I was in great form. I embarked on the round of shopping and ablutions that a first date calls for and Saturday night couldn't come fast enough.

But on Saturday afternoon my phone rang. It was my hero and he was yawning so hard his jaw cracked. 'I'm sorry, Kate, out on a job last night, just got back, need some sleep, on a shift again tomorrow.'

Another huge big yawn.

What could I say? Huffiness simply wasn't an option – no sniping about freshly done nails, new sandals, having turned down four other invitations and now what was I supposed to do, spend my Saturday night cleaning the bathroom? (Like I'd done every previous Saturday for the past month.) Instead I had to sympathise, even praise, and for the first time I saw the downside of having a boyfriend who saves lives for a living.

We rearranged for Thursday night and he promised he'd be wide awake and full of beans. I came to work on Thursday in my going-out clothes and Mark watched me click-clacking in my high sandals to the photocopier, but said nothing.

But that afternoon – minutes after I'd got back from spending my lunch hour getting my hair blow-dried – my fireman rang. He'd just got home after a fifteen-hour stint dousing a huge conflagration in a rubber goods warehouse.

'I'm sorry, Kate.' A five second yodelly yawn followed. 'I really need some zeds, I'm so sleepy.'

The disappointment was intense and as I thought of my good hair and my inappropriate clothes, I swallowed, braced myself – then went for it.

Brazenly, I said, 'I could come over and keep you company.'

He was shocked. To the core. He made interfering with a fireman's sleep sound like a criminal offence, and as I hung up I suspected I wouldn't be hearing from him again.

But there was no time to be miserable because within days I'd met Charlie – at a party where he walked straight over to me, pointed a finger and said, 'You, babe, are the woman I'm going to marry.'

'What a fool,' Siobhan murmured, and even while one

part of my brain was agreeing with her, another part found his confidence strangely alluring.

'The name's Charlie,' he said. 'Remember it because you'll be screaming it later.'

'I don't think so,' I replied, and he just laughed and said he wouldn't take no for an answer.

Over the next two weeks he pursued me rapaciously and he seemed so sure he'd win me over that in the end he managed to convince me of it too.

When I finally agreed to go out with him he promised he'd show me the best night of my life and I must admit I was intrigued.

First he took me to a party, but he made us leave after fifteen minutes because he was bored, then he took me to a bar which I'd read about but hadn't been to, but we were barely there half an hour before he wanted to be off again. Two more parties and a club followed – he had the shortest attention span of anyone I'd ever met and in a way all that variety was exciting.

There were three or four more nights like that. At the time I thought of myself as glamorous, but now what I remember most is the number of times I had to gulp back the drink which had just arrived, while Charlie eyed the exit and tapped his foot impatiently.

So convincing was Charlie's wide-boy swagger that it took me some time to notice that he was shorter than me. A lot shorter when I wore my boots. And when he couldn't sit through a film – and we're not talking *Dances With*

Wolves or *Heaven's Gate* here, only a normal ninety-minute one – his attention deficit disorder began to annoy me.

Worse still, he always seemed to have a cold and his constant sniffing was driving me mad. *Mad.* As soon as one sniff was over, I was tensing my shoulders in irritation against the next one. Occasionally he sneezed, and he baffled me by treating it like a major disaster.

Then I discovered the cause of the constant sniffing – and the short attention span – when I accidentally walked into his bathroom and found him crouched over the edge of the sink, a rolled up fiver at his nostril.

It wasn't the cocaine itself that shocked me. It was that he was taking it for a Saturday afternoon's shopping. And that he'd been snorting it all this time and he'd never once offered me any. Marching orders were swiftly dispatched, and not even him prostrating himself and swearing that we'd get a video and a Chinese takeaway and stay in for an entire evening made any difference.

The disappointment of Charlie set me back, and I was missing Mark a little too much for my liking, so to take my mind off things I decided to throw a party, which is where I met Owen.

The moment we made eye contact he began to blush. I'd never seen anything like it. It roared up his neck and face like red-hot lava, rushing to the furthest reaches of his head, then kind of 'pinged' on the outer edges of his ears. For some reason I thought of an advertising slogan: Come home to a real fire.

Flustered, he turned around and bumped into a bottle of red wine with such violence it splashed Siobhan's dress and my pale-gold curtains, and the only reason I didn't start shrieking like a termagant was because I felt attracted to him.

Owen was, quite simply, the shyest man I'd ever met, but after the cocaine-fuelled arrogance of Charlie, I liked his self-effacing charm.

And though he was short, he was very good-looking – a neat, handsome little package.

He asked if he could take me for a drink some time and when I said yes, he was so pleased that he knocked over and smashed my good flower vase into smithereens.

Our first date wasn't much better. He came to pick me up, said, 'You've lovely eyes. Even though they're quite close together,' then swept the phone off the wall with such force that it never worked properly again.

I urged myself to give it time, that he would eventually relax with me. But each outing was as bad as the first time – the blush that could be seen from outer space, the stammering compliment that managed to be an insult, then the ceremonial knocking over and breaking of something.

I had to end it with him before he'd destroyed all that I owned.

And into the breach stepped Shane, a friend of Siobhan's youngest brother. He was too young for me but I didn't care. He was cute-looking – another dinky one, actually,

I was having quite a run of short men asking me out – and he was sweet.

He took me to Brittas Bay to fly kites, which might have been fun had he not told me that we were going to an art exhibition and had I not dressed accordingly. Shane claimed to have no memory, no memory at *all* of telling me about the exhibition. Then he raced off down the beach with his big, yellow kite and I almost ended up flat on my back as I chased after him and my four-inch heels sank into the sand.

Eventually the kite-flying torment ended, we went to the pub and the real date began. But within minutes Shane disclosed that he thought: (a) Jack Nicholson and Jack Nicklaus were related; (b) that flour was made from flowers; (c) that the Mona Lisa's real name was Muriel.

At the Muriel bit I sighed heavily; this was awful. And thick and all as he was Shane said, 'You're not really into this, are you, Kate? Some guy wrecked your head, yeah? Siobhan said.'

I sighed again; Siobhan was so indiscreet. But all of a sudden the idea of spilling the beans about Mark to this dim, sympathetic boy was enticing.

'It was great for ages and I don't really know what happened but in the end he just rode roughshod over me.'

'He rode who?' Shane was all indignation.

That was it! But Shane was mad keen to see me again. 'We could go to this exhibition you keep talking about,' he beamed.

Gently I turned him down. I couldn't see him again. He was simply much, much, much too stupid.

Then I was depressed. I'd gone out with so many men and I was still thinking about Mark. I saw him at work but we never spoke. He'd been smiling a bit at me lately – probably because he thought enough time had elapsed for us to start behaving like civilised people again. Well, he could think again.

I squared my shoulders and told myself it would all be fine eventually. I thought the good times had finally arrived when I met a short, clever doctor who kept trying to get me into bed by tugging at my clothes and saying, 'Let me through, I'm a doctor.' It was funny the first time he said it, though not funny enough for me to sleep with him. Quite funny the second time, too. By the fifth time I was worried. Was this what counted as a sense of humour with him? Unfortunately it was and I stopped letting him through.

It was Siobhan who twigged what was happening.

'Hiho,' she greeted me with. 'How are you enjoying your fairytale romance?'

'Still waiting for it,' I said glumly.

'What are you talking about? You're slap-bang in the middle of it. You're Snow White and you're working your way through the seven dwarves.'

I told her she was off her rocker and that I wasn't going to play, but she insisted. 'They've all been very short, haven't they? Haven't they? And their personalities fit. The fireman who couldn't get out of bed? Sleepy, obviously. Charlie the coke-fiend is Sneezy, of course.'

'There wasn't much sneezing, mostly sniffing,' I said, but Siobhan was undeterred.

'Poor shy Owen is an open-and-shut Bashful. Shane is Dopey – the funny thing is that's what his friends call him anyway. And the doctor? Well, Doc, obviously.'

'So which ones haven't I done?' It's impossible to remember the names of all seven of them.

'Grumpy and Happy.'

Mark asked if I'd meet him for a drink after work. With a heavy heart I agreed. It had been five months now, I supposed he was entitled to his stuff back.

But we'd barely sat down when he blurted out, 'I'm sorry, Kate. I was such a grumpy bastard.'

As soon as I heard the word 'grumpy' my heart almost stopped in my chest. But Mark couldn't be Grumpy! He was too tall!

'You were right not to put up with me. I've had plenty of time to think and, Kate, I feel small. I feel so very, very small.'

'Small?' I repeated.

'Small. Tiny.' He held up his thumb and first finger, barely leaving a gap. 'This small.' Then he told me he loved me, that he was miserable without me and asked if there was any chance that I'd take him back.

'I know I don't deserve it.' He hung his head. 'But if

you'd give me just one chance I'll make it up to you and
I'll do everything I can to make you happy. If you come
back to me, Kate, I'll be happy. I'll be so happy.'

IT HAD CLEARLY BEEN A BIG MISTAKE
ALLOWING ERIC OUT ON HIS OWN AGAIN

Glen Baxter

Eric

Adam Spencer

The Songs That Guys Play and What They _Really_ Mean

- **Rolling Stones** – This guy probably hasn't had a good date since 1980 . . . about the same time the Rolling Stones wrote their last good song.
- **Enrique Iglesias** – Notice that when your date plays really sexy music he turns the lights down so low you can't see his face anymore . . . there's a reason for this.
- **Geri Halliwell** – If you think the words to her songs aren't original, it's because she doesn't write them. This guy's smooth lines aren't original either – two songwriters in Sweden came up with all of it. Even the 'Hey, your hair looks great' wasn't his.
- **Kenny G** – Ah, the old elevator music. Well, if spending all night just going up and down, up and down and occasionally stopping is your idea of a good time, you've found the guy for you.
- **Limp Bizkit** – Need I say more?

- **Tchaikovsky's 1812 Overture** – A bit predictable, but hey, it goes for more than four minutes and there are cannons at the end.
- **Britney Spears** – Head straight for the door, totally disgusted that he'd even suggest you'd find this romantic. Guaranteed to leave him thinking Oops I Did It Again.
- **Obscure American college Indie band you've never heard of** – The old 'impress her with how trendy and underground I am'. Call his bluff – 'Yeah they're cool, but they're no Yo La Tengo' is a good start.
- **Milli Vanilli** – Well, at least this guy is genuine and trustworthy.
- **NSYNC** – The problem here is that if you start making out at a nightclub, you'll suddenly find that there are five other guys fully choreographed moving as one.
- **Village People** – You're destined to end up just being friends, but he'll be keen to meet your brother.

David James's
Top Ten Hits

1. **'Planet Rock' – Afrika Bambaataa & the SoulSonic Force**

   The guys on this track were like gods to me when I was young. Afrika Bambaataa steered the gangland mentality away from violence and into a whole new music scene. The composition on this track and the rapping are so superb and, even though my taste in music is very broad, this track had a big effect on me and is one of the key reasons why I now have such a big interest in hip-hop.

2. **'Good Vibrations' – The Beach Boys**

   This is a song which I didn't take much notice of at first, but on hearing it again it really did something for me. I actually listened to it properly and realised that the composition is quite phenomenal. (When I was younger my grandmother played the piano in church and I used to play the cello, so I appreciate good song composition.) For a pop song there is such depth to this track – it's so outstanding that it almost seems out of place in pop-music history. It's a song that I can listen to over and over again in the car.

3. **'Four Seasons' – Vivaldi, Nigel Kennedy**
I do have a taste for classical music and this is awesome music! It is very difficult to stipulate one season from the other as being my favourite. It's such an energetic piece of music and Nigel Kennedy's interpretation is so inspiring, it blows all other variations out of the water.

4. **'No Woman No Cry' – Bob Marley**
I chose this song as it is so soothing. Bob Marley is such a fantastic artist. I'm not really an emotional guy but this is such a moving song, and in everyone's top ten there has to be a caring or moving kind of song. When I was young my dad was living in Jamaica and if I heard this song it really made me want to be there too, eating cornmeal porridge. Definitely a 'wish you were here' song for me.

5. **'Californication' – Red Hot Chilli Peppers**
When I first saw the video for this song I thought it was a bit cheesy and I think I had my anti-pop-music head on. The second time I heard it, it dawned on me how absolutely fantastic it is. The lyrics describe California to a T. Having had two holidays there in the last two years and having seen and heard what I did while there, the song totally sums up the state very well. Such a catchy song.

6. **'Going Underground' – The Jam**

   The drums and the bass line are awesome on this track. I've always really liked Paul Weller's lyrics too, they can be so profound. He's such a versatile performer.

7. **'Happy Birthday' – Altered Images**

   The great 'happy birthday' song not sung just at birthdays. This was (and still is) a great party song in the 1980s that made me chuckle.

8. **'Walking on the Moon' – The Police**

   I have a very profound memory of this song which is engrained on my brain. I was on an England under-21s tour to Toulon and on one occasion we had an evening off. We went for a walk down to the harbour and someone in a bar was doing a live rendition of this song. It was such a great performance that it made me go out and buy the Police album!

9. **'Staying Alive' – Bee Gees**

   I remember the video to this song so well, with them singing on a disused film set with a deserted train track. It's such an uplifting song and a great mood enhancer. Top song for a big night out.

10. **'Ashes to Ashes' – David Bowie**

    I think I noticed the video first with this song. David in his psychedelic all-in-one. I chose this track because I find it soothingly hypnotic.

Nick Earls

The Italian Job

Mal mentions the implant on our way out of the campus, just as he's taking a loose-toothed old leer at a couple of girls by the roadside.

'They don't wear much these days' is more the kind of remark I'd expected, but he used that one up on the way in. Besides, they haven't worn much for decades, and the look on Mal's face suggests he's known all along.

'Those were the days,' he says, though I'd rather he didn't. 'The days when nature could take its course. Before I got the pump-action equipment for the potency issue. Dunno that I mentioned that before.'

He shuffles in his seat, rearranges his belt as if it's constricting something. I wish he wouldn't.

This is the second day of our association, and the self-disclosure is hitting a new high. Why is he telling me? Why is he leering at that girl and then staring straight ahead and grinding his old choppers and telling me that, a few years ago, nature went missing and he went for the deluxe top-of-the-range pump-uppable penile implant instead?

'Italian she is. She's a beauty,' he says, like a man who carries his favourite sports car in his pants. His old hands are all knuckles and veins, and he grips the wheel a little harder as the Maxi Taxi hits a speed bump. 'Not that —'

And that's when I stop him and say, 'I'm sorry, but do you tell everyone this?' And is it really a 'she' for that matter?

'Don't have a lot of fares for two full days, love. Breaking new ground for me, this is. Anyway, I've been listening to you on the radio. I didn't think you'd be bothered. You talk about that kind of stuff, don't you? In your act? I got the impression it could get a bit blue sometimes, for a lady. That's what comes through in your interviews.'

'I guess, but no more than anyone else's. Lady or otherwise. I'm a comedian and, well, have you seen a standard-issue non-sports penis lately? They're pretty funny-looking. They're fair game for comedy. There's a reason for pants, you know.'

'That's not bad.' He gives half a smile, and about a quarter of a laugh. 'Do you use that line? The pants line?'

'Occasionally.'

So we're like co-conspirators now, it seems. After two days of this, we've got our van talk going, and then I go and handle the public stuff every so often for fifteen minutes at a time (at the most), doing radio interviews all over town. Mal knows that in the van he gets the quieter me that's perhaps even taciturn, and the problem is that that looks like intimacy compared to the radio version (which is up, up, always up). He doesn't know that van time is down time. I think, from his perspective, I'm a little more thoughtful in here, away from the razzamatazz (his term).

So he talks. I get his views on lots of things – politics (state and federal), the importance of roughage and a good breakfast, his penis and the war. That's how this goes. Mal, me and his cab-company van on day two of our road movie around the streets of Perth.

Yesterday, day one of the Festival publicist's illness, brought us together. They hired Mal for the day – some well-intentioned volunteer did – to get me around from interview to interview. Then one day became two, and here we are. They said that the only available festival person didn't have a car or a licence, but she could come with us, if I'd like, to shoot trouble should trouble come along. And I said No, of course, since you don't want to look like a complete prima donna who can't help herself.

I make mistakes like that all the time. We could have done with some carless girl these past two days, some carless girl without a blue stand-up act. With her around the implant wouldn't have rated a mention. We would just have made do with stories of disease and death, and complaints about young people nowadays, and all of that.

Actually, Mal hasn't been so bad with youngster complaints. He's in favour of the dress code, for a start. And disease has worked him over good and proper, poor bastard, and left him close to alone in the world. (There's a son over east, but they don't get on: Matthew, two kids, both boys, both at primary school.) I've become too used to cabbies who play shock-jock talkback and believe it, but they aren't all like that. That's the lesson I should learn from Mal. Weeks of touring makes you shut down possibilities and expect cliché, that's my excuse.

We got the obvious details behind us early – the fact that I'm in town for the Perth Festival, that I'm playing a venue called the Watershed, that I'm talking the place up on radio based only on the picture in the program, that I'm appearing on the telethon tonight, that it's much hotter than it was in Christchurch two days ago and, yes, I make a living out of this and, no, I don't do exactly the same routine every night, not exactly, but . . .

I liked the publicist. She did make the same inane remark about Christchurch, but that's okay. Everyone's entitled to a few of those. Rebecca, her name was. Or was it? Someone in the Festival office was called Rebecca. I met them all in one go.

But I'm with Mal now, cruising van-high through the traffic from one interview to another. Mal, in his sky-blue cab-company shirt that's ironed sternly but not well and his navy Sansabelt pants, getting me places and then crunching the seat back to read his battered paperback of *Silence of the Lambs*, or stepping out of the van for a smoke or to go in search of a toilet. The prostate started getting talked about midafternoon on day one, so it's old news now. I thought it only got a mention because it had to be factored in. There's no excuse for the penis.

Mal and disease are long-time companions. Skin cancer

has cost him one ear and he lost two fingers in a sawmill when he was fourteen, so his opening line to me was, 'Sorry about the ear and the fingers, love, but the company's downsizing.' He gave me a big wink and he laughed, and I laughed too though I felt a bit guilty about it, and he said, 'Thought you'd like that one. You're one of them comedians, aren't you? Here for that thing? The festival?'

And we got into the van and I handed him the itinerary and he went, 'Hang on a tick, that's the wrong eye.' I stopped the laugh as quickly as I could. It wasn't a joke this time. He said that one of his eyes has been out for ages, but the other one's fine for distance, and he quoted me the law on driving and vision. I think he's had to do that a few times.

So, he has one eye, one ear and eight fingers and he said, 'I know, love, if it keeps going there'll only be half of me left. It's like there could be some other fella somewhere made up of my spare bits . . .'

Another laugh, another joke. By lunchtime on the first day I was reading them better. Mal did most of the talking. I talk for a living and he drives, so his talk was recreational and he willingly kept it running most of the time. Mal lives alone, and he probably talks in the house. To the cat, to the silences.

So I heard it all. Pig shooting, for instance, and I've never had a conversation about pig shooting before. Mal didn't mind shooting the odd feral pig, till the shooting eye went and he picked up a case of the shakes. So, the feral pigs are safe now and, instead of a weekend out shooting them every few months, he drives the Maxi Taxi six days a week every week. He's got some regulars, most of them wheelies (his term) since he's fitted out for wheelchair access at the back, or old people booked in each pension day for a trip to the shops.

And his wife died a few years ago, but it took a long time coming.

Mal's stories lurch, one into the next, and the expression on his face doesn't change much. He looks ahead into the traffic, eases from one lane to another, tells me things and his craggy face and pale eyes hardly shift with the topic. He's had skin cancers on his lips, too, seared off surgically from the look of it.

For hours yesterday I blocked it out, batted it back with the right sounds and not much more. But then I realised it'd be rude to forget his son's name for a fourth time (Matthew . . . Matthew . . .), and that this was my chance to improve my record as a listener. I'm not one of the world's great listeners. I'm a better talker, and that's not always the best way to be.

The van's nine years, eleven months and two weeks old, he told me, and that means it has two more weeks to go. 'They reckon if I stay on till they pension her off I'm up for a limo next, but I've heard that kind of talk before.' And I'm sure he has. Don't we all hear that kind of talk often enough, one way or another?

We're back in the CBD now, our second campus interview of the day behind us, and two at the ABC up next.

Today, we've had Korea as the forgotten war and,

until just now, Mal's penis as the forgotten penis. But his impotence is an official war-caused disability, so he says he got the new one on the Repat.

What the hell. It's question time. 'Okay, war-caused disability . . .' How can this pass without clarification? 'Was your penis actually involved in the Korean War?'

'Well, it was there,' he says. 'And it had its moments away from the front line. But, no, I got diabetes. It's why the eye's bung as well. And the diabetes went down as war-caused. And the diabetes gave me the Mister Floppy, so there you go. The taxpayer spots me the Italian job. Fair's fair, hey? Of course, then Hazel died not so long after. Well, she had the first stroke and it was downhill from there for the next couple of years. Sometimes I pump it up when I'm bored, just to see if it's still going.' He pauses, as if it's for reflection, but I'm not sure which bit he's reflecting on. He moves his hands restlessly around on the wheel. 'Did you know that the penis is actually made up of three tubes running in parallel?'

'I think I was aware of that, yes.'

He taps the wheel, hums along with the radio, which is playing 'Calendar Girl'. He clears his throat, checks his mirrors and changes lane needlessly.

And I want to say, 'Mal, did you take drugs at that campus while I was doing the last interview?' but he's lonely. That's what this is, I think. He's lonely and he's heard me use the word penis playfully on radio, several times. Penis and euphemisms, but with Mal we're going to keep it medical, I think.

'They gave me pictures of it,' he says. 'Diagrams. There's more of your penis on the inside than you'd think. So, I've got a couple of excellent pump-up tubes courtesy of the Repat, and one that's mine but it's buggered up by its own prostate. It's ironic really. Well, not so much ironic as bloody unfortunate. But life's like that. It gets to a point where irony doesn't play such a part, but misfortune's pretty much behind most things. How's that for philosophy, love? I got the new equipment, then the prostate business only came along in the past couple of years.'

So I ask him how it works, and he tells me. I don't want to know, but Mal needs to talk. Why couldn't I have worked that out back at roughage? Why couldn't this be a discussion about glycemic indices? A dietician explained all that to me once. I'm sure I could carry my half of a conversation about that in any taxi in the world.

I imagine Mal at home, by himself in the evenings, eating without an appetite, watching TV he isn't interested in, gazing at the screen and talking as though there might be someone there to hear him. I could be wrong, but it's hard not to see his evenings that way.

So I get to hear about the groin reservoir, the pump mechanism, the valves, the long slow squeeze to bring it down after action. 'Sophisticated plumbing', he calls it, because that way we can both set aside the idea that it's actually his penis.

We tune in to the ABC so that I can listen to the person I'm talking to next. He's interviewing the state

Education Minister about class sizes and keeping small schools open in remote areas.

'Does a bit of politics,' Mal says. 'There's a lot of interviews on this show. The Premier's got a regular spot on Mondays. And there's a bit of artsy stuff. He seems like a nice enough fella, the guy who does it.'

'And who listens?'

'Oh, a mixture of people. Thirty-something and up, I suppose. People in the car on the way home from work.'

'Who needs a publicist, Mal? This is exactly the conversation I'd be having with some skinny girl in black if she hadn't got sick.'

And Mal says hmmm and gives a bit of a smile. 'Publicist, hey? All part of the service.'

I can see the ABC now, or at least the ABC logo on a building ahead of us, with the city to our left, and the river to our right.

'And you've told that fettuccine story twice today,' he says, as if I've misbehaved and he might have caught me out. 'The one about the spitting. Twice out of the three interviews I've been able to listen to. You told it at the uni, and you told it to the fella before that.'

'Yeah, that's the job, Mal: go about in public armed with a range of funny stories about yourself and give them a run when the chance arises. That's the real punishment for the publicist, staying chirpy through twenty tellings of the same story. They learn to tune out, I think. Hopefully I sounded charming both times. And spontaneous, hopefully that too.'

He nods. We turn left, and then right, and then park at a meter just near the studio.

'Spontaneous, hey?' he says. 'Yeah, you had me fooled. I thought you must have forgotten it in between.'

'Like I said, it's the job. You could ask me just about any question now and I should be able to get around to that story as the answer if I want to.'

'Okay, who's the only woman to have won Nobel Prizes in two different disciplines?'

'I was thinking more of questions people might actually ask me.'

'All right.' He clears his throat, ready for a fresh start. 'So, Meg, how are you finding Perth so far? What are your highlights?'

'I'm having a great time, Mal. I'm always happy to come to Perth, and it's a real bonus to be here at Festival time. It's a great chance to see some things you otherwise never will and to see an old friend or two in action. There's the band Women in Docs, for instance. They've been friends of mine for a while. I'd seen them play a few times and they'd seen me a few times before we actually met in Townsville a couple of years ago. I went up and introduced myself to them after the show, and we finally had the chance to talk. We might have exchanged a couple of emails before then, but that was it. So I went out to get something to eat with them, and Roz got a bit hyper about us finally meeting and she spat a piece of fettuccine alfredo onto my arm. And we got past that, of course, but then half an hour later I was back next to her and she was still eating and she said, "I can't believe we just met and I spat pasta at you." So I laughed and my head must have leaned back, and Roz laughed and a piece of fettuccine flew up my left nostril. So it's always a highlight catching up with them, particularly if Roz is eating. And the other highlight'd be Mal, of course. Mal's the guy who looks after the limo and keeps everything running smoothly, publicity-wise.'

He nods, as though there's careful assessment of the performance going on. 'That's good,' he says. 'You're good. It sounded like it just came off the top of your head, and you finished up with a nice bit of flattery, for me and the Maxi.'

'Charm and spontaneity, that's what I promised. And you smiled while I was telling the story, even though it was your third time listening to it today.'

'Did it happen? The fettuccine spitting?'

'Yeah. Yeah, it did. Just like that. I'm not so manipulative I make up my anecdotes from scratch. Well, it was pretty much like that. And who knows, in about seventeen minutes from now I could be giving it another run. I've got the local station here first, which'll be after the news, then I've got one from a tardis – a booth you go to when you do ABC stations in other places. It's for somewhere down south, I think. Somewhere else anyway. So I could be a while.'

'No worries. Might get out and stretch the legs.'

It's Broome, in fact, so not down south at all. I borrow a pen, I circle the interviewers' names on the itinerary and I leave Mal there, easing himself out of the cab and onto the road, book and cigarettes in hand, scowling at the traffic that's onto him quickly.

And in the first interview I tell the story just the way I did in the van – including the Mal parts – but when it's all done and I'm back outside he's still in the café next door and he hasn't heard any of it.

'Got fifty pages read then, and a cup of coffee,' he says. 'That's not bad. So, where to now, chief?'

'The hotel, I think.' We take a look at what's up next. 'Yeah, it's the telethon now, so I should get changed into something telethony and we should get out there. I'd go for a swim, but . . . no, there's not enough time.'

'The hotel and then Channel Seven. Done.' We get back into the van and he says, 'This has been good, you know. I don't get a lot of conversation, not with people with a bit of life in them. My regular customers are mostly old ducks who can't get out on their own. Any load of groceries could be their last, frankly. What's the telethon for?'

'I'm not sure.'

'Well, how do you know you support it, then?'

'Support what? It's a telethon. People don't have telethons for bad causes. There are no bad causes. There's just an almost infinite number of good causes, and you say Yes to what you can. Anyway, the festival wouldn't have put me up for it if it wasn't good. Except, I suppose it was a publicist who got me on there . . .'

I take another look at the itinerary, but it just says

'telethon'. Apart from that it tells me I get around two-and-a-half minutes on camera to do my stuff, and it gives me a call time and a contact person.

So, what do I wear? Mal's not likely to be a big help there. Okay, the lighting'll be wrong, so don't overdress. It'll be too bright, and the newsreaders will be in suits or slightly more casual, most of the people visible will be working the phones. Dress for a middling club, not for a ball.

I still end up with three potential outfits on the bed before I pick one. I wash my face, since there isn't time for a shower. Yet again I'm heading for a studio in a mess. There's a reason smellovision never amounted to much. A few quick squirts of Lou Lou is as good as it gets, and everything else can be sorted out at the station.

Mal's reading in the foyer, since it's brighter there.

'Thought I'd come in,' he says, 'once I knew there was a change of clothes involved. I can still remember what it was like having a lady in the house.'

He tells me I don't need to get stressed, we'll be okay for time, and he's right. The traffic's already dying down, and he knows a way that'll get us there with time to spare. So, more talk then. The conversation picks up where it left off.

We're nearly there when I find myself saying, 'You miss Hazel a lot, don't you?' without necessarily meaning to.

And he says, 'Yes. Most days, yes. But I missed her when she was sick, too. It wasn't the same, but it's what you get, isn't it?'

He stopped doing a lot of things when Hazel got sick, since they did most things together. There were years there when things slipped away from him, and most of them haven't come back.

The security guy at the TV studio tells us where to park, and I tell Mal it'll take ages – TV takes ages for two-and-a-half minutes – but there'll be food, so he should come in.

We're met at the door by a girl who strides straight up to me and says, 'Meg, hello, I'm Polly. I'm looking after the talent, and everything. Thanks so much for doing this.'

She has a headset and a clipboard and a mildly frantic look in her eyes, maybe slightly more frantic when she's noticed Mal looming up behind me.

'It's good to be here,' I tell her. 'And this is Mal. Mal's my publicist today.'

'Oh. Oh, right. Hi Mal.' She looks at the cabbie uniform good and hard, reading the cab company name on the epaulettes of his shirt. But even then she keeps talking business, keeps us moving. 'Well, would both of you like to come this way? We've got a Green Room for you and we'll come and get you when it's time for make-up and everything.'

We follow her down the corridor and Mal says, almost certainly to himself, 'It's more like a warehouse than I would have thought. It looks a lot better on the box.'

Polly glances over her shoulder but doesn't quite catch what he's said. She looks at me – I'm the talent, my comfort is everything – and I give her a smile that says all's well, so she doesn't break her stride.

Within a minute she's clipping the mike pack to my belt while I'm starting a good long graze at the chip 'n' dip.

She hands me the lapel end so that I can tuck it up inside my shirt, and she says, 'Oh, shit, the waiver. I nearly forgot to get you to sign the waiver. It's just the standard sort of thing that lets us broadcast bits for promotional purposes and all that.'

'Sure.'

I haven't eaten for hours, I realise all of a sudden. I sign and she goes, probably to meet another guest. Instantly, it's calmer in here. Through a mouthful of hummus I tell Mal to eat up.

'It's not bad, this,' he says.

'There's usually meals – pasta, chicken pieces, that kind of thing. They'll probably come out with it soon.' Meals with glycemic indices for all requirements. But, no, we talked penile implants instead.

The Green Room's half full, two-thirds full, with bands and TV people and local celebs. We can watch the telethon on a couple of wall-mounted TVs, but there's no sound. There's a guy on stage at the moment doing a routine with three kelpies. Across the room, I can see a few people I know from other things, and Roz and Chanel from Women in Docs.

Someone whose badge says 'Val – Volunteer' sets a platter of steaming meatballs on the table in front of us.

'Now you're talking,' Mal says, and Val tells him she'll be back with a plate and a fork.

He watches her go – I watch him watch her go – and then he looks away as though he wasn't watching at all. She's sixty-ish, and wearing a neat skirt and blouse with an apron over it. She's bustling around in an organised kind of way, and she's gone to some trouble with her hair, I think.

'Hey, Meg.' It's Roz, over this way to scoop some more food onto her plate. 'Saw you on the list. When did you get into town?'

'A couple of days ago. I've been out doing interviews, mainly.'

Val the volunteer comes back with a plate and fork for Mal – just for Mal – and Mal says, 'You're too kind,' in a joking sort of way. Then, as she's bustling off again, he reaches his hand out to shake Roz's and says rather loudly, 'I'm Mal, Malcolm, the new publicist.'

'I'm Roz, hi.'

'Roz and Chanel are Women in Docs,' I tell him. 'The band.'

'Oh, the band, yeah. You're the one with the pasta,' he says, and gives me a wink.

'And Mal's the guy with the penis implant who didn't realise he should keep the pasta story to himself.'

'Hey, I'm only publicising, love. Besides, you've been telling that story all over town on radio.'

Roz laughs, then realises he's serious. 'Thanks, Meg. Good on you. In future I'll try to limit my food-spitting to people without media commitments.'

'You already put it on your web site. I think the story's out there.'

'Meg . . .' It's Polly again. 'We'd better get you off to Make-up. You can bring your plate. Oh, you don't have a plate. We can get you a plate, and you can bring it. Or we can get you one when you're done.'

'That'd be fine. Mal, if you see Val while I'm in Make-up, could you get me a plate?'

'No worries, love.'

And I leave him with Roz and Chanel and get taken down the corridor to Geneva in Make-up ('Gen, every-one calls me Gen . . .') and she makes flattering remarks about my okay cheekbones and my average hair and starts to pink out any skin blemishes with a sponge. She talks in a way that's no better than nattering, and I could do without it. How many times has she had this very same one-sided conversation tonight? I shouldn't have men-tioned the penis implant to Roz and Chanel. That wasn't fair. But he shouldn't have mentioned the pasta either.

'Can you find your way back to the Green Room?' Gen says when she's done. 'Or shall I call Pol?'

There's nothing as dumb as the talent, I figure, since the Green Room's three doors away, and no corners. Or maybe we just never pay attention and accept no responsibility.

I make it all the way back alone without an error. Mal's standing by himself with three chicken drumsticks on his plate.

'They had to go off and do something,' he says. 'Your friends. Polly came to get them.'

'Yeah, look, I'm not sure I should have brought the implant up before. That was . . .'

'Oh, no, it was fine. You know, it sort of worked. They were more interested than I thought they'd be.'

'What?'

'From a conversational point of view. Not sexually, or anything.'

'Your penis is now a talking point?'

'I don't have a lot going for me, love. Give me a break. What am I going to use with the ladies? War stories? No one's interested in Korea.'

Up on the monitors, Roz and Chanel perform something but, without the sound, I can't work out which song it is.

Am I supposed to give Mal advice about conversation now? I have no idea. He takes a bite of his second drumstick and he keeps talking, giving me his views on television people and then on the sort of folk who do things for charities, unheralded behind the scenes things, year after year. He actually uses the expression 'salt of the earth'.

Polly says I'm on in ten, and shows me ten fingers (nearly dropping her clipboard in the process). I've got to think, I've got to be ready. I go to the toilets and lock myself in a cubicle. In my head, I run through the act, the particular two-and-a-half minutes I decided weeks ago would be right for tonight. If I hadn't got caught up in all this Mal stuff, I could have got everything straight in my head before now. But it's there, it'll be okay. Two-and-a-half minutes for a family audience, nothing blue, no penis implants.

I go back to the Green Room in five – that'd be the fingers on one hand – and Polly's at the door, missing me already. Over her shoulder I can see Mal talking to Val again. She laughs at something he says, and then Polly's fussing me away, getting me backstage.

A guy comes up to me, and he points out the mark I have to hit on the floor and the camera I'll be working to.

'You're straight up after the ad break,' he says. 'We'll get you there during the break, Tony'll do an intro and when you're done he might come back over and take you to the phones. Some people take a call. It just depends. Tony'll take you through it. If you take a call, it's only you going to air, not the caller. Okay?'

'Sure.'

So I get to watch the act before me, and it's always tougher at telethons. I was right about the lighting, and no one's got the crowd worked up beforehand.

Then they're done, it's the ad break, I'm there, we're back, I'm on.

I give it my best family-friendly two-and-a-half minutes, but that's a full 150 seconds, and seconds can each take a surprisingly long time. It runs its course, it runs as it should, it stays clean.

There's applause, and Tony – a newsreader for sure – is there at the end and he puts his arm around my shoulders and says, 'Why don't we take a call?'

And I give him a perky, 'Sure, Tony, let's do that,' as if we take calls all the time.

We're there in four steps and he shows me the nearest

ringing phone, shaping his hands in the style of a game show model, so that we can all know which one I should be picking up. Suddenly, this feels a little odd. I've done talkback, but I haven't done this.

'Hello, it's Meg Riddoch here,' I say to whoever it is when I pick up the receiver. 'Here at the telethon.'

'Who?'

'Thank you. What a nice thing to say.' And out comes the practised self-deprecating laugh designed to follow a compliment. 'Can you see the TV from where you're sitting?'

'Sure. I'm watching the telethon. Hey, that's you who's talking.'

'That's right.'

'I know you. You're that comedian. Singer or comedian. I've always thought you were a bit of a spunk. I'm Greg, by the way, Greg from Freo.'

'Now you're talking. Two hundred dollars sounds pretty generous, Greg from Freo.' I say it with the over-emphasis of an announcement, and the studio audience applauds. 'Why don't I hand you over to Jenni and she can take down your details?'

'Two hundred . . . ?'

The smiling girl with the Jenni badge takes the phone and gets to work, Tony crosses to the next act, there's a hand on my shoulder, gently shepherding me backstage.

'Well, that's it then,' Mal says, pretending he hasn't been talking to Val the volunteer all this time, but pretending it a little too quickly, glancing at one of the screens and making himself sound close to business-like.

'Yep, so we're out of here. How did I look up there?'

'Um, I was a bit . . .'

Val turns to the table and tidies a plate that was tidy already.

'That was great, Meg,' Polly says. 'Terrific.' She's unclipping my mike, talking, listening to the voice in her headset and giving me the 'that was great, Meg' face, all at the one time. She's good. 'We're really glad you could make it. Now, you're right to get to the after party?'

'Sure. Are we all going? Performers and volunteers and everyone?'

'Whoever wants to. I think I'll even get there myself eventually. It's at a club back in the city. The Toucan.'

'The Toucan,' Mal says. 'Righto.'

And already Polly has us moving, out of the Green Room and down the corridor towards the door and the car park.

'Well,' Mal says, and then he leaves it at that, and all the way to the van he jangles the keys around in his pocket with his hand.

'You still haven't said how I looked on screen. If you're going to be a publicist you have to learn to flatter the artist. I come off stage, you come up to me spontaneously – having ignored everything I've done – and you tell me how wonderful I was.'

'Sorry, love. You were marvellous,' he says as he gets the engine started.

'Thanks.'

'Bit late now though?'

'You're learning.'

'And tomorrow it's all over, hey? It'll be useful for next time, I suppose. So, I'll drop you off at the party then?'

'Drop me off? You'd be coming in wouldn't you? For a drink, at least. You'd be off duty then. Everyone'll be there. Performers, volunteers . . .'

'Well,' he says, but it's a more optimistic 'well' than the one on the way to the taxi. This time it's a 'well' with somewhere to go. 'For a drink maybe. I'll get a hell of a shouting at from the cat when I get home though.'

He drives us back into town, humming along to whatever he recognises on the radio, most of which is very forty years ago so it works pretty well for him.

'The Toucan,' he says as we're parking. 'Never been to the Toucan.' A new song starts just as he turns the engine off. '"Twenty-four Hours From Tulsa", that'd be. You know it? It's not that easy to tell from the intro. It was special to me and the wife, that one. It's just a song to those people though, isn't it? The radio station people. Life goes on, hey?'

And he shrugs, as though it might or it might not. There's a complicated mixture of things in Mal, a duty to Hazel that he still feels, an unfixed pain, a life going unlived. Today might have brought it to the surface again, but that might be all it's done. It might leave it there, too.

My artist pass gets us into the club, and I go off in search of a couple of free artist beers.

When I get back, Mal's talking to one of the handlers from the dog act, and he's saying, 'It's just the two chambers that are inflatable. One's still the regular thing.

41

That's how you can still go to the toilet.' He takes the beer and says, 'Ta, love. And before you think I'm going round bringing it up spontaneously, so to speak, it's your pasta-spitting mates who have put the word out about me. You know me – I usually keep myself to myself.'

And I've no idea when in the past two days he's kept himself to himself, but I let it go. He's better now we're out of the van again, and better than yesterday. I only realise now that there was a grimness about him, and I realise it because it seems to have lifted a little. Not all the time, but at least when things are at their best.

We get talked into dancing, Mal and me, a couple of dog handlers and a juggler. Roz and the band's violinist wave at us from the dance floor and then start mouthing 'Come on,' and this is so much like another life for Mal that he figures he's got nothing to lose. It's Frankie Goes to Hollywood's 'Relax' playing and he tells me he doesn't really know much about this new stuff but he'll give it a go. So there he is in his cabbie's uniform, cigarette in one hand, swinging his arms around to a song he's managed not to hear these past sixteen years.

A couple of drunk girls from a tap-dancing school start dancing with him and trying to teach him a move or two. He puts his cigarette in his mouth to free up his hands, but it doesn't help. We're all dancing to Frankie Goes to Hollywood, Mal's walking like an Egyptian and he doesn't even know it. Right decade, wrong song.

And that's when I notice his pants. The bulge in his pants. And he shrugs. The word is more out than it should be about his Italian fashion accessory and the tap dancers have found his groin reservoir and they're pumping him up while they're dancing – pushing rhythmically against him in some kind of move that shifts the fluid millilitre by millilitre into the business end of the system.

I should never have got him into this. And I shouldn't have looked at his pants just then. I don't know what's worse – me setting Mal up for humiliation, or Mal noticing me noticing his bulge. Hours of talk about that penis, and never once did I look at his pants until now.

'I'm sorry,' Roz shouts into the side of my head. 'I didn't think people'd actually do anything.'

But it's not over yet. There's someone new at the edge of the group, pushing in round at Mal's side. Val the volunteer, cutting in on the tap-dancers just as they've got him fully erect. And she's dancing in a jiggly way, and there's something different about her. The apron's gone, but it's more than that. It's the hair and make-up. They've been done for her, redone back at the TV studio, worked on professionally, ready for her close-up.

She dances with Mal, right in front of him, and concentrates on the jiggling and the eye contact, and that's a good thing.

I make a move from the dance floor when the song ends, but they stay up there for the next one. I try not to watch. Mal's hardware is betraying his feelings and Val might notice any second.

I'm about to get another drink when they turn up beside me and Mal says something about getting me back to the hotel for my early start. Which won't be that early, and isn't his problem, but I know I'm supposed to just take his lead.

'Sure, good idea.' That's what I go with, as if we're still on the job, and we each say an awkward goodbye to Val, but two different kinds of awkward, and she's still smiling when we leave her at the bar.

I wait till we're out the door before trying to work out what's going on.

'What early start?'

'Whatever early start you like.' We're walking briskly past the bouncers and along the street, around the corner back to the van. 'Sorry, I was just using you. I was heading for disaster in there.' Then he drops the volume, even though there's no one around, and says, 'The toilets were really crowded last time I went, and this needs a bit more privacy. You saw the reservoir action going on out on the dance floor, didn't you? And I'm pretty bloody risky down there. My fly's only held together by a couple of dodgy safety pins and I've really got to . . .'

'Detumesce?'

'Detumesce, yeah, that'd be it. Before I'm in danger of being done for indecency. Remember, the outside part of it's still flesh. There could have been trouble with that showing itself at the wrong moment. So, ah, cover me, love.' He steps into the shadow behind the van, and I hear him take a deep breath. 'Not a bad night, though,' he says, as I'm fighting to ignore the pants noises. 'Not a bad night at all. It wasn't the full workout . . .' Do we really need to maintain conversation while he does this? Have we really become so familiar? Could I possibly have imagined that this night would end with me guarding an old man while he squeezes his penis behind a van? '. . . but it's nice to know the gear'll still do the job if the chance comes.' There's a pause, the noise of hand shuffling in pants. 'When the chance comes. That's what you reckon, isn't it? Be positive, hey?'

'Sure.' Did I say that?

'And, ah, I got her number, you know.' His free hand appears around the back door, with a crumpled piece of paper in it. 'Val's – the volunteer lady. So, there's hope. I haven't totally lost my touch. We might get together on the weekend. Somewhere a bit more normal.'

And he gives one final squeeze, and he's ready to go home.

Karen Moline

Ready for My Close-up

'The tall one is Otto, and the short one is Luther,' Max told me.

We'd been wondering about the two heavy-set Germans who sat by the pool all day long and into the evening hours at our hotel in Negril, smoking long, thin cigars. No matter what time Max and I staggered down after one of our big nights out, there they were, eyes hidden behind thick dark sunglasses, their legs propped up on stools, listening to Julio Iglesias songs on the hotel's cheap boom-box. They were dressed in identical red-and-white polka dot shirts, unbuttoned to reveal their beer bellies and hairy chests, Panama hats, baggy shorts, and Birkenstocks. The only time we saw them move was to take a sip from their ever-present glasses of rum punch, or to light a cigar, or to change one of their beloved Julio CDs. They nodded politely as we sat down nearby.

'I am so sick of Julio-Fricking-Iglesias,' Max muttered under his breath as we waited for dinner one sultry night.

'We're in Jamaica, for God's sake. Why can't they put on some reggae once in a while?' He picked up the palm-sized Sony digital camcorder he took with him everywhere, and panned around the grounds.

'Have a hit,' I said, as I inhaled deeply. 'When you're whacked out of your tree, Julio sounds great.'

I'd never been so whacked out of my tree in all my life. I wasn't a pot-head, and rarely smoked back in LA, where we lived. But guilt was making me light up, and the pot here in Jamaica was so lovely and green, so freshly cut and damp, so cheap and delectable. The fragrant smoke erased all my worries.

For a moment, that is.

So I inhaled a joint for breakfast. Max would gobble his eggs and passionfruit, then go zooming off on the motorcycle he'd rented from some dodgy character he'd met on the beach. I'd lie down on a chaise in one of the thatched huts near the surf so I wouldn't get fried to a crisp – the only part of my brain that was still functional knew it should stay out of the sun – dozing till Max came back midafternoon for a late lunch. I never asked him where he'd gone. It didn't matter.

I didn't want to know.

Max would pick me up and throw me in the ocean, which was about six inches deep and as warm as a baby's bath, and I'd just sit there and splash around like a little kid and laugh. He laughed, too. Then he'd quickly down several glasses of spiced rum punch, and we'd pick at some jerk chicken and breadfruit salad, but I was too high to be hungry. We'd retire for a siesta, and make love like two ravenous wolves, our bodies slick and sliding every which way on the rumpled sheets. Even my sweat smelled faintly of pot, and that turned us on. Guilt turned us on. I had to stay turned on so I could turn off the memories of what was waiting for me back home. Namely: my husband, Johnnie.

Max picked up one of my joints at our dinner table and idly rolled it around in his hand. Chagrin was seeping out of his pores in the humid heat. That's because his wife, Lucy, was waiting for him to come back home, too.

Max directed rock'n'roll videos, and I was his personal assistant. Normally, sexual favours didn't factor in the job description. We'd known each other since high school, and were really good friends, and had gone to each other's weddings, and confided in each other about everything. After Johnnie and I'd had a huge fight, the last in several weeks of fighting about everything and nothing, Max caught me crying my eyes out in the office. 'I hate him!' I said, sobbing into a Motley Crue T-shirt left over from a shoot we'd done ages ago. 'I've got to get away from him. I've got to get out of here.'

'Talk about timing,' Max said. 'Lucy and I had a huge fight this morning, and when she threw my MTV award at me I packed a suitcase and told her I was never coming back. She's never going to understand me the way you do.'

Max looked at me, and I looked at Max. Next thing I knew, we were in the Hotel Splendide, perched on a cliff in Negril. It was the off-season and there were few tourists lurking about, which suited me fine, because I wasn't in the mood to talk to anybody. And thanks to the torrential downpours every afternoon – the kind of thick curtains of rain that kept the sun-worshipping island-hoppers away – it was so humid my hair had the texture of a banana bush, and the airconditioning was barely functional. I didn't care at all. The warm raindrops trickling like contrition down my back felt good. Everything felt good as long as I stayed stoned as a quarry.

'Are you enjoying your honeymoon?'

Otto had finally spoken. Max and I looked at each other and burst out laughing. Before this week, we'd never so much as kissed each other properly. We hadn't wanted to. It would have been like incest.

'Yes,' I said, smiling at Otto and nervously playing with my wedding ring. Of course he and Luther thought we were married.

Why wouldn't he?

'Are you enjoying your vacation?' I asked.

'Yes, thank you. Most enjoyable,' Otto replied. 'Quite a splendid change from winter in Berlin.' He had a beautifully mellifluous voice, completely at odds with his lumpen body.

'Most splendid,' Luther echoed. His voice, too, was deep and suave.

'Entirely splendid,' Otto said.

'How splendid!' I exclaimed.

Otto and Luther smiled indulgently at me, candlelight flickering over their faces, then exchanged a glance.

'May I see your camera?' Otto asked Max, who handed it over with such alacrity I thought he'd drop it. I looked at Max, puzzled. He must have been entranced by Otto's silken tones, because normally he'd go mental if I so much as put a pinkie on one of his super-expensive digital toys, here or back at the production office.

'Brand new,' Max said proudly. 'I used it on my last shoot.'

'Ah, you are a director,' Otto said.

'Ha,' Luther said smugly, holding out his hand to his friend. 'I told you so.'

Otto reached in his back pocket for his wallet, and pulled out a huge wad of five-hundred-dollar bills, then peeled one off and handed it over.

'A friendly wager,' he said. 'My friend Luther wagered me that you were a director.'

'How on earth did you know I was a director?' Max asked.

'The way you are looking at the landscape,' he replied.

'The way . . . how do you say . . . the way you squint,' Luther added.

'He squints, all right,' I said, laughing.

'Let me guess,' Max said, grinning widely, 'you're directors, too. Or producers.'

'Yes,' Otto said, beaming. 'We've made one hundred and seventy-three films.'

'One hundred and seventy-three?' Max asked, incredulous. 'I can't imagine directing one hundred and seventy-three videos, much less films. What are they about?'

'What are they about?' Luther said. 'They are all about love.' He looked right at me, his eyes kind and cajoling. 'All about the many different aspects of *love*.'

I blushed beet red to the tips of my frizzed-out hair. Stoned as I was, I had a pretty good idea of the different aspects of love he had in mind.

Max looked at my cheeks which were so red he could have spied them in the dark, then quickly back at Otto and Luther. He'd obviously figured it out, too.

'Might you be interested in directing a short segment for us?' Otto asked Max. 'You could shoot it right here, in the hotel. At night, when there will be few interruptions. We could shoot it out, or we could shoot it in.'

'Depending on the weather,' Luther said.

'Depending on many factors,' Otto added.

'The moonlight would look so lovely.'

'Contrast is always a selling point.'

'You would be handsomely compensated,' Luther said.

'Most handsomely,' Otto echoed. 'Most splendidly handsomely. Five thousand dollars. Cash, of course.'

'Especially splendidly,' Luther said, 'if your dazzling young wife here is the star.'

'Five thousand for her,' Otto said. 'Ten, if she takes easily to direction. After all, she is your wife.'

Max, whose eyes had gone all aglow at the thought of easy money for a night-time shoot, frowned, opened his mouth to say something, then quickly shut it again. I knew what he'd been about to say.

Not: How dare you ask me to direct a scene in a porno flick produced by two dodgy Germans in a hotel in Jamaica?

But: *She's not my wife.*

I'll show you, Max, I thought momentarily. I'll do it just to mess with your head, you bastard. And you can forget about ever laying a finger on me again.

Even if you shouldn't have been laying a finger on me in the first place.

'I take very easily to direction. Especially for that kind of money,' I said, inhaling deeply on the joint Luther had just leaned over to light. He caressed his thick gold lighter with a pudgy finger. 'And I love shooting at night. Who else would be in it?'

'One of the young gentlemen who's been working here, repairing the jacuzzi. Or perhaps two. Depending on how easily you take to direction.'

Depending on how many I'd be willing to have pounce on me at the same time, he meant. I took another deep drag. I knew exactly who he was talking about. I'd seen them working, strapping young studs, their muscles rippling. And best of all, I'd spied on them from my window, hiding behind the shutters to watch them clean up at the outdoor shower at the end of the day, totally naked and totally glorious. Once, one of them looked up at my window, as if he could feel my snooping, curious gaze upon him. I quickly backed away, and ran out of the room. The mere sight of how well-endowed he was had been enough to send me out in search of Max. And now here was a golden, lucrative opportunity to have that strapping young stud doing whatever I wanted, for all posterity to see. I'd been cheating already, so what difference would more shameless behaviour make? Max would never tell. I certainly would never tell. I closed my eyes for a second, and thought of the workman's beautiful dark fingers lingering on my pale white skin that I'd so carefully kept out of the sun.

'They love shooting at night, as well,' Otto said.

'In that case, better make it fifteen thousand,' I said. 'For that kind of money, you will easily see how well my darling husband and I work together.'

Max stood up. 'I have to go call my friend Johnnie, to discuss the matter. I never shoot anything of this importance without asking his advice.'

'Suit yourself,' I said, knowing he was bluffing. And not about to tell him whether I was or not. 'I'm ready for my close-up.'

Max and I left late the next day. Johnnie was so overjoyed to see me, so contrite that we'd fought, and even happier when I told him I was quitting my job and going back to school to get my Master's Degree in library science. He never asked me what happened in the Hotel Splendide. I never told him.

I never told him our trip had been all about the many different aspects of love.

John Eales's

Favourite Songs

1. **'To Her Door' – Paul Kelly**
   This is a song that we often sang in the Wallaby
   showers after a win. We probably sang it for a couple
   of reasons – it's a great song and also a lot of the
   guys knew the words. Despite the song being great,
   the vision of people like Tim Horan, Matt Burke, Joe
   Roff and myself belting it out in the shower (maybe
   I should just say *singing* it in the shower) was
   somewhat more ordinary!

2. **'Throw Your Arms Around Me' and 'The Holy
   Grail' – Hunters and Collectors**
   As above.

3. **'Closer to Fine' – Indigo Girls**
   A great tune with words that make you think. It's a
   good song to either sing along to just for the sake of
   it, or one to ponder in a thoughtful mood. They are
   a group that I have seen perform in concert twice
   and I love them. For me they are the female

equivalent of Simon and Garfunkel, with their great tunes, voices and harmonies.

4. **'For Emily Wherever I May Find Her' – Simon and Garfunkel**

This is a song that for me is categorised by the faultless tones of Art Garfunkel, and the soft and emotional images it conjures. It allows you to think of the important women in your life. At different times I think of my wife Lara or my daughter Sophia. It was a song that I knew I wanted to have played at my wedding long before the event took place.

5. **'The Only Living Boy in New York' – Simon and Garfunkel**

Another great S and G song. It's so hard to narrow down all their songs to just a few. I have chosen this one because I think in some ways it represents the simplicity yet relevance of their lyrics. To me the song is about a bloke who has no worries in the world, and I think that that is a good way to be.

6. **REM**

Any number of tunes from this band – it's hard to be specific. I think that they have tunes for all occasions. When you're melancholy you can listen to 'Everybody Hurts' or when you're up you can move to 'Shiny Happy People'. And if you are a kid you can listen to the version they did for 'Sesame Street' – 'Happy Furry Monsters'.

I particularly like the song 'Superman' off the album *Life's Rich Pageant*. It is an extremely up-beat song that is a great party sing-along.

The uniqueness of Michael Stipe's voice was the first thing that attracted me to this band, and the fact that he is such an enigma always makes me want to know more about the band and, in particular, him.

7. **'Time to Say Goodbye' – Andrea Bocelli**

This is one of those very special tunes that everyone associates with in some way or other. I often find it amazing that a song with virtually no English – it is written in Italian apart from the line 'Time to say goodbye' – is so powerful across different cultures. It was played at my Italian grandmother's (Nonna) funeral and there wasn't a dry eye in the place. It is both uplifting and sad. It takes you through all the emotions and I don't even know what it's about aside from saying goodbye.

8. **'Advance Australia Fair' – Peter Dodds McCormick**

Our anthem is so special to me because it is the only anthem that I have known. It has for a long time been my favourite moment when playing a test. We used to sing it before the test with the crowd, and after every win with the team in the shed. The Wallabies are very proud of being Australian and take great pride in singing the anthem at both times. When singing the anthem before the match I used to pick out a person in the crowd and sing along with them. At that time I imagined myself in their shoes, and thought about how much they would like to be in my shoes. This charged me with the responsibility to perform to the best of my ability out on the field. And besides, it was the only time that I would ever get the chance to sing in front of 110 000 people!

Senator Natasha Stott Despoja's

Songs for a Big Night Out

To ease into a big night out at the pub, there's nothing more fitting than Natalie Merchant (10 000 Maniacs) singing 'These Are Days' from the *Our Time in Eden* album. Merchant delivers folk-pop at its best with graceful poetry and an upbeat tone. How could it not be the start of a big night out?

To pick up the tempo it's one of the original 'girl power' groups: The Go-Gos. 'Our Lips Are Sealed' proved just how sexy a bit of attitude could be.

Time to dance. Next on the jukebox would have to be the Princess of Pop, Kylie Minogue. While everything by Kylie deserves a spin, 'What Do I Have to Do?' is funky, fun and unabashed pop – a dance anthem that has stood the test of time.

To keep the legs moving, Paul Mac's 'Just the Thing' is next. With an infectious chorus and a beat that gets bigger, it doesn't take much convincing to stay on the dance floor.

Brit Pop – Blur, Pulp or Oasis – sits you back down and ensures the night continues at a more leisurely but vocal pace. 'True Faith' by New Order is a must, but if there's one song guaranteed to get a room singing with gusto it's 'Wonderwall'. It's not too hard to picture – pub, people, beer and an out-of-tune rendition . . .

A big night out is not complete without my favourite band: Jesus and Mary Chain. Their 'Cherry Came Too' and 'April Skies' – hard-edged and raw – satisfy the dying hours of the night until . . .

. . . that point in time when everyone is finding love on the dance floor, in memories or the bottom of the glass. The Go Betweens' romantic and angsty ballad 'Quiet Heart' signals the time to leave.

Fruit, a local band, are not on the jukebox, but I see some of the band across the room and, as I leave, one of their songs, 'Finally', plays in my head: *Sharing secrets with the rain . . . Is this freedom finally . . . Finally, it's time to be alone. Finally, I'm finding my way home.*

James Holland

Getting to the Party

It was wartime. The Germans might not have invaded, but the Blitz had rained hundreds of thousands of bombs on Britain's cities, bringing destruction on a scale never before witnessed by a civilian population. There was rationing – of food, drink, petrol – of everything, it seemed. Abroad, Britain had suffered one disaster after another: Norway, Dunkirk, the loss of the Channel Islands, Crete, the debacle of Dakar. Her lifeline, the convoys from America, were suffering such losses that Hitler's promise to slowly strangle Britain into submission looked sure to become a reality. In short, things were not going well. The future looked rather bleak.

Not that Edward Gregory worried unduly. He had survived thirteen months of almost continuous front-line action and was still alive, and, if the truth be known, enjoying it in a way.

During the Battle for France, they'd lost half the squadron's Hurricanes in twenty-four hours. They'd been hopelessly outnumbered. Without radar, no one had the faintest idea what was going on. After twelve days of frenetic action, they had been pulled out. Edward had been just about to take off to fly back to England when yet another bevy of German bombers had roared past their decrepit airfield; he'd been lucky not to roll into a bomb crater. Certainly he hadn't been able to see much: the huge engine cowling in front of him made forward vision impossible on the ground and what with the smoke – well, it had been pure chance that he'd managed to get airborne. Several others hadn't been so lucky. He some-times wondered what had happened to them. Did the Germans ever bury them, or had they burnt to nothing with the remains of their planes?

After a month, during which time the squadron had been brought back to strength, they were sent into front-line action again. Firstly based in the north of the country, and then, from late August onwards, to the south-east, to an airfield in Kent. This was the Battle of Britain, and although they were still bombed every day, at least they now had radar and could get themselves airborne before the bombers arrived.

Those had been long days: up at dawn – which in summer was very early indeed – then up to twenty-thousand feet with eleven or so other planes (or whatever was available), to intercept 150-plus enemy bombers and fighters. Then back home, bit of a rest, up again, back, rest, up again. Sometimes they were in the air fighting the Germans as many as four times a day. In the evening, a few beers, bed, and then the whole thing started all over again.

Every morning he knew he might well never make it through the day. He didn't dwell on the matter, but it was *there*, in the back of his mind. Lots of friends had gone. Colin had ended up in the Channel. Brian had never escaped his burning Hurricane. A faulty parachute had done for Tony. Bill and Roly had crashed into each other and both been killed. Only yesterday, Dougie had been seen spiralling down to the ground, shot out of the sky by one of the new German Focke-Wulfs. Perhaps he'd been picked up as a prisoner of war, but the way his plane had trailed smoke, Edward was pretty certain Dougie had had it.

Those were just his good friends. He couldn't even remember the names of half the others – some had been with the squadron less than an hour. Of course he missed them, and their deaths upset him dreadfully, but he'd become an expert at not dwelling on it, even if one of his close friends died. He would have his nightly bath and think about them very hard, imagining them in the place he thought was most appropriate. He felt sure, for example, that Dougie would be best going to Tahiti, or one of the other South Pacific islands. As soon as an image of his friend's burning plane came into view, or he thought of the screams in his earpiece, he concentrated for a few moments and there was Dougie surrounded by nubile Tahitian girls, the shadows of the palms above flickering gently across his face.

It was as though they had gone off on their travels,

only they liked the place so much they'd not bothered coming back.

So Edward carried with him a 'what will be, will be' attitude that had served him well. He'd always been like that, even as a child. And he liked flying. He *loved* his Spitfire. What a plane that was! He liked most of his fellow pilots, and he particularly liked Diana Mortimer, a WAAF who worked in the Fighter Control Room at the station. Really, he had a lot to be thankful for. Far better flying around the sky at three hundred miles an hour in one of the most beautiful machines ever built, than slogging your guts out on the ground. If he had to die, far better to do so in style. And as a fighter pilot, rationing barely affected him, especially since they had started taking the fight to the enemy. Instead of waiting for the Germans to come over when they chose, it was the turn of the RAF to decide when attacks would occur. Since the previous December, he'd had three hot meals a day. He felt a bit guilty that his family in London were going hungry, but then, as his mother had said in a letter to him, he needed his strength kept up if he was to fight to his best ability. And he'd got to meet Diana. He couldn't help thinking she might not have let him know her *quite* so intimately had the circumstances been different.

It was a beautiful midsummer's day. A few wispy white clouds, but otherwise blue all over. Edward and the other pilots had moved some of the old chairs from the dispersal hut outside, and it was in one of these that he sat, his backside low in the seat, legs stretched out, his eyelids flickering gently in the brightness. A bee was busily visiting the daisies in the grass about him. In the distance an occasional clang of a spanner or wrench on metal could be heard. Otherwise, all was still and peaceful. No one spoke.

He was thinking about Diana: the creaminess of her thighs and breasts, the smoothness of her skin. The way her eyes had looked deeply into his and she had said, 'You know, I'm really rather crazy about you.' He was so glad they'd done it; after all, it had worried him a bit that he might die before ever knowing what it was like – this amazing thing that was supposed to be so wonderful. And it had been. He couldn't imagine ever tiring of waking up next to her. Perhaps they would get married. Mrs Diana Gregory. He liked that – a good ring to it. Married and living in a little cottage somewhere. With a baby boy. A boy who would be mad keen on cricket, just like him.

The telephone rang, shattering the peace of the slumbering pilots. It was rarely a scramble these days, but after the previous summer, living on a knife-edge waiting for the dreaded call, it still made him jump.

'For you, Edward.' Tom Wilson, the Intelligence Officer, was standing by the open window, holding the receiver.

Edward eased himself out of his armchair with a sigh, wondering who it could be.

'*Edward?*'

'Hallo.'

'*Edward, it's me – Diana.*'

Edward looked around to check no one was listening, then said in hushed tones, 'Diana – hallo, darling.'

'*Sorry to ring you on this line, but I was worried you'd forgotten about tonight.*'

Tonight. Tonight? His mind raced. What was happening? Then he suddenly remembered: the party at her parents' house near Tonbridge. He cursed to himself. How could he have been so stupid?

'Course I haven't, darling. How would I ever forget that?'

'*Well, I didn't think you had, only I was wondering about how we're going to get there.*'

'Oh, don't you worry, I've got it sorted. Tell you what: why don't you meet me outside the Mess at six-thirty. Sound all right?'

'*Perfect. And Edward?*'

'Yes?'

'*I can't wait to see you. Mum and Dad are so looking forward to meeting you. Bye.*'

'Bye.'

Edward put the receiver down and thought for a moment. Damn! He hadn't a clue how they were going to get there. The car was no good as Barnie Fuller had crashed it two days before. The train would take too long, so would a bus, and it was unlikely he'd be able to find a motorbike in time. Anyway, Diana wasn't going to thank him if she got oil all over her clothes. Bollocks! Why was he such an idiot? He gently thumped his head against the doorframe, then ambled back outside. There *had* to be an alternative.

✱

At six-thirty, Edward was pacing up and down outside the Mess when Diana appeared. She had changed from her WAAF uniform into a sleek pale-blue evening dress, with a small cape to keep her shoulders warm.

'You look wonderful,' said Edward, meaning it.

She smiled at him, and lightly kissed his cheek. 'Thank you. So do you.' Then she looked around and seeing no obvious means of transport said, 'Did you manage to get a car?'

'No – I've done better than that. Follow me.' He took her hand and led her round the back of the Mess towards one of the airfield hangars.

'Edward?' A note of alarm in her voice.

'Trust me,' said Edward, and he beamed, then even gave her a quick wink. Round to the front, away from the main buildings of the airfield, stood a lone Spitfire, its wings and perspex canopy glinting in the early evening sun. Edward stopped and bowed.

'My lady, your carriage awaits.'

'Edward!' exclaimed Diana, her hands clasping her face. 'We can't really be going in that!'

'We can and we will. Come on, it'll be fun.'

Slowly her face turned from an expression of shocked horror to one of capricious delight. Inwardly, Edward gave a sigh of relief. Outwardly, he hoped he was maintaining the debonair attitude he'd been trying to convey.

'Edward, you are wonderful,' said Diana, gripping his hand tightly and giving him one of her most radiant smiles.

Edward gave a signal to his ground crew, already waiting by the plane. They waved back, and then the propeller slowly and silently began to turn until, with a puff of smoke and flame from the exhaust stubs, the engine roared into life.

'Come on,' said Edward, 'let's go, although we've got to be quick.' Glancing around, he led her briskly to the plane.

'Thanks, you two,' he said to Barlow and Lucas who were now standing by the wing waiting for them.

'Let the lady get in first, sir, then you,' said Barlow.

Edward nodded, them clambered onto the wing and held out a hand for Diana. Holding up her dress, she took his arm and allowed herself to be pulled up. Balancing gingerly beside him, she looked at him apprehensively, then hopped into the cockpit.

'Good job you're not some huge fat oaf,' she laughed, as Edward lowered himself onto her lap.

'Sorry, but there's no other way. Normally I'm sitting on a parachute, you see.' He was a bit closer to the instrument panel than he was used to but, actually, his all-round vision was improved by sitting so far forward. Now he knew how people had managed before.

'Are you all right, darling? I'll try not to squash you completely.'

'I'm fine. Anyway, I'm far too excited to mind.'

Edward signalled to Barlow and Lucas, then slowly opened the throttle. The Merlin engine roared and the airframe shook, and they began rolling briskly towards the start of the runway.

'Great thing about a Spit,' shouted Edward, 'they don't need much to take off. Let's hope no one spots you.' He released the brakes and opened the throttle further, the engine responding with a deep and guttural bellow. They surged down the grass strip. Either side, the wings began to wobble with the increased power. It felt as though they were racing over a rough, pot-holed track. Then they were airborne, and the shaking had gone, replaced by a soothing gentle vibration. In moments, the horizon had slid beneath them as the Spitfire sped skywards.

Edward had to remind himself that he was not climbing into battle, but taking Diana on a gentle jaunt. Like a thoroughbred, the Spitfire always seemed to want to fly faster and turn tighter, revelling in its own speed and manoeuvrability; but today, he must reign her in. He gently pulled the canopy shut and turned them with the gentlest of sweeps. The horizon slowly tilted as they turned back and circled wide.

'Are you all right, darling?' yelled Edward.

'Couldn't be better!'

Edward grinned. What a good idea this had been. He took them higher – although not too high: six thousand feet should be plenty, as he wanted Diana to be able to see the countryside clearly below.

In the calm evening light, England lay spread out before them. A patchwork of green and gold. Ridges of hills clearly defined by the shadow of the sun. Snaking rivers silvery and gleaming. Dense woods. Such a shame, Edward thought, that they could only be doing this because of the War. And what a shame that his Spitfire, so beautiful, so sleek, such a joy to fly, should be designed not for pleasure, but for shooting other planes out of the sky. For killing people.

'I can see our house!' shouted Diana. They'd been airborne for about twenty minutes.

Edward brought the plane lower and circled, looking for the right field. There was a long grass paddock running alongside the house. It looked to be flat enough.

'Do a fly-past, won't you?' said Diana in his ear.

'If you want – hold on.'

Pushing the stick forward and opening the throttle, Edward dived towards the house, then pulled back as they whistled past. Diana screamed with delight.

'Hang on tight!' shouted Edward. As they turned and swept past again, he rolled the plane.

'Oh my gosh!' yelled Diana, then began laughing.

Moments later, they were coming in to land. The field was perfect – quite long enough, and Edward was thinking how glad he was that he'd forgotten about the party earlier and not organised a car.

'Thank you, darling,' said Diana as they came to a halt. 'I think that was the most wonderful thing I've ever done. I can't believe I've just been in a Spitfire! Mum and Dad will be *so* impressed.'

Edward kissed her cheek. 'Rather fun, wasn't it? England looks pretty good from up there, don't you think?'

'Beautiful. *Thank* you.'

✦

Diana's mother and father had some concerns about the sense and safety of two people flying in a single-seater plane with no parachute or harness, but were polite and kind to Edward all the same, and they and their friends had all enjoyed his fly-past. To make it home before it was completely dark, they had to leave just before ten o'clock, but neither Diana nor her parents seemed to mind.

'That's all right, young man,' Diana's father told him. 'Jolly good of you to come at all. After all, there is a war on.' They shook hands, Edward thanked him and his wife profusely, then they turned to wander back to the Spitfire, standing in the field with its nose pointing imperiously towards the sky.

'Do be careful though, won't you?' Diana's mother called after them.

The rest of the party had come out to watch. Edward prayed the starter batteries would work, but having primed them, the propeller turned and the engine fired almost immediately. Soon they were airborne once more. Edward couldn't resist one last sweep past the house, waggling his wings in salute. Diana giggled happily and tightened her arms around his middle.

'I think I'm in love with you!' she laughed.

What a perfect evening, thought Edward as they landed back at the airfield safely and taxied over to the hangar. He knew that even if he lived to a hundred, he would remember every part of it. He'd never been happier in his life. And Diana had told him she loved him! What a strange thing war was.

✶

He awoke the following morning still thinking happily about Diana and their trip to the party. Outside it was raining. It was impossible to believe the previous day had been so warm, clear and sunny. To make matters worse, at breakfast the adjutant told Edward the CO wanted to see him immediately afterwards. 'Brace yourself,' said the adj.

Edward felt a knot tighten in his stomach. He must have been spotted the previous evening.

He was right. The CO was furious and gave full vent to his anger: What the hell did he think he'd been playing at? Did he have any idea how expensive those planes were? What if something had gone wrong? And to take a young girl out just because he was trying to impress her! Really, it was unforgivable. 'I need people like you,' the CO yelled, 'experience doesn't grow on trees, you know. It takes time, not to say money. If anything had happened to you just because of some silly prank – well, I'd be bloody furious. I *am* bloody furious.'

Edward could say nothing. The CO was right, of course. Standing there, in front of the desk, he no longer felt so pleased with himself. In fact, he felt rather ashamed.

'You should be court-martialled for this, you know,' the CO continued.

Edward nodded meekly.

The CO sighed, rubbed his forehead vigorously, then pulled out a cigarette and lit it. Through a cloud of smoke, he reached into a drawer and pulled out a letter.

'Here,' he said, handing it to Edward. 'This has just come through.'

Edward took it silently, slowly tore open the envelope and read the perfunctory note. He'd been promoted from Flight Lieutenant to Squadron Leader.

'Congratulations,' said the CO.

Edward stood there, stupefied for a moment, then said, 'Thank you, sir.'

'You're going to need to act a bit more responsibly from now on. And by the way, you're grounded.' The CO rapped his fingers on the desk. 'If this had been peacetime, you *would* have been court-martialled, you know. Now leave me alone.'

By that evening the CO's anger had cooled, although he made Edward buy drinks for everyone. The other pilots thought the escapade hilarious, and were glad for the drinks; twelve shillings a day didn't go very far, even in the Mess.

The following morning, just after dawn, Edward led the squadron over France, escorting fifty bombers to attack German airfields. He had a headache, but couldn't stop thinking about Diana and their flight together. Then he spotted some Focke-Wulfs, and ordering the squadron to attack, entered the fray for the last time.

Such things happened in wartime.

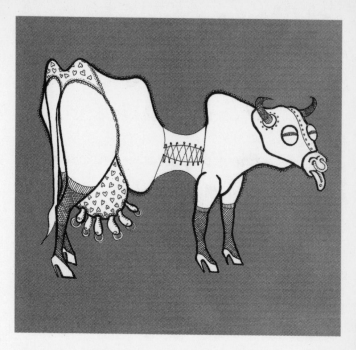

Paul Livingston

Party Animal

Titania Hardie's

Chemistry Lesson on How to Be the Perfect Sex Kitten All Party-night Long!

(Sorry chaps – this is for girls only!)

We often make the most impact at parties when we haven't tried too hard at all. There's something so desirable in a woman who's a bit laissez faire or enigmatic. If you perform the ritual below, you can go to all the fuss and trouble before you don your stilettos, and then exude just the right amount of ennui . . . ! Venus, goddess of love, rules the hour from 5 until 6 p.m. (6 until 7 in summer), and this is when you should start your ritual if possible.

Absolute essentials: tuberose perfume (try Annick Goutal, or Gaultier's 'Fragile', or my favourite from Paris: Maitre Parfumeur et Gantier, 'Fleurs Blanches'); one white feather; two drops scentless pheromone; stockings; one rose petal; one glass champagne blended with five drops damiana essence.

Glue a rose petal to the calendar or date-diary for the party's date, and say simply, 'Honour to Venus, Goddess of Love.' Then, on the day itself, at the aforementioned hour appointed (or as near as possible), dab three drops of tuberose perfume on the inside of each ankle, and one on each temple. Close your eyes and see yourself relaxed and in control. Sip some champagne, into which you have infused some damiana essence – five drops per glassful. Use your own words again to toast and honour Venus and the Moon. Lightly rub the outside of each ankle, just behind the ankle bone, for a moment: this releases the sex kitten in you like nothing on earth.

Recharge the tonic throughout the evening, rubbing one foot against the other! Put on some stockings (NOT tights!). Careful with your perfumed hands if you are using thigh highs: scent will encourage them to creep downwards. (Sip your champagne!) Spritz a little tuberose onto the feather, and put it in your purse (you can use it imaginatively later . . .), then apply two drops of pheromone under your nose. It is unscented, but don't inhale it. It boosts your own feel-good factor, enhancing your powers of attraction. Touch the rose petal on the calendar page, down the last few drops of champagne love-potion, and set forth! You are positively bursting with inner sensuality, so let this do all the talking while you relax and feel quietly in control. The night ahead is all yours! *Bonne nuit* . . .

Andiee Paviour

The Neverwas

Big Night Out? Which one of them to fix on when life as you've so brazenly reinvented it is a slo-mo swan dive through blow-outs, burn-outs and freak-outs? When *every* night – especially those doozeys you somehow can't recall – has been supersized for fourteen years and counting? And when the shameful-gainful job you do (which stains your consciousness like ink on skin but which you're pretty goddamned good at if you dare say so yourself) is to bring Big Nights to life, over and over again? To take the raw material of paunchy fools in polyester, interstate for three days on blah blah blah, with wedding rings abandoned on their hotel nightstands and twenty-dollar Rolexes on their podgy little wrists and, squeeze it, eyes clenched tight in a coffin lid of darkness, into a shuddering moment of ecstasy? And while you're Doing It, to quote to yourself the words of your soul sister Monet (that's 'Mon*ay*' after the painter and the dosh), that this act of copulation isn't so much one of 'prosti*too*shon' as a service to their used-up wives back home? Fact of it is, compadre, that from where this little black duck is sitting, there've been one too many Big Nights Out, you know what I'm saying?

And then there's the Neverwas.

My working name is Madonna, which none of my clients is ever likely to forget, but the girls at the service call me Gigi, which was a name I used back when, starting out, and it stuck like glue, go figure. Gigi bears no relation to my 'real' name, which, the fact of it is, you don't need to know. But it feels so much more *me* now than the handle I grew up with that last year I went and did the deed poll thing. So now I'm Gigi everywhere I turn, except at work when I slide into the M Girl like a blade into butter. I do a city hotel circuit, either by appointment or flying blind from the bars, and the routine is always the same: Frock up, front up and cosy up to whichever schmuck with a wallet is panting to blow his load. Drinks first while we skirt like skittish greyhounds around the issue of cash, then dinner in the five-star hotel restaurant (they all take a cut, of course, but Giles handles that side, along with the bookings), and off we scoot upstairs, vroom vroom. You might expect that's where the real work begins, but the fact of it is, it's listening to these losers that's most likely to send you to sleep, you know what I'm saying? Best advice I was ever given, back when, BC: make the marks feel wanted, and they'll worship you forever. 'Cause when you boil the B.S. down, how many people could really care less?

It's a cigarette-shaped restaurant with padded velvet booths along the walls and an ankle-deep runway of swirling Peruvian rug. The décor is a ruby cocoon with cerise lace trimmings on the trailing drapes and gilt-framed studies of dimpled French nymphettes, twinkling naughtily from a pillowed mound of cream and strawberry flesh. Miniature table lamps throw spotlights from conical parchment shades, and candle chandeliers flicker like swooning fireflies in burnished twists of metal. The maître d', bone-thin in matt-black tails, greets you with obsequious delight at the discreetly recessed front door, which for those in the know looks out onto . . .

How I got started was, I was eighteen years old, slinging hash in a suits' luncher on the trendy side of the Docks, and a girl on my shift threw the invite my way. Bella was her working name. *Mistress Bella Ball: B&D, U&Me.* Bella Ball was as tiny as a grounded Tinker Bell, with liquid, possum eyes and terrier bowlegs in hot-pink fishnets. Horsetail hair, which she assured me hung to her tush, was piled in sloppy bunches around her narrow little face. Her bee-stung brown lips were barely beginning to crack. *Give it a whirl, why don't you,* she husked with ground-in exhaustion, shovelling leftover pork rinds and half-chewed onion rings into an industrial trash bag with the same robotic efficiency I imagined she applied to spanking her paying monkeys. *It's easy dough and the guys are a pushover.* The thing about the business is it's as simple as wham-bam to fall into and canyon-deep to crawl away from. Give it a whirl. Pop on a frock. Time to time, you'll even get off on the sex. Fourteen years later, I'm still holding out for that particular performance bonus, you know what I'm saying?

. . . which for those in the know looks out onto . . . a cliff-side? A surfing beach? Or could it be the open sea; a crumpled throw of foam and spray shivering to infinity you can barely comprehend? Perhaps it's a streetscape, lacquered like an antique vase with candy-coloured lights? Banished behind the mirrored windows, a frazzled stream of outsiders peers wistfully in at where you are, unseeing but envious, desirous to desperation but des-tined to a life without . . . But hold up just a minute: I've gone and lost the plot. The Neverwas is wherever you want it to be, and this particular – this ultimate *– Big Night, its billowing drift of curtains obliterates the world outside, like a mother's embrace against the pain.*

The fact of it is, I never did get cosy with my ma and pa. Which, by the way, was their choice, not mine, them being the pampered monsters they were. I wasn't *neg-lected* exactly – we had the whole nanny, camp and country rellies thing going for the twelve years before they shipped me and my big brother off to boarding school – but I didn't take precedence over the parties, either. (Would it shock you if I said that the first person I Did It with was my brother? If you are freaked, don't sweat it: it was no biggie in any sense of the word, you know what I'm saying? We were kids, we were bored, and you'd be amazed how many 'regular' families are at it behind the scenes.) So, yeah, Mother was sexy and tart-mouthed and Father was dashing and smart, blah blah blah. It wasn't the raw material that did it for them, though, it was the way they wore what they had, as if they'd both been dipped in silver. They sparkled. They shimmied. They worked their rooms like a hired act even if they were the only ones in them. Who knows? Maybe that's where I picked it up.

You met the man you're with at a poolside barbecue two weeks ago. It was Some Enchanted Evening and then some: you looked, you clicked, and you haven't spent a night apart since. He's everything you've ever wanted from every man you've ever met: dishy, attentive, loaded, clever and so fall-about funny you can hardly keep a straight face, even now, with the skeletal Neverwas waiters curving over you like orbiting crescent moons, and the double-cooked gruyere soufflé a creamy daydream in your mouth. When your flute of Cristal is magically refilled, you tilt it towards him in an impromptu toast, and it's then that you notice the seductive glimmer at the bottom of the glass.

The first one was a tubby podiatrist from Cheltenham, with photos of his wife and kids in heart-shaped plastic frames beside the motel bed. He was clammy and hairless like a baby animal, and soup to nuts, I swear to God, we're talking two minutes. Afterwards, he paid me extra to hang around so he could bang on about what a terrific lay he was. I could hardly stand to look at him but it suited me to cool my heels since my second stop was a single two floors down and I had twenty minutes to kill until showtime. Sure, I was nervous to start with. Terrified out of my wits, in fact. In a sense it's a fear you're never going to lose – we've all heard of girls who've been torn apart by psychos. But what you really should be frightened of is the stuff you don't want to think about.

'It was my grandmother's,' he says. 'I would love for you to have it.' You cup it in the palm of your hand; a pear-shaped emerald prism alive with the dancing restaurant lights, and surrender to tears you won't try to explain. 'The colour matches your eyes,' he says. 'No one could wear this ring but you.'

Monet has a theory that the reason our john-boys blur into one is that since all men think with their cocks, we're basically balling the same dude over and over again. I met Monet ten years ago at Our Pleasure, a house I spent some time in when the bars were starting to get to me. She's roughened some around the edges now (you know the look: when the chins kick in and the laugh lines dig trenches under your eyes), but back then she was one of the industry's top earners. When business was slow, we'd do a cut-price double act, which I normally wouldn't come at (too whiffy, squishy and strained for me), but with her I didn't mind so much since Monet is a trannie and it was sort of like Doing It with a guy, you know what I'm saying? And plus, we'd have some fun with it; vamping and camping for the benefit of Mr Wrong. *Ooh bay-bee*, she'd wail, shaking her scrawny ol' groove thang inches from his slackjawed face in a classic Marilyn meets Miss Ross, *You shoah is wicked fine!*

You settle on chateaubriand for the main course: OTT and hopelessly old-fashioned, but it's something the two of you can share and besides, you don't swing by the Never-was for a salad. The champagne is an icy wash of burnished bubbles whose fizzy afterglow melts the licking candlelight and blurs the harsher lines. 'You are so beautiful,' he says. Azure eyes you can bathe in. A downy fuzz of stubble to nuzzle all night. You could curl like a kitten in his safe-haven lap and purr there for eternity, never moving or speaking again. Somewhere in the background (you're too cosy to check or care), a lone violinist begins to play.

I didn't take a shine to life at Our Pleasure. The pay was an improvement but the trade was as rough as they come, stomping like stampeding cattle up and down the stairs, and the hours killed. And plus, there were some Additional Services I totally couldn't deal with, you know what I'm saying? You wouldn't believe how many glasses of water a girl has to scull for a decent Golden Shower. And don't get me started on the Pleasure (not) of a three-way or the gob-stopping nightmare that is the Full French.

These days, I set my own limits and I make my own rules. Half French only, no showers or role-plays, and I don't care how much cash you're holding, no three-ways or B&D. Rubbers essential, prior inspections a must. I give it straight, I take it even straighter and I've got more clients than I know how to deal with. I like to think it's because I'm goddamned good at what I do, but Monet (who'll do anything with anyone – including her pet lizard, don't ask, won't tell) assures me that since your average john-boy is a yellow-bellied, wife-despising, closet-poofter pussy, the five-minute fumble is about all he's got in him.

'Windmills of Your Mind'? 'Both Sides Now'? 'Moon River'? Or maybe a medley of all three, the Neverwas being a medley state of mind? For dessert, you share a zabaglione, which in its honeyed filminess seems more like an air kiss than an actual dish, then liqueur coffees and petits fours, by which time you're spinning in your private seventh heaven. 'This is the happiest night of my life,' you tell him, swaying through the restaurant like reeds in the wind, his arm wrapped around you, pulling you close, and the raw silk of his whisper caressing your ear. 'It isn't over yet, my sweet,' he says. 'Not now and not ever.'

I live alone in a serviced townhouse in the Far North Sector and I work out of a studio on Airport Drive. I mostly use hotels, of course, but my local regulars get off on a homey vibe and, since they tend to linger longer and drop more dollars, Giles is all for the place, even fronting up with a slice of the rent. Every girl in my biz knows a lowlife like Giles. He's the reptile in the nylon shirt, spruiking outside strip clubs. He's the lech in mirrored wraparounds, leering from a car. In my case, he runs the service, pays the bribes and the bills and checks in for free nookie (his word, not mine, what can I tell you) three times a week. Father would have called him a pimp, and God knows he looks the part with his snakeskin boots and his wispy goatee (concealing, I would wager, a total lack of chin). I call him the closest to a boyfriend I've ever had – and judging from the experience, he's the closest I ever want to come, you know what I'm saying? At least when he hits me, he never touches my face.

The night air is syrup-sweet and when the Neverwas valet rocks up in the silver Alfa, you decide to fold the roof down for a spin out to the beach. The city thrums around you like the mirrored heart of a carousel but the sand dunes are deserted and the teasing wind is as warm as your blood. Without thinking, you wriggle free of your ivory satin sheath, he strips off his pants and shirt, and you dive in together, as deep and as daring as you know how to go.

My townhouse is pastel-toned Ikea issue, fitted out by someone I don't wish to know and swept and polished by people I try not to encounter. Courtesy of Giles, the working room is a mug punter's wet dream with soft-core portraits, shag-pile carpets, a circular king-size bed and mirrors out to Here. There's a bar in one corner (scotch, bourbon, Perrier, beer), and a hot-pink bathroom spa. Strawberries, cheese and pâté are on tap in the kitchenette fridge. I can't stomach food when I'm 'entertaining' but the john-boys do love their post-nookie nosh. The fact of it is, nowadays I barely eat at all. At thirty-two, every kilo you gain will be with you to the grave and besides, Giles prefers his ladies skinny. Count yourself lucky you still look so young, he tells me. Twenty-eight is dead-and-buried in this game.

'You look so young with your hair loose like that,' he tells you, wrapping you like a precious gift in the beach towel he naturally thought to bring. You snuggle beside him on a still-warm bed of sand, the two of you cold and salty from the glacial sea and the waning moon raining white light like a blighted sun, and you want to freeze this moment because you know there may never be another. 'Come to think of it,' he whispers with a wickedly playful smile, 'have you ever told me how old you really are?'

I turned thirty-two this month. My big brother popped my cherry when I was thirteen and I serviced my first client six years later; two random facts which may or may not be connected. I haven't seen my so-called family in fourteen years and in that time all I've ever amounted to (shades of Father, hard to shake) is a waitress and a working girl. I don't want children and I have no pets. He who travels fastest blah blah blah. My only unpaid sex is with a bully who beats me and my one true friend is a tough-cookie transsexual with a weakness for mean-spirited, unhappy men, who discovered her first lesions in a routine clinic test last week. I'm goddamned good at what I do but I'm too goddamned old to be doing it, and all the skin peels and collagen shots in the big, bad world won't give me back what I so blithely gave away.

For an agony of seconds, there's a make-or-break silence, then with the tiniest of sighs, he turns towards you and tilts your face to his. Crushed with shame, you won't meet his eyes, humbled by the judgement you are certain you will see there. That you tried to masquerade for him as something you were not. That you dared to shoot for happiness when you don't know what it is. That a girl – a working *girl – like you has no place in the Neverwas, or in his life, or in any scheme of things that believes, expects, accepts and gives thanks. You want to explain that you know the score but that in him you saw something you didn't realise you could see. No one can absolve you and you don't feel you deserve it, but can't he see how desperately you needed to escape?*

Meeting me the first time, you'd for certain think I'm hard. If you were a woman I'd tell you that all men are tarred with the one toilet brush and if you were a man I'd tell you whatever I thought you wanted to hear. But what about the secrets I could never say aloud?

✱

And then he speaks. 'Is that it?' he whispers, his eyes crinkled softly in what seems to be a smile. 'Is that what all the fuss is about?' You do look then, into a face so alight with love you know this has to be a dream. 'It's you I care about,' he says. 'Not what you've done, or where or why, not who you think you are. Because I know who you are, my sweet. You are the woman who I want to spend my life with.'

Like the face I impose on the faces of strangers? The way my old mantras ring hollow and false? The realisation that people despise me? The solo life sentence I didn't deserve?

The moonlight has faded, the tide has gone out and the time has come to return to the world. You lace up your sneakers and shoulder your backpack, readying yourself for the trudge back to town. It's a hike to the beach but the walk is a comfort, through lanes and back gardens you've known all your life. You're never afraid to come out here in darkness: it's the one journey you make where the destination is a place you want to be. Passing your parents' house, you peer from beneath your baseball cap at the shuttered front windows, wondering if they would know you as you are now and what they might make of you if they did. And picturing, despite yourself, the priceless gifts of childhood. Picnics by the river, Saturday matinees. Christmas cake and birthday candles. Bathtime bubbles and sleep-aways. 'I was happy then,' you think aloud, smiling in surprise at the memory.

Or the day my brother let me know exactly what was what? Give it a whirl, why don't you? he said, pinning me down like a moth on a board. It's no biggie. Tons of kids I know are doing it. I never believed that I might have had a choice. After the first time, it was almost every night. If you tell, he whispered as I kicked, thrashed and bit, I'll bring my friends around.

You were happy then.

Fourteen years later, I'm the one in control. I set my own limits and I make my own rules. Half French only, no showers or role-plays, and I don't care how much cash you're holding, no three-ways or B&D. I give it straight, I take it even straighter, and I like to think I'm god-damned good at what I do.

And now there's the Neverwas.

You know what I'm saying?

Barbara Else

A Little Mikado

Silence was the secret. That's what you held in your mouth like something precious. Some people would never understand and they could take a running jump.

'Would you like your cuppa in the lounge?' asked the new girl.

Maisie did up her cardigan, settled the cuffs, and stayed on her straight-backed chair. The girl put the cup and biscuits (one cheese cracker and one Tim Tam) on Maisie's bedside table, gave a fresh young smile (a vacant smile, to tell the truth) and pushed the trolley to Rowena's room next door. Even before it stopped, Maisie heard Rowena gabbing.

'She's never said a word since she came in, ask till you're blue in the face. Never leaves her room, either, didn't you know? If you want to learn what's what, dear, come to me.'

Maisie's blood frothed. She went down to the bathroom night and morning with a nurse. Other times she took a step or two into the corridor on her own. Sometimes, she took three steps. That Rowena had a tongue that flapped for miles. Just because she'd been a schoolteacher, Rowena thought she knew it all, but the woman wouldn't have the sense to salt the cabbage.

'Do you want tea in the main room?' The girl sounded patient. The vacant ones usually were.

'Of course, dear, I'm a social person, not like some souls.'

The trolley clattered off to the lounge. Rowena followed, still chattering as if she was the only one who ever got things right.

Cabbage reminded her, and the fresh young smile. And flouting the rules. That appalling boarding house in . . . somewhere near Manchester, where Maisie's own fresh smile led to all sorts of monkey business as that leering old man must have guessed. What smirks he gave, perched on his wooden chair between the cooker and the toilet door. And the name of the theatre was . . . gone entirely. Half a world away, a lifetime ago – sixty years, anyway, the smell of cabbage and the snaggle teeth of that old man. He'd made Maisie's flesh creep. But he'd still been fun to tease with a flick of her pink petticoat.

Maisie sipped her tea, ate a third of the cheese cracker, and dropped the Tim Tam in her wastebasket. A bulldozer wouldn't keep Rowena out of the lounge for afternoon tea. There she would have two Tim Tams and more. Maisie had kept her figure all these years and would go to her coffin in the white silk suit she'd worn on her wedding day, the brandy stain no drycleaner dared touch hidden by her folded hands. Anyone who came to view her would see exactly why she'd been an . . . the word, the word? . . . an ingénue.

Cries of delight and a riffle of laughter sounded from the lounge. Maisie smoothed her skirt and sat. It was like waiting in a dressing room, your make-up on, dress perfect, for your call. All that was lacking – apart from the fresh young face – was stage fright. People found it hard to understand about stage fright. If you said how terror surged about you, they dribbled fatuous remarks like how marvellously you acted, that you didn't need to worry. Now she thought of it, Maisie almost pined for stage fright. As soon as she had stepped in front of an audience, it hoisted her along on its pitch and billow. Happy exhaustion afterwards had flung her into several entertaining places.

More wheels came down the corridor, smaller, slower, from the other end. Funny as a fight this place could be, much funnier than a play, if only Rowena wouldn't try to rule the roost. And yes, Betty Matchett stopped in the doorway, hunched almost to the handles of the baby stroller. She swivelled it so it faced Maisie.

'This is Boy Pinkerton,' she said in her hoarse voice. 'Say hello nicely, Pinkerton.' She adjusted the ginger teddy's waistcoat. 'He never gives me a moment's trouble. Come on, little man, bath time.'

Last week it had been a blue velvet monkey. The month before, a koala, one of those unappealing toys made of wallaby skin. Few of Betty's boys survived more than a bath or two but the nurses were kind about it. No, you didn't need a night on the tiles to have a good time, just sit in your room, wait and watch. Better than the movies – Maisie held the thought a moment – no, she'd not have liked being caught on film forever, not able to do it any different.

Rowena waddled up again, chock-a-block with Tim Tams, no doubt. There was a hint of the nautical about Rowena's gait because she needed a hip replacement. She leaned in Maisie's doorway, puffing. 'You've eaten your Tim Tam.'

Maisie didn't glance at her wastebasket. She laced her fingers and smoothed the back of one thumb with the other.

'Here's a piece of news, I'm first to tell you. There's an outing tomorrow night. It's *The Mikado*.'

Maisie felt a jolt like a little splash of stage fright.

'We're going to a special performance, those of us who like a jaunt,' Rowena said. 'I was always one for the theatre. *The Mikado* is nonsense, of course, do you know it? It should go down very well with some. I can tell you all about it, every detail.'

Maisie felt she'd like to throttle something. No rewards for guessing.

'I will wear my blue pashmina. It's pure wool, from Pakistan. We'll all dress up to the nines. It was always rather fun to cut a dash.'

The inference was that Maisie had never cut a dash

and didn't have anything to wear even if she did want to go out. Maisie turned her hands until they made a little trap.

'It will be the last outing some of us have.' Rowena nodded towards a door across and down the corridor where the nurses had been busy for some time.

Did Rowena have the brain to pick up anyone else's inference? Maisie tilted up her chin. *Stuff your pashmina up your jacksy*, said that tilt. But Rowena rattled on about how she'd encouraged drama at school, how the mail was late today (silly old bat, it was Sunday, and who sent her letters anyway?), how perfect the pashmina was for the theatre, what a good thing she had kept it.

Maisie's blood was in a froth again.

Rowena shuffled aside as somebody approached. 'A visitor for you.'

It was Anne, Maisie's daughter-in-law, and she visited each week with a bouquet. Pink, of course. Always in shades of pink. Anne was a gem.

'How are you, Rowena?' Anne asked.

'I'm getting on like a bomb.' Rowena cocked her head towards Maisie. 'But there's not much joy in that one.'

Maisie's fingers tightened. She'd like to shove Rowena down some stairs, just give her the chance. Anne came in, sat on the second chair and took Maisie's hands between her own.

'Dougie found those magazines,' she said. 'I hope they're the right ones.'

It was hard not to react at the sight of Rowena trapped like a fly with curiosity: *how did Anne know what Maisie wanted when Maisie didn't even write things down?*

Maisie squeezed Anne's fingers instead of laughing, and began to sort the *Gaieties*. Rowena stood there, frowning.

A shriek sounded down near the bathroom. Captain Riley from Room Twenty-three who took terrible offence if anyone used his first name, silly old goat. He should know better than to interfere with Betty and bath time, but he couldn't keep away from water. A nurse hurried past Maisie's door, then another. By the time Maisie had the magazines in chronological order, Betty crept past again. The stroller left damp lines on the carpet and Boy Pinkerton dripped between them.

'Never a moment's fuss,' Betty panted. 'Not a bother, this wee man.'

'She'd better not be going to *The Mikado*,' Rowena said. 'There are standards to keep up. It's a pity Maisie won't be going, the nurses and I would keep an eye on her.'

Anne frowned a little and glanced at Maisie.

'My blue pashmina will be ideal. It's genuine, from somewhere, it came in the mail.' Rowena wobbled as she turned to do a skite.

Maisie – after a moment – tipped her head and glanced at Anne. Anne was a remarkable daughter-in-law. She patted Maisie's hand again and gave a smile of mischief.

Rowena had completed her laborious twirl, and bridled. 'What does that one think she's up to? What's going on?'

✦

The nurses seemed as bubbly as the patients while everyone got ready – to be more accurate, as everyone was
bossed around by the staff. Maisie heard it all from her
room. The bus had been ordered for six-thirty. Some
people like Captain Riley took so long over dinner they
had to be dressed beforehand. That meant being extra
careful about them not spilling. There'd been argument
about whether Captain Riley should go to *The Mikado*
anyway. He expected everything he saw on TV to be *The
Poseidon Adventure*, and was perpetually disappointed
when the ship didn't sink.

Rowena had already paraded by in her pashmina, so
big and blue she could have played the sea around Japan.
Maisie put her after-dinner cup of tea down on the tray.
She'd drunk only half in case of accidents, or at least of
being uncomfortable if the show went on too long. Not
that it was a full production. It was a shortened *Mikado*
put on by the pupils of a local singing teacher. But you
never knew, with bladders, which was why the old man
had sat between the boiling cabbage and the toilet door,
so teasable, that half-a-world-away lifetime ago.

Anne arrived with the garment bag over her arm.
Rowena rolled up to stickybeak but Anne eased Maisie's
door shut.

'I don't think the nurses believe me, but they're keeping a seat on the bus.'

Maisie felt the rise of fright. Anne understood entirely
and gave a smile that warmed her as well as any hug.

As carefully as Maisie might have done herself, Anne

unzipped the bag, making sure the garment inside wouldn't catch on the teeth. So many hasty backstage changes, zippers breaking at the worst time – oh, the marvellous fear!

'There,' Anne whispered and drew out the fine wool dress. She held it so Maisie saw the detail of the shoulder stitching, the pencil-thin pleats of the skirt, the weight and flare. Maisie had forgotten how it glowed between mist and sundown, a magical pink.

Anne helped her stand. They both took it very slow. The dress still fitted, almost perfectly. The hem was a little long now at ankle level, and the bust a little loose.

Maisie put a hand over the skin below her throat where panic waited, and looked in her mirror. Oh, the long-gone girl, and oh, the woman. She laughed – a rusty laugh but there, yes, there. For a second, Anne didn't move. Maisie held out one side of the splendid pleated skirt as if to take a bow.

'We couldn't find a matching coat.' Anne's voice was husky.

But Maisie felt warm enough for anything – the bus ride, the church hall where *The Little Mikado* was being performed, and champagne afterwards. Of course, there wasn't likely to be champagne tonight, only Milo and hot milk once they were all back in their rooms. Those with forethought, mind you, and a sensible son such as Dougie, always had a small bottle of Napoleon tucked in their bedside lockers.

Rowena still hovered outside when Maisie made her entrance into the corridor, but Maisie didn't glance her way.

Step by step, she floated to the bus, Anne beside her for support. Just as well she had talked to the nurses. Betty insisted Boy Pinkerton – soggy, but a bear with staying power – have a seat of his own, and Captain Riley fussed about being next to the driver so he could keep a lookout. It was anybody's guess what for, but apparently only a sea-faring man could be relied on.

All the walking frames, wheelchairs, and Pinkerton's stroller, were stowed. The nurse in charge made Maisie sit next to Rowena for the bossy old bint to keep tabs on her. Bollocks she would. Anne looked edgy as she waved goodbye.

The back seat was crammed with younger nurses gossiping about the drugs and boys they'd sampled lately. What a hoot, the way each new generation imagined itself the first to discover how to get blind drunk, as if sin were a new invention. Maisie could have scorched their eyebrows with stories of Blackberry Nip, Pimm's Number One Cup, and cabinet ministers in three countries of the Commonwealth.

'See the bulldozer!' Betty held Boy Pinkerton up to the window. 'No, not over there, it's some postulants.'

Rowena gulped with middle-class horror at the decline in standards. Maisie thought about waving, but it was a trio of sorry creatures in short black skirts, their hair sticking up as if they'd been electrocuted. No class – so Rowena was right.

'What do you mean by that grin?' Rowena asked. 'What did I say?'

The church hall was another matter, as was the singing teacher, tone and class to spare. Polished wood and brass railings for the one, a crimson floor-length skirt for the other, and a glamorous smile. She welcomed the busload with the air Maisie herself had found worked marvels at The Pink Apple in making the girls and the customers relax. The woman also had an eye for quality, because she noted Maisie's gown.

'Oh Lord, it's such a colour. I'll give you first offer of a sherry. The flor fino, or the sack?'

Flor fino had been just the thing for the voice before a show. Out the corner of her eye, Maisie saw Rowena and the nurse in charge move to object so she whipped her arm out for a glass and nodded thank you. It was always a matter of timing – and of balance. Some of the others showed how fast they were as well, when it was needed. The nurse retreated. The teacher offered Rowena a glass, but she spluttered like a panto dame.

'It's against church regulations, too,' the singing teacher murmured to Maisie, 'but I'm calling it medicinal.'

It was easier to move by now. The sherry helped. Maisie poured herself one more glass with aristocratic gestures she had used in plays by Shaw. The singing teacher prevented Captain Riley from taking off with a bottle to the back row.

Rowena wanted an aisle position but Maisie beat her to it – timing and balance. Rowena glared and muttered in the next seat. Maisie nodded *Look at the stage, you silly moo, the show's beginning.*

The citizens of the little town of Titipu scurried on and took up attitudes. Maisie hadn't realised – nor had anyone – the singing pupils were all children. There was a gaggle of other young ones in the front rows, brothers and sisters of the cast. They pointed and sniggered in the opening moments. Betty encouraged Boy Pinkerton to sing *Ying tong, ying tong* till the nurses shut them both up.

The Lord High Executioner loped across the stage and swung his sword.

'Where's the lifeboat!' Captain Riley shouted.

The Lord High Executioner flourished his little list. Rowena, despite her earlier comment about nonsense, made an inadvertent bleat about the mail, then shook herself, disconcerted. Maisie felt a nudge of pity. After all, Maisie had Anne and Dougie while Rowena never even got a mouldy postcard. The three little maids from school came on – Rowena's mouth softened and she murmured to herself. Captain Riley muttered, too, about three little life preservers.

Maisie's respect for the singing teacher increased each moment, at the innovations in the shortened script and her control over the cast of mixed ability. The young singers managed to ignore the unusual audience and kept up a creditable pace but some of them had no voice, not to mention a grain of talent. Only Katisha, the nasty old woman in the cast, rendered by a girl about thirteen, had real stage presence. She played her part with a mingled rage and elegance that endeared her to Maisie. She had a good strong voice, and showed a sense of fun in the way she rustled her yellow kimono.

Light-hearted nonsense *The Mikado* definitely was, but the citizens of Titipu changed the regulations as they went along, as happened in real life, if you asked Maisie. It was all playing parts but sometimes you adopted one with more enthusiasm than others. Nothing wrong with that.

The love tangle was as tricky in this shortened *Mikado* as the full-length, again like real life. Love made you burst out of your boundaries for a while – vivid moments, passion to carry you, secrets to treasure, that was what stayed inside you like the scent and taste of sherry. Maisie dabbed her eyes at the absurdity of Yum-Yum's song, how the pretty thing would rule the earth because of her beauty.

The Mikado finally appeared, played by a girl with shoulders like a weight-lifter. Maisie longed to cry out with delight when the troops marched in: the smallest singing pupils, solemn faced, dressed in shiny emerald green and with their hands thrust in their sleeves. This must be their first performance, some of these little ones and how brave they looked, how funny. Stage fright still lodged in Maisie's throat – how wonderful to know that friend again.

At the end of *Merrily Marry*, the Katisha did a bump and grind – but she hadn't been taught it properly. She got herself in a tangle, lost her nerve and blushed like fire.

Rowena began her prim and proper gabbling. Maisie's hands twisted on her lap, her blood seethed far too high.

The Katisha child knew she'd mucked it up, that was enough.

In a commotion of clapping, the children took their bows.

'Heroic! Not a man was lost!' cried Captain Riley.

The cast broke away. Through the chatter and laughing Maisie saw the Katisha, close to tears, sit on the edge of the stage.

'Ashamed and I should think so,' said Rowena.

Maisie felt near choking. She rose to her feet.

'Nurse!' Rowena grabbed Maisie's arm. 'Here, quick!'

Maisie shook Rowena off. On the pitch and billow of fright she walked to the Katisha.

With a puzzled, tearful smile the child stood up. Maisie gestured and flirted her marvellous pleats. The child hesitated, then gave a tiny smile and twitched the hem of her kimono. Maisie raised her arms and set them gentle as the licks of cabinet ministers on her hips. Again the child copied. All it took was understanding and control. Within moments the Katisha's bump and grind would have earned her tips in international currencies. Maisie touched her fingers to her lips – the girl copied that as well.

The singing teacher and the staff applauded softly. Captain Riley, Betty Matchett, and the other old folk were open-mouthed. The captain drooled, but the nurse in charge had a handy pack of tissues.

Maisie's blood calmed. The stage fright was a curve surrounding her. The blur of sherry. For a moment she wavered and leaned on the edge of the stage.

Rowena barrelled up in front of her, looking anxious. Maisie smiled and pulled herself up straight. Rowena gave a sigh of real relief. Very odd. For a change, the woman was speechless.

Maisie held out both sides of her skirt and took a bow.

'You – suit that,' said Rowena. 'Very nice.'

Pink had always been her colour but Maisie would not stoop to say so. The hot calm of her blood, the satisfaction.

Anthea Paul

Tanha Bar

Jill Dupleix's

Big Night In Cocktails

All you need to make a party rock is something lemony-limey, something bubbly, and something pink. It could be citron vodka or Limoncello (made from sun-dried lemons) and a whack of fresh limes. Champagne, of course, for the prerequisite fizz. Then cranberry juice, Campari, or pink grapefruit juice for pinknicity. And crushed ice for all: wrap ice blocks in a clean cloth and bash against a brick wall or hit with a hammer for instant frappé.

Serve with: prawns with wasabi mayonnaise, spicy pork sausagettes with freshly opened oysters, pesto toast topped with oven-roasted cherry tomatoes, salt-and-pepper calamari, or just big wedges of grilled sourdough bread topped with silky smoked salmon. Party on!

Lemon Fizz

120ml Limoncello
500ml chilled champagne
1 lime, thickly sliced

Chill four chunky glasses. Squeeze a slice of lime into each one, then toss in the squeezed lime slice as well. Add Limoncello and crushed ice, stir, then slowly pour in the champagne. Makes four.

Bitter & Twisted

200ml Campari
100ml blood orange juice
Chilled soda water
1 lime, cut into wedges

Peel a blood orange and cut the peel into long, thin strips. Fill a tall glass with ice cubes, and stick a twist of blood orange skin down the side. Add Campari and blood orange juice, lime and soda water. Makes four.

Pimm's Plus

100ml gin
100ml Pimm's Number One
50ml lime or passionfruit juice

Combine gin, Pimm's and lime juice over ice, and shake well. Strain into four well-chilled martini glasses.

Allegra McEvedy's
All-time Favourite Party Eats

Oysters Rockefeller

Undoubtedly the best way to eat oysters is raw. Having said that, this recipe wins on three fronts. Firstly, the name: how would anyone refuse an oyster Rockefeller; and secondly, a lot of people who have allergies to oysters, like me, can eat them cooked. Good pre-dinner nibble because they're pretty filling. Thirdly, you don't have to fret about knocking your friends out with food poisoning. Makes six.

6 rock oysters, shucked
2 shallots, finely diced
4 tbsp fresh breadcrumbs
½ bunch flat-leaf parsley, chopped
½ bunch chervil, chopped
3–4 rashers streaky bacon, finely diced
50g butter

Fry the bacon and shallots in half of the butter, stirring constantly until golden brown and starting to catch on the bottom of the pan.

Stir in the breadcrumbs and add the remaining butter in knobs.

Sauté the breadcrumbs until brown and crunchy, picking up as much of the bacon residue as possible.

Turn the heat off, stir in the herbs, add a little seasoning and then pack the mix on top of the shucked oysters.

Grill for around five minutes, then eat straight away. Preferably served sat on a pile of rock salt.

Deep-fried Salmon with Ponzu

This is one of my all-time favourites. If deep-fried salmon doesn't sound like your bag, think again – it goes all crunchy and delicious. The oiliness of the fish is beautifully opposed by the Ponzu, which is a light dipping sauce. The Ponzu is best if left to sit overnight, but can be made on the day if necessary. Serves three to four.

250g salmon fillet, tail end, skin on but scaled
Flour
Veggie oil for frying

For the Ponzu:
3 tbsp lemon juice
3 tbsp dark soy sauce
2 tbsp rice vinegar
1 tbsp mirin

½ tbsp soy sauce

1 tbsp bonito flakes

Radish to serve, daikon is best, shredded or thinly sliced.

Put the mirin in a pan and ignite it once it gets hot. Allow the flame to burn away, which takes the alcohol out of it. Add all the other ingredients for the sauce, warm everything through together, and sit it in the fridge for as long as possible. When you are ready, strain through a coffee filter to clarify.

Heat the oil to 180°C. Holding a long sharp knife at right angles to the salmon tail, cut it into slices around 1cm thick and then into bite-size pieces. Use a pastry brush to coat in flour, then drop into the oil (it should immediately start fizzling if hot enough) and cook until the fish gets properly crispy (approx. four mins). Drain on kitchen roll, and warm up the Ponzu. Put some sauce in a bowl for dipping, and arrange the crispy fish pieces around. Don't forget the radish, which isn't essential, but just goes nicely flavourwise and visually.

Ben Hatch

The Cruise

The Day Before

'Janine's a lovely girl. Good luck!' says my dad in his email.

'She'll be telling this story all her life – make it romantic,' emails my sister.

Day One
1 p.m.

We boarded the ship an hour ago, and opened our bottle of complimentary champagne as we cruised under the Golden Gate Bridge. Pedestrians leaned over the bridge to wave us off, the ship sounded its horn, and Janine let off the party poppers just as I noticed a pod of dolphins swimming alongside. It felt like they were our own personal escorts into the open seas.

It's going to be the press trip to end all press trips. The *Diamond Harmony* is the most luxurious cruise ship in the world and makes the *Titanic* look like a P&O ferry. Half a mile long, twelve decks of teak and marble, it gleamed above the wharf rooftops two miles out from San Francisco harbour. We have a deluxe stateroom on Deck 9 bigger than our flat, and our own maid and butler.

4 p.m.

We were warned in England by Debbie, the *Diamond* press officer, that the San Francisco to Alaska cruise tended to attract older passengers, but Janine and I are still surprised at the mandatory lifeboat drill. On the staircase leading to the mustering point, a steward's hand reaches into the crevice between my elbow and forearm as if I'm infirm. When the Norwegian Captain Okland reels off a list of safety precautions at the mustering point, we find one of these concerns getting into and out of the bath. It isn't striking midnight icebergs in a dead calm that's the biggest hazard aboard, but broken hip joints from passengers slipping on bath enamel.

After also warning of the perils of setting the gym Travelator walking machine to 'brisk', Captain Okland gives a semi-technical description of how the lifeboats are powered and operated, and says they are lowered from the deck by – he uses the next word as if talking about some new and exciting energy source – 'gravity'.

I say to Janine, 'This is very patronising. It's like he's talking to a bunch of pensioners', and then I look around and discover that that's exactly what he is doing. Everyone who has reserved a place in our lifeboat is over sixty-five. A thought occurs to me: I'd bumped into an elderly American woman by the lifts on my way down for the drill and she'd hidden her glass of champagne as if she thought she might get in trouble. Now it makes sense. 'I get it,' I say to Janine, 'nobody knows we're on a press trip. And we're so young nobody can believe we're rich enough to be here – they think we're members of the crew.' This is confirmed on our way back to Deck 9 when another elderly American woman compliments Janine about the jacuzzi on the sundeck.

5 p.m.

We discover our Filipino maid, Rita, lying outside our room with her hand over her eye. I ask her what the matter is and she says that it's nothing, but when I press her she reveals she scratched her cornea on one of the stems of dried flowers she was delivering, but didn't want to make a noise in case she disturbed us. She won't come in to wash her eye because fraternising with passengers is frowned on. 'No, I will lie here a little while longer and be all right in a minute,' she says meekly.

When she's better a little later she apologises profusely all over again, then informs us that room service operates twenty-four hours a day and everything is free. We can at any time of day or night order anything and everything from that day's five-star menu, including caviar. We laugh, but she is serious. A couple in a room along the corridor have already done this. More than thirty-two dishes were brought to their room. Their food included lemon sole, caviar, steak, chicken dishes, soups, cheese boards, cherry pies, and pasta. There was so much it had to be laid out on the king-size bed and floor because there wasn't enough room for it on the table.

We also meet the butler, a fussy Portuguese man called Pablo who's already in a flap about what I'll be wearing for the Captain's Gala Dinner tomorrow.

7 p.m.

Bon Voyage cocktails in the Vista Lounge. Debbie the press officer tells us the ship was chartered for Bill Gates' fortieth birthday. The Rolling Stones, Robin Williams and Tina Turner were among the guests. She says there's enough caviar aboard to sink a rowing boat, and with a ratio of 500 crew to 900 passengers we'll never be more than five seconds from a canapé.

As we sip champagne in our formal evening wear, the Manila Trio play 'The Girl from Ipanema'. White-gloved stewards gravitate towards our elbows with falafel hors d'oeuvres, and as the sun sets over the ocean, Janine leans over to me.

'It's like being in *The Matrix* – someone's going to yank a plug out of my neck in a minute and send me back to reality. This trip's going to be really special, Jez.' She looks at me hard. 'I mean, how *could* it get any better?'

Janine grins at this not very subtle hint, and luckily my flustered reply is drowned out by two American women in front of us. They've had so many facelifts they look like Gianfranco Zola, and are discussing whether they've seen

Bette Midler having a facial in the ship's spa centre. To thwart more probing from Janine, I point out the first woman's ears. They're so far back on her head they look like the grip suction pads on the bath slip-mat in our stateroom.

Day Two

We're sailing along the Oregon coast when Pablo arrives with the in-ship magazine, *Reflections*, on a silver tray with our breakfast. *Reflections* lists activities aboard, and Janine and I check them out. Mainly geared towards pensioners, they include beginners' bridge, jackpot bingo and foxtrot classes with James and Audrey Braithwaite. In the Diamond Cove, Jeff Rogers plays the diamond piano for our 'midday cocktail pleasure'. There's an art auction, a golf clinic at the Tiffany Deck driving range, paddle tennis and American TV chef Anthony Robson-Jones's preparation of smoked Sonoma range chicken on crispy wonton. There's also a casino, swimming pools and beauty-therapy rooms.

After a wander around the boat, we attend a Diamond Enrichment lecture in the Hollywood Theatre on looking after precious stones by gemologist Deborah Astle. Although we laugh at the end when a special chamois is given out for passengers to polish their diamonds with, Janine then worries me by insisting we visit Facets Jewellers in the Avenue of the Stars shopping mall to point out an amethyst ring she 'absolutely loves'.

1 p.m.

After lunch, I seek out Debbie for advice. I fell asleep in the Palm Court after breakfast and woke up with blueberry muffin crumbs around my mouth. I've taken part in no activities since we boarded and, more worryingly, I've already found myself browsing in the Avenue of the Stars for pastel resort wear.

Debbie warns that the slide into pensioner-dom is hard to avoid. She says passengers get so institutionalised by the luxury that they cancel the off-shore activities they've booked on day one because leaving the ship is considered too traumatic by day three. I know how they feel. Janine wants to do a helicopter trip to the Misty Fjords, but already I've got used to high tea in Palm Court and don't think I could go without my buffet lunch in the Trident Grill.

Another thing to watch, according to Debbie, is getting carried away with the five-star service. Apparently a journalist on a previous cruise got so swept up in it all she forgot she wasn't a millionaire herself and bought a Salvador Dali at an art auction that cost her the deposit she'd been saving for a flat.

3 p.m.

At the champagne art auction we're given a glass of champagne, and when Janine leaves complaining of sea-sickness, I foolishly buy a Jean-Claude Picot painting for more than $800. Janine is not impressed when I return to the room. 'But it's a marvellous example of the post-impressionist application of colour combined with the expressive qualities of line,' I say, reading from the fine-art brochure. Janine reminds me what Debbie told us – I am not a real passenger – and I am ordered to quibble about the transportation costs and use this as an excuse to get out of paying for it.

Sat in on jackpot bingo in the afternoon and fell asleep again. All the numbers called seem to have associations with pensioners. Number sixty-five – retirement age for some. Number seventy-four – you're a grandmother.

Trouble later, too. Men are requested to wear dinner suits in all communal areas of the ship after 6 p.m., and Janine thinks I'll show her up because of my M&S tux which still has all the labels on so I can take it back when the cruise is over. Why is Janine using the word 'special' so much? It is making me feel pressured. Special evening, special trip.

'I just want it all to be nice. And *please* get Pablo to do that cummerbund properly,' she says. 'You don't look . . .'

'I get the message. Special.'

11 p.m.

The Captain's Gala Evening in the Diamond Dining Room. I get away with my M&S garb until the label stating the percentage of cotton in my clip-on bow tie falls into my soup.

The waiter, Darren, fishes it out with bread tongs and, to demonstrate unflappability in high social circles, I engage him in conversation, bringing up the subject of crew parties. We have decided we must attend one. I no longer use staircases, and am prepared to wait a full five minutes for the lift even if I'm going down a single deck, and Janine thinks being around young people might reinvigorate me.

'In *Titanic*, Kate Winslet gets pissed and there's all that dancing,' I say to Darren. 'What's the chance of an invite?' But Darren feigns ignorance, pretending not to know what I'm talking about, and asks if I'd like to try the sorbet.

As usual, by 7 p.m. the ship's deserted. Everyone's in bed preparing for their power-walk around the Promenade Deck. A group do this at 6 o'clock every morning, walking super-fast and working their elbows like violin players, listening to headphones telling them things like: I will achieve my goals; I will conquer stress.

We consider sneaking down to the crew decks but feel too full after our foie gras. So, back in our room, and worried by Janine's continual hinting – she'd wanted to get *Father of the Bride* out from the ship's video library – I decide to test her.

'The reason women want to get married so much is because they spend their childhood putting wedding dresses on Barbie. It's different for men, who spend theirs attaching camouflage webbing to GI Joe. Don't you think?'

'It's true,' I say, ignoring Janine when she asks what this is all about, 'you expect us to go along with your infant fantasies, but you'd never go along with ours.

Admit it – you'd never parachute behind enemy lines in a commando unit with me to take out a Nazi bridge, would you?'

Janine goes to bed pretending not to be in a huff, but gives herself away by refusing to spoon me, claiming she feels seasick.

Day Three

My progress towards pensioner-dom escalates. A killer whale is spotted at the bow of the ship. There's a lot of excited chatter about it. But rather than climb up to the sundeck, I watch it on the ship's bridge-mounted video camera showing on Channel 54. It's the attitude of all hardened cruisers, many of whom only ever leave the ship for duty free.

After breakfast, when the plates had been cleared away and we were sitting there looking out of the porthole, Janine sighed and, apropos of nothing, suddenly fixed a stare on me and asked how long we'd been seeing each other, as if she'd forgotten it was four years. Then, when I told her, even though I wasn't doing anything at the time, she said just as a waiter approached to sweep away crumbs, so I had no chance to reply, 'Hurry up, Jez.'

We dock in Victoria. It's the capital of British Colum-bia, and we go on a Grayline bus tour of the town. It's very English, with double-decker buses, Devonshire cream teas and people dressed as Beefeaters. It's also Canada's Eastbourne, with 22 per cent of people retired.

Everywhere, old ladies shuffle for buses or join post-office queues. It's like being on the ship, only with worse service, and we decide to return.

On our way back, we see Rita. She's out of uniform and luckily doesn't see my reflex to summon her.

'You can't order her to fetch high tea – she's off duty,' says Janine and, chastened, I lower my arm. It's weird, the luxury is so all-encompassing that after a while you do find yourself moaning about small things. I tut-ted when the sun was on the wrong side of the balcony for breakfast, and I was annoyed with Pablo this morn-ing for tidying away my T-shirts in a different drawer to normal.

At the afternoon's press briefing with ship's officers it is revealed there are more than 200 crew that passengers never see. They don't come up from the lower decks and even have their own discreet gangplank for going ashore.

In the deserted Avenue Saloon later, listening to Jeff Rogers playing 'The Girl from Ipanema' for the hun-dredth time, Janine and I fantasise about the crew decks. She's never heard the ship's engine and wonders if it's actually powered by Filipino slaves operating giant oars.

'Maybe they live below deck for years, have children down there, never see daylight and are slowly mutating into a new species of half-blind crew-human savages,' I say.

'On every cruise,' says Janine, 'they're appeased with the blood of one passenger. An old lady plucked from the Diamond Dining Room, thrown into a dumb waiter, lowered to the waterline deck to be skinned alive with

Ulu Eskimo knives and devoured. Nothing left except a pearl necklace and a trail of offal in the ship's wake, picked over by seagulls.'

We don't say anything for a moment.

'What's the time? Oh, 8 p.m. I think *Some Enchanted Evening*'s just started in the Galaxy Lounge,' I say. Then, realising what I've said I add, 'We *have* to get invited to a crew party. We're going insane.'

In the end we have a romantic walk.

With the soft breeze off the water on my face and Janine looking sexy in her black dress against the shore lights, I find I'm rehearsing a groom's speech as we stop and kiss on the sundeck. Then one of the terminally ill passengers draws alongside. There are several on board. The man's wheelchair is being pushed by his wife. She pulls up a lounger and begins crocheting, but it's more the sound of his respirator that ruins the moment.

Day Four

When I was ten I can remember my mum telling me that one day I'd be married. I can remember exactly how I felt at the time. I was horrified. I was standing by the sofa in the living room of our old house in Hounslow, and I looked down at my luminous wristwatch and said I'd never get married. She said she'd remind me I'd said that when it happened, and I deliberately memorised the incident so in later years I could turn around and tell her she was wrong.

What is it that's magnifying Janine's bad points? She's

not making it easy. She spilt a glass of water this morning and I heard her make the *grrr* noise. Janine only makes the *grrr* noise after a clumsy blunder, and she only makes clumsy blunders when she's distracted because of a bad mood she's in about something to do with me. Normally I think, Oh no, the *grrr* noise, better keep out of her way. Now it sets my teeth on edge and makes me think, Can I live with that? It's the same with Janine's habit of sniffing me when we kiss, to decide if I need a bath or not. Do I really want to be smelt like a Labrador for the next fifty years? Every little thing she does that I don't like I am mentally multiplying by the number of times I think she will do this if we stay together forever. I am then totting all this up in my head and working out if it is more or less than the total sum of laughs and love I will get out of her over that same period.

We cruise through Queen Charlotte Sound towards the Alaskan town of Ketchikan and, during drinks in the captain's quarters, giddy on champagne, I quiz Debbie about below-deck parties. We have to meet some young people. She says passengers aren't invited because it ruins the mystique. Because I am annoyed about the crew-party rebuff, when Debbie reveals the average age on board is seventy-five, I ask her what's done with the bodies when someone dies. There are more than 900 passengers, they're all very old, it must happen.

Debbie looks nervous and says, 'There's a morgue.'

I ask about burials at sea, how bodies are shipped home and if there's a body in the morgue right now.

Debbie politely excuses herself and leaves to speak to another journalist about the ordering of fresh salmon.

Janine surprises me at dinner. 'Now I know that you're never going to ask, let's just enjoy ourselves and not fight,' she says. I say that I didn't think we'd been fighting. I can't work out if it's the ship pitching, the pheasant and sweet potatoes I had in the Galaxy Lounge earlier, or the reverse psychology that makes my stomach lurch as she adds, 'I'm not even sure I want to any more, anyway.'

I take the elevator to the business centre afterwards. The satellite link's open and I've got sixteen messages from my family asking if I've popped the question yet. I don't reply to any and Janine's not in the room when I return. I try the sundeck, look in the gym, search the Lido deck café, the Vista Lounge, and eventually find her back in the room. I kiss her on the ear as she turns her head away. She says she's going to the gym. Unable to think what to do, I find myself lying disconsolately on the bed, flicking the TV remote, saying in a genuinely bored voice when Janine half-heartedly asks about my plans, 'I suppose I could order some caviar.' Despite the frosty atmosphere we both burst out laughing at my spoilt tone of voice, and how it has come to this level of complacency. And for another split second I imagine doing it.

Day Five

We arrive in Ketchikan, our first Alaskan town. It's set against the beautiful snow-capped Deer Mountain. We wander around the tiny town and try to befriend Alaskans, but only meet a madman who claims he pilfered Hermann Goering's corpse in the Second World War. We tell him we're heading for Sitka next, and he says his niece runs a gift shop there and will give us a discount on Fabergé eggs if we present her with a card he gives us. On the card it says: 'I was sent by Uncle Conrad.' We give up befriending Alaskans.

On a sea-kayaking excursion we fail to spot any humpback whales but our guide says I'm in the boat that Alan Rickman used during Bill Gates' fortieth-birthday cruise. Tina Turner apparently performed an impromptu concert on the ship when it was moored off the wharf, and everyone in the town spent the night straining their ears to listen in to 'Private Dancer'.

'There isn't much entertainment in town, then,' I say.

He looks at me blankly and says, 'I hunt raccoon and there are lots of bars.'

We're back on the ship just in time to witness an American woman patriotically breaking into a rendition of 'Stars and Stripes' at the sight of a bald eagle swooping overhead. '*So* beautiful. They move me *so much*,' she confides with a tear in her eye, and then disappears below to meet the Friends of Bill W in the Bridge Lounge, a euphemism aboard the ship for Alcoholics Anonymous.

I watch Americans lose money in the casino in the afternoon, and when Janine catches up with me she's having an existential crisis after attending an enrichment lecture in the Hollywood Theatre about Promise and

Peril on the Pacific Rim by celebrity geographer Dr Harm de Blij. She's got so bored of the mollycoddled life on the ship she's been fantasising about Mount Edgecumbe volcano erupting and the ship sinking in an earthquake.

'Imagine it. Passengers tumbling into Charlotte Sound clutching their walking frames. Agonised millionaires crying for their butlers. "Pablo, Pablo – bring me my buoyancy aid." James and Audrey Braithwaite foxtrotting beneath the surf, unable to stop their slow-slow quick-quick rhythm as they go to their watery grave.'

I talk sternly to her – the way to combat the decadence is complacency. At dinner I demonstrate this by ordering French fries instead of haute-cuisine vegetables. 'Treat the pampering as normal and then abuse it and act common.'

She nods but then immediately has another crisis when the lights are dimmed and we witness the Parade of the Baked Alaskas. In near darkness, hundreds of waiters emerge from choreographed corners of the room and begin what looks like the figure-of-eight mating dance of the bumble bee, carrying above their heads flaming baked Alaskas while moving their mouths silently to Russian military music.

Before bed I ask Janine if she's serious about what she said yesterday. She says yes. She got swept up in what all her friends said – that if I was ever going to do it, I'd do it on this trip. She's sorry I felt under pressure. I feel terrible and want to tell her I have been thinking about proposing but that every time she mentions it I'm put off. If she could just leave it long enough for me to kid myself into thinking the whole thing was my idea.

Day Six

We're in Sitka, another tiny Alaskan town. We wander around and I try on a hat made from a Timber Wolfpelt. The wolf's jaws are open and its paws are used for earmuffs. Janine considers it too tasteless to buy, unlike lots of the American women.

For my article I interview my first passenger, Claudia, who claims she's just blown out a man worth $200 million because she's a genius-magnet and only goes for men with PhDs. When she asks if I know the Guggenheims I find myself pretending I'm a vague acquaintance of theirs.

'Peggy's nice, isn't she?' I nod and take a picture of her in the necklace she bought after the gem lecture. Claudia says jewellery on the ship is incredibly cheap. 'But I suppose you're married to that lovely girl,' she says as coquettishly as anyone can with varicose veins. I'm strangely thrilled by the misunderstanding, but just in case Claudia's coming on to me I make sure she's aware of my A-level results. The truth is I want to surprise Janine, but it has to be in the right setting. And in a way I'd like it to surprise me, too – be spontaneous. Maybe this afternoon in Glacier Bay.

5 p.m.

Glacier Bay. It's freezing cold. The water's green. The ice is minty blue and icebergs drift past the boat. Activities on board are suspended when the park ranger comes aboard. He's a serious man with a beard who, over the loudspeaker, says things like 'Here landscape is a noun not a verb', and when a woman asks to play paddle tennis she's not allowed to in case a tennis ball's hit out of the court, over the side of the boat and ends up being sucked into the blowhole of a humpback whale.

The ship draws to within 100 yards of the glacier, and the ice snaps and crackles as it moves down the valley into the sea. We see a brown bear on the mountain top, eagles swoop, and basking sea lions float by on pan ice. It's an awe-inspiring sight and for the first time it might be the moment to pop the question. There's a loud crack like the whip of a rifle shot, and a tremendous intake of breath all round as a lump of ice as big as a car shears off the glacier and plummets into the ocean. And just as I'm gearing up, thinking that it's the moment, Janine interrupts me. 'Bollocks,' she says. 'That reminds me – I forgot to defrost the fridge.'

Claudia's started following me around, which doesn't help, and an incident occurs. Still light-headed because of what almost happened, when she sidles up I inadvertently say she reminds me of the old woman in the film *Titanic* who loses her necklace. It turns out this woman is ninety-four. Claudia's a mere eighty-two and she stalks off claiming her ex-beau is a Nobel prize winner and that she'll sue my ass if there's anything in the article she disapproves of.

Then in Prego's we get a lucky break. Through a loose-tongued waiter we hear of an end-of-cruise crew party on Deck 6 tomorrow night. Perfect.

Day Seven

I need to keep busy to distract myself from tonight. If I think about it too much it won't be spontaneous. But if I don't think about it at all, I'll cock it up.

In Juneau, the state capital of Alaska, we visit Mendenhall Glacier. 'Not as good as the last one,' I hear myself saying peevishly. We ask the tour guide what people do in these towns – there seems to be nothing but gift shops selling Tlingit Indian totem pole fridge magnets. The guide says drinking is popular and so is McDonald's. Apparently when the Juneau McDonald's got its franchise, everyone in nearby Skagway was so bored and desperate for something to do they chartered a floatplane to pick up an order for the whole town. They brought their microwaves to the airport and all ate their Happy Meals together – 700-odd people. The day's remembered as one of the best since the Klondike gold rush. When in Rome we think, and over McChicken Nuggets, feeling strangely comforted by the inferior cuisine, Janine and I work out how we'll get into the crew party. We'll walk around the promenade deck aft, descend a flight of stairs and come in through the fire escape.

Midnight

My nerves build all day. Janine assumes I'm worried about gatecrashing. 'This isn't *Under Siege*, you're not Steven Seagal. We're off the ship tomorrow anyway.'

Our plan works a treat though. As we sweep through the curtained fire escape, the party's like that scene in

Chitty Chitty Bang Bang where they find all the children in the sewers under the castle. It's surreal and startling. There are hundreds of young people partying. People our age drinking, laughing, dancing, snogging. The Manila Trio's playing 'Wonderwall' by Oasis. James and Audrey Braithwaite are *foxtrotting* to it. Rita's dancing, Pablo's drinking Heineken. Darren, the waiter, is kissing a waitress from the Trident Grill. Suddenly everyone seems real.

It's perfect. I'll pop the question on the sundeck on our way back to the room, I think. Except pretty soon we begin to feel self-conscious. On the fringes, trying not to stick out, I begin to panic. It's unsettling seeing these people living double lives. The scene's so noisy, lively and removed from the piano tinkle we're used to, it feels like some dangerous tribal ritual we've stumbled upon: Robinson Crusoe witnessing the cannibals boiling a human head.

Janine feels it, too, and we sit in the shadows, watching, hoping we don't get spotted. 'What would we do if they dragged a passenger onto the dance floor and slit his throat like a chicken?' says Janine. 'Imagine how scared we'd be.'

Bloated on tender meats and cutlets, pampered to within an inch of our lives, we'd be no match for them and have to make a decision: pluck up the courage and get a drink or go. I feel the amethyst ring I bought from Facets this afternoon in my pocket, but as I see Rita approaching, I do something stupid.

'We've heard there's a morgue,' I say to her. At the time it seems the most blasé thing to mention.

Janine says, 'No, Jez.'

Rita looks blankly at me.

'We've been told there's a morgue – a place where they store bodies – I've been told it's on this deck. How many passengers have died so far?'

Rita moves away, Janine disowns me, and we're steered to our rooms by a large man with 'Diamond Security' written on his back.

Day Eight

We disembark in San Francisco. It's a rude awakening. There are noises we'd forgotten. Raised voices. The sound of children, mobile phones. We don't speak much on the flight, or on the Heathrow Express, and back at home it's straight to sleep.

Janine's alarm sounds at eight the next morning. We're both shocked to find we're not on the ship. I'd mistaken the answerphone message from my dad in the night for the captain on the loudspeaker.

Janine makes cereal, eats it catatonically on the green sofa. I'm not back at the magazine until tomorrow, but I sit with Janine in the living room to keep her company while she gets ready for work. When she does her make-up I follow her to the bathroom. We exchange a look in the mirror.

'Why are you following me?'

'I feel funny,' I say. 'We should be eating muffins in Palm Court now.' Janine dabs at her cheeks and doesn't say anything.

After she's kissed me goodbye she clomps down the corridor. I follow her to the front door. I don't want her to go. Standing on the doorstep she says goodbye. I say the same. Then, when she's almost out of sight, I decide to shout, Have a good first day back. Or something like that. But when I open my mouth, 'Will you marry me?' comes out.

It's a cold day and the breath of the words leaves a vapour trail from my mouth. It's the only evidence I've said it until Janine stops. All the way back to the flat she's repeating one word: 'What? What? What?' I keep repeating one word, too: 'Well?'

'What?'

'Well?'

'What?'

'Well?'

It goes on until she says: 'YES.'

She phones work to tell them a radiator's leaked and she'll be late. We sit in the living room. It's 9 a.m., but feels like 2 a.m. I feel drunk, so does Janine. We can't believe what we've done.

'Sorry it wasn't romantic,' I say, then remember the ring. Janine admires it on her finger even though it's miles too big, then she goes to kiss me.

'Just don't sniff me,' I say.

Janine laughs, does it anyway, then joins me in the bath she decides I need. 'Don't think this means I'm blowing up anything over the Rhine with you,' she says turning to face me. I laugh; she laughs. The ring must

129

have slipped off as I'm soaping her arms although neither of us notices this at the time, and it's as we're climbing out and Janine reaches down to rescue it from the plug-hole that I hear the *grrr* noise.

David Smiedt

C'est la guerre

He'd pleaded for no strippers. In fact, he'd begged us not to organise a stag night at all. However, these protestations only made me – his best man – all the more insistent.

Tim and I had been friends long enough for me to know that he was no prude. It was more that he had an aversion to being the centre of attention. He had also witnessed my own disastrous stag night some years earlier, when an extensively tattooed erotic dancer sat me on a chair in the middle of the venue, removed my glasses (thus rendering her performance an indistinct blur of inky flesh) and proceeded to squirt copious amounts of Vaseline Intensive Care down the front of my trousers.

Tim had a point. But I had one to prove.

Eventually, Tim relented on the condition that I would provide a no-nudity guarantee, and I set about organising an event he would never forget and that his mates would reminisce about for years. With the flesh factor prohibited, it needed to incorporate a smattering of the traditional features associated with such celebrations. That meant alcohol and a degree of ritual humiliation for the groom – all to take place under the cover of darkness. There was no way he was going to be home before sunrise.

The solution lay in violence – or at least a mock version thereof. On the city outskirts, where light-industrial meets semi-rural, was a Skirmish centre boasting infra-red night-vision goggles as standard equipment. 'This,' the brochure assured, 'lent the dusk till dawn covert paint bath an authentic operational feel.'

I hired a bus and driver and, after piling into the fifteen-seater at the designated rendezvous, we swung past Tim's place in the cream taffeta light of the late afternoon.

Having made me swear yet again that I'd keep my promise, Tim boarded the bus with an air of excited expectation tempered by trepidation. The balance soon shifted when he was handed a catheter bag of rum and Coke, and ordered to drain the contents. Tim was a newly qualified doctor, so his mates were primarily university friends and colleagues who took great delight in replacing the traditional yard glasses associated with stag nights with bedpans and other assorted medical paraphernalia capable of holding liquid.

Holding a fair amount of liquid himself, Tim was the first of the would-be combatants disgorged by the bus when we pulled into the Skirmish parking lot at twilight. A competitive beast by nature, he reeked of virility, and was gagging for a dose of sanctioned aggro.

Although his attitude was initially infectious, our

collective confidence dissipated like confetti in a sea breeze when our competition arrived. Perhaps it was the fact that their minibus entered the compound to the strains of 'We're going home in the back of a paddy van'. Perhaps it was the fact that some owned their own paintball guns.

Casting a nervous eye over the Guinness-swillers that were to be my brothers-in-arms for the day, I wondered briefly what the protocol was about swapping sides. After all, our competition were already exchanging stories about previous Skirmish adventures and were focused enough to have selected their team name – 'The Grunts' – during the bus ride over.

All was not lost, however, as our crew experienced a metamorphosis. As soon as Tim, Andy, Steve, Howard and the rest of the 'Coagulators' emerged from the provisions shed in camouflage jumpsuits, black ammo vests and wrap-around visor masks, what had been a bunch of blokes in jeans and football shirts now fancied themselves warriors, freedom fighters, soldiers. No longer were they an assortment of security guards, bank workers, solicitors and tradesmen in their mid-twenties who had been drawn together by impending nuptials. They walked taller, stood prouder and had the unmistakable air of the mercenary about them.

We walked the walk and talked the talk. 'It's kill or be killed now,' grinned Howard, an actuary with a wife and two kids.

'To win a war you have to become one,' agreed Tim, whose fiancée was being straddled by a stripper dressed as a policeman as we spoke. But Tim cared not a jot – there was a war to fight. 'I love the smell of napalm in the evening,' he bellowed – the combination of testosterone and alcohol amplifying his voice to such a degree that it rivalled the bullhorn being used by the Skirmish referees to explain the game.

'Skirmish is a contest between two teams of around twelve people,' yelled referee Dave, an ex–army reservist, his words rebounding off the gullies and corrugated-iron sheds in case the trembling-to-kick-arse participants didn't quite catch him the first time around. 'The teams have forty-five minutes in which to either eliminate all their opposition or attain an objective specified by the referees. Once a player is hit, they are out of the game and have to retire to the "eliminated area" holding their weapon in the air.'

Armed with a pair of thermal-imaging goggles and a matt-black two-kilogram carbon-dioxide-propelled weapon that fired grape-sized gelatine capsules filled with luminous red food dye, I remembered how utterly miserable I am at games of ruthless cunning. An obvious defence was therefore to take the piss out of it.

With our competition in a tactical huddle, I said to Tim, 'Give them some camouflaged gear and a gun and everyone's Rambo.'

From behind me rumbled a voice so deep that it would have made James Earl Jones sound like a castrato: 'Don't say Rambo.' Standing with his massive legs astride and wearing a pair of mirrored sunglasses that reflected my apprehension, a bull-necked Skirmish regular pointed his custom-designed pump-action weapon in the general direction of my testicles and spat out, 'It's not about war. We're pacifists – we just like killing small animals occasionally.'

Before I could piece together any type of appropriately humble response he continued, 'You'd better listen to the briefing, son. You might learn something.'

The referee barked out the rules of the game: 'Goggles on at all times, one whistle starts the game, two whistles freezes play, three whistles ends play meaning time is up or the objective has been reached, if you get within three metres of the enemy and call "surrender" they are obliged to leave the field. Or you can shoot them.'

'You'll get no mercy from me,' announced Steve, a hospital security guard who had spent the entire briefing telling us that 'on the streets there are no rules'. In the tradition of true mateship, we humoured him by looking in his general direction but not listening.

Dave seemed to share their sentiments and carried on oblivious to this tirade of toughness: 'There will be no alcohol or wacky backy on the course – leave that till the end of the day. There will be no butt stroking – leave that till the end of the day, too. If you get caught intentionally shooting a referee you'll be put up against a ten-man firing squad.'

It was a slick shtick, well rehearsed, well delivered and well received. The referees addressed all the players as 'sir' but had an air of the 'tough-as-tungsten, don't-fuck-with-me' Hollywood drill sergeant that only added to the atmosphere.

Before I could figure out whether Dave had modelled his performance on Louis Gossett Jnr in *An Officer and a Gentleman* or Chris 'All-purpose psycho' Walken in *Biloxi Blues*, we were squeezing off a few practice rounds at cardboard targets. Each shot was accompanied by a puff of carbon-dioxide gas and a sound not dissimilar to that made by my late Uncle Harry after a particularly spicy meal.

The first course of the evening was the Speedball scenario: an undulating clearing the size of a football field in the woods with a pole on either end, a dry creek in the middle and littered with 1.5-metre-high barriers built from planks. A flag hung from the pole at either end of the field and the objective of the game was to snatch the enemy's colours without being taken out.

A blast sounded from Dave's whistle and the game was on. Players scampered towards the barriers as the refs pumped five or ten rounds into the inky night to create the illusion of rapid fire coming from the battlefield. This sound was soon replaced by the thwack-thwack-thwack of paintballs slamming into the thin boards behind which my comrades dove feet-first like baseballers. Matters were complicated even further by the night-vision goggles, which rendered the surroundings varying shades of luminous green.

Howard shared my shelter but was immediately taken out by a projectile that slipped under the lowest board and was abruptly halted by his scrotum. With his groin covered in red slime, all he managed to wheeze was 'Where the hell did that come from?' before hoisting his weapon above his head and retiring to 'The Graveyard' – where dead men resided until the next game.

Over the din, a passing referee yelled, 'He's got the mark on you. I'd move.' Too late. The paintball collected me square in the chest like a well-trained knuckle finding the bony area just above the sternum. Looking more like a walking Jackson Pollock than a combat vigilante, I trudged back to The Graveyard determined to last longer in the next game. All the while my comrades in arms were scattered around me, communicating in complex strategic codes like 'Is that bloke on our side?'

While the war raged on, my fellow casualties gathered in increasing numbers. First it was Tim, who was soon taking great delight in the fact that he'd lasted longer than Howard and me. A considerable feat since he had complied with a Skirmish tradition which dictated all grooms-to-be wear an orange tutu while in the field of battle.

Next emerged 'there are no rules on the street' Steve, looking decidedly unhappy. He copped a paintball square on the crown, decided the entire Skirmish thing was 'stupid and childish' and announced that he didn't want to play any more. He spent the rest of the evening in the car park with a red stripe across his noggin, moaning 'What's wrong with strippers anyway?'

By game two, there was talk of the best positions to cut off crossfire and of covering your team-mates when they scurried to better vantage points. Dirt was being spread on faces for extra camouflage and Tim was commanding his allies to 'Take out the fucking bastard on the left' – who just happened to be me.

'To your left,' screeched Tim, having realised his mistake. I flung myself behind a tyre wall that was bombarded by a volley of paintballs from the enemy. Tim's selfless act was to be his undoing though. By telling me to take cover he'd given away his position and collected a projectile in the gut for his trouble. Charging forward to the next barrier, I squeezed off round after round towards none of the enemy in particular, like a grizzled Hollywood infantryman bent on avenging the death of Timmy (the eighteen-year-old farm boy who'd been sliced in two in the trenches beside me while reaching inside his jacket to retrieve a photo of his sweetheart Betty-Lou Comeuppance who he was gonna marry the minute he got home to Sweetwater, Arkansas).

Meanwhile, as he had been retiring from the battle-field, Tim had been the recipient of several paintballs, which, judging by the intensity of his ensuing discussion with the referee, were stinging like jellyfish and leaving bruises the size and colour of squash balls. 'But ref, he shot me when I had my gun above my head,' he whined. 'He says that paintball stain was from the last game but it hit me a minute ago. It's not fair.'

As the games went on and the referees led us to different courses, proceedings took on an increasingly earnest and single-minded air. In The Graveyard, the combatants shouted out instructions to their 'living' comrades. 'Dead men don't talk, gentlemen,' yelled a referee in their direction, but to no avail.

As members of the losing team, we had moved beyond developing winning strategies and were now pointing out each other's incompetence.

'Why didn't you call for help?' asked Howard.

'Then they would have known where I was, you dickhead,' replied Tim.

'They would have known anyway 'cause you were shooting at them,' said Howard, his voice edgy and rising.

'I can't just sit there like a coward. I've got to do something so I attacked them,' retorted Tim.

'Next time I see a stupid prick like you running along,' snapped Howard, 'I'll shoot him.'

At 5.30 a.m., with sunlight peeking over the horizon, it was time for the final and longest game of the night. I lost the infra-red goggles and entered the war zone one last time. Entitled 'Last Man Standing', the game worked like this: each team was given a building to protect while trying to capture the one held by the other. It was up to the gladiators how they would go about achieving this goal, but as long as you terminated all of your enemies and had one team-member alive, you were deemed to have won.

Wizened and wearied by our war experience, we decided on a strategy of divide and conquer. Tim and I would guard our building while the rest of the team assaulted the competition's.

The Grunts had different ideas. Theirs was a 'death or glory' attitude, with a policy of all-out attack.

Tim and I stationed ourselves on either side of the only entrance to our building and waited for the attack.

It came sooner than we expected as the remainder of our team had been woefully outnumbered and swiftly decimated by the enemy. But with the sounds of the fire fight still in the distance, I turned to Tim and said, 'Better than a stripper?'

He replied, 'Jane's pregnant.'

Every time Tim has shared a personally momentous event with me, it has been while we've been engaged in some activity. Before a second serve in tennis he told me that his parents were getting divorced. He revealed that his sister had a heroin habit while gutting a snapper. I guess being otherwise occupied made these discussions easier for him and, for my part, having something else to do – besides react – sliced the earnest nature of the topic into manageable portions. Unsure of how he was feeling about his impending fatherhood, I hedged my bets.

'How are you feeling about your impending fatherhood?'

'Well, I've been reading up on it,' he replied with a typically detached medical objectivity, 'and, Christ . . .'

A sizzling paintball grazed the top of his visor and he pumped a volley of shots in the direction from which it came.

'I'm actually pretty happy about it,' he continued. 'But fuck knows what kind of father I'll make.'

'I know what kind of father you *won't* make,' I said. 'You won't be one of those guys who buys his kids the best sports gear but never makes it to any of their games.'

Behind the paint-speckled visor, the skin around Tim's

eyes crinkled into a smile. 'And I'm not going to be one of those pricks who insists that their kids "can always do better" no matter how hard they try,' he replied, his eyes far away.

'So what's the problem?' I asked, poking my head into the open door frame to scan for enemy movements.

'Think about it,' he said. 'It's not like the old days where all you had to do was come home with a pay cheque and your job was done. We know what's at stake now and I don't know about you but I've got the neuroses to prove it. Incoming!'

Half a dozen paintballs whistled through the doorway and squelched against the far wall.

'I don't know about that,' I said while reloading. 'I reckon that whole "I'm a fuck-up because my dad never threw a ball to me" is a crock. My dad did all right by me and if I could do half as good a job as he did, I'll be happy.'

'No one's attacking your dad, dickhead,' said Tim. 'I like the bloke but we live in a more aware time . . . DIE, YOU COCKSUCKER!'

Tim found his mark twice and an enemy duo left the battlefield with guns held aloft. I knew he had something important to say when he took off his visor. 'How do I know I'll be supportive when my child needs me to be? Or attentive? Or encouraging?'

I've always had difficulty answering rhetorical questions, so I said, 'You'll make a great dad.'

He treated my response with the shallow disdain it

deserved and continued, 'If it's a girl, how do I make sure a pussy-hungry bastard like we once were doesn't break her heart?'

What was I meant to say to that? 'They'll be harder to pick if you can't see them, so put your visor back on before you cop a paintball in the eye,' I countered. But Tim had lost his concentration. 'And what if it's a boy? How do I make sure he has confidence but isn't an ego-driven prick who doesn't know the difference between strength and power?'

No sooner had the last syllable exited his mouth, than he was nailed by a paintball to the temple by the trio of blasting Grunts that had stepped from beside both sides of the doorway we were guarding. His vision obscured by the streaks of paint across the visor, he slumped against the wall defeated, as I was peppered with high-gloss bullets. The Grunts high-fived one another and walked off in the direction of The Graveyard.

Crouching over him, I hammed it up in a Saturday-afternoon double-feature style: 'Hang in there, Timmy Boy, I'm gonna get you out of here. Texas needs you.'

Tim immediately slipped into his repertoire of war-movie clichés. 'It's getting cold, Sarge. So very cold. Tell Jane I love her.'

'I will, Timmy. I will.'

He closed his eyes and shuddered. 'Tell her I wanted to name our baby after you.'

'What, call him Sarge? He'll get a hell of a time in the schoolyard, don't you think?' Sarcasm was the only way I could prepare for saying the one thing I was certain of during our entire conversation: 'How are you going to make sure your child has confidence but isn't an egotistical prick who can't tell the difference between strength and power? All they will have to do is watch their Dad.'

INXS's

Top Ten for the Best Night Out

JON FARRISS

1. **'Fly Like an Eagle' – Steve Miller Band**

   This song is so cruisey and funky. It collects and combines so many memories of big nights out I had during the 70s, and I still listen to it today.

2. **'Do It Again' – Steely Dan**

   Now, this track is also such a cruisey number. A little bit jazz, little bit Californian . . . It never ceases to amaze me how cool these guys are. This is another track that conjures up the wonderful memories I have of the 70s . . . timeless.

3. **'Once in a Lifetime' – Talking Heads**

   This song is so exciting. It just pulses excitement with that hypnotic bass line and drum pattern. You can hear Eno all over it. This song was revolutionary. It changed my way of thinking musically, and I think it had a huge influence on INXS and my peers at the time it was released. It still is a massive influence on me today, especially on a big night out. We used to use this track as an 'intro tape' before we came on stage to get the audience vibed up.

4. **'Move on Up' – Curtis Mayfield**
   This song is so upbeat and positive, I listen to it all the time. It is a permanent member of my CD stacker in my car and at home, and I find it encouraging when I'm feeling down. It really trucks along with that driving percussive rhythm and sexy horn section. Curtis has such great energy . . . very cool.

5. **'Superstylin'' – Groove Armada**
   If you want a tune to get you in the mood to party, this is it! If you are in a position to crank this baby up, it will take you to all the places you wanna go. Groove on it.

6. **'Everything in Its Right Place' – Radiohead**
   I find something very emotive about this song. It's sort of uplifting and haunting all at the same time – I find it really exciting. I get all juiced up before going out when I listen to this song.

7. **'Could You Be Loved' – Bob Marley**
   This is just an all-round up-vibe party tune. I love the guitar riff at the beginning of the track and the chorus is 'sing-along', and the rhythm track and vocals are so cool.

8. **'Bitter Sweet Symphony' – The Verve**
   Every time I hear this song it reminds me of happy times and sad times. I find it very powerful, it touches my heart deeply, and I know everything is

going to turn out fine. This song reminds me of going out with my friends – driving along and listening to it cranked all the way up.

9. **'Tomorrow Never Knows' – The Beatles**

I love Ringo's beat in this one. It's hypnotic and trippy and lends itself to psychotropic fantasies. Eno covered this song in the 70s with his group 801. The melody slides around like some dream. This is one of my favourites.

10. **'Digital Love' – Daft Punk**

For some reason I find this song synonymous with going out. I guess when I first heard it I *was* on my way out (for a big night), and it got me kinda amped up. It's 'doof doof' enough with some interesting production tinsel. It's kind of romantic, in an electronic way!

KIRK PENGILLY

1. **'King of the Road' – Roger Miller**
2. **'Little Ole Wine Drinker, Me' – Dean Martin**
3. **'Spanish Fly' – Akasha**
4. **'Bob's Your Uncle' – Happy Mondays**
5. **'Don't Fight It, Feel It' (Weatherall mix) – Primal Scream**
6. **'No Ordinary Morning' – Chicane**
7. **'Exodus' – Sunscreem**
8. **'All I Need' (White label 'Rough Diamond' remix) – Air**
9. **'Belfast' – Orbital**
10. **Donny Hathaway**

A big night out always starts somewhere . . . so why not at home and with a cocktail.

'King of the Road' by Roger Miller is always a great one for that first martini. A hard drinkin' tune with a melody to kill for, fantastic delivery and an entirely admirable ethic.

Deano Martin's 'Little Ole Wine Drinker, Me' is on next. He prays for rain to make the grapes grow and make more wine. Cheers, mate.

Getting a bit more Latino loungey, Akasha's 'Spanish Fly' for its sexy percussive groove – perfect for mixing that next drink, too. It all goes a bit pommie here with Happy Mondays, Weatherall doing Primal Scream and production gods Chicane and Sunscreem. Then a whiz-bang white labelly remix thingo of a fine Air tune.

By now we're back at the pad, and lying between the speakers for 'Belfast'. How loud can we go? Yeah, just that bit more thanks . . .

And who else to fall over to than Donny Hathaway – any album, any time. Ya gotta love it. Zzzzzz.

Tomorrow is another day . . . Go forth and conquer.
Kirk P.

GARRY BEERS
1. 'Respect' – Aretha Franklin
2. 'Superstition' – Stevie Wonder
3. 'Home' – Skunkhour
4. 'From Out of Nowhere' – Faith No More
5. 'Voodoo Child' – Jimi Hendrix

6. 'Grace' – Jeff Buckley
7. 'All That You Dream' – Little Feat
8. All of side two of *Abbey Road*
9. 'My Cherie Amour' – Stevie Wonder
10. 'Letter to Alan' – Cold Chisel

To be honest, my list could go on and on . . . Obviously my choices are heavily influenced by the stuff I grew up listening to – they remind me of great times, big nights out and make me feel instantly good.

Motown, soul and funk shaped the way I play bass, and will always put me in party mode . . . Rock music played by people who know how to play it gets my attention faster than the speed of light . . . I basically love music and a big night out . . .

ANDREW FARRISS
War Child is an incredibly important charity. Please support it if you can.

1. 'Once in a Lifetime' – Talking Heads.
   Well, how did I get here? 9.00 p.m. Best song ever . . . tonight.
2. 'Rock DJ' – Robbie Williams.
   Things are looking up. 11.00 p.m.
3. 'Pusher Man' – Curtis Mayfield.
   What was that? Did you say something? 1.00 a.m.
4. 'Superstition' – Stevie Wonder.
   Great Funk. Great song. 2.30 a.m.

5. **'Devil's Haircut' – Beck.**
   I knew this barber once . . . 3.15 a.m.
6. **'Precious Heart' – Tall Paul/INXS.**
   And why not. 4.30 a.m.
7. **'No Woman No Cry' – Bob Marley.**
   5.00 a.m. Sums it up, I guess.

TIM FARRISS

1. **'Come Together' – The Beatles**
   One of my all-time faves. Brings back great memories of growing up, both physically and musically with my brothers.
2. **'Bust a Move' – Young MC**
   Great bass line, brilliant vocals. What else can I say? I just love the song.
3. **'One of These Nights' – The Eagles**
   Whoever said The Eagles were a country band? This is pure funky 80s disco with Bee Gees–type harmonies on top. Great guitar music. Great band!
4. **'More Than This' – Roxy Music**
   Great song to listen to under the stars, especially at night!
5. **'This Is Radio Clash' – The Clash**
   Great live band, probably my favourite live band ever. This song, like 'Magnificent Seven' and 'Rock the Casbah', is an icon of its time.
6. **'I Got You' – Split Enz**
   Great song. Along with 'Dirty Creatures' and 'I See Red', these are brilliant 80s Enz classics.

7. **'White Room' – Cream**
   Wheels Of Fire was one of my prized albums as a young fella and to this day I have great memories of this song.

8. **'Get on Top of Me Woman' – Tim Buckley**
   Not that this song needs much explaining, but I used this record a lot with my girlfriend (who I ended up marrying). If you catch my drift.

9. **'What a Wonderful World' – Louis Armstrong**
   I would like to get the music for this tattooed on my arm one day, if I get drunk enough.

Grant McLennan

Party Piece

when dorothy parker and lord byron invite you over, you should arrive early and smell like an orchid. be sure to bring some peaches for your horse, because you can never have enough friends at these kinds of things. dean martin told me this as he swooned to *divine hammer* by the breeders. be careful not to spill your sapphire martini on your hosts' sarcophagus as juniper stains. attempt the watusi to *goin' down* by the monkees, but only if your dance partner is over eighty and looks like jonathan winters. if marlene dietrich begins singing *virginia plain* by roxy music, put on a gorilla suit and try to pick up the closest cat. when robert mitchum drawls *be my baby* by the ronettes, humour him, and go borrow catherine deneuve's bongos. if there is a pool, never take your clothes off. throw salt 'n' pepa's *shoop* into the water, load up the commodores' *machine gun* with raw indigo and spray ultra violet's mix of *ray of light* by madonna over those jesuits in the jacuzzi. if someone whispers *papa was a rolling stone* by the tempations into your mouth don't worry, it's only bianca's daughter. it is advisable now to *get yr freak on* by missy elliott and cut *loose* by the stooges. when *jean genie* by david bowie resurrects you in the powder room and coos this is *my favourite game* by the cardigans through a periscope, it is considered proper etiquette to reply, mine's *rock and roll* by led zeppelin. remember, a little bit of *sabotage* by the beastie boys and you *see no evil* by television. if the cops haven't shown up yet, you should hightail it *soon* by m.b.v., or by your horse, if luis bunuel hasn't proposed to it. always carry shades.

Candace Bushnell

Which One?

When William Dickerson's girlfriend was five months pregnant, he went to Los Angeles to get away from her for a week. He went to visit this friend of his, Holt Bixley. William and Holt had been friends for something like fifteen years, and they both sort of thought the other one had screwed up his life but they never talked about it. Holt had finally gotten married at forty but then his wife had an affair with a Senator and ended up posing in *Playboy*, where they airbrushed out all the stretch marks on her breasts even though she was only thirty-two. William had been married ten years ago for three years and he still didn't know why his wife had suddenly walked out on him one day, but it was all just sort of . . . typical.

William Dickerson's girlfriend, Layla, was twenty-three and she'd started going to fortune tellers to find out what to do about 'the William situation'. When William arrived at Holt's house on Beverly Glenn, Holt already had a couple of lines on the table and a couple of girls on the line. Holt snorted the lines of cocaine and wondered if the fortune teller could predict that 'the William situation' now included a week in which he planned to snort 'whiffy' and sleep with as many girls as possible.

The two girls came over at seven. They were just some dumb Los Angeles girls who were actually too dumb to even want to be actresses. Then, while they were snorting the cocaine (one of them was actually trying to steal some of the cocaine by slipping it into a folded-up dollar bill), Holt got a phone call and took it in his bedroom. It was Cindi, this dumb girl from New York who had been in love with Holt for something like ten years, even though Holt actually treated her like shit and only saw her when he felt like doing it up the butt. Cindi was in Los Angeles supposedly producing a movie about ice skaters, and was staying with the screenwriter who was supposed to be some big deal, but they'd gotten into a fight when he invited sixteen-year-old hookers over and now she wanted to come over to Holt's. Holt and William had a conference and decided to tell the two girls that Cindi was Holt's girlfriend, which was fine with William because then he might be able to get the two girls in a threesome, or, at the very least, have sex with them consecutively.

Holt went back into the living room where the two girls were talking about highlights. Half an hour later when Cindi came over, the two girls were still talking about highlights. They told Cindi that she should really get her hair highlighted, which was the wrong thing to say to a girl like Cindi who hated all other girls, especially girls who were younger and could eat more than one lettuce leaf a day without getting fat. Cindi took Holt out to the pool and screamed at him about his 'fucked-up lifestyle'. William went into Holt's bedroom and started watching the Bulls game. Sure enough, the two girls came in and wanted to know 'What he was doing. By himself.'

He said, 'What do you think I'm doing? Waiting for you.'

The girls thought he was 'nice' so one girl climbed on top of him and had sex with him while the other one snorted more whiffy and made phone calls. Then Holt came in and said that Cindi wanted to go to a party for some independent film company and that William could come but the girls couldn't, which was Cindi's way of getting rid of the two girls.

In the car on the way to the party, Cindi said to him, 'Well, I see you haven't changed. You're exactly the same way you are in New York. A big womaniser. Isn't your girlfriend having a baby?'

And then she laughed like she'd actually made a joke, so he said, 'How's your asshole?' and she said, 'Which one?'

The party was on Mulholland. Right away he saw a girl he wanted. She was really good-looking, and was probably exactly how Layla would have been in a couple of years if she hadn't insisted that she had to have his baby, acting like it was some kind of puppy or something that would 'always love' her. The girl's name was Michelle and she had some dumb small part in some dumb small movie that starred one of those dumb little actors who was hot-shit five years ago and now was something like twenty-seven and 'making his comeback'. The dumb actor was now her dumb boyfriend. He was walking around the party with a clear plastic tube stuck in one nostril, which so far wasn't attached to anything. William figured the actor was good for another two hours or so and then he would probably be passed out somewhere and he'd be able to make his move on Michelle. Nobody asked him what the tube was for.

In the meantime, this other girl kept following him around. She was short and kind of pretty but not that pretty by LA standards and she was English. Every time he got a drink she got a drink. Every time he did a line she did a line. Then she said he looked like the only intelligent person in the room, which he thought was quite astute of her, and she gave him this stuff about how she was starved for intelligent conversation in Los Angeles being from London and it was all sort of a shock and then she dropped the name of her father, who was some famous English actor whom William had actually heard of and had seen some of his films and then he really couldn't get rid of the girl who was twenty and wanted to be an actress but not because of her father. Finally, the girl, whose name turned out to be Fiona, followed him into the bathroom and gave him a blow-job, which made him happy but seemed to make her unhappy, especially since afterwards she went all around the party and confessed to everyone that she'd given him the blow-job. That was what Los Angeles did to these girls.

Fiona gave him a ride home and wouldn't let him out of the car until he promised to call her the next day. By noon.

Inside the house, Holt and Cindi were still up snorting whiffy. Cindi said, 'Oh. Layla called. Three times. She sounds pretty pissed off, Willy-boy.'

William said, 'You know, I think I'm the only man in New York who hasn't fucked you.' And by then it was four in the morning, 7 a.m. New York time, so he went to bed.

The next morning he got Michelle's number from Holt who got it from some girl he knew and called her up. She had to go to lunch in Malibu at some producer's house and she was all freaked out that the producer was going to try to sleep with her and it was such a fucking insult. William said he would go with her to protect her and she was really dumb enough to buy it, especially when he suggested that they pretend he was her brother. Which was really crazy because everybody, including himself who didn't care about anyone in LA, knew that this producer was gay. Everybody, it seemed, except Michelle. She was so into herself that she probably couldn't imagine that there was anyone who didn't want to fuck her.

Michelle talked about herself the whole way to Malibu – so much so that she didn't even notice when William 'got lost' three times on purpose, because he actually didn't want to go to this producer's house because he didn't want anyone competing with him for Michelle's attention, which was one of the tricks to getting laid a lot. Then, when they were almost at the producer's house he said he had to stop at Joffrey's for lunch because he was so hungry he couldn't drive any more without eating something.

By then, Michelle was on a tear about Layla, whom she'd been in Paris with two years before. She said, 'I hope you don't mind me telling you this, but Layla is really a slut. She slept with all these photographers.'

He tried to tell her that Layla had changed, but Michelle wasn't having any of it. The truth was that Layla sort of was damaged goods, but overall, she was a good girl. She'd just fucked too many guys and taken too many dugs and gotten too fucked over, so that now, at twenty-three, she was trying to get her life together, going to AA meetings but, luckily, still snorting coke 'on special occasions' when she wasn't reading new-age books and watching 'You and Your Baby' videos. When Michelle got up to got to the bathroom at Joffrey's, William sort of waited outside in the hallway, and when she came out, he cupped her face and started kissing her. That usually worked, cupping the girl's face, because most guys didn't do that and girls thought it was really romantic or something. Then right after that, he usually tried to fuck the girl like a horse. He wasn't really crazy about giving oral sex, but he would if that's what it took.

Michelle said, 'Hey, isn't Layla having a baby?'

And he said, 'Yes, she is,' but kept kissing her.

'Good,' Michelle said. 'I hope she gets really fat.'

'She probably will,' he said. 'Then I'll have to dump her and start going out with you.'

'I'd never go out with you,' she said. 'I only go out with movie stars. Don't you know that?'

They went to the producer's house and the producer was probably really pissed off because they were two hours late, but William didn't pay any attention to it because he didn't have to. Instead, he sat on the terrace, annoyed, drinking lemonade and not saying anything unless he was asked a direct question.

The producer said, 'You're Michelle's brother?' and he said, 'Proverbial brother,' and the producer said, 'What do you do?' and he said, 'I have a PhD in European Literature and Biology from Harvard,' which was true.

This usually shut people up because no one knew anything about European Literature or Biology but the producer said, 'Oh, you mean like Jane Austen.'

And Michelle said, 'He's intelligent,' and William said, 'I think I'm going to take a walk,' and he gave Michelle a hurt look over his shoulder as he walked to the stairs that led down to the beach.

He was kind of pissed off because he didn't like wasting his time having to listen to other people's stupid conversations unless there was something in it for him at the end, like when he sat for hours listening to some gorgeous dumb model whinge on about her life. At the rehearsal dinner for his wedding, his best friend had talked about how William never had any conversation for his friends, how he would only pay attention to beautiful women no matter how stupid they were, and William had laughed and laughed but he didn't see any reason why he should change.

Right away on the beach he saw this girl he thought Holt had slept with. At first he thought maybe she was dead, because she was lying on a towel, sort of crumpled up and bruised. But then he saw that she was actually smoking, taking hits off a cigarette that another girl was holding up to her mouth.

He said, 'Uh, Nancy?' to the bruised girl and she rolled her eyes around and looked at him.

'Yeah?' the other girl said.

'Is she okay?' William said.

'She's fine. She's been having too many massages. And not taking enough Vitamin C. You know?' And then this other girl came down some steps talking into a cell phone. She was wearing a long flowered skirt and a cheap tank top and flip-flops and her breasts were sagging and her hair was in her face but William recognised her right away – she was that actress, Jessie. She was even less attractive in person (other people thought she was beautiful but William thought she was a freak) but she was so tall, like 6' 2" or something – his height – that you had to admit she had something.

She walked by and she looked at Nancy and the other girl and she said, 'Oh Jesus Christ.' She walked down to the surf and William followed her.

'I want a car now,' she said into her cell phone. 'No, not fifteen minutes from now, now. I can't stay here another minute. This whole thing is just inexcusable. And I'm going to tell everyone. No one will work for him. No actress, anyway. No legitimate actress anyway. Well, I don't give a shit.'

William said, 'Excuse me,' and she looked up and said, 'Who the FUCK are you?'

He said, 'I'm William Dickerson. I met you a few years ago but you probably don't remember. I think you were about fourteen.'

She said, 'Fourteen was a million years ago and I'm only twenty-one.'

He said, 'I know, but your father was my English professor at Harvard.'

'How do I know that?' she said.

'His speciality was Proust and Balzac. He wrote his dissertation on *Cousin Bette*.'

'So?' she said.

'So . . . I couldn't help overhearing your conversation.'

'No, you couldn't, since you were standing right behind me. Listening.'

'I'm going back into town now. I could give you a ride.' He waited a second. 'I was just having lunch at X's,' he said, naming the producer.

'Uh-huh,' she said. 'What was your name again?'

'William Dickerson. I'm from Boston.'

'Boston, huh,' she said. 'Is your father . . . ?'

'Yes,' he said.

'Okay,' she said.

They went back to the producer's house. William wanted to leave immediately but Jessie and the producer had to make small talk. Michelle was steaming. They all three got into the car and Jessie offered to sit in the back seat and Michelle let her.

'So, what are you doing in Los Angeles?' William asked.

'A play. Can you believe it? *Cat on a Hot Tin Roof*. In Los Angeles,' Jessie said.

'I'm up for a part in X's new movie,' Michelle said. 'I was just wondering what you thought about him. Have you ever worked with him?'

'He's divine,' Jessie said, as if she were talking to a tick. 'I'm reading *Beowulf* right now,' Jessie said to William.

'Fascinating,' William said.

'I'm thinking about adapting it for the screen. But I have to find someone to play Grendel.'

'You probably need one of those fat actors,' William said. 'One of those fat actors who's already died from a drug overdose.' Jessie laughed.

Michelle said, 'That is not funny. Overdosing is very serious.' And that was the way it was all the way back into Los Angeles.

At Holt's house, both Michelle and Jessie wanted to come in for iced tea. Jessie invited him to be her guest at her play the next night.

When Jessie left, Michelle said, 'I want to come with you, as your date. I love the stage.'

Then a small metallic green Honda pulled into the driveway and Fiona got out.

'Oh no,' William said.

'What is that?' Michelle said.

Fiona came in. 'I was worried about you. You were so fucked up last night and I didn't hear from you today I wanted to make sure you were okay.'

'Why wouldn't I be okay?' he said.

'You were kind of fucked up.'

'Everybody was kind of fucked up.'

'I wasn't,' Michelle said.

William went into Holt's bedroom to get way from them.

Holt was watching the game, recovering. Fiona followed him.

'I should have known. You American men,' she said. 'You're so spoiled. I should have known you only date models.'

'He doesn't always date models,' Holt said. 'Sometimes he dates former pregnant models.'

'Oh, that reminds me,' William said. 'I saw Nancy. On the beach in Malibu.'

'Nancy. How's she doing?' Holt asked.

'She was bruised,' William said.

'She's been having a hard time,' Holt said. 'She can't get any parts.'

'She could probably get a part playing a dead person,' William said.

'Yeah. It's that S&M thing. Very chic,' Holt said. 'Say, you know that guy Jason?' Holt named a guy they knew from New York. 'He came out here and got involved in a master–slave relationship. I hear he lives in a cage.'

'I don't know, Holt,' William said. 'I think a cage would go very nicely with your décor.'

It was like that for the rest of the week. By the third day, William had sort of stopped paying attention. He could remember that he slept with Jessie and Michelle and Fiona, who appeared naked in his bed one night, but couldn't really recall the details. Layla called several times, but he couldn't remember their conversations either. All he knew was that his end of the conversation was always the same: 'Yes, hon. You're right, hon. Of course you're the most beautiful girl in the world, hon. Well, everyone gets fat when they get pregnant.'

On the seventh day, his father called him from Boston. He only remembered because he and Holt were looking for vaseline and they found the phone instead.

'Yeah. Daddy,' he said.

'Hello, William. I wanted to congratulate you. I just got the good news from Layla. You've agreed to set a date for the wedding. I'll certainly be there.'

'Oh. Right, Daddy,' William said.

'I'm proud of you,' his father said. 'But now that you're going to have a wife and child, I really think you should find a job.'

'Yes, Daddy.'

'You're forty-three years old, William.'

'But Daddy,' William said. 'Mom . . .'

There was a long pause. Then his father sighed. 'William,' he said. 'Your mother died over twenty years ago.'

Jasper Fforde

A Spot of Bother

Firstly, it was a gorilla. Secondly, it was big. To Alex it might just as easily have been *firstly* big and *secondly* a gorilla but it was the third feature of this powerful-looking primate that Alex found the most agreeable – it was, for the moment at least, asleep. Two regular jets of hot breath were blowing out of its nostrils and condensing into vapour in the cold air. The creature's massive chest rose and fell, and now and then its hands twitched as it dreamt of bananas or lady gorillas or whatever else gorillas like to dream about. Understandably, when Alex first saw it he had been surprised. Partly because the gorilla was asleep in a tree four sizes too small for it, but mostly because this was *not* the mountains of Rwanda but Weybridge, and the gorilla in question was in Alex's back garden.

Alex bit his lip anxiously. He didn't have time for this. He would be giving an award that evening at the *Daytime Drama Awards*, which, although *not* a prestigious event, required his attendance for reasons of exposure. Humility about one's roots was quite fashionable these days, and roots don't come much more humble than the midday medical drama *Dr Prongg's Casebook*. He had recently escaped the grind of daytime TV to mainstream features, and his newly found wealth and fame had transplanted him from a dingy flat in Tooting with a view of the Happy Haddock Fish Restaurant to a seven-bedroomed house in Weybridge with frontage onto the Thames, two gardeners, a Picasso and neighbours who drank Pimm's.

The gorilla, who up until that moment had remained quietly inanimate, suddenly and without waking, scratched his ear with a large hairy index finger. Alex took a step back in alarm. The prospect of the gorilla waking hadn't entered his mind, and his imagination was suddenly flooded with several unpleasant ideas about what might happen if it did. Deciding on the face of it that cowardice was merely valour with a clearer view of the situation, he cautiously retraced his steps to the house and searched through the telephone directory under 'gorilla'. When that failed and his agent's phone was engaged, he started to dial the police – until his eye chanced upon a circular lying amongst some junk. The heading that caught his eye read:

TROUBLE WITH PRIMATES?

DON'T DELAY!

CALL SIMIAN SEIZURE

AND CONTAINMENT TODAY!

All types of primates catered for: chimps,

bonobos, orang-utans & gorillas.
No job too small!

Call 02734 870582 for *free* quotation
(Gibbon work undertaken with surcharge)

He hurriedly dialled the number and wandered back into the living room from where he was able to keep a safe eye on the gorilla.

'Thank you for calling Simian Seizure & Containment,' said a woman's voice after a couple of rings, 'my name is Dawn. Will you hold please?'

She didn't wait for a reply and spoke into a two-way radio in the background about an orang-utan loose in Richmond. After giving an address and contact name she came back on the line again. When she spoke it was with the languid and bored manner you might expect from someone whose hobby revolved around traffic cones.

'Sorry about that, sir. Bit busy this morning. Can I help you?'

'Well,' began Alex, unsure of how to proceed, 'I saw your advert. There's an ape up a tree in my garden.'

'If it's a gibbon I'm afraid you'll have to pay a surcharge. It's our operatives,' she explained, 'they don't much like to handle them. They find them *disrespectful*.'

'Well, it's not a gibbon, it's a gorilla, I'm fairly sure of that.'

He heard the sound of rustling paper as a notepad was folded over.

'Thank you, sir. Can I have your name and address?'

'The name's Alex Corby.'

There was a pause.

'The actor Alex Corby?'

'Well, yes, yes I am,' replied Alex with well-rehearsed modesty.

'I thought you were fab in *Above Us The Sky*,' said Dawn, somewhat breathlessly.

'I wasn't in *Above Us The Sky*,' sighed Alex, feeling deflated, 'you must be thinking of Buck Stallion.'

'Of course. Silly me. Buck. Now *there's* a star. Have you ever met him?'

'No,' returned Alex, beginning to get annoyed, 'I was in *Trample & Hawkwind*. It was last summer's block-buster. Did you see it?'

'I don't know – was Buck in it?'

Alex groaned quietly to himself. Sometimes it was not easy being a major international star.

'You say it's a gorilla, sir?' she asked, returning to the job in hand. 'Are you quite sure?'

'Yes – I think so. It's very large and covered in black fur – how about *Saddlesore In Purbeck*? You must have seen that, surely?'

'No, sir.'

'Well you should. *The Mole* thought I was "A new star risen on the horizon". *ToadNews* described the film as "One not to —"'

'Sounds like a mountain gorilla,' interrupted the tele-phonist again, who obviously had more on her mind than the Corby filmography. 'Adult male. We don't often get calls about them.'

'Okay,' replied Alex wearily, 'what happens now?'

'Well, we're a bit short-staffed at present. Geoff was bitten by a gibbon in Battersea yesterday, so he's having a day off. I've got an orang-utan in Richmond that's been cornered in a spare bedroom and is trying to eat the flowers off the wallpaper, and we've had a report of a chimp on the Jubilee line at Stanmore fooling about with the signals, so I don't think – excuse me.'

She spoke into the two-way radio for a few moments before coming back on the line.

'Hello, sir? Good news. The orang-utan at Richmond was a false alarm. I can send someone round in half an hour. Our standard recapture fee is £230 *plus* VAT. Is that okay?'

Alex glanced at his watch and replied that this would be fine, told her to go and see *My Sister Kept Geese*, which was a great film – even if it didn't have Buck Stallion in it, and hung up.

He looked out of the window at the gorilla. It did not seem to have moved, so he went downstairs, posted a few more messages at the buckstallionstinks.com bulletin board and was just beginning to wonder how one might even *begin* to tempt a 300-pound gorilla out of a tree when the doorbell rang.

There was a shock of wild frizzy ginger hair on the doorstep, and beneath that a small, rotund man who appeared a little over fifty. He wore pebble spectacles and a lumpy red boiler suit with *Simian Seizure & Containment* embroidered on the top pocket. Behind him in the drive was a dirty and dented Toyota van with the *SSC* logo painted on the side.

'Sorry about the pong,' said the small man cheerfully. 'Got pissed on this morning by a bonobo. Poor chap was terrified.'

'Bonobo?' queried Alex.

'Looks like a chimp but isn't,' explained the man, delighted at having his knowledge tested. 'Known as a pygmy chimp until it was recognised as a separate species. He'd got himself trapped in a phone box. I understand you've been having a spot of bother with a gorilla?'

'Not exactly *bother*,' replied Alex truthfully.

'Is it angry?'

'No.'

'Sarcastic?'

'I don't think so.'

'How about ironic? Has it displayed any tendencies towards irony or pathos?'

'No.'

'Good,' murmured the gorilla-catcher in a relieved tone. 'We have a saying that goes: "If the gorilla's ironic, the situation's chronic." I suppose you've heard of that?'

'I wasn't even sure gorillas *could* be ironic,' said Alex, feeling confused.

'Oh, yes,' replied the small man cheerfully, 'it just takes an expert to spot it. May I come in?'

The gorilla-catcher scrubbed his feet diligently on the

doormat and followed Alex through the house, looking around at the opulent interior.

'Nice place you have here. I've seen you at the pictures, haven't I?'

'I've had some success in a few films recently,' replied Alex quickly, introducing himself before the small man had a chance to confuse him with Buck Stallion.

'Fancy that!' grinned the small man, 'I like to go to the movies. I've seen all your films – *Above Us The Sky* was my favourite.'

The small man carried on speaking before Alex could tell him his mistake.

'The name's Roy. Roy Stone. Will you sign something for my wife? She thinks the world of you. We wanted our son to play the classics but he has no aptitude. He sells carpets in Newbury. Children rarely turn out the way you want. A bit like parents – and gibbons. Do you have any children?'

'My agent thinks I should adopt some. About the gorilla?'

'Ah!' replied Roy. 'Of course. Where *is* the little scallywag?'

'There,' said Alex, pointing out of the window.

The little man pulled open the sliding doors and stepped into the garden. He pushed his glasses up onto his forehead and studied the creature at length through a pair of binoculars.

'Well,' he said after a pause, 'it's certainly a gorilla. Highland silverback. Wonderful creatures. I'd gladly swap all the gibbons in existence for a dozen more breeding pairs. Timid beasts and very peaceful, but if you annoy them they can snap your limbs like breadsticks.'

'Why,' began Alex, 'would anyone even *consider* annoying a mountain gorilla?'

Roy shook his head sadly and made a few tutting noises.

'The things kids get up to.'

The little man looked at the gorilla again through his binoculars and made a few notes on a pad.

'Been doing this long, then?' asked Alex.

Roy sucked air in through his teeth and thought for a moment.

'Twelve years this autumn. I studied gorillas in the Central African Republic for nearly a decade. I tried working in zoos but found it just too depressing. Caged great apes have a sad and empty look that is hard to describe. I eventually ended up doing this.'

He shrugged resignedly.

'Well, it's not the best job in the world but at least I'm preventing some cowboy who doesn't care about apes from doing it. Any fool with a pick-up truck, a net and two dozen bananas thinks he can handle simians, but it's more a science of this.'

He tapped his temple knowingly.

'To trap apes you've got to know what makes them tick. Get inside their heads, learn to know how they feel, how they will react. Use a bit of simian psychology – and have a good supply of bananas. Can you give me a hand with the cage?'

'Sure.'

They walked out to Roy's van, unloaded a small aluminium cage on wheels and then manhandled it down through the side entrance and across to where the gorilla could see it. Roy set the vertically sliding door, tied a length of string to an unlatching device and then stood a dozen paces away, Alex by his side. The gorilla, who had been wiggling his toes and gazing at them vacantly, now stared at the cage instead and furrowed his brow.

'If he lives inside a cage most of the time, he *might* associate one with home. See there? He's looking for food.'

Roy pulled a banana from his pocket, peeled it and ate it with a great deal of dramatic yummy noises, then chucked another banana inside the cage. The gorilla didn't move, so Roy walked up to him and offered him a third banana. The large ape looked suspiciously at his puny and hairless cousin. After a couple of seconds of deep thought, the gorilla leaned out of the tree and delicately took the proffered gift, unpeeled it with his feet and ate it in one gulp.

'Don't you wish you could do that?' whispered Roy reverentially. 'Peel a banana with your feet?'

'I think of little else.'

The gorilla shifted its weight sharply and stared at Alex with his deep-set brown eyes.

'Careful!' hissed the small man. 'Sarcasm can throw these peaceful-looking creatures into a mad killing frenzy. Stick to plain speech, and at all costs, *don't attempt hyperbole.*'

Roy held out another two bananas which were dispatched as quickly as the first. The gorilla wasn't impressed by the cage, though – and started to snooze. Roy offered it more bananas and it ate these too, but steadfastly refused to come down. After about half an hour and a seemingly endless supply of bananas, Roy walked slowly back to where Alex stood, shaking his head sadly.

'Problems?'

'I'm afraid so. He's very happy up that tree. This could turn into a bit of a waiting game, I'm afraid.'

Alex looked at his watch.

'I've got to be out of here in an hour. Couldn't you just tranquillise him or something?'

Roy looked at him with a shocked expression.

'Have you ever tried to lift a 300-pound dead weight? The first rule in capturing gorillas is that you get *them* to do all the walking.'

Alex thought about this for a moment.

'So what do you propose?'

'Well,' began Roy, patting his pockets, 'the first thing – Oh, blast!'

'What?'

'Out of bananas. Never mind. Where's the nearest greengrocer's?'

'The high street.'

Roy handed him the string.

'Good. Keep an eye on him. If he goes into the cage, pull the string. Don't let the door fall on him, otherwise you might annoy him. Okay?'

'Wait!' exclaimed Alex, who had never annoyed a gorilla in his life and had no wish to start now. 'You're not going to leave me alone with a 300-pound mountain gorilla?'

'You'll be fine,' replied the small man with a reassuring smile. 'Just don't make any sudden movements – and watch the sarcasm.'

'I've a better idea,' announced Alex hurriedly. '*I'll* go and get the bananas and *you* can keep an eye on him. After all,' he added, just in case Roy thought he was being windy, 'I do know where the shop is.'

Roy shrugged.

'Fair enough.'

'Good,' returned Alex with some relief. 'I'll be back in twenty minutes.'

As he walked back across the lawn he could hear Roy talking to the gorilla.

'Mr Corby is going to fetch some more bananas, Gus, so sit tight. We'll have you out of that tree in a jiffy.'

Alex opened the garage, chose the Jeep instead of the Porsche and drove off into town.

As it turned out it took him forty minutes to find a shop with bananas in stock; the local greengrocers had sold out so he ended up at Sainsbury's in Walton. On his return he was surprised to see that the Toyota van had gone. His first thought was that the gorilla had been caught, and when he walked into the garden and saw the empty tree, this did indeed seem to be the case. The gorilla and the cage had both gone. But that wasn't all. The tracks of the cage were still clear in the damp grass, but with the gorilla's footprints *between* them – as though he had helped Roy to push it back to the van. As Alex stood on the path with a bunch of bananas in each hand, a slow feeling of uneasiness welled up inside him. He sprinted into the house. The gorilla and Roy Stone were not the only things that had gone missing. The Picasso had gone, too.

'Bananas,' said the Detective Inspector.

'Pardon?'

'You said the local shops had sold out.'

'That's right.'

'They must have been round this morning buying up all the stock. Perhaps the shopkeepers can give us some more details. You're sure you didn't see the van's registration number?'

'I'm afraid not.'

The policeman grunted.

'Never mind. Stolen, I should imagine.'

He scribbled some remarks in his notebook.

'You shouldn't have left them alone, sir. You could have locked the house. They were only in the garden.'

'I know,' said Alex miserably, 'but they seemed so authentic.'

'Authentic? Gorillas up trees in Weybridge? Everyone knows gorillas don't climb trees. Didn't *that* make you suspicious?'

They were standing in the living room where under an hour ago a Picasso had hung. The hi-fi had also gone, as had the jewellery, the Porsche and a large sum of cash that Alex decided not to tell the police about.

He placed his head in his hands. He had never thought of himself as the sort of person who could be duped so easily. Falling for a confidence trickster is, like lottery wins and triplets, something that only happens to other people.

'Did the man tell you his name?'

'Sorry?'

'The man. Did he tell you his name?'

'He said his name was Roy Stone. He told me he worked with gorillas in Africa.'

'He tells that to everyone. You may be interested to know that his real name is Gordon Taverner and he's never been out of the country. Did he call the gorilla anything?'

'He referred to him as Gus.'

The policeman shook his head slowly.

'Not the gorilla's real name, either. He escaped from Paignton Zoo eight years ago and his name's Bongo. They've been working this little scam for the past six years. They target a wealthy homeowner, post the leaflet through the door and Bongo sits up the tree and waits. It always seems to go the same way – the homeowner heads off to buy bananas, leaving them to go through the house. He's a particularly clever operator. Always goes for paintings and expensive cars, jewellery and money.'

The Detective Inspector shook his head sadly.

'He's one step ahead of us all the way.'

Alex agreed.

'And he looks so innocent in those pebble specs.'

The policeman stared at him for a moment.

'No, sir, I'm talking about Bongo. Gordon Taverner is just his accomplice. The ape is the draughtsman behind this little tickle.'

The detective patted Alex reassuringly on the shoulder.

'Don't worry, sir. They must have liked you – if they didn't Bongo usually does something unpleasant in the bath.'

Another officer walked in.

'It's Bongo all right, sir. Prints all over the place. We found his dabs on the garage-door remote.'

Alex groaned.

'You mean Bongo stole my Porsche?'

'We need to speak to him about that, too, sir. We suspect he has no insurance.'

The policeman coughed politely.

'And if I might add, sir, I thought you were excellent in *Above Us The Sky*.'

Reg Mombassa

Australian Jesus in the South Pacific

Maggie Alderson

The Lord of Misrule

My Uncle Charlie was a real terror. A 'Lord of Misrule', my dad used to call him. 'Trouble', my mother called him, although I noticed she would take on a certain twinkle whenever he was around. He had that effect on everybody. Even our dog seemed to wag his tail harder when Uncle Charlie came to see us.

He wasn't really called Charlie. I'm not sure what his real name was, but he was always Uncle Charlie to us. Sometimes, after a good Sunday lunch, when Dad had imbibed a few sherries and a bottle or two of claret, we would get him to tell us the story of how Uncle Charlie got his name.

'Charlie and I were going to the rugby in Cardiff,' he'd say, reaching for the Scotch. 'He turned up to meet me in his Morgan wearing a terrible suit. It was made of really shiny material and the trousers were as narrow as ladies' golf pants. He said it was the latest thing – mohair. He'd bought it in Rome. Should have left it there, I told him. He looked a right Charlie in it, so that's what he was called from then on. Charlie.'

So he wasn't called Charlie and he wasn't my uncle either, he was just my dad's friend. Or partner in crime, as they preferred to say, but he was a big part of our lives when we were growing up. I don't know what it was about Uncle Charlie, but you could never just have a quiet time with him – as soon as he arrived anywhere, it was an event.

He'd turn up out of the blue, straight off the plane from Uganda, or East Germany, or whatever exotic place his work had taken him to, brandishing a bottle of the obscure local liqueur.

He'd stay for dinner, regaling us with marvellous tales of his trip and then he and Dad would disappear into my father's study to 'inspect the bottle', as Uncle Charlie used to say. I don't know why Dad called it his study. All he ever studied in there was *Playboy* and the racing form. Or that's what Uncle Charlie used to say, anyway.

He also used to claim that he'd only stayed friends with a 'tearaway' like my father because we lived conveniently between Heathrow and his place in Dorset, and it was a handy place to stop over en route, but we knew he was kidding. He didn't have any kids of his own and I do believe he was genuinely very fond of us.

He always brought us brilliant presents back from his travels. Not the predictable national costume dolls, or cuddly toys Dad would bring back from his occasional foreign business trips, but something quirky from the local supermarket, or that he had found in the street, or had to arm-wrestle a Lascar sailor for, or at least that's what he would tell us.

For years I treasured a bottle of shampoo from Nigeria called Ebony Brand, which had a beautiful sultry lady on the label. Once he gave my brother Roly an arrow from an Amazonian tribe, which he swore still had curare on the tip.

While Dad and Uncle Charlie were locked away in the study, Roly had held me down – with my full consent – and scratched my leg with it to see what happened. I didn't become paralysed so the effect must have worn off on the plane, we decided, which was a shame as we'd had plans for it involving the soppy boy who lived next door. Nigel. We really hated him.

Partly because of the presents, but more because of the general increase in energy levels when Uncle Charlie was around, Roly and I always adored his visits, but even better was going to his place. He had a very large modern house, built right on the edge of a cliff, which he had commissioned in the late 1960s, specifically in the style of Frank Lloyd Wright.

He was a forward thinker, Charlie, Dad used to say. From the mohair suit onwards, he was always interested in the latest thing. Mind you, I suppose you would expect that from someone who designed aeroplanes for a living.

Uncle Charlie's place was so different from any other house we had ever been to it was a treat just to be inside it. We – and everyone we knew – lived in old houses and it was thrilling to explore this sprawling open-plan palace, which had bare brick walls on the inside as well as the outside. And there were so many interesting things to look at in it. There were real African spears on the wall, chairs that hung from the ceiling on chains and the biggest fridge we'd ever seen, which made ice cubes all on its own.

There was another fridge in the bar area and Uncle Charlie would lift me and Roly up onto the zebra-skin bar stools – he said they were made from real zebras – so we could watch him make us special cocktails all of our own. Always based on Coca-Cola (which we weren't allowed at home) he'd make them in huge brandy balloons, dripping with maraschino cherries and pieces of pineapple on special cocktail sticks he had brought home from bars in Hawaii, Cuba and other exotic places.

He would always let us take the cocktail sticks home with us afterwards and the best ones we ever had were little plastic people in grass skirts from a bar in London called Trader Vic's. I still have mine. I keep it in the pencil pot by my drawing board.

No one ever left Uncle Charlie's house empty-handed. He seemed to have a special store of quirky things especially to give away to friends, and it was always part of the excitement of going to his place.

Once he gave my dad a tie with an anchor motif all over it, with the letter 'W' on top of each anchor. Charlie and Dad thought it was hilarious, but we didn't get the joke.

Uncle Charlie told us it was the team tie of the White

Water Rafting Club, which made Dad laugh even more, while my mum and Uncle Charlie's wife Nancy just looked at each other and shook their heads.

They did that a lot while Dad and Charlie were together. Then they would light up another cigarette each and go back to talking about whatever it was that seemed to fascinate them. They hadn't known each other nearly as long as Dad and Charlie had, but they always seemed to have a lot to talk about.

Uncle Charlie had met Nancy in Africa. On top of the grand piano at their house, there was a picture of her in a large silver frame, wearing a safari suit with her arms draped round the neck of a leopard. The leopard didn't seem to mind.

We never called her Aunt Nancy. From the first time we met her, she said we must call her Nancy. She was the only grown-up I had ever called by their first name and I really liked her. She was very pretty and always had her dark red hair done beautifully and her nails painted. She always wore high heels and never trousers. Apparently Uncle Charlie didn't like women to wear trousers, but he liked women who smoked. He said it was a good 'indication'. Nancy's cigarettes always had bright pink lipstick on the ends of them in the ashtray.

Mum always smoked a lot more than usual when we went there. I used to sit in one of the chairs on a chain, swinging round and watching them talking, with smoke wreathed around their heads, their high-heeled feet crossed at the ankle, the ice clinking in their cocktails.

Dad and Uncle Charlie always stood up to talk, leaning against the mantelpiece, the piano, or the bar, and they smoked big cigars. Uncle Charlie would always give Dad a box of Cuban cigars to take home with him, as he had an excellent supply, direct from Havana.

Sometimes he would give Mum presents, too, which used to make her blush. She always tried to refuse them, but she gave in eventually, every time. People found it hard to say no to Uncle Charlie, Nancy had said once after one of Mum's protests, and then she had laughed a funny little laugh.

Uncle Charlie always used to win Mum round saying all he wanted in return from her was 'one chaste kiss' and that used to make her blush even more, but she always did it in the end.

I could never understand why she pretended she didn't want his presents, because he always gave her such nice things. Once he gave her a scarf from Paris with the most beautiful pattern of butterflies printed on it. She never wore it and eventually she let me have the orange box it came in to keep my Barbie shoes in. Now I have the Hermès scarf, too.

It wasn't just the grown-ups who got presents. Once, when I was eleven, Uncle Charlie had given me a very special bottle of champagne, which had beautiful art nouveau flowers all over it.

He gave it to me because I had said something that made him laugh a lot. I couldn't understand what he found so funny about it, I'd only said that the nuns at my school were 'too Jesus Christy', but I was thrilled with the champagne. It was the most grown-up present I'd ever been given.

Mum tried to make me refuse it the way she always did, but I didn't want to. I wanted that champagne. Uncle Charlie got round Mum for me by making a joke of it, saying he wouldn't tell the nuns and I was to save it until I was twenty-one. If I did, he said, he would give me the rest of the case as a reward for 'abstinence'.

As it turned out, the champagne didn't even last until my twelfth birthday, because Roly had some friends to stay one school holidays shortly after and we opened it and drank it as a dare. It tasted horrible and I was sick afterwards, so Mum and Dad found out.

I was really humiliated when Dad rang Uncle Charlie and told him what we'd done, but he was laughing as he told him, so I didn't mind so much. Two days later a huge parcel turned up addressed to me and it had another eleven bottles of the special champagne in it. Dad locked it away in his cellar.

After that it seemed like we didn't see Uncle Charlie as often as before. He did call in a couple of times – once on his way back from Moscow, when he gave me and Roly the most brilliant fur army hats, and once after a trip to Romania, when he gave us special crosses made from dried grass, which he said were made to keep vampires away.

But although he was still wearing his big black sunglasses and was driving a new car – a silver Aston Martin –

he didn't seem quite as Uncle Charlie-ish as normal. He was thinner and his suntan didn't hide a tired look around his eyes.

Even more surprisingly, after giving us the Romanian presents, he didn't stay for dinner and overnight like he normally did. He just had a cup of tea with us in the drawing room, gave my father a bottle of plum brandy, which he warned was 'an evil brew concocted to a special recipe devised personally by Vlad the Impaler' and sped off down the drive, gravel flying from his alloy wheels, one brown hand waving out of the window.

Mum and Dad were quiet at dinner that night, and when they were having a nightcap later, as they always did, they had one of those conversations which stopped suddenly if Roly or I went into the room.

The next piece of news we had about Uncle Charlie was that he was bored with his Frank Lloyd Wrong house – as he had taken to calling it, when rainwater started to leak in through the flat roof – and that he was drawing up plans for a new one.

This was to be built according to the principles of Buckminster Fuller – a geodesic dome. I heard Mum talking on the phone to Nancy about it and it was clear that she was not hugely impressed with the idea of living in a glass house. Then my father rang them back and made a lot of jokes about stone throwing, but it was never an issue in the end because Uncle Charlie died before the house could be built. Liver disease.

Daddy was so sad when Uncle Charlie died, it was

terrible to see. After we got the news he locked himself away in his study and didn't come out. Mum sat on the sofa in the drawing room with tears running down her cheeks.

Later on that evening, I went past her bedroom and saw her going through her jewellery box. I stood by the doorway, where she couldn't see me, and watched. She never let me touch her jewellery box and I wanted to see what was in it.

After fishing around for a while, she pulled out a little gold brooch in the shape of a bow and arrow, with one diamond on the tip. She sat looking down at it for a long time, then she kissed it and cried a bit more. Then she put it away again, right at the back of the box. I'd never seen her wear that brooch.

Roly and I were very sad about Uncle Charlie, too – it was really hard to believe that he would never turn up on our doorstep again, in his white linen suit, like an unexpected extra Christmas. But we were quite excited when we found out that he had left things for us in his will. He had always promised to, but we were thrilled that he had actually done it. A lot of grown-ups didn't keep promises we had found out by then, but Uncle Charlie did.

He left Roly a real African drum, which was made from the skin of a lion that Uncle Charlie claimed he had shot himself, and he left me his gold Dunhill cigarette lighter. Dad locked it away in his desk and said I could have it when I was grown-up – but only to light candles.

Uncle Charlie's funeral was really sad, but it was strangely happy, too. People laughed a lot when a man got up and made a speech about Uncle Charlie. There were some really funny stories in it – well, they must have been funny, because everyone laughed, but I didn't really understand them.

Roly and I had only ever been to one other funeral – our grandfather's – and that had been very different, really boring with lots of hymns and organ music. Uncle Charlie had eight Scottish pipers at his funeral, playing mournful tunes on their bagpipes, which made my eyes sting with tears. And as we left the chapel, someone put on a tape of Frank Sinatra singing 'Fly Me to the Moon'. I thought it was a mistake, but Dad said it wasn't. He had tears in his eyes then.

There were loads of people there, but apart from a few men that Dad and Uncle Charlie had been in the Navy with, who sometimes came to pick Dad up to go to rugby matches and to the races at Cheltenham, we didn't know many of them.

As well as lots of couples my parents' age and some distinguished-looking older gentlemen, there were quite a few women there on their own, including the most beautiful black lady I had ever seen, in very high heels and a fur coat. Her hair was done like Nancy's, a smooth glossy helmet, curling round her face. She reminded me of the lady on the Ebony brand shampoo bottle.

She was so beautiful, it was really hard not to stare at her. I saw Mum looking at her, too, and the amazing thing was that they were both wearing the same brooch – the one with the bow and arrow. It was such a coincidence

I pointed it out to my mum in case she hadn't noticed. She told me to be quiet and not to be so silly.

When we went to the funeral drinks afterwards, back at Uncle Charlie and Nancy's house, I saw that Mum had taken her brooch off. But it didn't matter because the beautiful black lady didn't come to the party anyway. I was really disappointed, as I wanted to stroke her coat.

After Uncle Charlie's funeral, we didn't see Nancy again. She'd always send us a card at Christmas and judging by the stamps she'd moved back to Africa, although one time the stamp had a dragon on it and a Singapore postmark. I always knew which card was Nancy's from the envelope. She had really big round writing and used a thick black fountain pen. That Christmas I asked for a fountain pen with a thick nib.

I missed Nancy almost as much as I missed Uncle Charlie. I wanted to sit in the hanging chair, the way I used to, and watch her smoking and hear her charm bracelet tinkling on her arm as she raised her glass to her bright pink lips.

Nancy seemed to me to really know how to be a woman and, now I was fourteen and turning into a woman myself, I wanted to pick up some tips from her. I wasn't feeling very comfortable with my newly sprouting bosoms and I thought Nancy would be able to give me some advice about it all.

She was more like Lady Penelope than the other women my parents were friends with, or one of the lady cats from 'Tom and Jerry'. I wanted her to show me how to use a lip brush and an eyelash curler, like she always did. They were both gold, like her powder compact. And how to walk in high heels.

Five years after Uncle Charlie died, my father died, too. He had a heart attack on the golf course. On the eighteenth hole, in full view of the clubhouse, during the President's Tournament.

All his golf buddies said it was a great way to go and at his funeral they formed a guard of honour as his coffin was brought in, with raised golf clubs. My mother thought it was ghastly, but she couldn't say so, except to me and Roly. She hated his new friends from the golf club. She said they were hideously suburban and the only people she loathed more were their ghastly suburban wives.

After the funeral, all the golf club people came back to the house for the wake and as Mum refused to speak to any of them, Roly and I had to take over her hostly duties. I was at university then, studying architecture, so at least I had something to say when they asked me what I was 'doing' with my life. When they asked Roly he told them he was sliding, with great pleasure, down a sleek and slippery slope to degeneracy, which usually shut them up.

After a couple of hours it didn't seem like any of the funeral party guests planned on leaving. My father had always told us that when he 'went' he wanted us to throw a big party and that he wanted the drink to flow until the very last person left voluntarily. He was categorical – the bar was not to be closed, so we were stuck with them.

After a couple of hours of it I went into his study to escape.

I sat on his leather swivel chair and looked at all the things on his desk. His cigar cutter. The silver ashtray he'd won in another golf club tournament. His tray of drinks. The fountain pen he'd had since he was twenty-one. A pile of unread *Spectator*s. Then I opened the top drawer.

There was a copy of *Playboy* in there; Uncle Charlie hadn't been joking. The only other thing of interest was the key to the desk's locked drawer. I opened it and took out Uncle Charlie's bequest – my gold Dunhill lighter. I clicked it and it lit first time.

I sat and played with it for a while, examining its smooth lines and running my finger along the initials engraved on the bottom: C. J. W-T. Maybe Uncle Charlie's first name really was Charles, after all.

At that moment I missed him with a pain like a stab from one of his African spears. He would have known how to get rid of the golf club crowd, or at least how to make it more bearable having them there. Uncle Charlie could make a WI coffee morning into a happening, as my father used to say.

Suddenly missing the smell of him and my father, as much as their physical presence, I went over to my dad's humidor and selected the largest, fattest Cuban cigar I could find, trimmed the end and lit it with my Dunhill lighter. After a few puffs, leaning back in my dad's chair, leafing through the *Playboy*, which seemed quaintly tame,

I felt ready to face the golf club again. I took my cigar with me.

When I walked back into the drawing room, the mood seemed to have changed. It was growing dark and no one had turned on any lights and there was a strangely hypnotic sound just discernible beneath the hysterical chatter of gin-fuelled small talk. Mum and Roly were nowhere to be seen.

Then I spotted Roly – he was squatting in a corner playing Uncle Charlie's lion-skin drum. Just as I saw him he looked up and caught my eye. He smiled when I took a big puff on my cigar and motioned with his head for me to come over. I walked across to him and he pulled a joint out of his shirt pocket and put it in his mouth. Without saying a word, I flicked open Uncle Charlie's lighter and sparked it up.

Then I had another idea. I went back to my father's office, took his keys out of the top drawer again and went down to the cellar. It took a few attempts, but eventually I managed to open the wooden gate he had always kept locked over his 'special' wines. There was my Perrier-Jouet, very dusty, but all eleven bottles still there.

With my cigar clamped between my teeth, I got the wooden cases up to the kitchen. Then I filled a couple of buckets with ice – we now had a fridge that made ice cubes on its own – and put the champagne on the bar in the drawing room.

Roly was still playing his drum, but louder now, and he had put some music on Dad's hi-fi, too. The unmistakable sound of Sergio Mendes filled the room and people had started dancing. I went and sat on the floor next to Roly and we swapped the joint and the cigar back and forth between us.

When we'd finished them I went back down to Dad's cellar. Someone else had clearly been down there in my absence, I noticed – the doors were hanging open and I knew I'd left them pulled to. When I looked inside I saw that there were several empty spaces that had held bottles before, but I didn't care, because the bottle I wanted was still there.

I pulled out a bottle of seventy-year-old Armagnac that Uncle Charlie had brought back for Dad, from a trip to Argentina – said he had bought it off an ex–SS officer, trying to pass himself off as a cattle rancher.

I re-locked the cupboard and went back up to Roly, picking up the largest brandy balloons I could find in Dad's drawing-room drinks cupboard, on the way. We clinked glasses and, sitting in our dark corner, Roly tapping his drum between sips, we watched the dancing, which was becoming extremely lively.

After a few minutes, Roly indicated for me to take over the drumming, while he went and thumbed through the record collection – I recognised the track as the last one on the LP and Roly clearly didn't want the mood to be broken by a pause in the music.

As it ended he seamlessly segued into a more intense samba record, like the successful club DJ he now was – or as seamlessly as you can with one old deck. Then he sat down and resumed his drumming in earnest, with the pop of champagne corks now adding another level of percussion.

Just as cranking up the beat could render one of Roly's Ibiza party crowds hysterical, the change of music had a powerful effect on the golfers, who were now gyrating much closer together and moving their hips like Rio carnival dancers to the Latin rhythms.

After a couple of tracks I noticed that the President of the golf club had both his hands down the back of the skirt of a woman who was not his wife, and was grinding his pelvis into hers. The solicitor who had been my father's golf partner on the day of the fatal tournament was dancing with the Club Treasurer's wife, and Roly and I turned and looked at each other with wide eyes as he put his hands up her blouse and blatantly began to squeeze her breasts. Roly beat his drum faster and I poured us more Armagnac.

Two tracks later, my father's accountant ran past in pursuit of the Club President's wife who was drinking champagne from the bottle. They collided in the doorway and I watched her take a deep swig from the neck of the bottle and then pass the foaming liquid into the accountant's open mouth from hers. Then they disappeared round the corner into the hall.

Roly's next choice of record appeared to heighten the excitement even more. Many of them were now drinking directly from bottles of champagne, if their hands weren't busy inside the clothes of their dancing partners. As Roly got up once again to turn the record over, I saw my mother's most-loathed golf wife – a shrill-voiced, sun-bed orange, bottle blonde – disappear over the back of the sofa underneath the manager of a local bank.

I'd seen enough and went upstairs to find my mother, stepping over the bodies of the accountant and the Treasurer's wife who were writhing on the Persian rug in the hall.

Mum was in bed, still fully dressed and passed out, a half-empty bottle of Chivas Regal on her bedside table. I recognised the bottle. It was one of the many gifts Uncle Charlie had pressed upon her over the years. I remember him urging her to take it, saying that even if she didn't want the whisky, she could use the special anniversary velvet pouch it came in as an evening bag.

The dark blue velvet bag was lying next to her on the bed and I could see it was full of black-and-white photographs. Careful not to wake her, I pulled the top one out. It was of her and Uncle Charlie and, judging by her hairstyle, it had been taken twenty years before. Mind you, I only had the hair to go by, as they were both stark naked in the picture.

Uncle Charlie had clearly taken it, because his arm was stretching out of the frame. They were both laughing and Mum was holding the bow and arrow brooch to her naked left breast.

A wave of fury passed through me as I looked at the picture. My poor father. His best friend and his wife. How hideous. How predictable. How ordinary. They were as bad as the lot downstairs, I thought, the smug suburban professionals my snobbish mother so despised.

I pulled Uncle Charlie's lighter out of my pocket, held it close to one corner of the photo and started to press my thumb down onto the trigger, but something stopped me. My mother's face in the picture. It was so radiant, her smile so open and natural. I didn't think I'd ever seen her look that happy. But Uncle Charlie looked just as I remembered him: handsome, smooth, slightly too well groomed, a world of mischief in his crinkly eyes. A Lord of Misrule with a Mediterranean tan.

I put the lighter back in my pocket, slid the photo back into the velvet bag and went back to find Roly. It was time to send the golf club packing.

Tara Moss

Psycho-magnet

What do you do when no one believes you?

What do you do when you're a girl like me?

Stalked.

Hunted.

A psycho-magnet.

I go to the police and what do they say? We can't press charges until an actual crime has been committed. 'Like when someone gets attacked, or killed?' I ask, as only a girl with experience can, but a young Constable doesn't know how to respond to a question like that. Truth is, we're just as much paperwork dead or alive, and were it up to the system, I'd be just another statistic. We must fend for ourselves.

It is late evening as I return from work, and there is another one following me. He is tall, very tall, and he walks with long strides, supported on strong legs cased in fitted jeans. From the corner of my eye, I watch his

malevolent reflection shift across darkened shop windows. He walks with his head down, slightly hunched at
his wide shoulders, wearing a black leather motorcycle
jacket. I cannot see his face.

It has been five blocks now, with only me and my faceless escort to inhabit the road. I have no jacket to protect
against the cool, summer-night air, and certainly, I have no
defence against this man who follows me. My purse is
empty, save for a sharp set of keys and a bit of cash. Were it
up to me, I would have a capsicum spray, perhaps even a
Saturday Night Special. But it is not up to me at all. It is up
to the system, and they say I cannot have such protection.

My high heels click on the pavement beneath me,
echoing off the empty buildings while his steps are
soundless in pursuit. For a man of such immense physical
stature, he moves with feline stealth. But though he is
wickedly quiet, I know that I would sense his presence
even were he invisible. He emits evil as he moves through
the night, leeching the freshness from the air.

My heart is racing, and my legs feel stiff and useless
with his eyes crawling over them. Walk. Just walk. I concentrate, and with effort my pace does not change. But
nor does his, and eventually I decide it is time to cross the
street, to administer the first test.

Dim street lamps flank the road on both sides, and I
pass between them with purpose. I walk with great strides,
held tall in my blue dress, my fists clenched as if to say, I'm
ready when you are. There is no traffic to require me to
look both ways, but I do anyway, to catch a glimpse of my

stalker. I only allow myself a split second to take him in; his face is long and pale, crowned with light, strawberry-blond hair. He is quietly observing me, and I quickly turn my head the other way, as if to check for cars.

There.

I see you.

You know that I see you.

I step over the curb on the other side and wonder, Will he follow?

I pass a lamppost, then another, glad of the space between us. My side. Your side. Slowly my heart begins to relax, to unclench just a little, because he is not following. With that reassuring distance, I steal occasional glances, to see what he will do. He is walking on his course, not even looking my way, and my heart slows, adrenaline retreating.

I see the intersection only a block away, and my house just beyond it. The faulty lighting on my porch winks, welcoming me home. I am almost there. As my legs propel me steadily forward, I imagine the safety of my abode, the sanctity of what is familiar and mine. Should I circle the block to make sure I am not followed? I am aware that I appear attractive and vulnerable, and I don't wish this tall man to know where I live.

From the corner of my vision comes an unwelcome movement. The man is changing pace. He is crossing the street. Oh God, he's crossing! Over the curb, past the median and moving in fast, his long legs transporting him swiftly to my side of the road. Quickly, he bridges the gap, closing in on my space, intimidating me. He is so close now that if he reached out, his hands would be on me.

My heart pounds mercilessly, fear beating against my temples. The hairs stand up on my neck, and every inch of my skin tickles as it rises in goose flesh. My knees start to give, to succumb to his command for collapse, but by a thin thread I hold myself up. The chaos in my head grows louder, screaming, until I cannot even hear my own shoes on the concrete as they slow down.

I cannot succumb to panic. I cannot, will not, be the prey. Not again.

Never again.

I will my heart to slow as I change pace. My breathing becomes deliberate, controlled. My blood cools. I feel myself transform.

I am not the prey.

Strike the first blow. Take control. I play on my terms.

I stop in my tracks and turn to him, only steps from my front door. In one of his long strides he is upon me, less than an arm's length away. He looks down on me and smiles with a crooked, sinister grin. He is a full six inches taller than I, which means he must be very tall indeed, for I am no petite girl. I can see now that he is strong and no older than thirty. His reddish hair is slightly greasy, and his long, ghostly white face is horribly disproportioned.

I say nothing, only stare with a level gaze into his pale eyes. They are so intense, they seem to glow in iridescent blue. Unfeeling. Psychopathic. He has eyes like Bundy, I think. Eyes like Dahmer. Eyes like a predator.

I dare him to act, to complete what he has started, but he only steps a foot closer, towering over me. I tilt my head up to hold his powerful gaze. The porch light flickers.

On my terms. We play on my terms.

He is so close that I can smell him. He has a sick, malignant reek that threatens to throw my senses into panic again. But I do not allow it. My heart is ice. Invulnerable. I am in control. Like a savage animal, I know that he can sense fear, but he will not sense mine, because my fear has fled.

I am not the prey.

'Would you like to come inside?' I ask, and offer a cool, thin smile.

He hesitates. A thought flickers past. Then his rough, eager hands go straight to my waist, to squeeze the young flesh of me, and the game begins. Together we take the final steps to my front door. One step. Two steps. Three. I remove the keys without fuss, and slide carved metal into the lock. It turns on command, the door creaking open. In silence we enter the house. My house. My playing field.

Once inside he wastes no time. I find myself thrown against the wall, his body pressing hard, grinding me up. The keys are flung from my grasp, falling with my purse in a clatter on the floor. His hands are greedy and brusque, pushing, pulling, claiming my body with no intention of anything mutual. I accept his angry kiss, his poison tongue. I am emotionless. A machine. No panic here. Control.

He works at the back of my dress. Fumbling. His passion rises firmly through tight jeans, eager with violent desire. My dress is torn, my smooth skin exposed, devoured by crude, slobbering jaws.

I am a psycho-magnet.

I am bait.

'A drink?' I propose, pushing away from his rough, unshaven face. He pauses, his body unyielding, and raises a hand to my slender throat, teasing in a strangler's grip to hold me fast. He stares me down, craving control with eyes that are wickedly consuming. But I am unaffected. Gradually, he allows me to pull from his hold, and I leave him to venture to my kitchen.

When I emerge a minute later with two brandies, I find him on my couch. His pants are undone and his shoes and belt scattered on my floor. He accepts his glass, then stands, and grabs me again.

I do not panic.

'Please,' I say. 'Can we drink this first?'

I take the first sip, and he smiles a predator's grin as I drink, not realising that he is the prey now. He seems to mock me as he tips his glass back, his mouth opening greedily to receive my gift in impatient gulps. I am the one in control, and I step back in anticipation. Suddenly, his face contorts, and he breaks into a confused sweat, grabbing his own throat as he gasps for air. His empty glass crashes to the floor, shattering into hundreds of razor-edged shards. A graceless creature, he jack-knifes violently backwards, hitting the coffee table with great force and knocking its contents to the floor. His powerful physique seizes and trembles, savage convulsions consuming him. He flounders like a fish out of water. Pathetic.

I walk away, dispassionate, and put my empty glass in the kitchen sink. I fill it with soap and water, and calmly, I clean it. It's a shame the matching one had to break. When I return he is twitching. My catch is unconscious, internally asphyxiated, his long, ugly face grotesquely contorted. Finally, the massive dose of cyanide sends him into one last death throe, and his heart stops.

I will tidy the room and dispose of him in my own time. My house. My rules. They will find his poisoned corpse cherry pink, with a blue, shocked face, his pale eyes unseeing. Powerless.

I am a psycho-magnet.

I am bait.

I weed them out and kill them.

The half-read newspaper has fallen off the table, and I pick it up. The front page headline is bold. SIXTH CYANIDE MURDER VICTIM. POLICE SUSPECT SERIAL KILLER IS LOOSE.

I shake my head, because clearly, I am no serial killer. Bundy, Gacy, Brudos, Kemper: they were serial killers. But not me. They have it wrong.

Why won't anyone believe me?

I am a psycho-magnet.

Helen Lederer

Story illustrations by John Hegley

My Cock Tale

Here is my story about a particularly memorable male member . . . Oh, sorry . . . MY COCKTAIL.

Precondition:

If you're going to the trouble of mixing your drinks don't go mad and include the whole drinks cabinet. You'll be sick and have to go to hospital with wood poisoning.

Preparation Time:

All day if you have it, as long as you pour very slowly – ten minutes if you've just got in and suddenly remembered you've invited five people who you don't know very well, and who also don't know each other, to come round for a cocktail.

Title Explanation:

Always label your cocktail so you can announce it grandly. This provides reassurance, authority and a sense of control over your party. One sip and they will soon acquiesce and do what you want them to do – which is to be nice to each other. Two sips and they will be very nice. Three (of the enclosed) and you may have to intervene.

Title:

'Failsafe Social Bonder' or FSB, which is easier to remember and less threatening for the more autonomous sipper.

Ingredients of FSB: (serves five friendlies or ten more cautious portions)

1 fluid ounce white rum
1 fluid ounce bourbon (not the biscuit, stupid)
1 fluid ounce green chartreuse (it's always green; if it's yellow you've got hold of some washing-up liquid by mistake)
1 fluid ounce of vodka
1 fluid ounce of Southern Comfort (which has the same effect in the north)
2 fluid ounces lemon juice
2 fluid ounces orange juice

1 fluid ounce sugar syrup (just melt some sugar without
   setting fire to anything)

1 fluid ounce of grenadine (nothing to do with the
   Grenadier Guards)

Method:

Mix them up in a pleasing jug and pour – without spilling –
into glasses (never plates). Attractive paper flags are optional
but may look as if you've tried quite hard. Which you have.

They don't deserve you. Get rid of the guests and drink
it all up yourself.

Imogen Edwards-Jones

Wishing on a Star

It was minus fifteen and Kate had lost all feeling in her toes. Her hands were pink, her cheeks bright red and the snot in her nose was starting to freeze. She had been standing in the cold for the last half-hour and still she hadn't even had a glimpse of him. The moon was up, the cloud cover disappearing and the temperature sliding even further below zero, but her resolve remained firm. She had come this far and was not going to go without seeing him. She was determined not to let this opportunity of finally meeting him – pressing his gorgeous flesh – slip through her ice-cold fingers, just because the Moscow winter had arrived a little earlier than expected. Dedication was apparently what one needed in life, and when it came to Karl Stanford, Kate was more than dedicated, she was obsessed.

Kate had been in love with Karl Stanford ever since she could remember. Her bedroom at home in London was converted into a shrine to Karl way back in his early days on an afternoon soap called *Doctors and Nurses*. Her love for him had been one of those instant, *coup de foudre* moments that teenage girls seem to specialise in. For no sooner had Karl walked on screen, carrying a heavily pregnant woman, only to deliver the baby without a bead of sweat forming on his upper lip, than Kate went into full swoon. And from then on her commitment was total. She would scan the teenage magazines for any interview with him. She would read up on the plot in the television supplements, and she would rush home after school on a daily basis, declining invitations to hang out on the King's Road with her precocious girlfriends. Why would she be interested in gawping at boys, making one cup of coffee last the rest of the afternoon, when she could lust quietly from the comfort and convenience of her own sofa?

Needless to say, her mother, Genevieve, a rather glamorous interior designer, was somewhat horrified by her daughter's behaviour. She blamed herself initially. Divorcing Kate's father when her daughter was at such a young and vulnerable age can't have helped. But all the same, falling in love with an actor, a soap star, it was all rather embarrassing. Genevieve lost count of the number of times she told her daughter that actors were silly, vain creatures who are only interested in themselves. 'They make love watching their own performance in the mirror,' she declared one evening, having had a bit too liquid a lunch. 'Honestly, Kate,' she slurred. 'I do wish you would grow out of this obsession.'

But Kate didn't grow out of it. The passion continued to burn just as brightly, only she learned to keep it under wraps. When she left school and won a place at Exeter University to read Russian, the Blu-Tack was removed from the teenzine centrefold posters and reapplied to Che Guevara, Lenin and a black-and-white Athena shot of a some semi-naked man in jeans, cradling a child. But the obsession remained.

Meanwhile, Genevieve breathed a sigh of relief, and Karl Stanford went on to reinvent himself as a serious actor. He left *Doctors and Nurses,* after a dreadful disagreement over his character's motivation, and shared his trauma with the press. He cut a pop record that reached number eighteen in the charts and went off to Australia to make a kung-fu movie that bizarrely received some quite good reviews. By chance he ended up co-starring in the hit movie of the summer. His fee went through the roof. He was an overnight sensation. Then he was photographed having sex on the beach with his married, female, love interest, and returned to London to act in a theatrical soul-saver project, where he earned £250 a week but got to rediscover his roots. The critics were kind, and the company went on a mini-European tour – Paris, Prague and now Moscow.

It was one of Kate's flatmates, in her small communal apartment off the Arbat, who told her that Karl Stanford was playing the Maly Theatre and staying at the Savoy Hotel.

'I seem to remember you like him,' said Sveta, over pickled cucumber, vodka and Bulgarian cigarettes. 'I have a friend who can get tickets if you would like.'

'Really?' enthused Kate.

'Possibly . . .' said Sveta.

'What? For a bottle of vodka?' suggested Kate.

She had been studying in Moscow long enough to smell of cheap soap, old garlic and to know that something no longer happens for nothing anymore.

'Maybe vodka, maybe there is no need, maybe they have many tickets left?' shrugged Sveta, her surly Slav lips sucking on a cigarette.

'Oh please, please, that would be wonderful . . . Could you find out?' begged Kate, barely capable of containing herself.

'Yeah, sure,' replied Sveta, nonchalantly stubbing out her fag.

Two days later, Sveta came up trumps. It turned out that her last theory was correct. Although Westerners were keen to purge their souls of commercial triviality watching Mayakovsky's satire on the bourgeoisie, *The Bedbug*, the Russians were less interested. Having only just discovered the heady delights of Versace, the idea of an evening of self-improvement was about as appealing as doing time in a gulag.

So tickets were cheap and Kate was on her own, walking through the October slush towards the Maly Theatre. In the month and a half that she had been studying in Moscow, she had never been this excited. The first couple of days were, of course, amazing. Walking into Red Square, the grim granite of Lenin's tomb, the beautiful tutti-frutti domes of St Basil's, the swanky gold of the Kremlin, the glamour of the Metro, the striking difference between rich and poor, the weird shops that only sell one product, the terrible smell of cat's piss that pollutes every stairwell and corridor, the beauty of the people, their ability to swing from sublimity to brutishness in a shot of vodka. It was all beguiling in its own way.

But tonight was different. Tonight was a little bit of home. Tonight was a little bit of innocence. Tonight was a little bit of her childhood coming back to play with her. This was the closest she had ever come to meeting a star. But what's more, this was the closest she had ever come to Karl Stanford, the man who she had loved since the age of thirteen. The man for whom she would have willingly sacrificed her mother and all her friends. The man who she had waited nearly ten years to kiss.

She stamped her feet again and blew on her cold hands. She took a scrap of paper from her pocket and scribbled in the corner with her pen to check to see if the ink still flowed. It hadn't frozen. It worked. Karl would be able to sign his autograph. Kate smiled and looked around. The other women clustered by the Stage Door had come much more prepared. Thick coats with fox and sable collars, hefty boots; their scarves were wrapped so tightly round their faces, they all had squashed fat cheeks like beach balls. Some carried programs for Karl to sign, while others clutched individually cellophane wrapped carnations of varying hues. Kate fingered her scrap of paper back in her pocket. Why was he taking so long? He could not have left by a side entrance. There was only one exit out of the theatre, she had checked with the caretaker.

Suddenly there was the sound of doors slamming and distant chatter. The crowd stood to attention and closed in around the entrance. The double doors swung open and out came two men who Kate recognised from the play. Their faces scrubbed pink, devoid of make-up, the taller of the pair still sported some eyeliner like a New Romantic. A couple of the waiting women thrust forward with their programs. Some of the others handed over their carnations. Surely out of politeness thought Kate, as neither of them was at all famous. Next came the leading lady; thin, wan and delicate like a rare bird, she stood in an enormous faux fun fur jacket freezing her PC backside off, signing autographs. Then finally, just as Kate was about to lose all hope of ever meeting her idol, he strode through the double doors accompanied by a swift hair-flicking assistant.

Kate held her breath. She sunk her nails into the palms of her hands. It was all she could do to remain perpendicular. Karl was less than a foot away. Karl was coming towards her. Karl was short. Karl had narrow shoulders. And Karl was wearing an anorak.

'All right?' he sniffed, as he approached the crowd.

'Oh, yes thanks,' beamed Kate.

'You English?' he asked, sounding surprised, as he signed her piece of paper in a flamboyant, yet illegible manner.

'Oh, yes,' enthused Kate, losing herself in his baby-blue eyes, his straight nose and his full lips. 'Bradford's

answer to Brad Pitt.' They weren't wrong, smiled Kate.
They weren't wrong at all.

'Where are you from?' he asked, wiping his nose on
the back of his hand.

'Oh, London,' she gushed, like it was the most
romantic place on earth.

'Wow,' said Karl, sounding impressed. 'London,' he
repeated. 'That's amazing. Hey, Lydia?' The rare bird
turned around. 'You'll never guess what?'

'What?' said Lydia, in clipped RADA tones.

'This girl's from London,' laughed Karl.

'Really? How fascinating,' she said, like it was anything but.

'Amazing,' said Karl, nodding his head, as he signed
a program. 'Do you know what?' he asked.

'No . . .' smiled Kate.

'You should come back to ours for a drink,' he
announced. 'Us Brits should stick together. Especially
when we're in a shithole like this,' he laughed. 'We're at
the Savoy, come back and have a drink at the bar.'

Kate could only grin in reply. It was as if a throng of a
thousand angels had tipped up outside the Maly Theatre
and burst into the 'Hallelujah Chorus'. For upon his invitation, Kate lost the power of speech, along with the
ability to hear and see. There is nothing like meeting
one's idol to render even the most garrulous of fans
totally mute. Kate could only stand and grin inanely in his
general direction. Karl continued to sign autographs,
unaware of his stellar effect.

'Right,' he announced, rubbing his hands together as he handed back the last signed program. 'I need a bloody drink. See you in a minute, yeah,' he nodded at Kate. She grinned right back.

It was only when Karl's tight, blue jeans disappeared into the back of his black Mercedes limousine that Kate finally came to her senses. She wanted to scream, execute star jumps, telephone someone to tell them what had just happened. Karl Stanford had asked her on a date. He had. Karl Stanford had asked her, Kate Moore, out on a date. She had waited nearly a decade for this moment and it had finally arrived. Well, she always knew it would. They were fated to be together. Ever since she had seen him walk on set, carrying that woman, she knew they were going to be husband and wife. And here, finally, was her chance. Destiny was calling and there was no way Kate was going to keep it waiting.

She jogged the three-minute walk from the Maly Theatre to the Savoy Hotel. She passed a rabble of young men, their woollen hats pulled hard down over their eyes, smoking cheap cigarettes on the corner. She overtook a smart-looking couple with a child in a pushchair. Stiff and snug, it was bandaged tightly up against the cold like a sausage roll. A collection of little girls with pom-pom hats and candyfloss bows in their hair swung on their mothers' arms, executing copycat ballet moves, while they waited for a trolleybus opposite the Bolshoi Theatre. At the end of the wide street, before she turned into Rozhdestvensky Street, there was an old woman hunched up on a square of cardboard, her head down, her eyes lowered. Her flesh-less hands were resting on a brown plastic begging bowl, a tarnished military medal by its side.

Bursting through the doors of the Savoy Hotel, Kate was greeted by a blast of hot air that immediately defrosted her nose. Nodding casually to the night staff, ignoring the golden baroque interior like an everyday phenomenon, she scanned the lobby and turned in the direction of the ladies toilets. Standing in front of the large mirror, the neon strip lighting did nothing to aid her beauty and confidence. Typical, she thought as she rummaged through her hand-bag for anything that might resemble make-up. *The* meeting with *the* love of her life and she had a spot on her chin. Kate spent about ten minutes making herself up – powdering her nose, running some kohl around her eyes, covering and re-covering the spot, to the point that it had completely disappeared unless you looked right up close, with your face squashed against the mirror. Smiling at herself, nodding and practising muttering 'hello', she concluded that she didn't look bad.

With thick, long, blonde hair, green eyes and a curl to her mouth, Kate was one of those girls who you would immediately class as attractive. Dressed in a pair of slim-fitting jeans and a black shirt temptingly unbuttoned, she could hold her own, when she took her dowdy coat off.

Coat over one arm, fixed grin on her face, she walked into the small, smoke-filled, pre-revolutionary hotel bar. All gold, with pink and blue frescos and fat frolicking cherubs, lit by the light of a chandelier, the atmosphere was

immediately decadent. The noise level was high and everyone was drinking bottles of sweet Russian champagne.

'Over here,' waved Karl, through the cigarette smoke.
'London girl, over here . . .'

'Right,' grinned Kate, waving back, as she zig-zagged
her way towards him.

'Do you fancy a drink?' he asked.

'Yes please,' she replied.

'You can have some of this sweet shit if you fancy . . .
It seems to do the trick.'

'Don't you like Russian champagne?' asked Kate,
accepting a warm glass.

'I've lost the ability to tell what I like and what I don't
like, I have been away that long,' said Karl.

'Oh, it must be terrible being away so much,' suggested Kate, hearing her own voice, watching herself
trying to flirt.

'Yeah,' said Karl, running his thumb around the waist
of his tight jeans. 'It gets a bit lonely,' he added. 'Um, do
you want to sit over there?'

Kate nodded excitedly and turned to follow Karl to a
more secluded table, away from the loud crowd of thes-
pians all competing for airtime.

'Karl, darling, where are you off to?' trilled the rare
bird from her bar stool.

'Just over there,' indicated Karl with a swing of his
shoulder-length hair.

'Just so long as I know exactly where you are,' she
smiled, wagging a thin finger.

'Jesus Christ,' said Karl, sitting down on the banquette. 'That woman is such a bloody control freak.'

'Really,' smiled Kate, sitting down next to him.

'Yeah, anyway cheers,' he said, raising his glass. 'What's your name?'

'Kate,' said Kate.

'Cheers then, Kate,' he said, chinking glasses and putting his hand on her thigh.

Kate went rigid. Karl Stanford had his hand on her thigh and she didn't know what to do.

'Cheers,' she said, inhaling through her back teeth.

'So?' said Karl.

'So . . .' repeated Kate, not moving.

'So, what did you think of me, then?' he asked. 'Or should I say did you enjoy the play?'

'Oh, God, sorry, yes, right, of course, no, no, you were great,' said Kate. 'The best thing in it . . . The only thing I watched was you . . . Your entrance, your exit, your . . . You acted everyone else off the stage.' Kate smiled, wondering if she had left anything out.

'I didn't overplay it at all?'

'Oh, no,' said Kate shaking her head vigorously. 'You didn't overplay it at all. If anything you underplayed it.'

'Under?'

'No, no, what I meant was you were marvellous. Marvellous in the play and, you know, marvellous in general.'

'Marvellous in general,' said Karl, running his index finger up and down Kate's thigh.

'I have been a big fan of your work ever since *Doctors*

and Nurses,' she said, turning to face him. 'Honestly, ever since you entered, carrying the pregnant women . . .'

'God, that,' said Karl, snorting as he lay back against the banquette, running his hands through his long dark hair, and reaching down into the neck of his open white shirt, to play with his St Christopher. 'She was a hefty old bitch.'

'Really?' said Kate. 'You made her appear as light as a feather.'

'Yeah, well,' he said, turning back towards her, placing his hand back down on her thigh. 'So you're a fan, are you?' he asked, raising an eyebrow and licking his full lips.

'I have seen everything you have ever been in.'

'Really,' he grinned, his eyes lowered towards her cleavage. 'When did you like me best?'

Kate was overcome with emotion. The champagne was going to her head. Karl's seismic caresses were sending her off the Richter scale and his teasing questioning was becoming too much.

'Oh, God,' she giggled. 'It's all gone clean out of my head.'

'Well, perhaps I'd better take you upstairs and help you remember,' he suggested.

Kate was hardly through Karl's bedroom door before he had her up against the wall and was taking her shirt off.

'I like sturdy girls like you,' he said, his face disappearing between her breasts.

'Oh, good,' said Kate, ruffling the top of his head for want of something to do.

Within a few swift moves of a true professional, Karl had Kate naked on the bed and was flailing around on top of her like a plaice in the final throes of asphyxiation. After what felt like a couple of prods from a short, thin pencil, Karl ground to halt, collapsed on his front and started to dribble in her ear.

'But Dr Cutler . . .' she whispered.

'The name's Karl,' he mumbled. 'I'll try again in the morning.'

Gay Longworth

Harvest

Thursday 29th November. 9 p.m. Bedsit.

At last I have good news. Today I met a pretty English girl. Lizzie (small for Elizabeth). She said she had seen me in the college bar. I did not want to tell she is mistaken. I do not go to the bar. It is not like home. People do not say hello and offer drinks. They look at me and talk in each others ears. But all that is finished. I will tell from the beginning. I was in the café drinking hot chocolate. A treat (new word) for getting an A in my essay on farming. Mad cow is not funny. The teacher liked that, she said I had a good 'grasp' on English humour. Lizzie was having a cup of tea with milk and much sugar. She wore yellow glasses and a woolly hat and a scarf. Like me, she doesn't like the cold I think. I walked her to a tube station of Marble Arch and then she asked me to a party. I need to be cool but I was too happy. She is beautiful, even behind the big yellow glasses. I have taken out my money and I have went shopping. This is my big night out in the town. I do not feel sick for Dubrovnik so much but I still miss the fish and ice cream.

Daniel placed the biro back in the ring binder and closed the notebook. The diary was part of a year-long assignment; his first entries had been abysmal. Miserable, homesick and unable to express himself. After three months life had barely changed for Daniel. Although his English was much improved, Daniel still chose not to fully express himself in his diary; he didn't want anyone reading about his loneliness or his fear of this giant, grotesque city. He looked at his newest possessions lying on the metal-framed bed. Things were going to be much better now he'd made a friend. Daniel had re-budgeted his month's allowance. By reducing his food to eggs and bread, and walking to and from the bedsit in Bayswater to the language college, he had found an extra £72 to spend on his first party in London. So far he had spent £3.40 on new hair gel, 75p on a new comb and £12.99 on a new shirt. It was denim. It went well with the jeans his father had brought for him when he left Croatia. He had carefully and painstakingly washed the jeans in the sink, wrung them out and hung them from the plastic curtain rail to dry. This new life was a shock to Daniel. In Dubrovnik he was someone. He and his father ran a boating business, which had greatly benefited from peace and the increasing influx of tourists from England, Italy and Germany. The sharp, clear coastal water of Dubrovnik enticed even the sea-fearing tourists, everyone wanted to hire boats, sip cold beer and watch shards of light dance on the sea floor. Daniel's father was too old to learn a new skill, so Daniel was the one sent to England to improve his English, Italian and German. Daniel could still taste the envy among his friends; *he* was going to London. London! But the city had not welcomed him into its arms, it was a secret society and Daniel didn't know the password. London didn't depend on him, it had no reason to throw open its doors and beckon him inside. Every day made him feel less and less significant. He wasn't weak by nature but London had the tools to mine your confidence, self-belief, your will to live. Daniel hung up his shirt and placed his gel and comb on the edge of the brown-stained sink. He regretted the money he had wasted trying to clean the sink. None of the expensive products would shift the mark left by indifferent tenants and rusty water. Daniel laid his socks on the cold radiator, lined his shoes against the wall and buttoned his pyjamas up to his neck. He lay on the thin mattress and listened to the building groan under the weight of overpopulation. But this night he didn't care that he could hear the Hindi music through the wall, he didn't mind that he could smell the smoke of the woman downstairs, he didn't tense up when babies cried or men shouted. Everything was going to change. The secrets of the city were beckoning and the password was Lizzie.

The following day Daniel plucked up the courage to enter the college bar. It was usually busy from Friday lunchtime onwards. The wealthy Italian students congregated in the corner and chattered at and over one another. Like machines guns, they stopped only to reload with lager and then they were off again, each one crowned with designer sunglasses. Daniel sidled around them and continued to search for a glimpse of yellow glasses and a woolly hat. He would have asked someone, but he didn't know her surname, or what department she was in. Standing in the middle of enemy territory, he realised he knew nothing about her at all. He retreated. It didn't matter, he told himself, he had one last purchase to make. The most important one of all. Aftershave. Daniel left the bar and returned to Superdrug where he spent fifty minutes smelling every balm, spray and splash on offer. He wanted sophistication in a bottle. With much coaxing from the girl behind the counter, he finally chose one – by Dunhill. She assured him it was a 'dead cert' with the girls, but Daniel didn't like the way her colleague smirked at him behind a gash of red lipstick. He raised his chin. No one was going to spoil this for him. Daniel stood on the pavement and checked his change. He had £24.86 left. This he would save so that he could buy Lizzie a few drinks, maybe a rose. He thrust the money in his pocket and headed for the bedsit. He had some ironing to attend to.

The woman downstairs rented her iron to him for £2.00. Her toothless, tattooed face made him want to cry.

'I'm not a fucking charity,' she balked when he tried to complain. If Daniel had written even half the truth in his letters, his father would have summoned him home.

That his neighbour slept with men for twenty pound notes to pay for vials of crack cocaine, that his landlord shirked health and safety laws to pack poor Indian families into one room, but Daniel hadn't told him anything. He wanted his father to be proud of him, he wanted to be proud of himself. Daniel folded his jeans and placed them on a towel on the floor. He spent fifteen minutes checking them and another forty-five meticulously ironing them flat. When he was finished he lifted them up, opened them out and checked the long sharp crease down the middle of each leg. He smiled. Perfect.

On Saturday Daniel woke early and put on his running clothes. He ran for a hour through Hyde Park, past the women in flowing black robes and the couples with matching children in the Princess of Wales playground. Back at the flat he did his daily sets of press-ups and sit-ups. He lived on the coast, draped in sunshine, he liked to look good on deck, it helped bring the punters in. German women liked triangular torsos, Italians liked them smooth and English liked them bronzed. No one in London knew what lay beneath the buttoned up cotton shirts and patterned knitwear. It was too cold, wet and dirty to strip down to the flesh. Another advantage he'd lost crossing the Adriatic. If Lizzie didn't like the cold, maybe she'd enjoy a summer in Dubrovnik. They could walk along the polished marble stones, holding hands so that she didn't slip. They'd eat sea bass and roasted potatoes high up on the cliff-side restaurants, all the bar and café owners would call out his name and wave to them and she'd know he was a popular man. Daniel showered, still felt the grime of the 'hotel' on him and showered again. A man hammered on the door for him to hurry up. Too brash for an illegal immigrant, he must have been yet another 'friend' of the woman with the iron. Daniel would never, ever bring Lizzie back here, of that he was certain.

He combed his hair until it was dry, cemented his side parting with the new gel and pulled on the shirt and jeans. He buttoned up the shirt, tucked it into the waistband, put on his belt and observed himself in the windowpane. He looked neat. Clean. One last splash of aftershave and he was ready. This was his night, the start of a new life; he could feel the excitement in his fingernails.

They had arranged to meet at Camden. Not in the station, she wanted him to walk a little up the hill past the cinema and wait down a side street. She would be waiting in a car. She had apologised for not offering to pick him up, but she didn't like driving across town on Saturday night because of the traffic. He didn't mind. He used the walk to rehearse his English and recall the newspaper articles he had read that day. He knew he was intelligent, at home he was top of his class, but in London he felt stupid as his vocabulary evaded him at crucial moments. Daniel arrived in Camden at quarter to seven. Not wanting to look like a tourist, he had made the journey without his trusted pocket A–Z. To avoid getting lost, he had studied his route, learning the street names by heart.

Now he stood and waited, checked his watch and continued to wait. Fifteen minutes after their arranged meeting time Daniel's nerves took on a new form. He reminded himself the traffic was bad on Saturday nights, and it did look bad, very slow; even so, had she forgotten? She didn't have a phone she said, so he couldn't even ring her to check. Maybe it was a set-up? A joke at his expense? Of course a girl like that wouldn't be interested in a Croatian language student, not when there were all those handsome wealthy Italians who never even bothered to go to their lessons . . . Damn! Daniel kicked the railings just as he heard a car horn blurt out noisily beside him. He looked up. He recognised the glasses behind the glass. She waved and beckoned for him to come quickly. He ran to the car, all fears forgotten. She had come. He still had a date, this was still his Saturday night and no one was going to take it away from him.

'Hello, Lizzie.'

'Seatbelt,' said Lizzie.

'Oh yes,' said Daniel. 'Sorry.'

'I got the address wrong, it is going to take a bit longer to get there. Why don't we listen to some music?' Lizzie slammed on a tape and the small car filled with a heavy thumping techno beat.

'How was the rest of your week?' shouted Daniel.

'What?'

'Week? Good?'

'Fine.'

'I didn't see you at college?'

'Revision,' mouthed Lizzie by way of explanation.

Daniel was confused. Exams weren't until the end of the school year. Lizzie was nodding her head up and down to the music.

'How did it go?'

'What?'

'The exam.'

Lizzie took her hand off the steering wheel and shook it from side to side. Daniel reached out for the volume control.

'Don't!' shouted Lizzie. Daniel turned to her. She didn't meet his eye. 'It helps me concentrate when I drive.'

Daniel leaned back in his seat. Fair enough, he thought to himself, it was her car, she was driving, and anyway they would have plenty enough time to talk at the party. Lizzie pointed behind her and mouthed the word 'beer', then she smiled and Daniel immediately felt better. He opened one and passed it to her, she took a swig and passed it back to him. She encouraged him to drink. Sharing a drink, he smiled to himself, now that was a good sign. A street name flashed past him. He recognised it. He had walked down the same back street over an hour ago on his way to Camden. She *was* driving across town. Daniel didn't say anything. Lizzie didn't have to know that he'd walked all the way.

They drove for nearly an hour. Daniel had no idea where he was and he didn't think that his £22.86 would cover drinks and a taxi home. He didn't want to be presumptuous but he was a little nervous when they pulled into a nondescript cul de sac.

'Will you drop me back?' asked Daniel as soon as the deafening music died with the engine. Lizzie looked at him with a strange expression, then nodded. It was barely a movement. Daniel got out of the car.

'Whose party is it?' he asked, looking at his disappointing surroundings.

'Um, just some students.'

'From the language school?' Daniel could hear the panic in his own voice.

'No, med students, don't worry.'

'What do you do at the school?'

Lizzie blinked at him. 'My employer wants me to learn Spanish. I'm a nanny and the family go to Spain every year. It's so I can go shopping and things.' She smiled at the thought of it.

'Nice job.'

'You don't believe me,' she snapped.

'Of course I do. Sorry,' said Daniel. 'I didn't want to embarrass you.'

Out of her bag Lizzie brought out two masks. 'I forgot to say. It's a mask party. I got you one.' She passed him a black-felt mask with holes for eyes and a space for his nose.

'Fancy dress,' said Daniel, pleased that he knew the word.

'Something like that,' said Lizzie, staring at the floor. She pulled off her glasses.

'Lizzie?'

She ignored him. The strap of her mask was knotted up.
'Lizzie?'

She looked up, startled. Then just as quickly turned
away. 'What?'

Daniel replied with a smile. Blue. She had blue eyes.
He committed her pretty face to memory and followed
her up a brick pathway, to a door with a red balloon tied
to it. She didn't use the bell, instead she knocked three
times on the door.

'We'll get a drink first,' said Lizzie, 'then go and find
a nice quiet place to talk. What do you think?'

The door was opened by a man in a mask.

'I think that would be excellent,' said Daniel and followed her in. There weren't many people in the dimly lit
room. Even so the masked man at the door brought the
red balloon in with him. Daniel heard it pop. It made him
jump. If he and Lizzie were the last guests to arrive, then
perhaps it was not going to be the night he'd hoped for,
a night to remember.

Daniel tried to pull the covers over him. The bedsit was
cold, but not usually this cold. He was freezing. It felt
like he was lying on a bed of ice. He must have drunk too
much. He couldn't remember getting home. He tried to
lick his lips, but had no saliva in his mouth. Slowly Daniel
pulled his eyelids apart, they were sticky with sleep. He
blinked, trying to make his eyes stay open. Frame by
frame a white bathroom appeared in front of him, he
closed his eyes again, adjusted his head. He'd gone to a

party, he'd had a drink, he . . . He couldn't remember. Jesus it was cold. He opened his eyes again. He was lying in a bath of . . .

'Ice,' his voice vibrated unfamiliarly. He raised his hand. It was blue with cold but the ice he lay in was pink. He tried to sit up but he was frozen numb. His uncle had once had a big party. He'd kept the champagne cold by filling a bath of ice. Had he fallen in? Could he have got that drunk? Where was everyone else?

'Hello?'

His back hurt when he spoke. On the wall was a mirror. Someone had written a telephone number on it in red lipstick. CALL ASAP. He didn't know anyone called Asap. He tried to sit again but the pain in his back forced him to collapse back into the ice. It was changing colour, the pink was getting darker. Redder. He felt terrible, he had to get out of this ice. Scared, he called out again, the effort made the room swim around him. He turned his head to the left. By the bath was a telephone. It was on a stool within reaching distance. It took him several minutes to muster the strength to move his arm towards the phone. He looked at the number on the mirror again. It was the only number he knew, so he called it. Maybe Asap had his clothes. Maybe this was the joke. The phone rang in his ear. Eventually a woman answered. Daniel nearly dropped the phone, the voice was suddenly too loud.

'Asap?' Daniel croaked in a whisper. Even talking was taking extreme effort.

'Asap?'

'Who is this?'

'Daniel. My clothes?' The room was darkening at the edges. 'You put me in ice?'

'Oh God,' Daniel heard the voice say. 'We've got another one! Daniel? Daniel? Listen to me. Where are you?'

'. . . Bath . . .'

'Daniel, you need to stay on the line, you understand, stay on the phone, we can't help you unless we can trace this call.' Daniel heard the words operator, intercept, emergency, but he didn't know what they meant. He was very cold. He couldn't concentrate. He just wanted to go to sleep.

'Daniel, are you bleeding?'

Daniel looked at the melting ice water again. It was pale pink at his feet. Brighter around his legs and waist. And to the right of him floated a red cloud of blood.

'I am bleeding,' said Daniel in a small voice.

'Where are you bleeding from?'

'My side,' he said, his voice cracking with fear. 'No, behind me, my back. It hurts.'

'Okay, Daniel, I need you to feel for an incision.'

'Inci . . . Help me. I don't understand. Where am I?'

'Daniel, you are looking for a cut, halfway down your back.'

His fingers slipped into a warm gash and he retched.

'Oh, my God . . .'

'Daniel, this is important, is there one cut or two?'

Daniel didn't respond. The white bathroom had turned black.

'DANIEL! LISTEN TO ME! ONE OR TWO?'

'One,' he whispered.

'Thank God,' said the nice voice. 'They're on their way to get you.' The voice got quieter. 'Single harvest.'

Harvest, thought Daniel disappearing into blackness, to gather a crop from where it has been growing. He got an A in that essay, his father was really proud, mad cow was not funny, soon they'd own a fleet of boats, he'd take Lizzie sailing, he could feel the excitement flutter under his ribcage, they'd swim, the water in Croatia was translucent, aquamarine, warm . . .

'You still have one kidney,' said the voice. But Daniel was back in Croatia, and the voice was far away.

Libbi Gorr's

Peach Bellinis

An age-old recipe by LIBBI GORR passed on to her from her brother DAVE.

Get ya blender out and stick in two fingers of each of the following (that's horizontal fingers):

Champagne
Peach Nectar
Peach Schnapps
Malibu

It doesn't matter if you aren't very accurate with your measurements. Trust me.

Put in enough ice so it begins to pile up over the liquid. Experiment with different amounts of ice. Not enough: too runny. Too much: loses flavour and hard to drink.

Blend like the Brady Bunch.

Strip naked. Pop on red gingham apron with frills, and fluffy mules.

Pour Bellini mixture into champagne glass. If none available drink straight from blender. Not too fast, mind, on account of ice headaches and sensitive teeth.

Have another.

Pop on potato gems.

Have another.

Eat potato gems.

Have another etc. After four, take care not to stray near bathroom and suntan lotion. Coconut oil and Malibu may smell deceptively similar.

Lauren Burns

Caipirinha

To me this Brazilian cocktail brings back feelings of being in Rio – one sip and I find myself salubriously lying on the Jericoacoara Beach. Images of big-bottomed beautiful women parading in G-strings, and of tanned muscular men playing soccer on the sand float dreamily through my mind. All of this haziness is gone with the jolt of the Cachaça hitting the back of my throat, and then wooooh! Am I ready to party.

The main ingredient of this cocktail is the Cachaça, a strong sugar-cane rum. Now one of the most popular drinks in Brazil, Cachaça was originally drunk in poorer circles and fed to slaves for reportedly increasing vigour. Cachaça goes by other names, two of which are Abrideira ('the opener') and Agua Benta ('holy water') but I will leave their meanings for your own interpretation.

There are many recipes for this festive summer drink but personally I am a big fan of the traditional Caipirinha recipe to get those hips swinging:

Caipirinha (little peasant girl)

1 fresh juicy lime, halved
2 shots Cachaça
1 heaped teaspoon brown sugar
Crushed ice

In a glass mull together lime halves with brown sugar. Add crushed ice and pour over Cachaça.

Drink with a lover and let this fluid of dreams take you across the Pacific Ocean to the moonlit beaches of Brazil during Carnaval, where the music is playing and the fire swells in your belly. Or simply slam it back with some friends and have a boogie at home before hitting the town!

Disclaimer: I cannot be held responsible for what the night may bring after consuming this potent beverage.

Theresa Byrnes

Big Night Out

I monitor a big night by # 1, if I fall out of my wheelchair tanked with chilly margaritas, face-planting the downtown sidewalks. It's happened twice. Those two particular big nights ended at 5 or 6 a.m., the first, in bed with Michael and Javier, the second, having a very early breakfast at 'Odessa' (a 24-hour diner on Avenue A) with Nigel and Bill while holding an icy-pole to my swelling cheekbone.

The good thing about projecting from your wheelchair drunk is that you relax into the flight. Before you know it, you've splattered safely. I spend the next few minutes calming down the lads, letting them know I'm okay. Sprawled on the cement, trying to look as glamorous as possible, I instruct how best to heave me back into the chair. Grabbed under the armpits and alley oop! I give a silent prayer of thanks that I didn't wear a G-string and a mini.

2 monitor – how many people, if any, have to assist me to take a piss. Even though most clubs in New York City have handicapped facilities, it is of enormous help on

a big night out if my chosen ally pulls my knickers down at the strategic moment when I stand and grab the rail. I swivel and land on the toilet seat in one fell swoop (usually ensuing in toilet-seat breakage). Inebriation is great, in that I don't have a skerrick of embarrassment or shyness. I kind of enjoy the opportunity to show off my powdery ass. No shame, baby!

3 monitor – taking the dance floor by storm, oozing joy, sexuality and having a man either straddling me for a seated groove or abandoning the wheelchair altogether, tossing my arms and legs around partner's neck and waist for vertical groove. The second option usually results in my girlfriends running around my empty wheelchair on the dance floor wondering where the fuck I am.

4 monitor – 6 or 7 a.m., searching the streets for an open bar with an entourage of wonderful freaks who have become new best friends. They say New York never sleeps; well, for that crucial hour before the new day begins, I have found that it goes into a brief coma. Worst of all regarding monitor #4 is that the pizza places are closed – Rosario's, Ray's, Sal's, Three Boots (really Two Boots) – shut, shut, shut. No cheesy oil to anoint my party clothes. I would invite the rage crew back to my apartment but it's full of wet paintings, and damage control forbids entry. Time to take my ass home, raid the fridge and hopefully make it into bed without falling.

5 monitor – purposely or accidentally 'exposing myself'. Wearing a boob-tube dress, rocking out to ambient trash at 'Parkside' on Houston with Jill. Numerous

tequila shots with wheat beer chasers later, we move to the back room where I thrash my head in punk fashion to corny, synthesised harmonics. Jill leans over, informing me to readjust my stash shoved down my top, the bag being more prominent than my tits. As I pull it out, a boob pops out – time to go. A week or two later, I go to Rockefeller Center with my friend Jessica to pick up some champagne truffles from Teuscher Chocolates. After purchase, we roll up Fifth Avenue where a young man runs up to me and asks, 'Didn't I see you the other week at a Downtown club?' I think for a moment and then remember. My face reddens in recognition. He chuckles, 'It looked as though you and your friend were having a great time – I wanted to join your party.' He gives me his email address. Three months in New York and already my reputation preceeds me.

6 monitor – ending up at 'La Nouvelle Justine', a love and hatred club in the East Village. I hung out there with gorgeous transvestite and Bette Midler impersonator, Aneeda Cocktail. We had picked each other up at 'Lucky Chengs' (a world infamous drag club) earlier that evening and totally clicked. Margarita after margi, a Polaroid together with a cobra, a joint in the dunny where I stripped down to my leather bra, free cocktails until closing, a queue of kisses, and a gift of a leather paddle with 'La Nouvelle Justine' inscribed on it. I was the toast of the leather set.

So, I am good at the big night out. Oh, the thrill of risk, the joy of the shocking and the abundant possibilities in destruction. The uptight walls crumble and there seems to be no limit to my all-encompassing exuberance. It's taking control of my own mortality, sacrificing brain cells to booze and bringing on cancer by sucking down cigarettes. There is something enlighteningly defiant about celebrating, letting loose, rejoicing by poisoning myself, not giving a shit. 'Contradiction in terms?' Life is so full of contradictions, opposites giving each other meaning. My idea of balance is back-to-back extremes: creative hyper-productivity, contemplation and isolation to full-on, out-there, party-mode. It seems that unity and truth reside in colliding forces and nothing is right or wrong in that moment of exalted obliteration.

I live outside the loop – no husband, children, mortgages or automobiles. I own nothing but my presence, my wheelchair and my art materials. I am one of the underground privileged. Not chained to the system – grateful to it, but also critical of it. I *live* freedom in the delirious joy of living my dreams, a self-sufficient artist based in New York, travelling the world exhibiting my work. It was the dream of my ancestors, being answerable only to one: 'I am the boss of me.' From a lineage of adventurers running from war, from arranged marriages, from strict family, from poverty, I have arrived certainly without a silver spoon, but with millennia of love and a knowledge that I can do anything, wherever I hang my hat. And now bloody civilisation comes tumbling down.

My entire adult life, as an artist, writer and vehement freethinker, has been about seeking truth – the way to live in ultimate freedom, on the firm path of destiny. I had always felt on the outside of the community or so deep within it I was avoided like a mutant. I don't want what most work for all their lives: financial security. I want only to understand life and to ride the adventure of it with no fear, facing all opposition as a means to bringing me closer to truth. Rebellious? I just want to cut the civilised crap.

I treasure my unstable life. I follow my bliss and my will to be a conscious global citizen. Added to my mix is a fatal, genetic disorder – Friedreich's ataxia – causing deterioration of my coordination. My nervous system is failing and clumsiness is increasing. Now wheelchair mobile, I speed down the path of freedom deconstructing. Wind in my hair, I know deeply that freedom is not about mobility and control of the body or about unabashed consumer choice. I miss the ball, but not the plot.

I live in the East Village, downtown New York, about fifteen minutes from the World Trade Center. One afternoon I was doing a little martial arts workout with my then-lover and friend Cameron, when a smoky stench flooded in, directed by the wind, that was to fill the air for months. We embraced and sobbed in each other's arms because we recognised that smell instantly – the smell of death, incinerated bodies, asbestos and CFCs.

It seemed that any light relief or joy was fleeting between trauma, as thousands of spirits let go of New York City, realising their death. And we too were realising death, not just the deaths of the victims but also the death of the world as we had known it. Once again I would have to examine the meaning of freedom.

Sirens reined in the hood. In the weeks after 'the crash' you could barely count to sixty without a screaming emergency vehicle ripping through your heart. Locals wore dust masks, NYPD on every corner, roadblocks, and an anthrax scare at 'Key Food' (my grocery store on the block). The military were in the East River, and in the sky. The City on high alert; lockdown.

I slunk with ease into depression. There were days I could barely raise my sobbing head off my chest. The following Friday evening, after crying most of the afternoon, my best friend and neighbour Irene (originally from Perth) invited me to go see Archie Roach and Ruby Hunter perform at the BAM café (Brooklyn Academy of Music). It was part of the Next Wave Festival. I crashed the opening party and ended up dancing with Robert Archibald (Manager Cultural Relations, Australian Consulate in New York) and Teresa Keleher (Cultural Ambassador, Australian Embassy in Washington DC), while sculling good Australian wine on the BAM stage.

Irene and I used to party at the same clubs in 1980s Sydney, The Trade Union Club, Manzil Room, Kardoma café. I was fourteen and she was thirty-one. After tracking similar paths and dancin' in each other's shadows, we finally met when I moved into the building a little over a year ago. We have become like sisters, joined by the spirit of good live music, a past of wild men, a ragingly independent tenacity and a sublime love for New York City.

Irene and I had a conversation shortly after September 11 about how we both felt we'd been in training for 'the fall' all our lives. Some of my friends had just moved from New York while others, like Jess Adams (author, astrologer and co-editor of this book), arrived from London the night before. If New York was an artist, her subject would be freedom. And maybe we are her scribes and her expression. The word on the street is that we feel selected by this place and although freaking out, couldn't bear to be anywhere else.

I am used to the whole death-sentence thing. We all have a fatal condition called life. But now more than ever, it feels like any day could be the end. I look at the Manhattan skyline and I can't help but see it collapse before my eyes. I listen to politicians of the Western world saying, 'Buy, buy, buy!' as friends lose their jobs and the ass falls out of the art market.

Archie and Ruby's first song was 'Took the Children Away', about stolen children. I burst into tears. Irene put her arm around me and held my hand. I had come full circle to realise that we are all stolen children: all born to the earth and swiftly indoctrinated into religious, moral, economic and political orders. Division is created, beliefs instilled – capitalism is mistaken for freedom: it enslaves, impoverishes and commodifies human rights. Desire delivered, consumer need expands – exploitation creates stability. I cried because I felt a renewed unity with the earth and a profound spiritual solidarity with my indigenous brothers and sisters, the entire humanity.

September 11 has had a sobering effect on the neighbourhood. In the past few years the East Village has fallen victim to a 'creeping fabulousness', the once notorious Alphabet City now gentrified. The young, hip and financially mobile come to get sloshed, on a crawl from one shi-shi bar to another. On Friday and Saturday nights I hear raucous, drunken Americans blunder by my storefront into the morning hours. I expected there to be an upsurge of public drunkenness after September 11, but no. In the weeks and months afterward, bars were empty. My sleeps were undisturbed. A strange peace fell over the hood. People were not escaping, or maybe they knew there was no none.

Now my 'Big Night Out' is rare and changed. The children dying in Afghanistan make it hard to groove. I feel their little souls. We are all connected. Victory needs to be mourned. And celebration of life has taken on a less destructive edge.

I had a vision when I was twelve: Dad was driving our yellow Valiant over the Harbour Bridge. I hung my head out the window at the sunny, Sydney day. Suddenly the buildings vanished, the bridge collapsed. Indigenous people were fishing with spears. The car had become a time machine. But was it going forward or back? Now I'm grateful every day to open my eyes and live again. I'm blown out by the beauty of life and the fragility of this technological society. From that day on, whatever followed was a bonus.

At BAM the twelve-year-old son of one of the filmmakers pushed me around the party like Queen VIP.

Gliding from food table to bar, I was introduced to brilliant Aussie actors starring in *Cloudstreet* and also its director. I caught up with many dignitaries, like Michael Baume, the former Consulate General who had come to my very first exhibition in New York and had now retired.

I danced with Robert Archibald, Teresa Keleher and sweet Irene. I spun my wheels and thrashed my hair. I had not had a drink for ages and the wine was going straight to my head. I was missing the beat but didn't care. I didn't care because I was letting myself become numb. I was feeling joy again for more than a moment. I had crashed the party and ended up being a big wheel.

Sacha Molitorisz

Highway to Heaven

'Who's the best flatmate I ever had at Bull Street?' It was 11 p.m. and Ange was calling from the pub. She sounded emotional, but I couldn't tell if she was smiling or crying.

Easy.

'Anthony.'

'Yeah, Anthony.'

The first time I met Anthony I was five years younger and five hours early. I was twenty-one and living in Sydney. I'd driven to Newcastle to visit my little brother Dave and little sister Ange. And escape my boyfriend. For a couple of years I'd been having this hot-cold-up-down-on-off rollercoaster-ride of a relationship. Lots of sex, lots of arguments. Just then we were in an Arctic phase. I was crying for half the journey, though I knew by the time I returned everything would be better.

Dave and Ange? They must have been twenty and nineteen. Dave was studying engineering and Ange was working almost as much as she needed to earn enough cash to go out every night till daybreak. That was pretty much her only expense. It wasn't like she had to spend much on rent. Not even the tightest landlord could have charged more than a few bucks for Bull Street.

The day, I remember, was fiery and hot, even at ten in the morning. That's when I arrived at Bull Street. I hadn't been before, but I found it straight away, tucked between a couple of radio newsflashes about the bushfires burning all around the State. Theirs was the only condemned house in the street. During the earthquake it had collapsed in on itself. I think it was only still standing because it couldn't decide whether to fall to the left or the right. I stepped down from the road and walked to the front door, which had sunk about a metre below street level. Like you were stepping into an antechamber for the underworld. I knocked and waited.

And waited.

No one answered. Shit, why would they? Belatedly, I remembered they'd probably only fallen into their beds a couple of hours earlier. Getting there at 10 a.m. was like getting to my mum's house at three in the morning. I drove to the supermarket. Dave and Ange spent all their money on Tooheys Old, so I figured they had no groceries – simple stuff even, like toilet paper and bread and milk and pasta and orange juice and shampoo. So I filled up a trolley with all the basics. Except cleaning products. Waste of money. Nobody at Bull Street would have known how to use them.

An hour later I returned with an armful of shopping

and the knowledge Bull Street would still be quiet. And it was, but the front door was open. So I let myself in and tried to find the kitchen. Hell's kitchen.

As I looked around, I noticed all the rooms were sloping. Not the same way, either. Each room was crooked in its own special way. And some of the cracks in the wall you could have passed a carton of beer through. With the darkness and dodgy angles, it was like I'd stepped onto the set of *Nosferatu*.

Which is when I saw the vampire, blinking hard against the light. Not scary, but just as good-looking as you'd expect a vampire to be. I had a good chance to look him over, because he didn't see me for ages. 'Oh,' he said finally, obviously just woken. 'Who are you?' Not rude. Just curious.

'I'm Jo, Dave and Ange's sister.'

'Oh.' Another minute lurched by. 'They're still asleep.'

'Yeah, I guessed.'

As we were speaking, I kept putting groceries in the cupboards. He didn't seem to notice. Bull Street probably had siblings and parents doing this sort of stuff all the time.

'You want a coffee?'

'Thanks,' I said. 'I can take care of it.'

'No, really,' he said, flicking on the kettle. He was smiling this big lopsided smile. He only had one dimple.

The 1989 earthquake hit Newcastle like a buck's party hitting the Cross. People died and buildings crumbled. Bull Street must have shaken and shifted so much no one would have backed it to survive, even in this town of gamblers and underdogs. Now it looked like a haunted house the earth had started to swallow before realising it didn't really like the taste.

I was sitting on the back verandah with Anthony, who wasn't a vampire after all. We had a cup of coffee each and he was smoking a ciggie he'd pulled from a Peter Stuyvesant soft pack. 'Your boyfriend sounds like an idiot,' he said. I agreed, but resented him for saying it.

Midafternoon, still hot as hell. We were on our second coffee anyway. In the sun, he looked less like a creature of the night than a doomed rock star: long hair, beautiful eyes. Obviously not a morning person.

'When I was a kid I was playing ring-a-ring-a-rosie with all these girls,' he said. Must have seen me staring at his dimple. 'And I fell into a rose bush. I cut myself on a thorn. Needed a couple of stitches.' The boy who fell in the rose bush and grew an extra smile? Sounded like a fairy tale, so I didn't believe it. Boys were always lying to get you to like them.

'You're at uni with Dave?'

'Yeah. I'm doing communications,' he said, letting his cigarette butt fall into a near-empty beer bottle. The garden had more empties than flowers. A party last night, probably. 'And I work at a bakery.'

'Right, for the hours?' Hard to imagine this boy I'd mistaken for a bloodsucker elbow-deep in dough at 4 a.m. Meanwhile, Dave and Ange were still sleeping. That was okay.

✦

I kept wondering if I should call him. I was about to ask if I could use the phone, till I remembered it had been cut off. I was sure I'd seen a phone box just up the street.

Dave emerged about three. Ange crawled out into the late-afternoon sun fifteen minutes later. Their body clocks were obviously battered but finely calibrated. Dave didn't say much, just sipped his black-as-oblivion coffee. When he was drunk he was quiet; when he was hung-over he was less a person than a piece of furniture. Ange was usually the bright one. When she was drunk, she was amorous and animated. Right now she was a shadow, cradling her coffee like her one true friend.

'How's uni, Dave?'

'Okay.'

They were pleased to see me. It was just that right now they weren't so pleased to be alive.

'How's work, Ange?'

'Yeah, good.' Anthony offered Dave a cigarette, which Dave took and lit and inhaled. Ange did the same. Smoke and silence filled the air.

'You been writing, Dave?'

He didn't say anything. Ange looked up. 'Yeah,' she said. 'He's writing a short story.' Dave didn't budge.

'Really? Can I read it?' Dave was the smart one. Ange was the wild one. I didn't know which one I was, but I knew if Dave had written another story, it'd be good. The silence started ringing out.

'So, tonight . . . ?'

'The pub.' I don't know who answered, whether it was Dave or Ange or Anthony or all three.

'I don't know how to end it,' Dave said, surprising me. He never usually said anything much before about 9 p.m. Ange finished for him. 'Yeah, the story,' she said, but I knew what he meant.

It was about 8 p.m. and we were at the pub. Dave and Ange were having breakfast beers. The beers weren't really for breakfast, but they'd only been up a few hours, so I was giving them a hard time.

The pub was called The Lucky Country, except that it wasn't. The Lucky was rough, although not nearly as rough as the pub down the road, which everyone said was like the rumpus room of Maitland Gaol. The Lucky had a pool table and sticky carpet and drunk builders and noisy students and crims too but not nearly as many fights.

That's how Dave described it in his story, and he was spot-on.

'I always have trouble with endings,' Dave said. I was smiling, Ange and Anthony were listening. 'I mean, I don't want some Hollywood bullshit guy-with-a-gun-bursts-in-the-hero-saves-the-world sorta shit, but I don't want some French nothing-happens-but-wow-isn't-life-just-like-that arty crap either.' I'd read what he'd written and loved it.

It was almost dark, but still hot, with TV newsflashes about the bushfires every half hour or so. They weren't so close anymore. You couldn't smell the soot and ash, but everyone was edgy anyway. Like we were simmering in a frying pan. In between the newsbreaks we watched *The Simpsons*.

'I reckon *The Simpsons* is just like *60 Minutes*,' said Anthony. 'Except with morals.' He was looking up at the screen. 'I'm serious. Look, both shows have these stupid, two-dimensional characters. Both shows are light entertainment. And both shows are really, really funny. The only difference is that every now and again *The Simpsons* teaches you stuff.'

'Like what?'

'Well, like . . . um . . .'

'Like how to drink beer and eat doughnuts?' asked Ange.

I'd been wrong about Anthony, but Ange really did look like a vampire. Her long straight hair was black anyway, but she dyed it blacker. She mostly wore long flowing dresses that were black too, and lots of jewellery, and ghost-white make-up and deep red lipstick. She looked like a satanist, but Ange was more like an angel.

It was the middle of the night but still the TV kept updating us on the fires. I think the reporters kept saying we were all going to burn, but I didn't care. Mostly because by now I was laughing so hard it hurt. Once I had to make myself laugh loud enough to drown out everything else. If I'd heard one more joke or dumb crack or whatever I would have wet myself.

At about midnight, I stopped laughing long enough to call him from the public phone in the corner. Couldn't help myself. But he was asleep. I'd had a bit to drink and wanted to tell him everything would be okay and I still loved him and couldn't wait to see him, but before I could say anything, he wanted to know why I'd woken him up and what was I doing up in Newcastle anyway, was I screwing around behind his back, and suddenly we were arguing again.

We were all very drunk now and Ange was speaking. 'Hey, Anthony, aren't you meant to be working tonight?' As the youngest at the table, she probably had the most brain cells for remembering that sort of stuff. Anthony nodded but didn't look bothered.

'What time does your shift start?'

Anthony thought for a moment. 'What time is it now?'

'Quarter past three,' I said.

'Fifteen minutes ago.'

'Shit,' said Ange, 'they've already warned you. I'll call them, okay?'

'What?'

'I'll tell them . . . you're sick.'

We were all laughing except Ange. She just grabbed Anthony's arm and led him to the public phone I'd been yelling into three hours earlier. Dave and I grabbed our beers and tumbled along behind, listening as Anthony reluctantly gave Ange the bakery's number.

She dialled and started speaking. 'Herro, I am friend of Anfony.' Ange was putting on a bad Asian accent. Interesting, I thought, till I realised it was because she was speaking to Anthony's boss, who was Chinese. A sympathy accent. She probably didn't even know she was doing it. The accent must have done her credibility some serious damage, particularly when it started wearing off. But Ange just didn't seem to notice. She was unstoppable. 'I'm calling from the . . . um, hospital. Anthony is very sick. He has . . . '

'You tell Anthony, he fired.' We stopped laughing because the voice on the phone was loud enough for us all to hear. 'You tell him, he fired.'

Eventually, Ange hung up. I didn't know what to say. 'Shit, Anthony, I'm so sorry. Are you okay?' Ange was asking, but looked like she was the one who might burst into tears.

'Nothing the Smashing Pumpkins can't fix,' he said. 'Or Accadacca. Look out, I'm on a hiiiiighwaaay to hell.' I think he was joking. He didn't seem like an AC/DC kind of guy. He didn't seem bothered, either.

'At least now I'll stop getting that fucking rash.'

On the way back to Bull Street Anthony told me his job had made him sick. He was allergic to flour. Seriously. Most shifts he would wear protective gear and be okay. But sometimes he'd go to work straight from the pub and forget and end up coming home all sneezing and itchy.

I wasn't sure whether he was joking, but Ange said it was true. 'You're better off on the dole anyway,' she said, and we finally started laughing again.

To celebrate, we bought a case of beer. My shout, because I was the only one with any money left. I don't remember the walk back actually, just snatches of conversation. And then the four of us sitting on the back verandah just like we had twelve hours earlier.

'Maybe you don't need a big climax, Dave,' said Anthony. 'I've always thought endings were overrated. They're just new beginnings anyway. Maybe your narrator or hero or whatever just has to have this moment where something important suddenly makes sense.'

'Like realising your job isn't that important?'

'That I knew already.'

Dave didn't say anything. I think Dave had drunk so much he'd come full circle and was a piece of furniture again. He just nodded, I think. I couldn't tell because it was so dark. I made a mental note to buy candles the next day, though I realised that the next day I'd probably have a snowflake's chance on Satan's BBQ of remembering.

Speaking of snowflakes . . . down in the garden, was that . . . ? I was drunk, sure, but I couldn't remember taking a trip.

Ange answered without me asking. 'Someone must have done some washing downstairs.' There was a downstairs to this crumbling wreck? That really must have been hell. 'We burst a pipe or something, and if someone washes their clothes all the soap suds go everywhere. We should get it fixed.'

It was beautiful. I felt a sudden stab of optimism. 'So, what's everyone up to today?' Getting the words out was a struggle.

'Not working,' said Anthony. 'I think I'll paint all day.'

'You paint?'

'He's really good,' said Ange. 'Does all these shelf-portraits. Self-portraits. He's too shy to ask anyone to pose.' She reached over and squeezed Anthony's cheek. 'Hey, Jo, did you hear how he got his one dimple?'

I nodded. Ange looked back at Anthony. 'The rose bush,' she said. 'It's hilarious. I never used to believe it was true.' Nor did I.

'What about you?' Anthony was looking at me. 'Any plans?'

'I'm gonna leave my dumb stupid prick of a boyfriend,' I said, the words all messy and tumbling over one another. I hadn't planned to say this. 'I'm gonna call him when I get back to Sydney and tell him it's over. Really over. Life's too short for that shit.' Anthony, Dave and Ange were smiling at me like I'd just discovered the cure for cancer.

It was warm now, not too hot, and everything looked so peaceful and beautiful, what with the snow and on top of that the pre-dawn light creeping over the horizon and colouring in everyone's faces like some uninvited Picasso. It felt safe here, like all the fires must have gone out.

Five years and one relationship later, the phone. 'Hey Jo, who's the best flatmate I ever had at Bull Street?' It was late, Ange was calling from the pub, and I couldn't tell whether she was smiling or crying.

'Anthony.'

'Yeah, Anthony. He's dead.'

✸

A patch of water on the freeway and Anthony's car lost grip and started sliding and kept sliding right into the safety railing at the side of the road. He was driving from his parents' place in Newcastle to his girlfriend's place in the Blue Mountains, and when the helicopter picked him up he was lucid as ever, probably positive as ever too, until he stopped breathing and his heart stopped beating, right up there in the sky, way, way high above Bull Street and hell and everything.

Clare Grogan's

Music/Cocktail Therapy

Five Tried and Tested Suggestions to Put You Right Back in the Groove

A perfect pairing of two of life's greatest pleasures –
listening to great music while sipping its sublime
equivalent in alcohol. Best done while having a Big
Night Out at a friend's house, just in case an immediate
lie-down is induced . . . Enjoy!

1. **For a truly fuzzy 'I am gorgeous' feeling:**
   Flirtini *with* **Madonna** – 'Ray of Light'
Sex and the City–inspired cocktail. Carrie and the girls
were feasting on these while my sister and I watched
enviously. Not having a clue as to what they contained
but not wanting to be left out, we decided to invent our
own. Champagne, fresh pineapple juice, topped up with
the smoothest of vodkas. Sparkling, healthy and with a
kick . . . And, hey, Mr DJ, put a record on. Madonna,

the best company any Big Night Out could ask
for – you really will feel like a dancing queen.

2. **Only if you have the potential to be the last one
   standing:**
   **Scotch whisky with Irn Bru *with* Belle and
   Sebastian** – 'Tigermilk'

Scotland's boldest beverages – whisky of the blended
variety matched with our other national drink, Barrs Irn
Bru, drunk at room temperature for maximum effect.
Team up with a little Scottish soul music . . . Rage and
sway as Belle and Sebastian fill the space with their
bittersweet harmonies. Tender and furious, you will
laugh and cry before the Big Night is over. It's always
wise to let it all come out . . .

3. **Suave – Moi? We've all got the pretension for it!**
   Classic Martini *with Ocean's Eleven* soundtrack

No need to shake or stir, simply sashay your way
through an evening dedicated to Frank, Dean, George,
Brad and all those other sharp-suited wise guys and pay
homage to a classic vodka drink, the martini. Take a
cocktail glass from the freezer, add a couple of drops of
Vermouth before pouring your favourite brand of vodka
(also from the freezer) and garnish with an olive. Not
too quietly in the background should be Quincy, Elvis,
Perry and friends. You'll feel like a million dollars and
without having to steal it!

4. Grown-up teeny boppers take a bow!
 California root beer *with* **The Partridge Family –**
 'The Definitive Collection'

Revisit the time when you didn't think there was
anything wrong with snogging the TV screen when the
object of your pubescent desire appeared . . . In my case
it was David Cassidy. In fact, I couldn't resist his entire
Partridge Family, yes even the ginger freckled one. Sing
along to their songs while swigging some California root
beer. Big girls need a soft drink with a twist, the twist
being a dash of Kahlua, with a splash of Galliano, fizzed
up to the top of a tall glass with soda water and cola.
Young hearts will swell with contentment!

5. For every heart broken, a good time awaits:
 Caipirinha *with* **Cesaria Evora** – 'Café Atlantico'

You are in good company, if you're one of the broken-
hearted, only the afraid won't let themselves fall. Grieve
a little with my favourite diva, in her sixties, usually
barefoot and all the way from Cape Verde. She has lived
like no other and her gravelled voice confirms this.
Intimate evenings were made for Cesaria and
Caipirinha. Fresh lime crushed with sugar and ice with
Brazilian Cachaça rum . . . Feel alive again, laugh in the
face of pain, and get ready to love once more.

Claudia Winkleman's

Best Songs for a Big Night Out

1. 'Moonlight Cocktail' – Glenn Miller and Orchestra

2. 'Vodka and Wine' – Murray the Hump

3. 'Cigarettes and Alcohol' – Oasis

4. 'Red Red Wine' – Neil Diamond

5. 'Tequila' – Terrorvision

6. 'Two Pints of Lager and a Packet of Crisps, Please' – Splodgenessabounds

7. 'Born Slippy (Lager, Lager, Lager)' – Underworld

8. 'Me and My Gin' – Dinah Washington

9. 'Rye Whiskey' – Tex Ritter

10. 'Little Ole Wine Drinker, Me' – Dean Martin

11. 'One Bourbon, One Scotch, One Beer' – John Lee Hooker

12. 'Beer Sex Chips 'N' Gravy' – The Macc Lads

13. 'However Much I Booze' – The Who

14. 'The Night They Invented Champagne' – Liza Minnelli

15. 'Vodka' – John Coltrane

16. 'Cocktails for Two' – Tommy Dorsey

17. 'Gin Soaked Boy' – Divine Comedy

18. 'Whiskey, Gin and Wine' – Joe Liggins and the Honeydrippers

19. 'Rum and Coca-Cola' – Andrews Sisters

20. 'Vodka and Tonic' – Dukes of Dixieland

21. 'Tits and Champagne' – The Joneses

22. 'Champagne and Reefer' – Muddy Waters

23. 'Champagne' – Kenny G

24. 'Beer Drinkers and Hell Raisers' – Motorhead

25. 'There's a Tear in My Beer' – The The

26. 'I Like Beer' – Tom T Hall

27. 'Gimme a Pigfoot (and a Bottle of Beer)' – Diana Ross

28. 'Whiskey Heave' – Fats Domino

29. 'Smoke and Strong Whiskey' – Christy Moore

30. 'Alcohol' – Bare Naked Ladies

and finally:

31. 'Puff the Magic Dragon' – Peter, Paul and Mary

John Gordon Sinclair

Big Knighty Out

'Hey, Knighty big-man! You coming at the weekend?'

David Knight turned to see Gary Neil lumber awkwardly towards him across the playground. David could never understand why it was that the only qualification required to become a 'Nickname' was to have a 'Y' tacked onto the end of your surname. It showed a certain lack of imagination, he thought. Not only that, but nicknames were supposed to be shortened versions of real ones; simply adding an extra letter went against the whole idea.

'Garshay!' Gary Neil's nickname; another product of profound thinking! 'How goes it?'

David tried to sound as casual as possible. When a guy who is renowned for shooting fellow classmates with an air rifle, deftly flicking a Bic biro into your forehead from twenty feet away, and stealing money from anyone and everyone – including his own mother – shouts out your name, it's a struggle to remain cool.

'You comin' at the weekend? Me and Wub are going

camping up the Duntocher hills.' (Robert Broadworth's nickname, 'Wub', stood for 'Wee Ugly Bastard'. Not bad!) 'You should come, it'll be a laugh.'

'Laugh! As in let's rub shards of glass in our eyes and stare at the sun for an hour,' is what David wanted to say, but instead he plumped for:

'Eh! I think I'm busy at the weekend.' Lame! Lamentably lame!

Garshay was onto him like a cat chasing a blind, amputee mouse. 'You think you're busy! Don't you know?'

'No, it's not that, it's just that I *know* I'm doing something but I can't *remember* what. That's *why* I said "I think".'

David reasoned that by emphasising a few words here and there, he might sound more convincing.

'Shite!' replied Garshay succinctly. 'If you cannae remember what yer doin' it cannae be that important. Come campin' wi' us. We'll pick you up at your place about half eight in the morning . . . Can you get your hands on a hatchet?'

David couldn't disguise his look of dismay. His eyes searched the heavens for a better way of expressing to Garshay that he probably could get his hands on a hatchet, but if Garshay thought for one minute that he would then let him get his hands on it, Garshay was even more deranged than he looked. The best reply he could come up with, however, was . . .

'Eh? I don't think so.'

Cat.

Blind mouse with no legs.

'You don't think so? You spend far too much time thinking, big-man. See you in the mornin'.'

If it was calculation on Garshay's part, or if he was genuinely unaware of the power he had to terrorise with a single phrase, didn't matter to David. What did matter was that Garshay's parting comment had him mumbling incoherently to himself for the rest of his journey home.

'Wub's nicked his dad's air rifle and I've got a bottle of whisky. It'll be a laugh.'

It had taken David several agitated waves of his left leg every half-hour for nearly three hours to get the duvet to lie in the correct position to regulate his temperature effectively. He was very hot.

Although he hated being ill he was secretly hoping that it might be the flu. He had lost count of the number of times he had 'flumpfed' his pillow. He also wondered if someone had sneaked into his bedroom and turned up the volume on his bedside clock.

Ridiculous idea!

The clock at the side of his bed didn't have a volume control; no clock did. His theory that if you weren't asleep by a certain hour you missed the beginning of your dream was being tested to the limit. At this rate he'd be lucky to catch the credits. Maybe he would invent a machine for recording dreams, then open a large store where you could rent other people's for £1. In no time he would be a millionaire and he could build remedial schools all over the country for the likes of Garshay and Wub.

Bollocks!

The mere mention of their names was enough to send his left leg flapping about like a landed fish on the deck of a boat.

Was he getting hotter?

The last time he looked at the clock it read 5 a.m.

The final image in his head before stumbling headlong into unconsciousness was of Garshay chopping his left leg off with a hatchet while Wub turned up the volume control on a fish . . . Fish didn't have volume controls though . . . did they? That twilight moment between consciousness and unconsciousness – where the brain loses all sense of reality – can be just as distasteful as it can be delicious in terms of the images it throws up.

This is what happens when you join a dream after it has already started.

Someone was shouting his name.

'David! . . . David!'

'Fuck off, Mum!'

David woke with a start. Had he just said that out loud? Somewhere between the fortissimo fish, having a leg amputated and being fully awake had he just cursed at his mother?

No!

Thankfully her voice was coming from downstairs. David glanced at the clock. 8.30 a.m.! Shit!

'There are two boys at the door for you, David.'

Garshay might be psychotic, but at least he was punctual. David's left leg spasmed involuntarily. Perhaps there was time to hide under the bed. His mother might think that he had been abducted in the middle of the night; to be held for ransom at some later date. In his present emotional state it seemed like quite a good idea.

He had only managed to crawl halfway under the bed when he heard the bedroom door open.

The edge of the valance lifted and his mother's face appeared. 'If you're looking for your balaclava, it's hanging up in your wardrobe.'

Balaclava! Sometimes the logic his mother employed astounded him. What on earth would he be doing under the bed looking for a balaclava! And who in their right mind would hang one up in a wardrobe?

He thought it prudent not to challenge her on this, however, in case she asked him to explain the real reason he was under the bed. The 'abduction theory' suddenly didn't sound so reasonable.

'There are two boys waiting for you downstairs. They said you're going camping with them.'

'Oh yeah! I completely forgot. I'd love to go, but I think I've pulled a muscle in my left leg and I've got the flu, so if you could tell them I'm really sorry. I don't want to hold them back.' The last little bit was inspired. It made him sound almost heroic.

'Nonsense! Hurry up and get dressed.'

Before he had a chance to protest, his mother was up and out of the room. As she headed back downstairs he heard her say, 'Come in, boys, and have a cup of tea, David's just trying to find his balaclava.'

He had read a magazine article once about matricide. The more he thought about it, the more the idea was gaining merit. David decided at that moment that if he survived the weekend the first thing he would do on his return was murder his mother.

The journey to Duntocher was fairly uneventful, which in itself was not entirely reassuring for David. By the time they had waited at the bus stop, boarded the double-decker and settled into the cold leatherette seats upstairs, they had run out of conversation.

David projected his mind forward. He saw the tent being erected in silence in the middle of a bleak, colour-less landscape. He saw a fire being lit to fend off the cold wind as it vibrated the taut guy-ropes without producing any sound. He saw the grey sullen faces of Garshay and Wub as they stared lifelessly into an empty whisky bottle; even *it* seemed reluctant to whistle as the air swirled around its exposed neck.

David's morbid reverie was broken by the bus-conductor shouting, 'Fares please, any more fares.'

David tilted to one side and rummaged in his pocket for some loose change. As he turned he noticed that both Wub and Garshay had dropped their heads forward and Wub was glowering at him.

'Put the money away you tit, or we'll all have to pay,' he snarled.

Suitably chastened, David slipped the money back into his pocket and dropped his head forward as well. The logic seemed to be that if you managed to avoid the conductor's gaze then you weren't required to pay your fare. After an hour of staring at the floor, however, David's neck was beginning to ache. He then made the fatal error of checking his watch. They had in fact only been on the bus for twenty minutes; it just seemed like an hour.

As he sat there, head drooped, he thought to himself that it would be worth paying the fifty pence just to be able to see where they were going.

It was midafternoon when the boys reached the foot of the Duntocher hills and a slight drizzly rain had started to fall. David's denim jacket soaked up the fine mist like a sponge and it wasn't long before he started to shiver with cold. He was secretly wishing he had brought along the balaclava. The realisation that he was woefully underprepared for this expedition in just about every area was exacerbated by the vague sense of panic he experienced when he thought about where his next meal might come from. The Mars bar and packet of crisps his mother had given him had long since been eaten and he knew it was highly unlikely that Wub or Garshay would have brought along adequate provisions for themselves, let alone him.

He fingered the box of matches he had lifted from the kitchen table. His grandfather had always told him, 'Whenever morale is low, light a fire.'

'Where's your tent, Knighty?' said Garshay, as he pulled a filthy blue nylon bundle from one of the two plastic carrier bags he was holding.

'Tent?' replied David with a hint of apprehension.

'Me and Wub are sharing this two-man . . . Where's yours?'

'Eh?'

Wub burst out laughing. 'Ya tit! You mean you haven't brought a tent. Are you going native on us, big-man, sleeping under the stars? Ho Garshay! Lend him one of your poly-bags and a few twigs and he can build a wee tent for his heid . . . Ye're such a tit, Knighty!'

Whether it was an act of true compassion or a further act of cruelty, David couldn't tell, but Garshay's solution to the problem did nothing to quell David's feelings of utter desolation.

'Don't worry, big-man! You can squeeze in with us; we'll go head-to-toe, it'll be a laugh.'

The prospect of lying with his head anywhere near Garshay's unpasteurised feet was almost too much to bear in itself, but Wub's as well! David wandered off to collect some firewood, feeling decidedly queasy.

The whisky drinking started at dusk and by the time the Black Hand of night had a firm grip of the evening, Garshay and Wub were drunk. It also seemed that the Black Hand's scrawny thumb was pressing down firmly on David's heart.

'Cheer up, big-man, have a glug.' Wub took a slug, then

passed the bottle to David who in turn raised the bottle to his lips and pretended to take a long, slow draught.

'That'll put a shine on your shite,' added Garshay glibly.

David could only guess at what germs were being passed between them, but took solace from a fact he had read somewhere, that at the time of the Highland clearances whisky had been used to sterilise wounds. He hoped now that it was having the same cleansing effect on the neck of this bottle.

It suddenly occurred to him that if he was pretending to drink, it followed that he would have to pretend to be drunk. A bead of sweat broke surface on his forehead.

His first ploy was to start slurring his speech and hope that Garshay and Wub were too drunk to notice it was an act.

'Ish, ish brilliant whishky, ish very tashty,' he said in order to test the ground.

'The drink's gone right to your head, big-man, you'd better take it easy,' Garshay replied, as he grabbed the bottle back from David and took a real swig.

David was sure he had passed the test but decided to keep the chat to a minimum just in case. He could tell from the way Wub's and Garshay's eyes were opening and shutting ever more slowly and from the evil scowl they had both simultaneously adopted, that it wouldn't be long before the fighting started. If the rest of the day was anything to go by he also knew that he would be first in line when the punching started.

David had a brainwave.

He wobbled slightly as he stood up (nice touch), staggered backwards a few paces (even better), then launched himself off into the night and headed for the relative safety of some bushes a hundred yards or so down the hill. He threw in a few stumbles for good measure as he went.

Wub shouted after him, 'Where the fuck d'yer think ye're going?'

David called back through the enveloping darkness, 'My bum has an appointment in the bushes with some dock leaves.'

As he stood there taking in long deep breaths of the cool, clear, summer-scented air he mused that under different circumstances this would be quite a pleasant place to be. The rain from earlier on in the day had been nothing more than a passing shower and his clothes had soon dried out. He could quite happily spend the rest of the evening gazing up at the pinpricks of light peppering the flat, black sky. The realisation that this was the first moment of calm he had enjoyed in nearly twenty-four hours made him feel slightly better.

How long could he stay there before those two baboons noticed he was missing?

All night, probably.

How long did it take to do a dump? He must remember to take his stopwatch with him the next time he went to the toilet. You never knew when information like that could come in handy. Now was just such an occasion.

The next conundrum that popped into his head was this: 'Where were the laughs Garshay kept promising and why had they invited him here in the first place?'

The answer to both of these questions came in a guise that not even David's vivid imagination could have dreamt up.

The first thing he noticed was the total silence.

A few moments earlier he had been aware of the faint mumbling and sounds of drunken squalor emanating from somewhere up the hill. Now, however, the only sound he could hear was the gentle rustle of leaves from the bushes nearby.

For a moment he thought he picked up a hint of Wub giggling but it was too faint to be sure. Suddenly there was a distinctive popping noise followed by a whoosh as something flew passed his head and smacked into the tree behind him. A huge guffaw of laughter erupted from the direction of base camp.

There was a moment's silence, followed by another pop and whoosh, and an even bigger guffaw.

It wasn't until the third whooshing sound appeared to terminate in David's thigh and he fell to the ground in agony, that he realised what was happening.

Wub and Garshay were taking pot shots at him with the air rifle. Pop! Woosh! Guffaw!

Three more pellets fizzed over his head before David became aware of the damp spreading through the cotton of his Y-fronts. 'Please tell me I'm not lying on the same piece of grass I've just pissed on,' he thought.

As he lay there he wondered what was the best strategy for dealing with two armed and dangerous psychopaths.

It occurred to him that the only other person who knew he was here was his mother. If he killed all three of them it could be the perfect crime. Even the bus-conductor couldn't identify them, they'd all had their heads bowed for the entire two-hour journey. Although someone was bound to have noticed the commotion Wub created when they discovered they had missed their stop. The first thing he had to do was crawl out of the line of fire.

It was while he was wriggling commando-style through the rough gorse that the idea came to him.

He kept crawling until he had circled round behind Garshay and Wub and was within two or three yards of the tent. He watched as they cocked and loaded the rifle, then fell about laughing as they loosed off one shot after another.

It was during this noisy salvo that David made his move. He crawled up to the back of Garshay's tent and used his matches to set the overhanging nylon flap alight.

His grandfather was right; as the flames started to lick around the bottom of the tent, his morale definitely improved.

He then quickly made his way back down to where they had been shooting at him and started shouting 'Cease-fire! Cease-fire! I've been hit, aaagh! I've been hit.'

The giggling turned to hysteria.

A torch beam swept the bushes.

'Where are you, Knighty? Stand up an' let us see you,'

shouted Wub, making no attempt to disguise his joy at another's misfortune.

David stood up and was immediately fired upon.

More raucous laughter!

In the darkness Garshay and Wub couldn't see the smile on David's face as he watched the cheap nylon tent almost explode when the flames finally caught hold. The conflagration took no more than a couple of seconds, but the satisfaction would live with David for a very long time. Garshay and Wub's rapture disappeared just as quickly as the tent and was replaced by accusations, foul language and flying fists. David turned and made his way carefully down the hill, picking his way through the long shadowy grass until at last he came to the main road.

The last bus home had long since departed, but he didn't care.

He smelled of urine and was limping quite badly as a result of the pellet wound, but the walk through the night, enjoying the quiet, the country air and the clear, sparkly sky would more than compensate for the events of the last few days.

The next time two psychopathic hooligans invited him camping, Big Knighty would be out.

Adèle Lang

Don't You Know Who I Am?

Tape 001 (unedited version): Transcribed 31/1/02

I am attempting the very tricky task of speaking into this Dictaphone, for the benefit of my ghostwriter, while slumped face-forward over one of the many toilet bowls I now own, and wondering why the view down there remains the same whether you're disgustingly rich and famous or not . . . It doesn't seem fair really . . . I mean, I drink a much better quality of alcohol these days, and the toilet's a genuine antique – and you'd think that at those prices the lid would be non-stick.

[*long pause*]

So, anyway. Where was I? Oh, yes, that's right. Ta-da! I'm still here! Still kneeling over the toilet bowl trying to avoid throwing up all over this dictaphone which, by the way, I really resent having to lug around for twelve whole bleeding hours. It's a total invasion of privacy, if you ask me. But this is what I've got to do apparently, if I want to [*adopts posh voice*] 'tell the world my story' . . . What gets me is how book publishers expect you to do all their work for them, like you're some sort of skivvy or something. And I'm going to have to flush this toilet live on air, which I know isn't very ladylike but I don't have any option now, do I? Since no one's actually shown me how to switch this sodding tape off – [*tape stops suddenly*] Oops! Still trying to get the hang of all the different buttons round here . . . Oh, right. There it is . . . [*sound of toilet flushing*] I mean, call me a stupid tart like the rest of my critics seem to do these days, but aren't I meant to be 'DALLAS – THE WORLD'S MOST BONKABLE BABE', as the tabloids so flatteringly put it before they turned on me like a flock of baying wolves and started getting really derogatory? . . . My mum says I should ignore them because they're just jealous cos they all want to shag me but know that they can't. Not anymore. Not now their publicity-hungry wives have found out and sold their pathetic lies to anyone who'll listen. Well! See if I care.

[*tape stops*]

[*rustling of newspaper*] You know, even if, say, I really was a fame-hungry home-wrecking bitch, I am only human and personal comments on the amount of Botox I've been doing recently really, really hurt . . . [*starts sobbing*]

[*tape stops*]

Sorry. Got a bit carried away back there. Like, I might seem older than my years but, as my publicist keeps telling me, deep down I'm really just as vulnerable as the next nineteen-year-old girl. A moment ago I was going to look in the mirror above this toilet just to check that I really am still nineteen years old despite what it says on my passport. But the mirror above the toilet is broken . . . [*nervous giggle*] . . . You know, it always surprises me what damage a brick can do when you hit a mirror really, really hard with it after you've just found out that you only got to number two in the pop charts.

[*long pause*]

Ow! . . . Ow! Fucking ow, ow, ow!

[*tape stops*]

I am now having to stand upright over the toilet while still talking into this dictaphone, and using my one free hand to wipe all the blood off my knees, which I think must have come from the bits of mirror on the floor. And so now guess what? Both my feet are bleeding, too! And I can't find any loo roll to mop it up cos I don't know where it's kept, and I know I'm meant to be a really down-to-earth sort of star who does her own grocery shopping and stuff, but this is fucking ridiculous . . . JUANITA!!!! GET YOUR BUTT IN HERE . . . NOW!

[*long pause*]

That was me shouting loudly just then. Not because I'm a prima donna or anything, but because Juanita comes from another country and her English is really crap . . . Here, listen. Juanita, honey! Come and speak into Dallas baby's new dictaphone!

[*female voice of Latin descent*] 'Si, senorita.'

See what I mean? I so love people with accents. Me, I always wanted to be French when I was little . . . like Audrey Hepburn in *Doctor Zhivago*. Course I also wanted to be as beautiful as her, too, but believe it or not, I was actually a complete moose as a child until I got my tits done.

[*tape stops*]

To be honest with you, though, I'm never really at my best first thing in the evening. Even when I haven't just found out I've been beaten to the number-one spot in the charts by a sodding glove puppet . . . I was woken up an hour ago by that particular answering machine message from my record company who – and I hope they are listening to this – are threatening to drop me just because I refuse to record my next album until the producers provide me with my own oxygen tent and flotation tank, and have repainted all the studio walls white. So, of course,

Juanita then had to rush to my bedside and give me a vitamin jab before I could even think about racing to this toilet and throwing up the dregs of last night's secret Malibu and Coke binge.

[*nervous giggle*]

I say 'secret' because, if the press find out what I've been drinking, I'll never hear the end of it. I'm meant to be on my third attempt on the wagon, and if my publicist finds out that I've just fallen off, the bitch will rat on me again . . . Then I'll probably be packed off to that poxy detox-farm-to-the-stars, the one which, if you ask me, turns previously interesting people into complete and utter morons. Call me a snob – which I'm not, I'm working-class and very proud of it, my dad's been unemployed for years – but the stench of a bunch of stars with night sweats was enough to make me vom the last time I was there. So, guess who then also got diagnosed with bulimia nervosa as well as borderline alcoholism? Even though, and I can promise you this – hand on heart – I never so much as touch food if I can help it.

[*tape stops*]

You know, it's really strange talking into a dictaphone all by yourself. I half-expect my publicist to leap out from nowhere and press the 'PAUSE' button because I've just said something that could totally wreck my career. Not that I've got anything to be ashamed of anymore . . . not now

I've become a born-again Christian-Buddhist-Scientologist. And, anyway, I'm sure whoever's editing this tape for the *Big Night Out* book will take out anything that makes me look stupid. Which is another thing that really pisses me off, by the way. Why is it that just because I'm blonde – and not even a natural one at that – the press automatically calls me a bimbo? You don't win Rear of the Year three times in a row and go on to host your own show on cable if you're as thick as pig-shit, believe you me.

[*tape stops*]

[*sound of echoing footsteps*] I am now walking down one of the corridors of my house – there's twelve of them, you know. Juanita's running me a nice hot bath because apparently I'm a water sign and water signs are always at one with water.

[*tape stops*]

Testing, testing. One, two, three.

[*tape stops*]

Good. I'm still here then. You know, it never ceases to amaze me how, the minute you take an electrical appliance into the bath with you, the thing always slips out of your hands and into the water. I've lost loads of Nokias, Palm Pilots and iMAC laptops that way.

I know that might sound pathetic . . . owning so many phones and stuff . . . but it's not. I need them to keep in contact, because being a famous celebrity can cut you off from the real world if you let it. I mean, me, I've definitely become a bit of a recluse. In fact, I can count on one hand how many times I've left my house this week . . . Once for my swimsuit calendar. Once for my cameo role in a soap. Once for my new pop video. Once for my keep-fit one. Once for the launch of my new fashion label, and my new website, and my new cookbook. I think that's it. Oh, and once for the guest appearance I made at that awful nightclub.

[*long pause*]

Between you and me, lip-synching to songs is so sodding difficult I think it would actually be easier to sing the fucking things. But, like my publicist said to me after-wards, if gay men want to hear live music they should go to a live-music venue, not to one of my gigs. Anyway, even when I did try to sing something out loud that night for some street cred, half the punters' ears started bleeding which I thought was a bit insensitive considering everyone knows I'm a vegetarian.

[*long pause*]

Anyway, to cut a long story short, because I think I'm meant to be recording a short one, I'm going to show up all the other authors involved in the *Big Night Out* book by appearing more caring and cleverer than them. I mean, let's be honest here. They're not nearly as famous or as attractive as me, and so don't have half as much to live up to. So, what me and my publicist thought was that, just to show that I've done my research, I would actually attend a glittering event hosted by the book's charity (which is for dead baby orphans with torn-off limbs or something). Normally I don't have time to do things like this because – and I'm sure the charity will sympathise with me here – I'm way too busy trying to get maximum press coverage myself.

[*tape stops*]

You can't see the gorgeous dress I've just changed into for my big night out . . . and neither can I! It's completely see-through! It's got long sleeves, a high neck and a full-length skirt, so it's actually really elegant . . . [*sound of doorbell ringing*] . . . Hang on a sec, I think someone might be at the door.

[*tape stops*]

[*whispers*] My minders have just turned up and I'm a bit pissed off, to be honest. I wanted black ones so I could look ghetto-fabulous, but the security agency I use say they have a strict equal-opportunities policy and – by the looks of it – an even stricter immigration one. My two certainly aren't going to fade into the background at night.

[*male voice*] 'Awright, Trace, how's it goin'?'

That's the ginger. Clearly from Essex. And if he thinks we're going to bond over our humble roots or the fact that he knows my real name, he's got another think coming. As a famous celebrity, I'm very wary of people who think that just because you both went to the same comprehensive and visited the same mates in prison, you've automatically got something in common. The skinhead's said nothing yet, though he did give me a salute, which was quite sweet I thought.

[*tape stops*]

[*sound of clinking bottles*] Hiya. It's me again. I've just told Einstein and Goebbels to help themselves to the non-alcoholic sports drinks from my cocktail cabinet. They won't find any though. I never drink the stuff unless I'm being paid to do it on an ad. But still, I guess at least for now they're just shuffling bottles, rather than breaking them over the head of a fan like the last minders did when I went to the opening of that up-itself art gallery. I was mortified, let me tell you, seeing as the cretins used the full bottle of champers I'd nicked from a drinks tray on my way out from the venue. I mean, how was I to know it was part of a sodding exhibit?

Anyway, as you can probably tell, I'm not particularly crazy about having minders watching my every move. Unfortunately, as a famous celebrity you can't be too careful these days, and I do have at least one stalker that I know about. In fact, he's sitting out there across the road from my house right as I speak. He just lolls on a blanket all day and night, and it's really starting to give me the creeps.

Einstein and Goebbels here reckon he might be a homeless person, but they can't fool me. Everyone knows that homeless people can't afford to live in my neck of the woods.

[*tape stops*]

[*sound of phone being slammed down*] I have just finished ringing round all my most recent ex-lovers because, unless I want to look like a sad cow who can't keep hold of a man like most of my other famous female friends, I need an escort for tonight. My exes reckon they're other-wise engaged – some have even got married – and haven't I read about it all in the gossip columns recently? As if! I only ever read my own press clippings. And, even then, I still have to get Juanita to do it for me because, like most highly artistic types, I've suffered from severe dyslexia ever since I left school with no GCSEs. But I'm determined to keep up appearances tonight because my great mate, Peru, is bound to be there with Bobbie (who dropped me the minute he realised that I wasn't going to do him any favours in the Sexiest Man Alive Under Thirty magazine phone polls – not when they're being voted by spiteful and bitter nine-year-old schoolgirls). Peru's in a soap at the moment and plays a right slag . . . which is a good thing, really, since she's not that great an actor.

My other close friend in the business, Tibet, will no doubt be draped around the one great love of my life, Wozza 'Two-Fists' Wanker. He's a footballer, but his game has started to suffer since he met Tibet. The way she's always all over him, you'd think she'd never had a man before if you hadn't read *News of the World*.

Course, I could try calling Bill, the old and ugly multi-millionaire who'll buy you a Porsche if you refuse to sleep with him first, but I'm really not that desperate anymore. Not now I can afford to buy my own . . . anyway, got to go as I've just had a brainwave.

[*tape stops*]

[*sound of man loudly protesting*] Juanita has just invited my stalker into my flat because he's going to get washed and scrubbed up for tonight's big bash. He's under strict instructions not to use my customised liquid soap and shower gel that I got sent for free from some shop that clearly wants a personal plug from me and won't be getting one. It's not that I'm a bitch, it's just that I really can't cope with people who beg.

[*tape stops*]

[*loud woofing in background*] I'm in the back seat of my limo with my minders, my stalker and my stalker's dog –

which I brought along because my arch-rival, Tennessee, is bound to show up with her stupid mutt as she's such a bloody show-off. Mine's not as small and white and fluffy though, which is why I'm going to switch off this tape – we're pulling up outside now, and I can't do as many drugs as I've just done and hold this dictaphone while keeping a fully grown German shepherd tied to a piece of string under control, too.

[*tape stops*]

[*sound of sirens*] On a stretcher. In an ambulance. Dying. Sorry . . .

[*tape stops*]

Surpri-ise! It's me! I am still in the ambulance but feeling a lot better. The medic's just plunged a needle into my chest, which perked me up no end! And he seemed quite perky, too, since I'm currently a 38DD! Anyway, you'll never guess what happened at the charity do . . . I was walking down the red carpet with my entourage in tow, following behind some foreign dignitary from some Third World country or another. And he obviously thought all the clapping and cheering was for him, so I quickened my step and caught up with him just to let him know it wasn't.

Then, just as I'd arrived at his side, all of a sudden I felt incredibly unwell, which I did think at first might have been to do with the small amount of recreational drugs I'd earlier consumed. But, just as I was about to pass out, shots rang out from the crowds behind the cordons, and I suddenly realised that Einstein and Goebbels weren't doing their jobs properly and I must've been hit by yet another crazed fan! That's what was making me feel so dizzy and sick.

[*tape stops*]

Hiya. I'm at the hospital now. You'll be pleased to hear that I am making a full and rapid recovery, though apparently the foreign dignitary caught a bit of shrapnel and is still in intensive care. But what do you expect when your job is to represent the peace process in a war-torn country by hanging onto the tailcoats of a famous celebrity? I'm certainly no scholar myself but I'd dare bet that if I was in his position, I'd be more than grateful to lose half my lower intestines if it meant saving the life of a cultural icon.

Anyway, I've just spent a pleasant three hours in Casualty signing autographs for all the medical staff, and now I've got an interview! With MI6! I think they must be a regional radio station because I certainly haven't heard of them before.

[*tape stops*]

[*muffled voice*] I am currently being wheeled out of the hospital's main entrance under the cover of a blanket to avoid the paparazzi. Despite all this, I am in an utterly filthy mood.

[*muffled shout*] No comment! Fuck off and stop following me around!

[*muffled whisper*] MI6 – who are spies, by the way – informed me that it was the foreign dignitary who someone was trying to shoot, not me. The fact that I collapsed at exactly the same time he was shot was pure coincidence. Like, don't these terrorists know anything? I mean, I've never been to whatdiyamacallit and I'm sure things are really, really bad there, what with the civil war and refugee camps and stuff. But still, trying to knock off a guy who's up for some crappy old peace prize when you could've killed a famous celebrity is a bit beyond belief.

[*tape stops*]

[*sound of a male snoring in background*] Hiya. Me again. I am back at home now, being consoled by my boyfriend who I met just a short time ago. We're very good friends, and I'm not going to say anything more at this stage.

It's early days and I don't want to do what my best friend Cairo – the supermodel, really sweet but a bit thick – does. I am not going to start banging on about how madly in love I am and then look like a complete loser when he dumps me in the morning . . . [*phone rings in background*] . . . Hang on a sec . . .

[*long pause followed by lots of yelling*]

That was my publicist. She's been fielding calls all night from journalists snidely inquiring after the state of my health. They still seem convinced that I'm suffering from nervous exhaustion even though I thought it would've been perfectly obvious to anyone that I collapsed from the shock of witnessing an assassination attempt. And the bastards also wanted permission to confirm the identity of my new 'mystery man' who was seen entering my house through the tradesman's entrance. Naturally, I didn't want them to find out so soon because my new boyfriend's not quite as successful as me, and he might find all the press jibes a bit demeaning as I haven't officially appointed him my chief choreographer yet.

Still, I guess having my reputation unfairly ripped to shreds yet again will guarantee me more ticket sales at the box office . . . [*nervous giggle*] . . . Yes, I know, I know. I've been a bit coy about that one. It's just that I'm feeling very shy about the whole thing. It's my first attempt at writing, producing, directing and starring in a multi-million dollar movie . . . what was that, babes?

[*long pause*]

My new boyfriend says that even if my movie bombs, at least the charity I'm representing for this book will get heaps of free publicity for all those [*adopts Scottish accent*] poor wee kiddies . . . Look, I don't want to go on like one of those whingeing, whining celebrities who all need a good kicking as far as I'm concerned. But, if the thought of helping underprivileged children at the expense of my own career is meant to make me feel grateful, then McPrat here obviously hasn't got what it takes to handle a sensitive famous celebrity like me. And that means – and it really guts me to say this – I'm going to have to boot him and his German shepherd back out onto the street.

Honestly! The pressures of fame. I am just hoping that whoever's ghostwriting this sodding story is ever so good at their job.

[*tape ends*]

Muriel MacLeod

Peacock Tail

Tracey Cox's

Flirting Techniques for That
Big Night Out

Seduce with science (practical stuff to help when you're on the pull)

As someone who specialises in body language, this is what most people want to know when they corner me at parties. Burning question No. 1: How do I tell when someone fancies me? Well, we all know about hair flicking and licking of lips, now here's the *really* secret stuff . . .

Ten Ways to Tell He's Definitely Flirting with You

1. **He's given you three looks in quick succession.**
   The first is a 'stranger look' – he's checking you out because you're a human being who's passed into his line of vision. He looks a second time simply because he's clocked you're female (I know, girls, shallow, shallow). Now, pay attention, because if he fancies you, he'll look back a third time. Even better if he darts the three looks while he's five or six feet away.

2. **He pulls his socks up.** I swear I'm not making it up! This one harks back to the days when men only dressed up on special occasions and teamed tired old socks with their ill-fitting suits, so spent half the night pulling them up to complete the (usually dreadful anyway) look. It's a gesture that's become second nature: if he pulls his socks up or adjusts them in your divine presence, it's an almost 100 per cent guaranteed sign he's trying to look his best and is interested.

3. **He's pointing to his genitals – literally!** If he puts his hands on his hips with his fingers splayed and pointing down towards you-know-what, he's subconsciously willing you to look at it. He'll also spread his legs when sitting opposite you, to give you a full display of his crotch. Hopefully he's still got his clothes on at the time.

4. **His feet point towards you.** If we find someone attractive, we point at them subconsciously with our hands, arms, feet, legs and toes. Check out the feet next time you spot a group of men with a particularly attractive woman among them. Even if they are pretending not to notice by chatting lovingly to their girlfriends, their feet give them away. Inevitably, they're all pointing in her direction.

5. **He's touching his face often, especially as he looks at you.** If he's keen, he'll stroke his cheek up

and down with the back of his fingers, touch his ears or rub his chin. It's a combination of nervous excitement, preening (smoothing clothes or eyebrows or hair to make sure he looks okay) and autoerotic touching (more on that delicious topic later).

6. **His eyes move in a triangle.** When we look at people we're not close to, our eyes make a zig-zag motion: we look from eye to eye, across the bridge of the nose. With friends, the look drops below eye level and moves into a triangle shape: we look from eye to eye but also look down to include the nose and mouth. Once we start flirting, the triangle gets even bigger. We spend more time looking at their mouth and the triangle widens at the bottom to include the good bits (like breasts and crotch).

7. **He's looking at your mouth, loads.** It starts with the flirting triangle and becomes more intense as the flirting intensifies. The more infatuated he is, the more time he'll spend looking at your mouth while you're talking. It's a very, very sexy gesture because you can't help but think *I wonder if he's imagining what it would be like to kiss me?* Which is exactly what he is thinking. Among other things.

8. **He's blinking a lot.** If someone likes what they see, their pupils dilate and their blink rate increases. If you want to up the odds in your favour, try

increasing the blink rate of the person you're talking to by blinking more yourself. If the person likes you, they'll unconsciously try to match your blink rate to keep in sync with you, which in turn, makes you both feel more attracted to each other!

9. **He's got you pinned up against a wall.** It's officially called blocking: using your body to create private space and establish a boundary around you and the person you fancy. Men often block by putting one hand up against the wall behind you, leaving you (rather effectively) trapped underneath his armpit (and yes, start praying he reached for more than just his toothbrush that morning). Another (sweeter) way he'll block is to lean his head close to yours to create your own little vacuum in a crowded room. Aw, sweet!

10. **He keeps squeezing his bottle or can of beer.** When men are sexually interested in someone, they start playing with circular objects. No real prizes for guessing why: circular objects remind him of your breasts (no, *never*!) and his body is 'leaking' what's happening in his subconscious mind. (*Cor! Wouldn't mind getting my hands on those!*)

Ten Ways to Guarantee She's Keen

1. **She flashes her eyebrows at you.** Okay, I admit it: you probably didn't notice. That's because it all

happens in about a fifth of a second. Well worth keeping your eye out for next time though because it's a way of telling if she fancies you – before she even knows it herself! When we first see someone we're attracted to, our eyebrows rise and fall in a small, rapid movement. If they fancy us back, they raise their eyebrows in return. We're not consciously aware of doing this rather bizarre Groucho Marx–type gesture, but it's supposedly the most instantly recognised non-verbal sign of friendly greeting in the world. It helps us to attract friends and lovers because it makes us look more attractive by pulling the eyes open and allowing more light to reflect on the surface of the eyes (hence the '*Your eyes are like large, liquid pools*' stuff). The trick is to watch for an eyebrow flash when you meet someone new. Even better, tell her you're interested on a subconscious level by extending *your* eyebrow flash for up to one second.

2. **She's fidgeting with her clothes.** If she's adjusting her clothing or smoothing it (particularly over her hips), she's keen. Other dead giveaways: looking down to see how many buttons she's got undone (and emerging from the loo with a couple more open). Before *you* nip off to the loo, see what position her skirt is in. It's all good news if you return to see she's hiked it higher up her thighs.

3. **She's flashing her wrists.** It's particularly obvious if she smokes, because she'll hold her cigarette high

and twist her wrist so it's turned towards you. If someone exposes their wrists to you it means they're open and honest. People find it incredibly hard to lie with their wrists and palms exposed (so if you think someone's acting dodgy and they're hiding their hands, you're probably right). It also means she's sexually interested. Wrists are a definite erogenous zone, probably because back in the days when women wore neck-to-knee clothing, the wrists and ankles were the only flesh ever exposed in public.

4. **Her hands keep moving into your space.** We use our hands to signal interest by moving them closer to the object of our desire. If she moves her hands across the invisible line that divides the table in two or into your personal space, her tongue really is starting to hang out.

5. **She's sitting with one leg tucked underneath her, so the inside of her thigh is exposed.** Check her head and body also point towards you, then consider yourself wanted. She's revealing quite an intimate part of her body: one you'd normally only see during sex.

6. **She's crossed her legs.** The leg-cross (twining one leg around so her foot crosses behind her calf and also the ankle) is a potent, yet polite, sexual signal. Why? Well, for a start, it makes her legs look good because it presses the flesh to give the appearance of high muscle tone. Which sends another subliminal

message: our bodies show increased muscle tone when ready for sex, as nerves and excitement make us tense and primed for performance.

7. **She keeps on crossing and uncrossing them ever so s-l-o-w-l-y.** The more a woman crosses and uncrosses her legs in front of a guy, the more interested she is in him. She's deliberately trying to draw his attention to her legs and genital area. (V. naughty. Which is of course why lots of women *love* doing it!)

8. **Now she's (blimey!) kicking one leg up and down, while crossed, or dangling a shoe from her toes.** Both are strong, deliberate and obvious signs she's up for more than just coffee. First up, she'll cross her legs towards you and begin to slowly and seductively kick her foot up and down in a thrusting motion. (If you need me to tell you why imitating thrusting is sexy, you seriously do need to get out more.) If she's really, really keen, she'll follow this up by slipping her foot in and out of her shoe (the old in-out-in-out thing again) or dangle the shoe from the tip of her toes (*I'm undressing myself already/Wouldn't you like these shoes off and under your bed?*).

9. **She's touching her neck, mouth and lips a lot.** It's called autoerotic touching: touching yourself where you'd like someone to touch you. As well as sending

a powerful subliminal message (get your fingers over here!), it feels good! When we're sexually aroused the blood pumps ferociously through the body, making nerve endings tingle and our skin much more sensitive to touch. (A super-sexy, sure-thing, get-the-bill-and-get-a-cab-NOW signal: she's touching her mouth while looking at yours!)

10. **Whatever you do, she seems to do.** It's called mirroring and if she's doing this, she's yours. Nothing bonds people more instantly or effectively than mirroring someone's behaviour. We do it subconsciously when we like someone but it's remarkably easy to manipulate, so if she's not mirroring you, try mirroring her and see what happens. If she leans forward to tell you something intimate, you lean in to meet her. If she sits back to take a sip of her drink, you do the same. The theory behind mirroring is that we like people who are like us. If someone's doing what we're doing, we feel they're not only on the same level as us but also in the same mood we are.

PS Before you sprint out the door to the nearest bar (or dismiss all this as a load of old bollocks), you need to know The Golden Rule of Body Language: don't ever judge on one thing alone. Like, sitting with your arms crossed *can* mean you're protecting yourself emotionally. But it can also mean it's bloody freezing or you're having a fat day or some silly bugger just spilt red wine down your shirt. So don't jump to conclusions (or pounce on every girl who happens to be dangling her shoe). Instead, follow The Rule of Four: look for at least four body-language signals saying the same thing before totally believing it.

Jessica Adams

Victoria Shepworth's Big Night Out

I have just seen an advertisement in the newspaper for speed dating. I'm thinking about it. But, as my friend Hilary pointed out, if I start speed dating, where will it end? Speed marriage? Speed babies? Speed death?

We are sitting in the Children's Library when we have this discussion. Hilary works there. She spends a lot of time rinsing out urine from beanbags. The kids sit in the corner, drinking blue power lemonade, reading *Harry Potter*, then they lose bladder control when they reach the part about the owl.

'The trouble with speed dating is the cost,' Hilary tells me, as we sit on tiny kiddie wooden chairs below a Tintin mobile. Every so often Tintin's feet swing around in the airconditioning, hitting Hilary squarely on the forehead.

'It's only $800,' I say. 'Small price to pay for instant love.'

'For God's sake, Victoria, for that money you could set up your own speed-dating agency!'

Later on, when I go home, though, it gets me thinking.

What if I did try to meet men in bite-sized chunks? Not that there's anything to bite on at the moment, of course. I split up with my computer-obsessed boyfriend Bill the Boffin ages ago (our love was like a modem, it went on, off, on, off and finally it just went off). And since then, I haven't even shaken hands with a man.

It's all right for Hilary. She's living with a bloke who looks like André Previn. And they have even committed to whitegoods together. The only intimate contact I get with men these days is when they pull out the supermarket trolley in front of me and it accidentally jams on my wheels. Or, sometimes, a man at work will ask to borrow my biro. That's it, really.

As I get ready for bed (I'm trying the left side tonight to make it more interesting), I wonder how all my ex-boyfriends would have stacked up as speed daters:

'Hi, I'm Greg Daly. I enjoy bushwalking and shagging German exchange students with hair like the lead singer of Bananarama.' (Five seconds.)

'Greetings. I'm Leon Mercer. I'm a mature-age student radical who enjoys drawing the winners of Socialist Workers' Party raffles.' (Eight seconds.)

My sales pitch, of course, would be as follows:

'Hello. You don't know me, but I think we should get married. My name is Victoria "Total Bloody Relationships Disaster" Shepworth and I haven't had sex since the late fourteenth century.'

I probably wouldn't do anything about this speed-dating idea, except it's 7 February, which means in seven days from now it will be the worst day on the single calendar. Valentine's Day. Twenty-four hours of loveless hell with nothing but bulk emails of donkey porn arriving on your computer, and Reader's Digest sweepstake envelopes in the postbox.

'You could fly to Melbourne to do your speed dating,' Hilary offers, when we talk about it again the next day.

'Why?'

'Do I really have to explain, Victoria? I mean, this is *Sydney*. You are living in *Sydney*.'

'Whoops, I nearly forgot.'

She waggles her finger at me like Osama Bin Laden in one of his early cave videos. 'Never forget, Victoria. We live in Sydney, a city ruled by inner-city boys in their late thirties with Triple J promotional condoms and Winona Ryder stickers on the fridge. We live in a city populated by ferals. 'Footy Show' men. Criminals. Paedophiles. People from Bondi who wear sunglasses that make them look like blowflies. Men who wear their baseball caps backwards. Failed performance poets. Ageing backpackers with small feet. Mummy's boys who own four-wheel drives and live on the North Shore. And barristers.'

I think about it for a minute.

'Well, it worked for you, didn't it?'

'Paul,' she says her boyfriend's name lovingly, 'is from Brisbane. He only came to Sydney by mistake. He was heading for Wollongong at the time.'

'Hilary, listen. What about this idea instead? What if I forked out my own money for speed dating? Put an ad in the newspaper, and set myself up in a bar somewhere? Or maybe I should double my chances, and set myself up in two bars, one in Melbourne and one in Sydney?'

'I still think you should forget about Sydney,' Hilary says, waving me aside.

'But I have to live here. At least for the moment. My job is here.'

'Well, all right then,' Hilary says grudgingly. 'But if you really want to build up your chances of successful speed dating, you should do both places in the same night.'

'What, get the Qantas shuttle from Sydney to Melbourne and back again in the same night?'

'Exactly. Think of the frequent-flyer points. Plus, you can pay my fare as well. I'll be your chaperone. And it's still going to cost you less than the $800 you were going to waste on that dating agency in the paper.'

So, call me Mad Miss McMad, but on Valentine's Day, I find myself placing the following classified advertisement in the Personals section of *The Australian*.

On Hilary's advice, it says: 'VICTORIA SHEPWORTH FREE SPEED-DATING OFFER. BE MY VALENTINE! MEET ME FOR TEN MINUTES IN MELBOURNE OR SYDNEY TONIGHT! WEAR A RED ROSE IN YOUR LAPEL AND BOOK EARLY TO AVOID DISAPPOINTMENT!' Then I give my email address, except Bill the Boffin has already pointed out that I've got that bit wrong. He rings me up, just as I'm about to send it to the newspaper.

'You don't spell the full stop in your email address as "dot", Victoria, you just put a dot. Okay?'

'That's what I hate about the Internet,' I tell him, 'it's all bloody dot this and dot that.'

'I don't know why you're doing this speed-dating thing anyway,' Bill sniffs. 'Why don't you just fall in love and let it happen naturally, like normal people?'

Bill, of course, has fallen in love. I knew it would happen after we split up, and it did, within weeks. Her name is Janet. How boring is that? She's a vegetarian. She's colour-blind. She likes Ricky Martin. She's stunning, but I saw her feet in a photo and they're ugly. Janet has the feet of a dinosaur.

No, really, I could care less what Bill the Boffin does with his love life.

'So, where exactly are you meeting these men?' he asks. 'And what deadline are you giving them?'

'I'm speed-dating from 6 p.m. to midnight, including flying time. I thought I'd give each man ten minutes, through the night. By my calculations, including flight time, that gives me thirty windows of sexual opportunity in two major Australian capitals. I'll do Melbourne first because Hilary says my chances are better there. Then, if I've met the love of my life in Melbourne by 9 p.m., I won't even have to come home and do the Sydney bit. I can just ring up the barmaid and get her to cancel everyone for me.'

'What, you're prepared to have a one-night stand in Melbourne?'

'As you know, Bill, I'll have a one-night stand any-where. That was how we got together. Remember?'

'You're insane,' he says, eventually.

'And I'm not telling you which bar I'm going to be in for the Sydney bit, Bill, so don't even try. You'll only come and stare through the window.'

'Janet and I are going out to dinner for Valentine's Day anyway,' he tells me.

'Ha! Vegetarian nut roast and tofu dressing. I bet you can hardly wait.'

Bill wanted to do the friends thing after we split up. I didn't, because I think it's pathetic and sad. He keeps ringing me up though, and I end up talking to him, so I suppose we've achieved some sort of weird friendship. It drives Janet insane. I suppose that's partly why I go on with it.

'Good luck with it anyway,' Bill says. 'I hope you get some replies.'

'Don't you worry about that,' I tell him. 'Once I've scanned the photograph of me side-on wearing my Wonder-bra, they'll be bashing down the door to get to me.'

'You don't know how to use a scanner. You're a techno-bimbo. You can't even work out how to open your own hotmail account.' Then he pauses. 'What Wonderbra?'

'Oh, piss off.'

I put the phone down.

He bought me the Wonderbra, of course, last Valen-tine's Day. It's bright red.

✱

310

On 14 February, I take two days off work – coughing up blood is still my excuse *du jour* – and I dedicate myself to organising the seventy-seven email replies I get to my advertisement, looking for the top thirty.

Finding forty-seven to delete is easy. I delete thirty on signs of sexual perversion, fifteen on signs of being married and wanting a bit on the side, and two on the grounds that they may be thirteen years old.

That leaves a total of three hours of men, with six minutes for each individual speed date, which I neatly divide into Sydney and Melbourne. In Melbourne, we are to meet at Polly's in Fitzroy, because Hilary likes the curtains. In Sydney, we are to meet at The Summit, so that if I get to the end of Valentine's Day without a new relationship, I can just hurl myself off the roof.

At just after 6 p.m., when Hilary and I are both on the flight to Melbourne, I find myself opening a designer cardboard box with a ham sandwich in it, and squirting plastic milk all down my front. Hilary saves the free Anzac biscuit to take home to her budgie.

'Show me the emails from the men again,' Hilary prods me. So I drag my handbag forward from the seat in front of me, drawing a poisonous look from the flight attendant, and find my folder full of instant dates, starting with Melbourne:

1. David from the Dandenongs. Divorced. Forty-five. Loves jazz, picnics in the country and current-affairs programs. 8 p.m.–8.06 p.m.

2. Warren from Footscray. A builder with allergies who enjoys *Lord of the Rings* and hopes to move into real estate. 8.06 p.m.–8.12 p.m.

3. Che from St Kilda. A political activist who has been single since 1982 and likes body piercings. 8.12 p.m.–8.18 p.m.

4. Trevor from England. A new arrival to our shores. Twenty-one years old. ('Jail bait,' says Hilary. 'Or possibly just out of jail.') Favourite program 'Neighbours', enjoys the music of Britney Spears. 8.18 p.m.–8.24 p.m.

5. Bob from Glen Iris. Offers cuddles. ('I'm gonna spew,' says Hilary, 'give him three minutes, not six.') 8.24 p.m.–8.27 p.m.

6. Robert from Toorak. Wonders if there is a woman out there who is as disenchanted with modern life as he is, and longs to escape to his hideaway among the vineyards of the Hunter Valley with a lady who cares. 8.27 p.m.–8.33 p.m.

7. Someone called Grunt from Carlton. ('No minutes for him, unless his name turns out to be Grant and it's a spelling mistake,' Hilary advises.)

And so it goes on, a list of brief email descriptions designed to inflame me with passion. At the end of his email about vineyards, Robert from Toorak tells me one of his former wives was a flight attendant. I wonder if that's her now, trying to read the emails over my shoulder, as she collects my cardboard box with the uneaten ham sandwich in it?

'Take care when opening the overhead locker as some baggage may have shifted during the flight,' she says, craning her neck to read Robert's words of wisdom on chardonnay.

Minutes later we are off the plane, in the cab, and heading towards Polly's.

'I've got my stopwatch,' Hilary says, producing it from her handbag. We are getting changed in the back of the taxi, which means the heel of my expensive Midas gold party shoe is impaled on Hilary's left breast, and her mascara wand is stabbing me in the eye, but otherwise, all is going according to plan.

'You girls going out somewhere?' the driver asks, in a guttural accent.

Hilary and I exchange a look. Could this be Grunt from Carlton?

'None of your business,' Hilary says firmly, jamming her lips together, which is difficult as she is trying to apply lip-gloss at the same time.

As we jump out of the cab outside Polly's, something occurs to me.

'Hilary, what if you fall in love with one of my speed dates?'

'Victoria, I am shocked. You know very well Paul is the love of my life. Besides, I don't fancy any of them.'

Once inside Polly's, we check the clock. We are early – but already a man with a red rose in his lapel is hanging around near the giant fish-tank by the entrance.

'Either he's here to clean out the fish or he's David

from the Dandenongs,' Hilary observes. 'I'll hang around near the bar and be discreet, okay? Just give me the nod when you want him to go.'

'Or not go, as the case may be,' I reply. The man near the fish-tank is quite good-looking after all, even if he is wearing a black velvet jacket.

Just as Hilary is about to set her stopwatch, though, and I am about to go and lure him over, the fish-tank man runs towards the front door – and embraces an equally good-looking man in a white velvet jacket, also with a red rose.

Hilary dashes over to me, spilling her gin.

'Did you see that?' she gasps.

'Yes, Poof Central. I thought you said my chances were better in Melbourne?'

'I can't believe two grown men can get around in velvet jackets and red roses.'

'Well – it is Valentine's Day.'

'Back to the bar, then,' Hilary says gloomily, and we hang around until 8 p.m., when a short, bald man wearing a white shirt, black bow tie and black pants – and black shiny shoes – stalks in.

Hilary gives me a dismissive look and mouths the word 'waiter' but before I can relax and sink back in the couch again, the short man with the shiny shoes makes a beeline for me. Reaching into his pocket, he produces a red rose.

'Hi, I'm David, sorry I didn't have time to put my rose on,' he pants, 'I was running late and I thought if I got here at 8.06 p.m. it might be awkward.'

'Well, it would be,' I tell him, 'because you'd be sitting on the couch with Warren from Footscray.'

I glance at Hilary, who scoops up two glasses of champagne from the bar (it's in our $800 budget) and rushes over, stopwatch dangling from her wrist.

'Here you go, chaps,' she says, 'your time starts now.'

I look at David. He looks at me. Hilary goes back to her perch at the bar and watches – nothing.

I can feel the time ticking over to 8.02, then 8.03. Still nothing.

David clears his throat. 'Well, I suppose I'd better begin by telling you a little bit about myself,' he says.

And then it begins. A gushing torrent of information that takes us all the way to 8.05.

'I was born of humble stock, my father lost a leg following an industrial accident in the Arnott's biscuit factory, my mother had been married before, to a bankrupt golf-club manufacturer, so although we had a lot of free biscuits and golf clubs in the house, we didn't have a television, and I don't remember seeing 'Skippy' until the early 70s when a friend lent me the money to buy one. I guess you could say I'm a gregarious type, I dip in and out of jazz festivals when I can, keep up with my old school friends, one of them became quite famous actually, he was on 'Water Rats' as a dead body in the water. I'm financially solvent, or I like to think I am, I own a Volvo, and although you probably won't like my sister, I'm happy to introduce you to her if you want a discount haircut – she works at Toni & Guy. I collect Federation-era antiques, and I'm building a water feature in my garden, or at least my ex-wife is, we're still friends, which I think is healthy. And sexually I guess you could say I have slightly better-than-average appetites, although I should be frank and say I have an allergic reaction to most condoms with Nonoxynol-9 in them. Is there anything you want to tell me about yourself, Victoria?'

But it's too late. A red-haired man with glasses and a sour look on his face – and a red rose in his buttonhole – is loitering near the entrance and checking his watch. 'Oh my God,' I say, 'it's Warren from Footscray who likes *Lord of the Rings*!'

He also looks like a deep-sea monster, but never mind that, anything's a relief after listening to David from the Dandenongs and his tales of Arnott's biscuit-factory accidents and condom allergies – not to mention inhaling his foul breath.

Hilary races over with her stopwatch. She's on her second glass of champagne, I notice.

'Thank you very much, David,' she says, waving him away, 'we'll be in touch in due course.'

'Oh,' David says, looking at her arse in what he thinks is a clandestine manner, 'are you available as well?'

'No, I'm the chaperone, now, can I just get you to move over here, please, so we can welcome our next gentleman in?'

It's too late though. When we look up at the entrance again, Warren from Footscray has already gone. Perhaps he thought I looked like a deep-sea monster as well.

Hilary shoos David away, writing all his details down

on her clipboard, and then she staggers back to the couch, spilling champagne all over the cushions.

'I can't believe Warren from Footscray just buggered off!' I protest. 'I mean, one minute he was there, the next minute he'd just vanished!'

'Never mind,' Hilary comforts me, watching the hands on the stopwatch whizz around. 'It's nearly time for Che from St Kilda. And,' she gives me a look, 'I take it that David from the Dandenongs was not to your liking?'

'Hilary, I would rather root some old wombat that's been killed on the side of the road.'

'Okay, point taken.'

When the hands on the stopwatch tell us it's 8.12 p.m., however, we can see no sign of Che, or in fact of any man at all. Hilary goes back to the bar for more champagne, stretching out the minutes until 8.18 p.m., when it's time for Trevor from England, the twenty-one-year-old Britney Spears fan, to make an appearance. By 8.24 p.m., however, there's no sign of him either – or Bob from Glen Iris, whose generous offer of non-stop cuddles so repulsed Hilary.

'Stuff this for a joke, Sydney's beginning to look better by the minute,' Hilary moans.

And then we see him. Tall, slightly harassed-looking, but not unattractive. Hair sticking up like a porcupine. Jeans faded at the knees, and Doc Martens.

'Bill the bloody Boffin,' Hilary breathes, 'how about that, Victoria?'

Bill comes over and joins us on the couch, sending a

red velvet cushion flying. 'I've stuck a note on the front door,' he says, 'so don't worry, there won't be any more men.'

'You did what?' Hilary hisses.

'Yeah,' Bill jerks a thumb at the entrance to Polly's. 'I could see you were just attracting no-hopers, Victoria, so I thought I'd save you both the trouble and send them all away.'

While Hilary storms out to see Bill's note, I make a show of standing up in disgust.

'Sit down,' Bill pats the couch. 'Do you want a drink?'

'How dare you fly all the way to Melbourne just to bugger up my speed dating.'

'It's called helping, not buggering up. Nobody knows you better than me, Victoria, so I thought I'd just do some elimination for you. And from what I've seen so far – who was that guy who looked like a deep-sea monster? – they all need eliminating.'

Then Hilary stalks back to the couch and punches Bill in the stomach. He groans.

'Thank you very much for your note, Bill. "Anthrax alert. All women inside this bar wearing a red rose may be contaminated. Proceed with caution."'

'I thought it was funny,' he says.

'Even funnier,' Hilary sniffs, 'is the fact that these men are so stupid they're actually taking it seriously and running away.'

'Just goes to show,' Bill nurses his punched stomach, 'they're all wankers.'

Hilary gets her handbag. 'Anyway, I'll leave you two to it. I can see this is going to be another episode in the continuing saga of Bill the Boffin and Victoria "Total Bloody Relationships Disaster" Shepworth.'

'Where are you going?' I squawk.

'Back to Sydney. To cancel your session at The Summit. Just one question, Bill, how did you find out where we were?'

'Remember Grunt from Carlton? You know, sexgrunt@hotmail.com? Well, that was me.'

Hilary pulls a face. 'Once again, Vic, we are confounded by our own technobimboism.'

I wait until Hilary has gone, then shift over to the opposite end of the couch.

'What about vegetarian woman?' I confront Bill. 'What about the big Valentine's Day dinner date with the nut roast? What about Janet the goddess of love?'

'She dropped me.' Bill shrugs his shoulders. 'Did it yesterday. She said she was watching other women buy cards with big love-hearts and kisses on the front, and she felt like a fraud. Because she didn't feel that way about me.'

'Wow.'

And I suppose, for a minute, that I feel sorry for him.

'I hate February the fourteenth,' Bill sighs, drinking the dregs of Hilary's champagne.

'Not as much as me.'

'What about that guy with the shiny shoes?' Bill laughs to himself.

'You were spying on me. I can't believe it, you were hanging around outside looking through the windows and spying on me.'

'Well, what else do I live for?'

'I don't know Bill, I really just don't know . . .'

Julia Morris

Future Husband Spell

It had been a great Sydney summer holiday. Tans, buddies and the odd chilled chardonnay at every available moment! Living in London I had forgotten what a really belting summer was like, so, as I returned on my flight to Heathrow, I was sad that it was over but excited at the prospect of meeting my future husband!

Emily had come up from Melbourne to stay with us at my friend's holiday home in Sydney's Palm Beach for a week. Now, when I say holiday home, I am not trying to be all sha-la-la, but you could have fitted my entire Soho flat into the laundry toilet, still leaving ample space for an industrial-sized washer and dryer! This home was big. It was on the cliff-side of 'Palmy', overlooking the Pacific Ocean and because it was facing the east, we could see the sun and moon rise from any one of the five levels, or the massive balcony. Emily had the guest bedroom next to mine on the top floor. We had a slanted roof above our beds that opened like a skylight and let in the warm evening breeze – mmm, heaven. The day she arrived I had my nose slightly out of joint because up until then I had been the only girl in a house full of lovely, bronzed Aussie boys. Emily had one of those bodies that almost hurts your feelings. Her slim, long legs arrived in the room a few minutes before her, making it easy for the rest of her fab figure to make a grand entrance, her hair cascading in a cavalcade of soft, blonde ringlets. Her bright blue eyes only just stole the attention away from her pearly white teeth, but here is the bad news . . . as the next few days unfolded she turned out to have a seriously great personality with a ballistic sense of humour. I think it is safe to say that I was a healthy cross between suicidal and homicidal!

We got on like we had been besties forever, even having to make an effort not to alienate everyone else in the house. She prepared meals like a chef, she used a beautifully manicured hand to clean surfaces better than Domestos, and she always managed to effortlessly wear just the right thing to look like she had leapt off the pages of *Vogue*! Emily was everything I wanted to be when I grew up (if I could only find the time). In the daytime we had our *Sex and the City* 'Most boys are bastards' discussions, and in the evenings we spent our time out at beach parties chasing after them. We seemed to have exactly the same sense of humour, and one afternoon devoted hours to making up those 'trendy spelling', 'new age' baby names. We made a list that caused us to laugh so hard we nearly coughed up a lung. Such gems as Shonette, Quelle-Beth,

Rondelle, Gayleen, Shari-Lee and not to leave the boys out there was Jarryn, Traviston, Kertle and what about Treven? Fantastic.

Emily told me one afternoon that she had a brother who lived in London, he had moved there from Melbourne about a year before. It was during a balmy sunset, while sipping a sneaky chilled rosé, that she uttered these magic words: 'You should meet him for a date, he's seriously the best. He's single, he's handsome, he has a very good job in banking and he loves outgoing girls. Actually, he could be a future husband. I'm going to email him when I get home and make him take you out for a drink.'

Well, I was officially beside myself. From then on he was all I could think about. If God had been as genetically kind to him as he had been to Emily, and if he had just a quarter of her outstanding disposition, well, I was in love. I don't really remember the rest of my holiday, I was just so excited to return to London and start my new life with my new husband (never one to overestimate a potential first date, but let's just say that I had already decided on the font for our wedding invitations).

London was snowing when I got back (just imagine my surprise) and the days seemed to be getting dark by lunchtime. The distant memory of Palm Beach was fading faster than my tan, I was well and truly back! The only joy in my life came from my visits to the Tottenham Court Road Easynet, ferociously scouring my hotmail for news of my date. Weeks seemed to go by, actually it could have been days (to be fair it could have even been hours), and I started to lose hope. The man in my local video shop was clearly getting concerned when he looked at my account to see my fifth screening of *You've Got Mail* in one week. It was then that I realised . . . I have no life.

BINGO, BINGO, BINGO, BINGO!!! Oh my God, there it was. I moved my cursor sooooo gently, making sure I did not accidentally press the delete button (which I do so often) and opened the file:

Re: Overnight Romance

Dear Shonette,

My sister tells me you might be into a bit of 'overnight romance', so where and when?

Seriously, I'm Ben, Emily's brother, she told me you two caused some trouble in 'Yabby Creek' this summer. So, would you like to meet me for a drink to tell me exactly what my little sister has been up to? Give me a call at work and we can organise a date.

Traviston-Keith.

Date, did you read that? Date, my future husband wants to take me on a date. My heart was pumping so fast and furiously that I could barely print the message out. I, I, I was speechless, typeless, witless, in fact just out of my mind with excitement. I signed off the computer and floated down the stairs and out onto the street with one of those smiles that you just can't harness. (Once I had a flatmate who was on the tablets and she used to smile like that all the time, lucky bugger.) And then it hit me like a steam train . . . What the hell was I going to wear???

Two days later I made the phone call, even waiting till the afternoon so I did not look too keen. He had such a grown-up boy's voice. Dreamy like a film star. He had left the location details to me, but we both agreed that Thursday is the new Friday, so the day was set. I had met some buddies for a drink in their glamorous hotel in St Martins Lane about a week earlier, so I was sure the Light Bar was going to be perfect. If it were up to me to pick a cool place, it would have been a Burger King (loving a 'Whopper, cheese, no pickles'). I phoned the hotel and blagged a booking, can't bear these private bars in London that are clearly designed to keep VUPs like me out!

I arrived at the bar first. I hate walking into a bar by myself, it always makes you feel like such a no-life! Securing one of those glasses of wine that looks like a bucket, I found a nice romantic table and sat down.

A tall man walked into the bar in a divine 'City' suit and walked straight up to me and said, 'Hi, sorry I am late, would you like a drink?'

'Nah, I'm cool' and he walked over to the bar. I had expected that he would be good-looking, but not like this. Dark hair, beautiful shirt and matching tie (I think it was a Danielle Wallace), broad shoulders and a smile to die for. How is my luck? I was sick to the stomach with excitement, or it could have been hunger – it had been such a busy day I had had no time to eat.

He sat down and undid his jacket button as I was thinking 'Do you want a big or a small wedding? Bondi or Scotland? Winter white or Ecru?' I was trying to be the very best version of myself, like we do on dates, just thinking I was faaaaascinating.

He had a great sense of humour and liked to talk as much as me. When does that happen? Conversation rolled out like a red carpet, could not have been smoother.

Two wines, three, four and the time had come for my first bathroom visit. I did not want to be too long but my gay flatmate had demanded a running text commentary . . . NW HSBND, V. GOOD NITE, C U HM, XXX . . . Send. I love it when that little envelope flies away! That first mirror check after a few wines is essential. Lipstick – check; eyes – check; teeth – check. The lights were a little bit blurry, but I didn't see that as a bad sign. Sensible, safe walking back to the table and ooooh he really is that handsome and he even stood up as I returned. What a 'mighty good man'.

We ordered another drink but the white wine had started to burn my tongue. I was sooo thinking about a cigarette but you know how boys hate it. Anyway, if we got married that would be an excellent excuse to give up (thank God dreams are free). I was enjoying myself so much that I unveiled that laugh that you only keep for dark cinemas, comes right up from underneath the tummy and almost sounds like a bark, even chucking my head back in that laughter that knows no bounds! More wine, more wine.

As I moved my head the lights were now on a short delay, not necessarily a bad sign? Ben then suggested we go and get some dinner. Great idea but I had a better one. 'Let's go to the all-night supermarket, then go to my place and cook.' So we headed off.

Making our way around the supermarket with that little basket was my idea of the best first date EVER. My flatmate was the best. I texted him to say we were on our way home and he made himself scarce. I put the water on for the pasta and whipped up a sneaky dish that would have made Margaret Fulton's mouth water. Needing a little wine to cook (to sip, not for the dish) he took care of the boy's job and opened a nice red. I am usually a bit shy of red, it can be quite cosmetically unfriendly considering the grey teeth and the 'Joker' mouth, but I was beyond caring, thinking the meal would sober me up.

The pasta was al dente and it was time to drain. Who needs oven mitts? I clearly didn't, picking up the saucepan with my bare fingers. Not wanting to create a very sad scene, I just moved the saucepan quickly to the sink. Cold water, cold water, cold water, sooooo not cold enough. The end of my fingers started to blister immediately and I felt like such a knob. He kissed them gently and we headed into the lounge to eat. My fingers were aching with white pain, so it was a little hard to concentrate on the meal! I tried to keep my pasta-slurping to a minimum, so as to regain some composure. We then called his sister in Melbourne and had such a lovely chat. She was sad not to be in London with us and a little pang of homesickness hit us both. While he was finishing the phone call I seized the opportunity to duck to the bathroom for another check and as I came back into the room I managed to dim the lights.

Returning to the couch I stretched out and snuggled in close. All the signs had been so good and to be honest with you I was getting tired (surely not the wine). It was at that moment that I decided to make THE move. Yes, I hear you, too soon, but it didn't seem like that at the time, but here is the cringe file . . . I lunged at him . . . LUNGED! Who am I? Larry the Lunger? Not only that but I slipped as I lunged and hit my chin on his front teeth. Oow. He then very politely told me that maybe it was time that he should leave. Leave? What do you mean leave? You can't leave . . . what about our wedding?

I saw him to the door, he kissed me on the cheek and started to head down the street. Having yet another brilliant idea I yelled, 'COME BACK HERE, SURELY A PASH IS NOT GOING TO HURT YOU . . .' He turned, he smiled and he kept walking.

I know, don't say it, I needed an entire filing cabinet for my cringe files. Opening my eyes the next morning, there was at least a three-minute threshold where I remembered nothing, then I noticed the end of my fingers. Oooow.

Then oooooooow, my husband. I rang him to apologise and he was so lovely. He said, 'It's not often that I am lavished with the affections of a beautiful stranger . . .'

I did not get to go on another date with Ben, but do you blame him? I blame chardonnay for ruining my wedding, and my advice? Oven mitts are essential.

Anthony Stewart Head's

Guarantee for the Best Party Ever

Now, it all depends on what kind of a big night out we're looking for, but, as far as music is concerned, I still don't believe you can go wrong with a serious bout of Soul. Whether it's just to get you in the party mood on the way there, or strategically played throughout the evening, there is nothing like a bit of Aretha, James Brown, Otis or Wilson Pickett to get you going. One of the best gigs we saw last year was Macy Gray and her band doing a charity event at the House of Blues on Sunset Boulevard, LA – just for the irresistible, irrepressible, unstoppable groove, you cannot beat good Soul, new or old.

When it comes to cocktails, I have to say I'm a complete sucker for a really good margarita on the rocks (no salt please). They're not as easy to find as you would think, since a lot of bars use a pre-made sweet-and-sour mix that is mostly sugar and tastes like crap. Since they are completely impossible to get in England (except for the occasional corner that is forever Mexico), I learned how to make them for myself. The recipe is unbelievably simple but the specific ingredients are very important:

Squeeze a lime into a cocktail shaker.
Pour in an equal amount of Heridura Silver.
Add half that measure of Triple Sec.
Shake with copious quantities of ice.
And serve.

Now, it has to be said that the Silver/Gold thing is debatable, but I personally find that Gold Tequila overshadows the taste of the Triple Sec. However, it is worth fighting to get Heridura (I bring it back with me from the States) because it's one of the only brands to be made on site at the distillery – most of the others import it from other sources, ergo, it's much purer than most and WON'T GIVE YOU A HANGOVER! In the event that you can't find Triple Sec (but if you can't find it then you don't stand a hope in hell of finding the above), Cointreau will do. It has taken me a long time to understand the physics of allowing the ice to melt a little in order to dilute the mixture. Consequently, for some years I served unfortunate recipients with virtually pure alcohol, which seemed to have the effect of quickly severing the neural connection between their body and their feet. My margaritas are notorious.

If you don't eat meat, the voyage into the land of canapés can be a perilous one (especially if the person holding the tray has no idea whether the small brown paste-filled things on the left are carnivorous fare or not). I'm sure it doesn't count as a canapé but the perfect accompaniment to my really good margarita on the rocks (no salt please) is fresh tortilla chips and fresh salsa (hot). For some reason, best known to the English, this is equally hard to find on this side of the Atlantic and I admit to bringing tubs of that back with me as well.

Alternatively, blinis (combinations of caviar, smoked salmon, cream cheese and capers on small Russian pancakes) are a superb, although a little messy, canapé. This, however, leads us into a totally different arena involving Kir Royale or champagne cocktails at the very least, and it's probably best not to go up that avenue now we've planted ourselves firmly in Tex-Mexland. On the other hand – as a Pisces who sometimes struggles with choices – I always have the exciting, if not a trifle nerve-racking, option of combining my two favourite drinks. La Entrada de Las Tequila Slammers. The less said about the effects of these the better. You'll be past caring after the second one anyhow. And will remember nothing after the fourth.

Drawing of FIESTA GILES from the Buffy Action Figure Set – about which I am still acutely excited, not least because it boasts that I articulate in fourteen places (hey – two more places than in real life! – Sarah) and am officially classed as a choking hazard. He has everything needed for a perfect night out in LA. Put pin in cross and swivel 45° to the left to illustrate the effects of Tequila Slammers.

Emma Tom

No Wuckers

The only good thing about Saturday night was that I didn't smoke an entire cigarette and I didn't end up kissing Chanel Levicki right on the lips in front of Matt Tripplehorn and both our mothers and EVERYONE.

Apart from those two things, the entire night was a write-off. In fact, it was probably the worst night of my life, although this news is unlikely to impress my mother.

Mum's the 'I just had the worst night of my life' queen. She's had fifty-six worst nights of her life so far (fifty-seven if you count the time she accidentally set fire to her nipple tape on parent–teacher night).

Mothers are HOPELESS. This is a scientific fact I plan to prove just as soon as I leave home and become an inventor or a forensic pathologist or an explorer or even a brain-dead bloody model, if it means I can get out of rotten bloody Rappsville.

Just joking. I wouldn't really waste my intellect by doing anything as shallow as modelling. That's what

Mum did and look where it got her. The woman's practically thirty-three and last weekend she went out and got a TATTOO.

It could have been worse, I suppose. Mum's just discovered Twisted Sister and wanted a spider web on her elbow. Luckily, the tattooist talked her round and gave her a dolphin on the shoulder instead. (It's definitely the lesser of the two evils, but she *has* been wearing way more than her fair share of boob tubes in order to show it off.)

Anyway. Where was I? Oh, right. Saturday night. Chanel Levicki's birthday party.

What I want to make clear from the outset is that unlike the rest of my generation, I *don't* think drugs are big and clever. Contrary to popular (or at least my mother's) belief, I'm not some reactionary fossil who wouldn't know a good time if it got me drunk and shaved off both my eyebrows. I am just highly observant, and it has become obvious to me that people who take drugs turn into complete and utter imbeciles who couldn't have an intelligent conversation about the situation in the Philippines or Latin roots or the dominant paradigm, if their life depended on it.

Take Chanel, for instance. She might have once worn a necklace made out of black jelly beans sewn onto a string, but she is not an idiot: (a) her dad is a professor of something at a university in the city; (b) she got to be second barrister in the mock trial team even though she uses hair dye; and (c) she's the only other person in the whole of Year Eleven who gets anywhere near beating me in English (even if it is due to the fact that Mr Swipe is too unreconstructed to appreciate GENUINE FEMINIST MASTERPIECES *BY THE* FUTURE FIRST WOMAN PRIME MINISTER OF AUSTRALIA). (Pleb.)

Chanel Levicki is the sort of girl my mum would call 'a very smart cookie', but her intellectual prowess is powerless in the face of drugs. Take the night of Matt Tripplehorn's pool party, for example. Matt (Neanderthal) and his brothers (Cro-Magnons) had made what's known in delinquent lexicon as a 'bong' out of an Orchy bottle, a length of hose and half a macadamia-nut shell.

And Chanel, of course, had to have a go.

One minute Professor Levicki's daughter was having a completely lucid conversation about the oxymoron that is legal ethics. And the next she was eating chalk and giggling like a blithering idiot. Matt made some witless remark about the number six sounding like 'sex' and Chanel laughed like it was the funniest thing she'd heard in her entire life. Then she pashed him on the day-and-night lounge, then she let him give her a love bite IN FRONT OF THE ENTIRE PARTY, then she put on Mrs Tripplehorn's roller skates and joined everyone else doing that stupid dance to 'Nutbush City Limits'.

It was so incredibly immature I can barely bring myself to talk about it. Quite frankly, it was the sort of behaviour you'd expect from a high school drop-out or an air hostess, not the daughter of a university professor. Outrageous. At sixteen, you're practically an adult. You should have got all that adolescent foolishness out of your system.

I certainly have.

Which probably makes you wonder what I was doing boiling up magic mushrooms in Mum's electric frying pan in the first place.

The truth is, I'm not entirely sure. Nothing terrible had happened to make me want to throw away my life and turn to drugs or anything.

True, Mum had just done another newspaper advert for concrete edgemakers in which she appeared nude under the headline 'Check the curves on this' (my relentless letter-writing campaign to *The Rappsville Examiner* has done absolutely NOTHING to reduce gratuitous sexism in the print media).

True, Dad had just rung reverse charges from Western Australia to wish me happy birthday for the third time this year (when I pointed this out, he said 'Good on ya' and hung up).

True, I probably was the only sixteen-year-old girl in the entire universe who still wore a training bra, didn't have a date for the Year Eleven formal and hadn't had my stomach pumped after overdosing on one of Matt Tripplehorn's bongs.

But none of this really explained why, when Chanel Levicki rang up on Saturday afternoon and asked if I'd bring a flask of magic-mushroom coffee to her birthday party, I let out a contemptible squeak and yelped 'no wuckers'.

GOD.

Normally I wouldn't be caught dead using a stupid

teenage catchphrase like 'no wuckers' (short for 'no wuckin' furries' short for 'no fucking worries'). It's the sort of thing my mother would get printed on the side of a mug.

And since when had I become the school drug dealer?

That's what you get for living in the middle of a cow paddock, I suppose. In fact, if I didn't have unshakeable ethics (not to mention a future as the first female Prime Minister of Australia), I could make an absolute fortune as a drug dealer. Every time it rains, the back yard breaks out in gold tops. Mum also has three marijuana plants behind the old chook shed. If she ever gets busted, she's going to tell the magistrate she's got cancer. Reckons she'll submit the lump in her breast as evidence and everything.

Having seen what drugs did to Chanel Levicki's neck, I refuse to go anywhere near the things. (Matt Tripplehorn has the sucking power of a vacuum cleaner.) That said, I'd definitely sleep better at night if Mum would agree to go to the doctor and get that lump checked out.

'I'm only trying to be a responsible parent,' she says each time she offers me a drag on a joint slash reefer slash scoob slash SIGH. 'If you don't try drugs at home you're only going to rebel against my authority and try them in the back of some boy's panel van and end up a teenage mother like I was, and then who's going to look after me?'

Mum's authority. That's a funny one. The only way I could truly rebel against her 'authority' is by becoming a nun, which, by the way, I would NEVER do because the church oppresses women and refuses to condone alternative lifestyles, and because as soon as I get out of Rappsville I'm going to become a famous feminist activist or left-wing political agitator or leader of the sisterhood.

(P.S. If it's true what they say and I turn into my mother, I will absolutely bloody well DIE.)

Of course, the big mystery is why Chanel Levicki keeps inviting me to parties in the first place. It's not like she rings up any of the other girls who sit in the library at lunchtime.

Chanel's real name is Katica, but her parents changed it to Chanel (after the perfume) when they moved to Australia from Yugoslavia. Thanks to the fact that she wears more eyeliner than anyone except my mother, she is one of the most popular girls in Year Eleven. The headmaster is always telling her 'This is a high school, not a circus', but Chanel takes no notice. Once she even turned up for a mock trial with dangly earrings and strips of her hair shaved off above her ears. Mr Swipe was scandalised. He pulled me aside to say that as the team's first barrister, it was my duty to bring my maverick associate into line. I didn't, but lucky for us, the magistrate hearing the case was wearing pizza-slice earrings even bigger than Chanel's.

After winning the regional championships (take that, Rappsville South), Mr Swipe took the entire team out for milkshakes and Chanel explained how in Yugoslavia parents think it is cute to teach little children to swear. When people met up in posh hotel lobbies, she claimed it was perfectly acceptable for them to yell something like: 'Fuck your mother in the mouth, how are you?'

Mr Swipe was scandalised.

I put the phone down from Chanel and waited until Mum had left for her Saturday afternoon Swinging Singles Disco Rodeo. There was no way I was giving her the satisfaction of knowing I was finally about to experiment with drugs. Then I put on my rubber boots, took a plastic bag up the back of the house and got to work.

'How can you tell the magic mushrooms from the toadstools?' I'd asked Mum last time it rained and she'd headed out with a plastic bag.

'Gold tops turn blue when you step on them,' Mum had said. 'Like this, see? Oh. That's not exactly blue, is it. It's more a kind of brown . . . But I'm sure you get the idea, right?'

I emptied the mushrooms out on the kitchen bench. They looked like puffy bruises that had been cut off someone's face.

The big problem was knowing what to do next. I used to be an aspiring chef (anything to avoid Mum's sausage casserole), but then I realised food preparation was yet another tool of the patriarchy and went on indefinite kitchen strike. (I've definitely felt more liberated since then, but life does seem to contain a lot more burned toast.)

I took Mum's 'My Other Mug's a Shot Glass' coffee cup out of the cupboard and tried her usual combination of three teaspoons of Nescafé, four teaspoons of sugar, hot water and cream. Despite precision measuring, the result wasn't exactly what you'd call show quality. The coffee congealed into black lumps on the bottom, and the magic mushrooms floated around on the top like a bunch of Pacific Islands that had just been nuclear bombed by France. I didn't like the way the cream came out of the carton in yellow strings, either.

Obviously making magic-mushroom coffee required more skill than anyone had ever suspected.

That's when I decided to apply the tyre-changing principle. This was a little something I discovered the first time Mum's Beetle had a flat. We'd driven over a sharp bit of cow's skull in the middle of nowhere and Mum (who'd given up on the tyre jack after tearing a cuticle) was having an absolute fit about how we were both done for and how it was only a matter of time until we were torn apart by matinee jacket–loving dingos blah blah blah.

That's when it struck me that thousands, maybe even millions of people with IQs nowhere NEAR the size of mine managed to change flat tyres every day of the week. That's when I realised that if they could do it, I could too – probably faster and with greater attention to detail.

Admittedly it took longer than I would have liked. Mum paced so much she had an asthma attack. But eventually I got the old tyre off and the new tyre on, and we got to the pub Dad was supposed to be staying at with half an hour to spare. As per usual, the XY contributor to my genetic make-up stood us up, but at least I got to spend the rest of the afternoon practising tyre changing out in the car park.

I got my drill down to eight minutes flat.

I was eleven.

'The point is that if a laboratory rat like Matt Tripplehorn can make magic mushroom coffee, then I should have no worries,' I said out loud in the kitchen, narrowly avoiding a repeat of the 'no wuckers' debacle.

I dug Mum's cookbook out of the dusty shag pile on top of the fridge, and went straight to R for Recreational. The recipe was located distinctly unalphabetically between Super Alcho Smoothie and Hash Cookies:

Soup à la Gold Top.

'Soup à la Psilocybin more like it,' I soliloquised while inspecting the instructions: *Boil chopped mushrooms with honey and water for thirty minutes. Add Nescafé etc. Blend in blender and bon voyage!!!*

It was classic 'my mother' to use 'etcetera' in a recipe. Well, it could mean anything, couldn't it? Sugar. Salt. Half a bucket of bloody paint thinner. I decided to use my discretion and interpret it as 'a teaspoon of Vitamin C' (as a token gesture towards healthy living).

The best thing about stirring the bubbling potion in Mum's massive electric frying pan was feeling like a witch who was about to be persecuted by the forces of religious extremism and burned on a stake but was really just an academic naturopath ahead of her time. The worst part was trying to decide what to wear when the time came to call a cab. I have a policy of never sporting skirts or dresses outside of school, but the last time I went to a party in overalls, Matt Tripplehorn asked if I was a council worker.

I absentmindedly assembled the blender, wondering whether it was worth doing the unthinkable and raiding my mother's wardrobe.

I guess it wouldn't be the end of the world if I tried on a pair of pants that had been made for a girl and not a boy, I thought, filling the blender to the brim with boiling mushroom mixture.

And it's not like there's a law that says you have to team EVERYTHING with a boob tube and stilettos . . .

And that's when it happened. That's when I switched on the blender and it let out a roar and the lid shot off and boiling magic mushroom coffee sprayed all over my face and throat.

A full minute passed when all I thought was 'Oh shit, now I'm going to have to clean up and start again'. And then it started to hurt. In fact, it hurt more than anything I've ever experienced in my entire life, including the time I got a running spike through my foot at the athletics carnival after Mum streaked during the relay.

The burning got worse and worse, so I ripped off my steaming shirt and my steaming bra and I ran to the fridge. Amazingly enough, Mum had done the shopping and the freezer was chockas for once in its life. I held a frozen pizza to my face and a frozen pizza to my chest, and ran to the phone.

The first number I tried was wrong. Some illiterate Rappsville pig hunter had to listen to me screaming hysterically for my mother for five minutes before I realised my mistake and hung up.

On the second attempt, I managed to get through to the Police Boys' Club.

'She's setting a record on the mechanical bull,' said the woman who answered the phone. 'I'll tell her it's an emergency, shall I?'

The one thing my mum is really good at is getting upset when I get hurt. It's the one time she turns into the sort of real-life mother you see on TV.

When I howled out the news that I was hideously burned, she shrieked 'Oh my God!' a few times, then told me to calm down. She said she was ringing the ambulance. She said she was ringing the neighbours. She said if anything bad happened to me, she was gonna bloody well kill me.

'Don't call the neighbours!' I screamed. 'Are you listening? DON'T SEND A BLOODY AMBULANCE.'

As you can see, even writhing in agony I remained completely rational. After all, if anyone caught sight of the half-blended spray of illegal drugs splattered all over the kitchen, my political career would be over before it had even begun.

'The important thing is to stay calm!' Mum continued shrieking. 'You get that, Cassie? CALM. I don't care if there's nothing left of the house. I don't care how much we have to pay for plastic surgery. All that matters is that you're okay. AND THAT YOU STAY CALM. YOU GOT THAT?'

The phone went dead and the next however-many minutes passed in what cliché-lovers like Mr Swipe would probably know as a 'blur'. I couldn't sit down because as soon as I kept still for longer than a couple of seconds the boiling on my skin became unbearable. I realised I was still screaming when I caught a glimpse of myself in the fridge-door handle and my mouth was wide open like what's-his-face in the Munch painting.

Bloody Mum did call the neighbours. AND the ambulance. AND the fire brigade. Everyone arrived pretty much at once.

'What have you done to yourself, love?' someone in a uniform yelled through the front door.

'Nothing!' I screamed back through the glass.

'I know you aren't feeling too crash-hot at the moment, honey, but I really need you to unlock this door to show us where the fire is and let us take a look at you . . .'

So much for my legendary stoicism. So much for my legendary commitment to my future. I'm such a wimp that I opened the door and let two ambulance officers and four firefighters and Mrs Reddish from down the road walk right into the house of drugs.

'Been up to a bit of cooking have we, darl?' Mrs Reddish said, surveying the carnage.

But all I could do was yodel.

Those burns really bloody well hurt.

All I remember about the ambulance ride to the hospital was lots more yodelling. It was weird. All I could think of was me. It was like I was right inside myself and all I could feel was this shell of pain, and there were people poking and talking at me, and in a way it felt good just to scream hysterically and utterly ignore them.

Arriving at the hospital brought me crashing back to reality. As the paramedics lifted me out of the ambulance and onto a wheelchair, it suddenly dawned on me that I was being wheeled through a public building screaming my lungs out and wearing nothing but a pair of shorts and a couple of half-melted pizzas.

Mum was pacing Accident and Emergency dressed in her tasseled pink jumpsuit and cowboy boots.

'Oh my God,' she said, running up and stinking everyone out with perfume. 'Are you okay? You can tell me, Cassie. I'm ready for it. You don't have to break it to me gently. But if anything happened to you, I mean if ANYTHING happened I just couldn't cope, really I just couldn't – WHAT?'

'She's going to be just fine,' the ambulance guy said, trying not to stare at the scabs flaking off my mother's new shoulder dolphin. 'She's just going to be a bit uncomfortable for a while. Not that we have any idea what she was up to in that kitchen of yours. No fire, but gunk everywhere. Maybe when she settles down she'll let us in on what actually happened.'

At that point, Mum stopped babbling and took a long look at my magic-mushroom-spattered shorts and my magic-mushroom-spattered thongs and the magic mushrooms that were still dangling in lumpy rats'-tails from my hair. I could see her putting two and two together, and for once in her life she didn't come up with 'Hmmm?'

'It was soup,' she said in a big, loud voice. 'You were making soup, *weren't you, sweetheart.*'

'That's right!' I said (voice hoarse from all the yodelling). 'It was just a batch of harmless, completely non-hallucinogenic vegetable soup . . .'

Life started looking up. A nurse buried me in ice and after a couple of hours the burning stopped.

'First-degree with a little second-degree one here,' the doctor said to Mum, pointing at the messiest spot on my chest. 'No need for IV fluids but you will need to bring her in daily to have the dressing changed. And get her some cooking lessons for Christmas, eh?'

It was 9 p.m. by the time Mum dressed me in a spare boob tube that had been lying on the back seat of the Beetle.

'How are you feeling?' she said, as we walked out to the car.

'Fine,' I said, trying not to bump the bandage under my chin as I got in. 'Kind of weird, but fine.'

'Great,' said Mum. 'Because we're dropping in to Chanel Levicki's party on the way home. Otherwise all this drama will have been for nothing. Right, sweetheart?'

After everything I'd been through that night, turning up at Chanel's place with a face like a traffic light and a lime-green boob tube was child's play.

'What happened to you?' Matt Tripplehorn asked when Mum propelled me into the darkened romper room and vanished onto the patio to drink sangria with Mrs Levicki.

'Magic mushroom burns,' I said. 'I'm going to be scarred for life.'

'Cool,' said Matt Tripplehorn. 'I never met anyone what took so many mushies they got burned before. Wanna durrie?'

All I can say in my defence is that I must have been in shock. There was simply no other reason why I, dux of Year Eleven and future Prime Ministeress of Australia, would accept a lit cigarette from Matt Tripplehorn and wash it down with a plastic cup of warm rum and Coke. Thank God I had enough presence of mind to 'accidentally' drop said cigarette into a small pool of vomit beside the Levickis' leather ottoman before I got addicted.

I was busy scanning the crowd for Chanel when I felt a dry slug in my left ear. It was Matt. He'd jabbed his tongue so far into my head I temporarily lost half my hearing (not such a bad thing given the volume of Adam and the Ants on the Levickis' stereo).

'What are you doing?' I yelped in disgust.

'Blggh,' he replied. 'Blggh blggh BLGGGHARA.'

'Jesus Christ, keep it in ya pants, Tripplehorn.'

It was Chanel, with a bottle of Bacardi under one arm and two cricket bats under the other.

Another glare from the birthday girl and Matt was scuttling off into the gloom like a Baygoned cockroach.

'Your mum told me what happened,' Chanel said, inspecting my features in a businesslike fashion. 'Are you, you know, okay?'

'Yeah,' I said. 'I guess so. Why are you carrying those cricket bats?'

'Am I?' said Chanel. 'Well, bugger me. You learn something new every day.'

She paused.

'Fuck-all room on this couch, though. Mind if I sit on your lap?'

Before I had the chance to answer, Chanel plonked herself onto my knees. Her necklace got snagged on the way down and dragged Mum's boob tube halfway to my navel.

If my face was red before, it was certainly luminescent by then. I yanked up the tube, hoping no one had seen, and took a long swig out of Chanel's Bacardi bottle. Her skirt was even shorter than usual and I could feel the edge of her underpants on my thighs.

She leaned forward and gave me an intense, up-close-and-blurry look right in the left eye.

'Look,' she said. 'I feel really terrible about what happened. I don't even like mushroom coffee. The only reason I asked you to bring it was to make sure you'd come.'

'That's all right,' I said, noticing Matt Tripplehorn slinking his way back across the room like a cockroach that had been Baygoned but had survived and was wearing a couple of lungs and a colon on the outside of its body.

'Listen,' Chanel went on, looking as serious as it is possible to look when you're sitting on another girl's lap and still have two cricket bats tucked under your arm. 'I know you probably hate me and think I'm a total idiot but the truth is . . . well . . . the truth is, I don't. I mean, I do. Really like you, that is. You're always telling off Mr Swipe and you organised that strike and you look like a totally cool tomboy and I fucking loved that essay you wrote about the chick whose fake boobs took over her body and made her start reading *The Female Eunuch*. You know the one? Of course you know it, you wrote it, didn't you. Told you I'm an idiot . . . The point is (and I've only got the nerve to do this because I'm pissed), the point is (tell me to fuck off if you like), the point is I really, really like you and I was wondering whether you'd consider going to the Year Eleven formal with me . . .'

I gasped. Then – God help us all – I squawked 'no wuckers' in exactly the same voice I'd used when Chanel rang up about the mushrooms.

JEEESUS.

I struggled to regain control of my mouth so I could explain that normally I wouldn't be caught dead using stupid juvenile brain-dead teenage catchphrases, but before I had the chance to say anything, Chanel was leaning forward and opening her mouth and showing off her glittery gold fillings, and I was having to use a polite kind of karate chop to stop her kissing me on the lips right there and then.

It's not that I have anything against lesbianism. In fact, I have often considered becoming a homosexual partly as a political statement and partly because lately I've been having funny dreams about Chanel and sometimes Olivia Newton John (but only in *Grease* AFTER the makeover).

No, the real reason I kung-fu chopped Chanel off my

face was because Mum and Mrs Levicki had appeared at the doorway and were wending their way towards us.

'Mother alert,' I hissed.

And Chanel leapt off my lap just in time.

'Taking care of our little patient, Chanel?' screeched Mrs Levicki.

'Yes, Mum,' said Chanel, looking more subdued than I'd ever seen her, EVER.

'That's the way, lovie,' Mrs Levicki screeched, yanking a pair of leopard-skin tights out of her bottom. 'Having fun, Cassie?'

'Yes, thank you, Mrs Levicki.'

'That's the way, lovie. We're just out on the patio if you need us, girls. Be good and if you can't be good be careful. Ha ha!'

'Yeah, right.'

'Boy crazy,' Mrs Levicki said to Mum in a stage whisper as they walked off together. 'Fuck your mother in the mouth, you know how they are at that age. Can't keep their hands to themselves.'

As she got to the doorway, Mum turned back and winked.

'I love you, Cassie,' she mouthed.

'Thanks for the soup thing,' I mouthed back.

'WHAT?' she said, still mouthing.

'DON'T WORRY, I'LL TELL YOU LATER.'

Mum shrugged her shoulders, gave me the thumbs up and disappeared.

'Fuck, I hate my mother,' Chanel said, looking at the

ground and poking the cigarette in the vomit with her toe. 'What Dad sees in her I'll never know. She's a fucking MORON.'

'Hey, Chanel,' I said.

'Yeah?'

'Wanna go outside or something? Your boyfriend is giving us the evil eye.'

'FUCK OFF,' Chanel said, cheering up. 'Matt Tripplehorn is hardly my boyfriend. I wouldn't fuck him for practice. Shall we take the Cheezels?'

'Nah,' I said. 'I'm trying to become a vegan.'

'Really?'

'Really. There's animal by-products in everything these days. For instance, did you know there's tropical fish in beer?'

'BULLSHIT.'

'It's true. And that's only the START of it . . .'

Later, much later, when Chanel and I came back down from her tree house and I said 'See you at school on Monday' and she said 'You better believe it', I got into the front seat of the Beetle and Mum twisted round in the driver's seat and gave me a long, funny look.

'I don't remember those shorts being on inside out back at the hospital,' she said, starting the engine.

'Oh, I'm sure they were,' I said, turning away.

'You're blushing.'

'I am not. I've got first and second degree burns and I've just had the worst night of my life. I am *hardly* blushing.'

'The worst night of your life, eh?'

'That's right.'

'Liar, liar, pants on fire.'

And the two of us grinned in the dark all the way home.

Gil McNeil

Carry On Camping

'What time are you dropping James off? Charlie's driving me crazy, he's so excited.'

'God, I wish I was.'

'Oh, Kate, stop it. I'll swap you if you like. You can stay at home with two boys camping in the back garden in a knackered tent, and I'll go out on a hot date with a gorgeous new man.'

'Graham is not a gorgeous new man. He's an accountant, and he knows my mother.'

'You said he had lovely eyes.'

'Well, yes he does. Actually he *is* rather gorgeous. Oh God, I don't know, I've been looking forward to this so much and now I'm so nervous I feel sick. I'd almost prefer to cancel. I really want it to go well, you know. And I'm so out of practice.'

'It's okay to be nervous. It sort of adds to the excitement, don't you think? Anyway, what are you wearing?'

'I can't decide.'

'I know. I'll come round, and we can do dressing up, and then I'll take James off with me early so you can get ready in peace.'

'Brilliant. You're a star. See you about twelve, I'll make us some lunch.'

We arrive at Kate's to find James is already packed, and standing by the front door desperate for the off. He's six, Charlie's best friend at school, and has all sorts of marvellous things planned for the evening. It turns out that one of these involves bringing his new hamster, Norbert, named after the baby dragon in *Harry Potter*, to play at our house. Over my dead body.

'James, I think he'll be much better off staying at home. He'll be frightened in a new house.'

'Norbert is never frightened, are you Norbert?'

Norbert replies by twirling round in his wheel for a bit, and then wandering over to eat a few seeds out of his food bowl. He is quite pretty, a sort of pale honey colour, with white blotches, but nevertheless I don't fancy being in charge of two small boys and a hamster for the evening.

'Phoebe's gone to Charlotte's, and they've got guinea pigs and rabbits and sheep and everything, and they're going to have an animal tea party. It's not fair.'

Phoebe is his big sister, and she's spending the weekend with her best friend Charlotte, who lives on a farm. I wonder if the sheep know they're invited to a tea party.

Charlie and James both get increasingly agitated in a

joint bid to convince me that it's vital that Norbert be allowed to come home with us, until Kate silences them by announcing that lunch is ready, and there can be Coke to drink, but only for boys that do not go on and on about hamsters. A temporary truce therefore reigns while we eat, and then we settle the boys down with a video so we can go upstairs and try on countless outfits in peace. Unfortunately they choose *The Wind in the Willows*, so the rodent motif is continued, and they claim if we leave Norbert at home rude weasels are bound to get into the house and bully him senseless. We beat a hasty retreat upstairs, but I don't reckon much on our chances when it comes to getting them into the car minus Norbert.

After trying on what seems like hundreds of different items of clothing, and getting her hair into a complete tangle in the process, Kate finally settles on black trousers with a new white shirt.

'The only problem is I'll look like a waiter. That happened to me once at a wedding, you know; some old git ordered two gin and tonics and a glass of champagne, and I was so mortified I went and got them for him.'

'You do not look like a waiter. You look lovely. Relaxed, but smart too, and those trousers are very flattering, you know, they make your legs look fantastic. Now stop it, or we'll have to start all over again. Let's get the boys sorted and we'll disappear and you can have a bit of peace.'

'Fat chance, I still feel quite sick actually. It's years since I did all this dressing up stuff. I feel like a teenager again, all this what to wear, what to say stuff. Do you know I actually found myself reading the business bit in the newspaper today to see if there was anything interesting about accountants.'

'Was there?'

'No. Well, there might have been, but I got so fed up trying to understand an article about pensions I gave up.'

'Look, I'm sure you'll have a brilliant time, and anyway, it's bound to be better than staying in doing the ironing.'

'Well, let's hope so, otherwise I'll be round by half past ten for a debrief and a large gin.'

'It's a deal.'

We finally get the boys into the car, but the Norbert issue resurfaces with a vengeance, and in the end James bursts into tears and sobs so pitifully I give in. Which is pathetic, and Kate is all for standing firm, but it's so much easier to be firm with your own children. Well, actually that's not strictly true in my case, as I'm a terrible pushover for any small child in tears. Anyway, Norbert is on the back seat next to James as we drive off down the lane. I really hope she has a lovely time, she deserves it. Apart from a couple of disastrous blind dates set up by well-meaning friends, she hasn't really had a night out for over a year now, while her ex-husband Phil has gone off with a blonde called Zelda, who has legs that go on forever and an IQ that doesn't. It's very annoying. We've even thought of renting some gorgeous young hunk just so we could have him slumped over the kitchen table when Phil arrives, with me lurking about so I get to see Phil's face when he's introduced to the young Adonis. But we couldn't work out who rents young hunks by the hour. Personally I still think it's a bloody good new business idea, and wonder if you could get a government grant: it would be so much more useful as a service to the community than another new restaurant.

The boys spend the afternoon rampaging round the house playing a series of games that involve pretending to kill each other, with very realistic sound effects. I decide to make some soup, which I hope will come in handy later, when they're in the tent in the garden and showing the first stages of hypothermia. I spend what seems like hours chopping up a succession of vegetables into small cubes, and then the boys hurtle in and grab a handful to give to Norbert. I follow them into the living room to watch them and make sure they don't let the bloody thing out of its cage.

'He likes carrot, Mummy. Look, he's nearly eaten that piece.'

Too late I spot a large piece of onion, which seems to have got mixed in with the carrot. I'm not entirely sure hamsters like onion, and this feeling is confirmed when Norbert bites a huge chunk out of it and then freezes, makes a series of coughing and spluttering noises and charges for his water bottle shaking his head. Oh God, we've fed the poor thing the hamster equivalent of super-strength chilli. I send Charlie off for a saucer of water, while James and I watch Norbert drain his water bottle. In between slurps he's giving us filthy looks. Charlie comes back dripping, with a large cereal bowl, slopping water all over the carpet. Norbert launches himself into it. I have a horrible feeling he might be trying to commit suicide. He holds his head underwater for what seems like hours but finally re-emerges, soaking wet. Then he shoots into his bed, and all the bedding stuff sticks to his fur, and he looks absolutely furious. He sits glaring at us, making little chattering noises, which I'm sure are hamster swear words. The boys try poking in more bits of carrot but he's having none of it. Finally they give up and wander off, and I apologise once more and go back to making soup. I wonder if you can be reported to Rolf Harris for inadvertent cruelty to hamsters.

The boys greet the idea of soup for supper with total derision and refuse point-blank to even consider eating it, until I tell them that it is official Boy Scout Soup, recommended for anyone contemplating camping in a tent all night, whereupon they slurp away quite happily. A hideous half-hour follows while we try to get the bloody tent up. Just as you get one bit up the other bit falls down. I end up bashing in tent poles with a bit of brick, and eventually it is sort of up, wobbling slightly and looking like the smallest breeze will cause a total collapse, but they are inside it quite happily arranging their sleeping bags and arguing over whose turn it is to hold the torch. Then they reappear and announce that they need weapons in case of invaders, and trot off upstairs to collect swords and helmets. I'm sitting in the garden waiting for the warriors to return, when there's a bloodcurdling scream. I rush back into the house to find that they decided to say goodnight to Norbert, and Charlie put his hand in to give him a quick stroke, whereupon he bit him, hard. There is blood. Charlie is making a tremendous fuss and James is examining the wound, looking very grave. There is no sign of Norbert.

'Look, Mummy, I'm bleeding, I need a bandage. It's urgent.'

'Charlie, a plaster will do, it's only tiny. Where's Norbert?'

There is a long silence, and then the boys confess that in the midst of the trauma over Charlie's terrible savaging, Norbert has escaped, and is now hiding under the sofa. They have poked a sword under, trying to get him out, but, understandably I think, he has chosen to stay put. I make them promise to stand absolutely still, and not tread on anybody, while I go off to get plasters from the bathroom cabinet. I wonder if hamster bites can be dangerous, but can't face ringing up the doctor to ask for guidance, as I suspect hamster bites might not really be his thing. I'm sure there's something about lockjaw from animal bites, though the idea of Charlie with lockjaw does have its attractions. No more mammoth conversations about how telephones work. But he's had his tetanus shot, so I'm sure he'll be fine. I'll dab it with some antiseptic, just to be on the safe side.

I get back to the living room to find the boys frozen to the spot, like they're playing statues. Charlie makes a huge fuss about the antiseptic, and claims his hand is on fire, but is mollified when the dinosaur sticking plaster is finally in place. Then we all lie on the floor and peer under the sofa. There is no sign of Norbert. Suddenly we spot him at the other side of the room, disappearing out of the door. We all run after him, and spend the next twenty minutes tearing round the house like we're in some mad Benny Hill sketch. James has got a sieve and Charlie is clutching a saucepan. Poor Norbert probably thinks he's going to be cooked, and has been fed onion as some sort of ready-made stuffing.

We finally end up in my bedroom, with Norbert under my bed. I make the boys sit on the bed and be very quiet, and see if Norbert peeps out to check if the coast is clear. They promise to remain absolutely silent if they spot him. I stand by the laundry basket, and pretend to sort through dirty clothes in an effort to con Norbert into thinking it is now safe to come out. It works, and he saunters out, and then freezes when he spots me. The boys go into paroxysms of pointing and rolling their eyes, but thankfully remain silent. I suddenly remember seeing someone on telly picking up a recalcitrant rabbit by hurling a tea towel over it, and decide to see if it works with hamsters too. I slowly lift up the first item of clothing from the basket and waft it towards Norbert. Unfortunately it turns out to be a large pair of black pants, but they descend onto Norbert who is suddenly plunged into total darkness. I grab him and rush back into the living room, clutching a small limp hamster inside a pair of knickers, followed by the boys whooping with delight and congratulating me on my unusual animal-capture technique.

I shove him back into his cage, and he sits looking daggers at us. Poor thing has had a very hard day, and being covered by a pair of pants was probably the final straw. He'll probably have some weird version of post-traumatic shock, and be unable to use his wheel for fear of flashbacks. The boys demand to be allowed to go back to their tent now the excitement is over, and I spend ages getting them settled, with pyjamas and fleece tops and hats on. The tent collapses, twice, which they both adore. We do lots of bashing tent poles with bricks, and finally they're both in their sleeping bags zipped up tight, despite protests, because even though it's June it's still freezing.

I spend the next hour creeping backwards and forwards into the garden to check they're still all right, and haven't found a way to set fire to the tent, because even though I've strictly banned candles, and provided a torch, I wouldn't put it past Charlie to find a way to rub two sticks together and burn down the garden fence. I refuse all requests for drinks, crisps, and a very polite request from James for a bacon sandwich, and they finally fall silent. I open the tent flap to check they're still actually in it and asleep, and haven't decided to go off exploring. They're both fast asleep, Charlie still clutching the torch with his hat right down over his eyes, and James holding both swords with no hat in sight. It's now pitch-black, and I walk into the garden gate on the way back to the house. Luckily they don't wake up and hear me swearing.

I'm just about to get ready for bed when there's a very

tentative knock on the door. It's Kate. She does not look happy.

'How did it go?' I ask.

'On a scale of one to ten?'

'Yes.'

'Luxembourg, nil points.'

'Oh dear. Why?'

She bursts into tears, and I put my arms round her and pat her on the back for a bit until she calms down and I can actually understand what she's saying.

'The next time I meet someone at one of my bloody mother's bloody dinner parties, I must remember that anyone seems sane compared to her and her barking old-bag friends. It was awful.'

'Why?'

'He was so right-wing he could have been in the SS. I made some comment about the new vicar, who my mother hates because she's convinced he's gay, and he went off into one about shirt-lifters, and how disgusting it is and how they're to blame for the state society is in, them and single mothers who've got no intention of doing a good day's work and expect honest taxpaying citizens like him to pay for their houses.'

'Oh, charming. And did you remind him that you're a single parent?'

'I didn't get a chance, I could hardly get a word in. He said he didn't mean me, of course, I'd been married and everything, and why did Phil leave actually, bit on the side was it? Or was there trouble in the bedroom department.'

'He didn't!'

'Well, not in those words, but that's what he meant.'

'I hope you hit him.'

'No, but I thought about chucking my lasagne at him. I wish I had now. Then I tried to change the subject and started talking about gardening. I thought it might calm him, so I said the only thing Phil was really handy for was mowing the lawn, and then I said I was thinking about buying a new lawnmower, and then he spent twenty minutes lecturing me about hover-mowers.'

'Oh.'

'Yes. And then he got started on strimmers.'

'Christ.'

'Yes. I got so bored I started making little figures out of the candle wax. When I looked down I'd made an entire village.'

'Did you do little houses, and a railway? I love those little railways you get in model villages.'

'Shut up, it's not funny. Anyway, nobody mistook me for a waiter, but the waitress did give me a rather pitying look when he got out his calculator to check the bill. In the end I couldn't stand it, so I just gave him my credit card and said I insisted on paying, to thank him for all the useful tips about lawnmowers. He seemed quite pleased, actually.'

'Christ, what a wanker.'

'Yes, but the thing is, I should have known. I mean, my instincts must be pretty crap, mustn't they, if the only proper date I have in years turns out to be with Attila the Hun. Oh God, I was so looking forward to it and everything, I must be mad,' and she starts to cry again, but this time more quietly, in a kind of my life is crap way, rather than a phone an ambulance I'm having a major meltdown.

'Oh, Kate, don't let it upset you. Honestly, I've been out with loads of men who seemed perfectly nice and then the minute they're on a date with me they turn into psychotic losers. We all have. It's his loss, you know, you're too good for him. Anyway, you missed a thrilling night round here. The boys slipped Norbert a bit of onion, and he went berserk. Take it from me, never give him onion again, and then he got out and we spent hours charging round trying to catch him. It was a real laugh, I can tell you.'

'I'm glad someone had a bit of excitement. I think we must be doing something wrong, you know, if the highlight for both of us on a Saturday night is the hamster getting out.'

'Oh, I don't know. I can think of plenty of dates I've had in the past where chasing a hamster round would have been far more fun.'

'I suppose so. And I don't really want a man in my life anyway, I've got enough on my plate coping with the kids.'

'And Norbert. The Steve McQueen of hamsters. Don't forget him.'

'Okay, I feel better now. Actually I'm totally knackered, can I stay here tonight? I don't fancy going home. Are the boys all right in that tent?'

'Yes, I've checked on them loads. You can have the spare bed, and have a lie-in. They'll be up at the crack of dawn if the tent stays up that long, so I'll be up anyway.

One of us might as well get to stay in bed. Stay for lunch if you like, I'll make pizzas and we can drink that bottle of wine you got me for my birthday.'

'That's a very good bottle of wine, you know, I meant it for a special occasion.'

'This is a special occasion. You can tell me all about lawnmowers. I've been meaning to get a new one for ages. Our one only sort of flattens the grass, it's hopeless.'

'Bugger off.'

'If you're still feeling a bit tragic tomorrow, we'll let Norbert out again and you can try to catch him. That'll take your mind off things, I can guarantee it.'

'Don't you dare.'

'Okay, but promise, no more doubting yourself and getting depressed. Sounds like you had a lucky escape to me.'

'Promise. Night, Annie, and thanks again.'

'My pleasure.'

'Liar.'

I check on the boys one more time, and they're still sleeping peacefully. As is Norbert. I stagger into bed at midnight, and am woken what seems like minutes later by two small soaking-wet boys. It is half past one and it has started to rain, the tent has fallen down, and they're both freezing. I'm tempted to send James upstairs to wake his mother, but resist in the spirit of friendship. But she owes me one, big time. They climb into my bed, and begin to tell jokes. This is going to be a very long night.

Lauren Laverne's

Ultimate Girls' Night Out Top Ten

Ladies' nights: a tricky beggar to DJ for. The track list must be adaptable enough to cover the full GNO spectrum; from a wine-fuelled gossip/bitch/whingefest at a cheap Italian with your best mate, right through to a no-holds-barred nightclub attack incorporating a bank-breaking dress, cocktails (also expensive – physically and financially), random sailors, the loss of one shoe and a taxi home at dawn. There must be enough funk to elicit inappropriate and perhaps involuntary booty gyration, but enough cold electro to pretend we're really ice queens. Cheese enough to raise a smile, but not a queasy 1980s hen-party portion. Above all, the perfect GNO soundtrack should make all the women of the world want to cut loose, be they your heartbroken little sister or your worryingly tipsy Nan. Here's my top ten: read, raid, tailor to fit and then get your freak on, madam!

Added Extras:

12. 'Femme Fatale' – The Velvet Underground

Short and sweet, this song is the kind of thing that's just perfect as a soothing background while you prepare yourself for a hardcore evening, or post-GNO. When you arrive at someone's house at first light, but want to close the curtains and keep last night going inside, at least until the booze runs dry. Critically, the tinkly noises will perfectly drown out the denial-shattering sound of the milkman making his first rounds. And if morning doesn't ever come, your hangover can never kick in – brilliant!

11. 'Hey Ladies' – The Beastie Boys

Hip-hop's cutest rich-kid trio in credible girls' night theme tune shocker! Ad rock and the lads implore us to 'get funky' over such a thoroughly danceable smorgasbord of funk, disco and eclectrica that it seems impossible to do otherwise. They also earn bonus points for sampling James Brown's dirty laugh and judicious use of cowbells. A hit!

Top Ten:

10. 'Sock It to Me' – Missy Elliott

One woman hit factory Missy 'Misdemeanour' Elliott brings the funk, as co-conspirator and femme fatale Da Brat waxes lyrical about it being 'The muthafuckin' bitch era'. Scary.

9. 'China Girl' – Iggy Pop

Now, this is what I call a love song. Miles better than Bowie's weedy version, Ig imbues this hymn to Eastern loveliness with an endearing undercurrent of lascivious filth. Get your cheongsam on and pretend he's singing it just for you.

8. 'These Boots Are Made for Walking' – Nancy Sinatra

Proof that having kick-ass footwear and a killer attitude is even scarier than a millionaire dad with the most infamous of hardman connections. Heaven help the boyfriend who dared suggest that Nancy tone down the eyeliner – listen and learn.

7. 'Genius of Love' – Tom Tom Club

After imbibing the correct amount of alcohol, the lyrics of this 1980s delight will start to make sense like some kind of aural magic-eye painting. If you're not quite there yet just sing along to the 'I'm in heaven/With my boyfriend' bit and bluff your way through the rest with your best coquettish disco moves.

6. 'Babylove' – The Supremes

The little black dress of ladyhits, this song is always welcome, and never out of place. Every woman in the room should be up and dancing by the fourth bar, including your Mam and Great Auntie Betty, which is arguably reason enough to leave it out. But I say why spoil their fun? Unless you're worried your

Mam will put shame in your game by knowing the proper dance routines.

5. 'It's Your Thing' – The Isley Bros.

If this doesn't make your ass move, get to the doctor's because, frankly, it's broken.

4. 'Doin' the Do' – Betty Boo

Ooh, Betty! Ms Boo's floor-filler takes it right back to the school disco. One of those songs that everybody inexplicably knows all the words to, this will remind you of the sweet taste of first freedom and first lip-gloss. Fantastic.

3. 'The Model' – Kraftwerk

'She's going out to nightclubs drinking just champagne.' That's us, that is. Okay, so we're drinking luminous alcopops and cheap trebles. But we still possess every bit of the Teutonic elegance of this song's heroine. Yes, those are ladders in my tights. Your point being . . . ?

2. 'Heart of Glass' – Blondie

Fantasy GNO companion and quite possibly the coolest woman of all time, Deborah Harry sasses through this piece of perfect pop, showing the whole world exactly how things should be done. Get up, get down and let some of Deb's mojo rub off.

1. 'Independent Woman Part 1' – Destiny's Child

All the best things about a GNO in four funkadelic

minutes: Beyonce and Co. are on one long ladies' night and we're all invited! No, he wasn't worth it! Yes, you look fabulous! Now shake that money-maker like tomorrow might never come! Girls' Nights Out rule!

Kathy Lette's

Top-ten Tips for
Looking Fab at Forty
Which Don't Involve Face Cream

1. Always be seen out with much, much uglier women.

2. Before resorting to facelifts, just remember the nasty side effects: cosmetic surgery can lead to women developing thick Californian accents.

3. Don't get a bellybutton stud to try to appear younger than you are. A woman does not need any holes in her other than those which are, strictly speaking, necessary.

4. If any bloke ever makes a crack about your ageing looks, tell him that they've finally found a cure for baldness, you know. Hair.

5. If you're feeling fat, just make sure you are seen standing next to a heavily pregnant woman. Take one with you everywhere you go. And wear pantyhose which control your excesses the way the Taliban controlled Afghanistan.

6. Just remember that the dimmer switch is the greatest sex aid known to womankind.

7. Acquire much, much older friends.

8. Some husbands think that their wedding vows include the clause 'Till Death Us Do Part Or Until Someone Younger Comes Along'. If your hubby trades you in for a younger model, take revenge. Hair-removal cream in her mascara wand will make you feel much better!

9. If you think he is going to trade you in for a younger model, do it before he does. 'For Sale. One Husband. Has Had Only One Careful Lady Owner.' And go get yourself a toy boy. A toy boy is a gift from the Self-Esteem Fairy. And so much more rejuvenating than a face cream.

10. And always remember, if your bloke prefers beauty to brains, it's because he *sees* better than he *thinks*.

Rebbecca Ray

Eden

'You know what story you never told me, my friend?'

'The night's got too short for stories now . . .'

'You never told me the story of how you got here. Never told me why you came.'

'You don't want to hear it,' I answered, and I smiled.

'I want to hear it. You tell me,' he said.

In the night-time here, the air is still. It settles with the dust, in the evenings. A man could call out then from the peak, from the valley's other side, and you could hear him. A man could clap his hands together, just a mark on the evening sky and, sitting here, sitting by my home, the air would move against your skin before the twilight settled back, between.

In this stillness now, I leaned across and took the bottle from him.

'There's no need to look sad. It has a happy ending. Because you're here.'

'It has a happy ending,' I said, and then I told him, 'I don't know.'

The fire sang low in front of us, pine that was burning down now. His face was smudged like mine must have been in the shadow here: dark as the glass round an oil-lamp's flame, and red like it, with the fire's heat. He smiled at me softly and I drank a little, heard my own coat shift as I sat forward.

'I lived in the city, you know . . .' I began. 'In the city, there were empty houses . . .' I looked over at a spit of flame and cleared my mouth for a moment, said nothing. 'There were one hundred and four thousand empty houses. I read the number once, remembered it. One hundred and four thousand empty houses, and people didn't glance, walking past them. You'd find them on their own, you know. A road full of perfect houses, and you'd come to one with its age spilling right over the street. Boards on its windows, the names of children scratched or painted on the walls. Weeds all around. Locked up,' I said. 'They were always locked.'

I saw a flake of ash like snow twist down and settle on my boot. In the morning, when the winds had come up again and I walked out here, the ash and dust would be stirred together there, pale colours over the burnt ground. I looked up finally, with a better smile for him.

'I used to steal houses,' I said. 'I lived in seventy-three. I took seventy-three out of a hundred and four thousand. Can you imagine a city – so many houses empty? And they were building, still there, all the time.'

'We love to build, man.'

'We all love to build. That's why we're grand.' I looked down at the fire. 'You find a house, left empty a few years, it becomes like a person, you know? Becomes more like a person each day that starts there and ends there with quiet. They become like people, then, they're empty long enough, they become like animals, man. You see them then.' I held the wine out to him; tipped to him. 'You see them then, in the middle of the city, they'll look like the landscape is breaking through.'

He pulled himself from the ground and took it and his fingernails were red in the light.

'You could live forever in that city,' I said, 'only moving between them. I thought for the longest time, that I'd do that. In the city, every person's got a goal. Achieving something, doing something, becoming something. Even if that goal's just getting through the week and having one big night out at the end. People wouldn't glance, walking past those empty houses. Eyes always, always forward. I thought for the longest time they didn't realise what they were leaving.' I smiled at him a bit.

'Look at what we've lost, for goals. But it's not that they don't realise, they see and understand. It's just that the goals are bright,' I said. 'It's just that they're beautiful.'

'You had no goal then,' he said. His face was gentle without a smile.

'No. I'd rather be here. Big night out,' I said, and laughed.

Here, where it's empty, the view can move you like it

pricks through the pores of your skin. The mountains hold this valley, dark in the mornings, when the sky behind them is as pale as words unspoken. And you can stand by my house here, look out, and never wonder about achievements you left behind. Here, where it's empty, where it's full of grace, there's no need to think of anything that way.

I looked out with him now, past the fire, and the mountains were a shape against the night. A thin, distant moon hung there over them, and my hands were warm with the fire's light. The porch step creaked but I looked back and it was empty. The house will make sounds only with the cold. Under a bright and hanging bulb, there were just the floorboards. There was just the rug and a stack of wood there, the open door that led to where she slept. I smiled, looking through the doorway, to that room where she'd left the light on, even sleeping.

'I don't want to live for goals,' I said. 'They may be beautiful but you can't ever touch them. And how would you know anyway, beautiful or ugly? You have no comparison if you're only looking forwards.'

I remembered the houses, empty so long that letters were piled inside the door. I remembered the shine of the envelopes. The same names repeated over and over, as if they still mattered in the dim light. Like a tree, an empty house grown wild across its skin will be hollow, will be still like this, inside.

'We opened the houses at night,' I said, 'and found the things that the people had left behind. A cup. Standing on its own, on the kitchen table, you know, and that table will be thick with dirt. The oven with its door left open . . . A picture of some place you've never seen, lying face down on the shelf over the fire.' Here, it was easy to remember, the way that it had looked, and felt, and sounded. 'We'd light a fire first. We'd go out at night to the city parks, and bring back the deadwood from the ground. We'd go out at night and find food. We ate from others' rubbish bins,' I said. I looked up at him and my smile was sad. 'You could live forever in that city on the things that the people throw away. Tools, material to build with, beds and rugs and lamps. Paintings,' I said, 'even paintings. We lived on the street at night. In the daylight there nothing belongs to you. It's a breaking of the law,' I said, 'to take any refuse away.'

'Build with one hand. Throw away with the other.' He nodded with contempt, empty-handed in the embers' light.

'They pass the whole world from hand to hand that way. There's no goal in what you leave behind. We used to hang blankets,' I said, 'ones we'd found, over the boarded-up windows. There wouldn't be a view of the street, no sound of it. We painted landscapes onto the walls.'

I remembered mountains in dark colours and sunsets; vivid, beautiful, unskilled.

'I was always living here,' I said. 'Wherever I was, I was always living here.

'We had a kitchen with a stock of every kind of spice, cumin and nutmeg and cardamom, juniper and cinnamon and allspice. Found them all in rubbish bins . . . There was a time when spice was the most precious thing in the world. We sent out ships to find it, across the oceans, for months, to countries we'd never seen before . . . saffron and turmeric.' I remembered it. In the light of candles, found and stolen, all their packets had been bright in the dimness. 'You find spices like that in a rubbish bin though, and they look like the most precious things in the world.'

Between derelict walls we'd cooked in candlelight: ginger and lemongrass. The room would be damp around us, stripped and peeling with age. We'd have some great pan on the stove. 'Everything's precious in a derelict house . . . like things are precious, for their first times, or like they're precious when you fall in love.'

He smiled and I turned to see the doorway. She has dark hair. She sleeps with it let loose.

'Like things are precious here,' I said. The room where we sleep looks out on the valley. The sun comes through in the early morning, and where she likes to sleep, it touches her.

In the still air, I heard him say, 'I'll never leave.'

I looked at him and he was smiling but only as you do, losing something; giving it away. His plate and his knife across it lay on the ground here, pushed from him and clean, but for reflections of the flames. He had four cigarettes left for us, for the night. Three we had shared already. I'd cut this wood in the morning today from trees that I'd felled in the spring. They'd come down with great sounds in the woodlands then, like trees had never fallen there before. I remember hearing the silence afterwards; it went on for so long a time.

The nights were longer now, the days diminishing, summer was leaving the air. And though the wine was washing at the bottom, really we were drunk already, both of us.

'I'll never leave here now,' I said.

I smiled a little, sad, and looked down.

'She said to me,' I moved my hand towards the doorway like saying her name might wake her now. 'She said to me, I want to live in the past. Do you think that's true?' I asked.

'At what time in the past?' he said. 'No, I don't believe that's true.'

'I would have liked to have stood up on deck, on one of those spice ships, you know? Seen a new coastline. A new country maybe. Stand there at night and watch it coming; see its outline against the sky.'

'There was only one moment,' he said, 'standing on the ship and seeing that coast, there was only one moment when they looked at what they found.'

It was the shape of the landscape that I thought of, empty as the mountains here.

'They were sharpening their weapons before. They were reading their Bibles afterwards. One moment,' he said, 'when they just stood there, when they just stood and looked at what they'd found.'

From his pocket, he took the four cigarettes and I saw him lay them out on the ground. He moved his fingers over them and chose one from the dirt. I watched him brush it clean, in the many small sounds of the fire.

'You can't live in a moment,' I said. '. . . I don't want to live in the past.'

There was a time then, he lit the cigarette and smoked some and he passed it over to me. There was a time then, just the crackle of the fire, and the movement of air through this valley.

'I loved my life for the longest time . . . It was timeless, in those places. We used to tell stories together, you know, sitting in a room with dereliction just falling from it, and we'd have the candles burning. The things we'd found, they sparkled there like they were the last of their kind . . . Like the end of the world. It felt that way. Like, outside the windows, the boards and blankets, there wouldn't be any street. There wouldn't be any city, just a landscape, like the one that we painted on the wall.'

Here now, the mountains were a shape against the sky-line, unreal, and beautiful because of it. Without a sound in this valley, without a movement, you might've touched their distant line, for there was nothing between. 'We looked for ten years for a house that we could stay in,' I smiled, 'like the Holy Grail, you know? Sometimes a month in one place, sometimes three, before we'd get moved on. Still, every next house felt like it could be the one. Like looking for Eden,' I said. 'The end of the world, it'll surely feel like the beginning.'

'We'd light the first fire again,' I said, 'another ruined fireplace. Ten years, we were looking for the house where we could stay, the one that was meant to be for us. I was worn out by it,' I said. I scraped the dust with my boot, with a small sound, and thought again of our footsteps here when the morning finally came.

'We found it,' I said. I looked up at him, trying now to smile. 'After ten years, we found it. It was beautiful . . . that was the house I left behind.'

I remembered now, in this still silence: the silence of the others, sleeping around me. I remembered the debris of the night's work scattered, drinks half-drunk and candles, guttering, sawdust on the rug in the space that I'd cleared between all our foundling things.

'The house was ours . . .' I said, 'it was our home. We worked, until it wasn't dying anymore. Had running water, hot and cold . . . Worked till we had running electricity. All the creature comforts.' I heard my voice, bitter then and for the first time. And the words still unspoken were pale in my chest, just like the sky above the mountains, come the mornings. 'We worked till our empty house was full. Not a dying place . . . It was growing, you know? Nature can't make anything that doesn't either die or grow.'

'That's why we love to build,' he said quietly, 'That's why we're so grand.'

I nodded in this fire's gentle light. I looked at his face and wondered how it could be, that we could want to spend a moment in building, or a week, a year, a life, when we could be sitting like this; talking together like this.

'I didn't know what to do,' I told him. 'The house was a home, just like we'd looked for, and I didn't know what to do. I thought . . . that I'd make some things, try to sell them, you know? Toys. Things for people to put on their shelves. You can find materials to build anything. Out on the streets, you know.

'There was a space on the pavement by our door. And it was a rich part of the city. People walking past us, all the time . . . I thought that I'd stand there in the days,' I said, 'with the things I'd made laid out.'

They'd sat behind me, brightly coloured painted wood, finished, in the sawdust on the floor. And I remembered the pale sound of traffic rising, the dim light that stretched from behind the blankets, to gutter with the last of the candles there. Even the small goals look beautiful.

I saw the reaches of light that were cast now from the door behind us, and where they ended, fell to shadow in the dust, I remembered the reaches of morning in that house as I'd taken the blankets down.

'I didn't know what price to ask for them,' I said.

She had looked at them before sleeping, turning them around in her hands.

She'd said they looked like toys from a storybook, Christmas stories, books with faded covers. I remembered holding the blankets in my arms and looking out, through broken glass and my reflection, to a winter street and to the people who were moving there, passing the house without a glance as they walked to work in their mornings. Something left me then, was lost. And I just stood there, I remembered. Just stood there, afraid of failing; looking out at that street in front of me, and afraid of the goal I could see.

'"Nature can't make anything that doesn't either die

or grow," she said to me. I wanted to live in the past, and I wanted to say to her then, that we were meant to live that way. I wanted to say to her, we've grown too much, everywhere, outgrown what we should've been. I wanted to say it to her . . . but it isn't true. All that nature ever meant for us, was to grow.'

I looked up at him and he had no answer. He passed me one of the three cigarettes we had left and his eyes were distant, some place he'd seen long ago, though he had been born here in this valley.

'That's why goals are beautiful,' he said, 'they're beautiful to draw us on.'

I remembered turning away from the window in that room and looking at the others, sleeping there. Every house we had ever lived in would have reached that point if we had stayed. The sound of the city is the sound of evolution. And I couldn't leave that house, I couldn't find another ruin, just to try and live in a moment that will not stay.

'Looking for somewhere where things are good . . . for Eden . . . is looking for an empty place.'

He turned away, with the end of my story.

'That was why I came here,' I said.

And it was beautiful. Morning or night, summer or winter. The skies are different every season. We've both said to each other that we'll stay, we've said we'll have children here. But even if there were no children, if we were the last, still it wouldn't have been for no reason. I told her. I said that to her. We would have had the days still, cutting the wood, and the nights, when it burned slowly on the fire.

Scarlett Thomas

The Old School Museum

'You can't dig up your own time capsule,' John says.

'Why not?' says Simon.

'You just can't,' says John. 'It's weird. You can't bury a time capsule and then dig it up again.'

It's dark and it's cold and we're standing in the field in which we think we buried the time capsule just over two months ago. I remember burying it (not where, of course – none of us can remember where). There were fireworks going off and the sounds of little kids shrieking far away. It was New Year's Eve 1999 and we were all a little bit out of it, in a nice way, of course. We thought we were leaving an interesting present for people in the future, or possibly aliens. But things change and I don't know why John's arguing now. We all agreed that we have to dig it up.

The three of us live in a flat above a shop in a small, slightly hippy town in Cornwall. The flat and the shop are Simon's:

he inherited them from his father a couple of years ago. John was Simon's flatmate in London, and I was (and still am) John's girlfriend. It went like this: Simon decided to move into his dad's old place because he's an artist and there'd be no rent. John decided to move in with Simon because he'd always lived with Simon and Simon offered him a room for £20 a week. And I moved there, too, because it was time John and I shared a place. I'd never been to Cornwall before I moved here. There are lots of artists around here. In the local paper they call them a 'community'.

We live on the main street: a steep hill with a pavement so thin that women with prams have to walk in the middle of the road and get honked at by out-of-towners in shiny off-road-style vehicles. There's a health-food shop next door to us and a traditional bakery next door to that. If you walk up the hill behind the shops you can see the old fishermen's cottages and the sea sparkling in the distance.

Between this town and the next, and joined by an intricate matrix of dangerous one-lane roads known as 'the lanes', are villages full of home-made *Buy British* signs and pro-capital-punishment creative writers with regular domestic help and a fondness for plays on Radio 4. Every village has a small local shop selling old fruit, out-of-date videos and powdery white pepper. In the villages, the people customise their own road signs. There is a sign in one village that says *No Goods Vehicles*. It used to say *No Heavy Goods Vehicles*. Another village has imposed its own ten-mile-per-hour speed limit. Most people from the towns stay out of the villages. They use particular words to describe them: *parochial*, *time warp*, *insular*.

You can always hear seagulls around here, day and night, especially in town. The locals say they don't even hear them anymore but I do. I hear them at four in the morning when they are at their noisiest. They sound like an alarm, or a distress signal.

Simon had already decided to turn his dad's old shop into a museum by the time John and I moved in. We asked him what kind of museum. He said, 'The Old School Museum.' He had a sign made. We asked him if it was an art project, like an installation or something. But he said it was just a museum.

The flat was cluttered with Simon's dad's stuff and all Simon's childhood things. John and I helped him go through the attic. We had fun looking at all the old photos of people in flares, and orange and brown clothes. Some of the people in the photos looked like ghosts or dead people but it was still fun.

The attic was full of toys and games from Simon's childhood. John and I felt nostalgic because we'd had a lot of the same toys. Everyone must have done. There was a space-hopper, a Rubik's cube, a Scalextrix, a Swing Tennis set, a wind-up Pac-Man toy, an old Atari, a handheld Frogger game, Play-Doh, a fake dog turd, a joke disguise set including a false moustache, nose and glasses, a book on how to be a spy and, among lots of other games, Kerplunk, Scrabble, Mousetrap, Operation and Buckaroo.

In an old box we found a *Blue Peter* badge, some football stickers, some dice, a rainy-day cricket set, an old address book with blue ink staining one corner, a mini kaleidoscope, a spinning top and lots of marbles. Elsewhere we found a couple of white tennis balls, some old Shrinky Dinks, several of those soft jelly-like spiders that would appear to walk down the wall if you threw them at it – until they got covered with dust, which was what happened to mine – and a huge pile of annuals with spacemen and naughty freckled kids and TV stars on the covers.

'What are you going to do with all this stuff?' John asked.

'It's going in the Old School Museum,' Simon said.

'Why exactly did you call it the Old School Museum?' John asked.

Simon frowned. 'All this stuff is "old school", isn't it?'

John looked blank.

'You know, like hip-hop,' said Simon.

'It makes it sound a bit trendy,' I said uncertainly.

'Well, I can't call it the Childhood Museum,' said Simon.

No one ever visits the Old School Museum. Well, that's what I tell people when I'm using the museum in an anecdote (there are several anecdotes: the time it almost burnt down, the time people broke in and didn't steal anything, the time the council objected to it because no one understood it and so on). In fact, in the two years it's been open, we've had maybe forty or fifty visitors. Mostly, though, people just look in the window, frown and walk away. It costs two pounds to get in. Maybe that's it. Or maybe people are just freaked out by being confronted with such a formal collection of stuff that, frankly, looks like junk. Or maybe the childhood on display is one they don't recognise and can't connect with. Or maybe they can and that's why. If I didn't have to go in there I probably wouldn't.

Simon made the display cases himself out of pine and glass. The things from the attic looked odd displayed in the cases next to little white cards explaining what they were. Simon mounted a white tennis ball on a golf tee and put it in a case by itself. He lined the case with bright green AstroTurf. The card next to the case said 'White Tennis Ball', which was unnecessary really.

When the museum first opened, none of us had any money. John and I were each supposed to pay Simon £20 rent a week but sometimes we couldn't even afford that. John was building a website and I was just doing all these abstract sketches for no particular purpose. We used to talk about how we'd go back and take London by storm one day when we were all famous. We knew it would never happen but it was still the general plan. Have you ever noticed how most people's life-plans are just totally unrealistic? Secretaries think about the day they'll run the company; cleaners dream of marrying a millionaire; losers always think they'll become famous.

While John and I were so skint, Simon suggested that we work in the museum instead of paying him rent;

polishing the display cases, sweeping up, letting people in, showing them around. It is quiet in the museum and slightly dark. Whenever I work there I think about how time changes the way people see things. I think about how items like the white tennis ball seem desirable because they are rare. I think about when people first started using green tennis balls and how fascinating and special they seemed. Everyone was sick of white tennis balls then. Now they're sick of the green ones. Well, I don't mean they're sick of them exactly. I'm sure people don't really think about it. But no one thinks green tennis balls are special, that's for sure. But they did once.

Sometimes when I'm sitting in the shop I watch people walk past and I wonder what I'll look like when I'm older. I wonder if somewhere down the line something will happen that will mean I can afford a big silver car or a Jeep and go around in department-store leggings with my hair done up in a clip. Or will I in fact end up like the large red-faced lady with the string shopping bags and the blue flowery hat? She always looks cheerful but there's something about her that seems lonely, as if someone she knows has just died. Other times I look at teenage girls and they really have something so special that I must have had but never realised. I look at them going past and wonder if I ever looked like any of them. There's one girl with big flared jeans and blue dreadlocks. I used to do things like that with my hair and then worry I looked really stupid. I wonder if she worries about that.

I thought I was really ugly from when I was about ten

until I was about twenty. Now I look at pictures of myself from then and I didn't look ugly at all. I actually looked really pretty, especially compared to the way I look now. Now I really am ugly. When I sit in the museum I wonder if at some point in the future I'll be even uglier, and I'll look at pictures of myself now and think I looked really pretty.

It was winter when Simon came home with the time capsule. They sold a lot of time-capsule products during 1999. There were huge plastic time-capsule-shaped confectionery collections on sale in supermarkets, and proper time-capsule kits in toyshops. Simon got his from a toyshop.

John and I were both in the museum that afternoon keeping each other company. Simon rushed in with the time capsule with a look in his eyes – as if he'd been given important instructions that had to be carried out immediately. Then he began stuffing the time capsule with his most prized objects from the museum.

'What are you doing?' John asked Simon.

'Making a time capsule,' Simon explained.

'Oh, cool,' John said, and started helping.

John's been obsessed with space for as long as I've known him. He collects toy robots and space ships and books about planets. I could tell by his excited expression that he was connecting time capsules with space in some way. Maybe it's the word 'capsule', or the idea of something travelling through time (kind of). I was just worried that Simon seemed to be putting all the best things from the museum into the time capsule. At the rate he was going there'd be no museum left.

'What are you going to do with the time capsule?' I asked.

'Bury it,' Simon said, slightly breathlessly.

'Where?'

'I don't know,' he said. 'In a field somewhere.'

'Why?' I said. 'What about the museum?'

'No one wants to go in museums,' he said. 'When the past is easy to get hold of no one's interested. But when they have to dig it up – well, that's different, isn't it? There's that TV program where they get those teams to do archaeology. Everyone likes that. Anyway, I know if I bury this stuff then people will take it seriously. They'll think about it and what it means. It might even be on TV.'

I've never understood why he's always been so obsessed with people thinking about what his things mean. I've sat looking at them for hours at a time in the museum and never really thought they meant anything. While Simon and John stuffed objects into the plastic case I wondered whether archaeological TV shows would still be popular when the time capsule was dug up. Things change, after all.

'Won't it be funny if people think all these 1970s things are from the year 1999,' John said. 'It'll totally confuse the aliens or the people from the future or who- ever digs it up.' He laughed.

Simon didn't laugh. He looked worried. Then he started taking everything out of the time capsule. He labelled each item with a date and description before putting it back. By the time he'd finished, the time capsule was overflowing like a Christmas stocking. Half the stuff ended up in a Safeway carrier bag that Simon sort of tied to it. Then he put it in a cupboard until New Year's Eve.

Then we buried it. My memory of that is a bit hazy. We drove out of town, down the lanes, through the villages and found a field with a public footpath. It was very dark.

The museum phone rang earlier today. It never usually rings. I was working in the museum all day, not that there seemed to be much point. Since we buried the time capsule all the best stuff is gone. There's no white tennis ball anymore.

The phone call was from someone at a magazine. He was responding to one of the press releases we'd sent out some time last year. He was called Hugh. No one else had ever got in touch as a result of the press releases. I'd forgotten we'd even made them. Hugh said he found it in his predecessor's desk and thought it looked interesting.

'So, it's like a retro thing?' he asked me. 'Like, loads of old school stuff?'

'Yeah,' I said. 'You know, white tennis balls, Buckaroo, 1970s TV shows.'

'Wow, cool,' he said. 'And this is, like, in Cornwall?'

'That's right.' I told him the name of the town even though it was on the press release. Then I laughed nervously. 'Middle of nowhere,' I added.

Then he started going on about how it was so weird and cool to have something like that in Cornwall and he wanted to do a feature with photographs for the magazine. I said it would be great to get some publicity for the museum. Then he got out his diary and arranged to come down with a photographer in the morning.

'Oh my God,' John said when I told him. 'Everyone reads that magazine.'

He was right. It's probably the most popular style magazine in the country. People our age read it. I suddenly imagined those people – in their trainers and London clothes – making important pilgrimages to Cornwall to look at Simon's museum in the same way people go to Stonehenge. But there was one huge problem.

'All the most important items are buried,' Simon said when we told him. He looked at me, slightly panicked. 'Did you tell him that?'

I shook my head. 'No. I sort of didn't remember.'

'We'll have to dig it up,' Simon said. 'If he's coming in the morning we'll have to do it tonight.'

And that's how we came to be here, on a cold dark night in February, trying to dig up Simon's time capsule.

John keeps stamping his feet and rubbing his hands together.

'Fuck me,' he keeps saying. 'It's fucking freezing.'

Simon's standing there with a shovel, looking sad.

'It was by a tree,' I say to him. 'I remember that. You said if we buried it by a really old tree then it was unlikely that the land would get built on or dug up too early, or, you know, farmed.'

I'm remembering more things now about the last time we came here, on the eve of the Millennium. Like the way the screaming and the firework noises in the distance made it feel like someone had left a radio on somewhere but apart from that we were totally alone out here. I remember wondering what would be left when we drove back into town after midnight. How long would it be before we saw the full effects of the Millennium Bug? All the way home we talked about how you could be out here on the lanes and the world could change and you'd never know. We wondered whether, when we got back to town, the place would be unrecognisable and chaotic, with people running in the streets and cash flying out of cashpoint machines. But when we got back everything was the same, except of course the Old School Museum, which looked a bit like it had been looted.

'Didn't we decide that it would be good if something was built on top of it?' John says, his breath white in the air. 'You know, to preserve it for a very long time?'

'My whole childhood,' Simon says softly.

I look at John. 'I can't remember what we decided.' I sigh. 'This is stupid.'

Eventually we start digging by a tree about half a mile further down the dark footpath. The ground is cold and hard. It's almost impossible to dig into it. But we're digging anyway, in torchlight, and I'm thinking about Hugh and his glossy magazine and the thousands (millions?) of readers and how this could have been the thing that made everything all right. We could have taken London by storm. We could have done interviews and chat shows and become celebrities. Everyone would have known us as those people from Cornwall with the weird museum. All evening John's been saying that he's not sure he wants to be famous, but I don't believe him. He also keeps saying that the time capsule is better as a time capsule than as a museum, and that he doesn't think we should dig it up at all.

We keep digging but we know we'll never find it. We're still not sure if this is the right footpath, the right field, the right village. Out here, beyond the towns, everything's empty and still and sometimes, at night, there are badgers and bats. It's like that in the next village and the next. It's like that in every field between here and the sea. On summer nights there are thousands of insects. In winter there's hard ground and cowpats frozen like hamburgers. We're going to have to ring Hugh early tomorrow and tell him not to come. John seems upset because Simon looks so sad. Eventually Simon puts down his shovel and just stops.

'It's lost,' he says sadly. 'Let's just go home.'

Suddenly I think that maybe John's right and it's better to leave it buried. Maybe it'll be good for Simon to stop thinking about the time capsule and the museum and use his dad's old shop for something else instead. As we walk back to the car John smiles at me in the torchlight and I'm fairly sure he's thinking the same thing. And then Simon smiles for the first time for ages and mumbles something about the museum that we can't hear because of the wind.

Paul Donnellon

The Boys

Andrew Humphreys

The Biltmore, 1934

Two men stood at the top of the marble sweep of stairs, tugging at the starched collars of their shirts. Their faces were as big and square and twitchy as their shoulders. The heat of an Indian summer swept across the Pacific Ocean and through the palm-lined boulevards, and even as the sun began to set, sweat ran freely down their faces from beneath the pomaded weight of their hair. They wore guns beneath their jackets, forty-fives in shoulder holsters, probably, conspicuous in outline.

He knew there would be trouble.

'Cute tuxedo.'

'Thank you.'

'Not you. The monkey. Cute. You could do with less spit and a little more polish. Hey, Al? You hear that? I made a funny. That was a good one, huh?'

'Yeah, Lew. You're a regular Eddie Cantor. You – what's your name?'

'Professor Doctor Jozsef W. Kiss, but you may call me

Captain Joe.'

'Captain what?'

'Captain Joe.'

'Where you from, Captain Joe?'

'Hungary.'

'Plenty of food when you get inside, buddy.'

'No, I'm from Hungary.'

'That would explain the slightly accented English, huh, Al?'

'It is slight, isn't it, Lew? Very difficult accent to reproduce, I would imagine. If one was a writer or such.'

'Oh, yeah, Al. Very difficult, if one was a writer or such. I expect it would be best not to even make the attempt. Have some character or something comment on its slightness and move right along.'

'That'd seem to me like a good way of handling it, Lew. As for you, Captain Joe, see this list? You're not on it.'

'Of course I'm not.'

'Of course you're not. But if you're not on the list, you're not going inside, see? So I'm going to have to ask you to take it outside.'

'But we're already outside. I would like to get inside.'

'What are you, some sort of wise guy?'

'I thought that was a pretty good one, Al. Almost a zinger.'

'Button it, Lew. And you, Captain Wise Guy, beat it.'

'But we are guests of this party.'

'Look, Cap – can I call you Cap, Cap? We've been

through this. If you're not on the list, you're not going inside.'

'I am not on the list.'

'That's right.'

'But he is.'

'Who is?'

'He is.'

'The monkey? Are you shitting me, Cap? Are you trying to shit me?'

'You don't know who this is?'

'Who? The monkey?'

'This is not a monkey, this is Siggy. Siggy the Wonder Chimp? Don't tell me you don't recognise his face. Siggy – here! You don't get to the movies much, do you?'

'The movies?'

'The movies. Motion pictures.'

'We know what movies are, right, Al?'

'Sure we do, Lew. And I ain't never seen this monkey before in my life.'

'It's probably the tuxedo that's confusing you. Usually Siggy appears *au naturel*.'

'You mean . . . ?'

'As nature intended him, yes. Surely, gentlemen, you've seen *Jungle Man of the Jungle*. It was one of the studio's biggest hits in thirty-two.'

'Thirty-two?'

'Two years ago, Lew.'

'Correct, Mr Al. And *Jungle Man and Jungle Woman*

is sure to be one of this year's finest and most profitable entertainments.'

'Oh, yeah, Al – now I remember. I read about that in *Variety*.'

'And what were you doing reading *Variety*, Lew?'

'I picked it up at the barber shop. They got a stack of them there.'

'So you're telling me this is a movie monkey?'

'Al, it's Siggy the Wonder Chimp! He's Jungle Man's faithful jungle companion. So this is a movie party, Captain Joe?'

'Of course it's a movie party, Lew. They're all movie parties in this town. We ain't in Detroit no more, are we?'

'So there are movie people here?'

'There are movie people here.'

'They're all movie people, Lew. Always.'

'I thought I recognised that guy with the big ears, Al. The one with the blonde dame. She was stacked like this, remember?'

'I remember, Lew.'

'I told you I'd seen him before. You know I ain't too good with faces. Or names. Reading, writing – that kind of stuff. It troubles me.'

'You don't say?'

'Sure he says. He just said, didn't he? What are you, some sort of wise guy? I've had just about enough out of you. Beat it before I beat it for you.'

'But Al, look. He's on the list. Right there – look: Siggy the Wonder Chimp. I think that's what it says.

I ain't too good with letters and stuff. That's what it says, right, Al?'

'Well, I'll be a monkey's uncle. He's on the list, all right. But you still ain't, Captain Wiseacre. The chimp can go in, but you ain't goin' nowhere.'

'But I must accompany Siggy wherever he goes. I'm his trainer. Show me that list. Look – there: Siggy the Wonder Chimp *plus trainer*. And I'm his trainer.'

'He's right, Al. He's the trainer. Look at the way the little monkey's holding his hand. Ain't it cute, Al?'

'Sure, Lew. It's cute enough.'

'How'd you get him to do that, Captain Joe? How'd you train him?'

'Science, Lewis. Punishment, reward, lack of punishment, lack of reward. Basic physiological principles.'

'That stuff works on monkeys?'

'Of course. He's just like a child.'

'Like a goddamned hairy, ugly child with banana breath, huh, Al? I made another funny.'

'Yes, you did, Lew. All right, Captain Wise Guy, you can go in. And take the monkey with you.'

'Can I pet him, Captain Joe?'

'You may, Lewis. But be very careful. Remember, he's still a wild animal at heart. He can only be properly handled in the presence of a professional trainer. He could turn on you in a second. Any second. Remember that.'

They walked hand in hand through the colonnaded ballroom, the professor and his monkey. The room was hung with brocaded draperies and decorated with palm fronds. Gold thread weaved through blood-red velvet in elaborate motifs. As he stopped and studied them, the professor fancied that he could see patterns swirling and forming, stitching and re-stitching before his very eyes. But he had learned never to trust his eyes. His face was flushed with heat and the whisky they had shared from his flask in the cab.

The women were dressed in red, all to a theme. Backless gowns flowed over their breasts and hips and spilled to the floor. Their arms and shoulders were bare except for the occasional sliver of jewellery. Blondes and brunettes spiced with the occasional redhead, all beautiful, all strangely interchangeable. Groups of men in tuxedos and tails gathered around them, proffering martini glasses and cigarettes. In other corners groups of women fluttered around single men, young and old.

This was the endless season of the Hollywood party. Summer nights were filled with buffet dinners around temporary wooden dance floors. Strings of paper lanterns led from one party to another, a peppermint-striped tent filled with music and laughter in every back yard.

Every night was an occasion, every night another show, each blended into the other. Siggy and the professor had seen them all. There were swimming parties, beach parties, tennis parties, croquet parties, country-club parties, cocktail parties, game parties, masquerade parties, invitations that required you to come-as-you-are, others to come-as-you-aren't. There were parties throughout Hollywood and downtown Los Angeles, big and small and invariably drunken. And then there was Mexico – a six-hour drive to the Agua Caliente, with its racetracks, dog tracks, casinos, tennis courts, hot baths and whores.

And here? Where were they now? And why? It didn't matter. The bar was in the far right corner, directly opposite the band. The professor could see raised arms and smiling faces lined around the counter three and four deep. He pushed his way to the front, Siggy wrapped around his right leg, nipping at passing thighs and buttocks with his teeth, and flashing his best show-business smile.

The professor pitched his voice above the noise.

'Two whiskies, straight.'

'Yes, sir, mister. Two whiskies coming right up! Best whisky this side of Prohibition!'

'But we are this side of Prohibition.'

'Yes, sir! That we are, and ain't we all thankful for it!'

'Of course, but I still don't understand your point.'

'My point?'

'About the quality of the whisky, specifically with regard to Prohibition.'

The bartender's fixed smile faded as he moved his head in close. He glanced left and right before he looked at the professor. Their foreheads were almost touching.

'Look, Mac. There is no point, see? It's a line, that's all. A lousy line. I ain't lookin' for no trouble here. I'm the bartender, see? The bartender. This is me behind the bar, and that's you on the other side. So why don't you let me play the bartender and you can play the customer, okay? And play nice.'

His tone was vaguely menacing. It was also familiar. Probably an actor, the professor thought. He was sure he knew the face.

The whiskies soon arrived with a smile and a flourish, the bartender clearly back in character.

'There you go, mister. Two of the best whiskies this side of Prohibition! Enjoy.'

The professor handed one glass to Siggy and held the other before his mouth in a formal salute, looking down at his charge. Siggy copied the gesture. They both emptied their glasses in one clean shot. Siggy shook his head and squealed and handed his glass back to the professor, who placed both glasses on the counter in front of the bartender.

'Two more, please.'

'Jesus, Mac! What have you got down there? A crazy midget or something?'

'Siggy is a chimpanzee.'

'A chimpanzee? You sure it's healthy for a chimpanzee to be drinking this stuff?'

'I am Siggy's trainer. Of course I am sure. Besides, this is the finest whisky this side of Prohibition, is it not? It cannot be bad for his health. Two more, please. And keep them coming.'

Siggy pulled on the professor's arm and lifted himself onto the bar. He sat cross-legged in his little tuxedo jacket and blew the bartender a kiss.

'Hey, Mac! You sure it's safe for him to sit up there?'

'Of course it's safe.'

'But is it, you know, clean?'

'Siggy's backside is far cleaner than yours or mine.'

A voice behind the professor's ear said, 'Speak for yourself, buddy.' Other voices laughed in approval. A crowd was gathering.

'I am Siggy's trainer and I will be responsible for him. He's perfectly safe as long as he is not provoked. Two more whiskies, please.'

'And keep 'em coming, huh?'

'Yes, keep them coming.'

The band picked up its tempo as Siggy and the professor continued to drink. The dance floor began to fill; only the committed drinkers remained. Siggy rewarded them with an impromptu performance, wowing the crowd with a series of backward somersaults and forward rolls – each less steady than the last – along the length of the bar. Glasses were displaced in all directions, but no one seemed to mind.

Siggy was irresistible, eyes wide, jaws stretched in a smile of flashing teeth, hands clapping, head shaking with laughter. He leapt from the bar and swung from the draperies, zipping above the heads of dancers and drinkers alike, swooping on waiters and their trays of canapes until the professor brought him back to ground with a sharp command and the offer of another whisky.

Soon he was scuttling across the dance floor, the professor in hot pursuit. He caught him with his arms around the neck of a platinum blonde, her ample breasts spilling from her dress as Siggy pulled her towards him and puckered his oversized lips for a kiss. He always went for blondes.

The woman was obviously drunk, unsteady on her feet and careless with her naked arms. There were bruises, soft and yellow on her pale white skin. Before the professor could reach her, Siggy had broken the embrace and dashed underneath her skirt. She reacted with anything but alarm.

She was laughing a little girl's laugh as a man grabbed her by the wrist. He was too tall to be an actor, his face brittle and torn. The professor marked him down as a writer.

'Goddamnit, Jean! Not again. You're not happy until you've got something between your legs, is that it? Even a goddamned chimpanzee? Get that thing out of there!'

'Why? He sounds happy enough to me, Paul. Ouch! That tickles! A little to the left please, little friend.'

Siggy pulled the folds of the skirt apart, flashed a wicked grin and then promptly disappeared. The professor was forced to admire his sense of timing.

'So, now he's your little friend, is he?'

'No, Paul. You'll always be my little friend. The littlest of them all.'

'You're a goddamned bitch, Jean. I oughta wipe that smile right off your drunken face.'

She laughed in reply and Siggy joined her with a sharp, infectious cackle from beneath the safety of her skirt.

It was time for the professor to intervene. 'Please, get him out of there.'

'Why, buddy? You got the next ticket?'

'Button it, Paul.'

'That is my monkey. My Siggy. Please, he can't see under there. It could drive him wild.'

'A few more seconds and he'll be driving me wild, mister.'

'Siggy! Out!'

'Aw! Let him play, mister.'

'You don't understand, he's a wild animal.'

'Oh, she understands all right.'

'He could turn on you in a second and rip you to shreds. Any second! Siggy! Out!'

'He sure seems friendly. Hey! Ouch!'

Siggy emerged at the third command, hands over his eyes in mock embarrassment. He looked to the ceiling, laughed sharp and loud, landed a perfect standing back-flip and then he was gone, speeding towards the stairs at the back of the room, the professor in his wake.

Her voice echoed behind them: 'Call my agent!'

At the top of the stairs was a full-length oval mirror with an elaborate gold frame. Siggy was standing before it, mugging at his reflection. By the time the professor caught up he was almost completely out of breath. Heat from his lungs filled his body. His head was, as the Americans so aptly put it, swimming.

'No more, Siggy! Understand? There are important

people here, people we might have a need of one day. Behave yourself. Do not make a fool of me. Breathe. Relax.'

The professor leaned against the mirror, clutching Siggy's wrist. They looked down on the red and black shapes twirling, entwining and falling apart below. The music was loud and insistent; it would not let them stop.

When he closed his eyes the professor saw the dance floor dissolve into a clam-shaped pool, filled with champagne. A dozen women swam naked in the bubbles, gliding on the frothy white surface, turning effortlessly from freestyle to backstroke, rotating their shoulders and parting their legs in slow, deliberate motions. He and Siggy drifted along the bottom of the pool in their tuxedos, watching the women above. Siggy raised a martini glass – the olive broke free and floated slowly towards the surface – and said, 'Obviously I would have preferred a larger dining area, but you can't beat the view.'

The mirror pushed suddenly against the professor's back. It was opening against him. A voice came from behind the glass.

'Hey! Give us a little room here, buddy!'

The mirror opened with a shove. It was hinged at its left side. A man stepped from the door behind it. He was small and bald. He mopped his neck and forehead with a clean white handkerchief.

The voice in the doorway said, 'Better luck next time, Sol. Rules is rules, right? I know you're good for it, but it ain't up to me. Come back when you've got something new to show us.'

The man shuffled away. The mirror stayed open.

'So, you two coming in or what? How long you been waiting? Don't just stand there, boys.'

The professor stepped through the door, Siggy by his side. The mirror closed behind them.

'Whaddaya know – a monkey.'

'Siggy is a chimpanzee.'

'Whatever you say, pal. Down the hall, first right.'

The hall was narrow, barely wide enough for the two of them. The professor ducked his head to avoid the light fittings that illuminated the plaster walls. But ahead was only darkness. A fuzzy light and the clicking sound of a projector spilled from a doorway to the left.

Siggy was already inside when the professor stuck his head around the doorway. It was a small screening room. Four rows of seats, upholstered in rich maroon velvet, faced the screen. Siggy had taken a seat at the front and was gazing up at the screen. Two other men sat in the second row. Another man sat slumped in the back left corner. Cigar smoke filled the room. It swirled and danced through the beam of the projector, thick and white by the lens, a hazy curtain before the screen.

The only sound was that of the projector; the film itself was silent. Old stock, probably. But it was not the kind of film that needed sound. It featured the blonde woman they had met on the dance floor, naked on all fours, smiling a dazed smile to camera. A group of men stood around her. The professor thought he recognised some of them. One was holding up what appeared to be a hot-water bottle.

He did not want Siggy to see this. Siggy, for his part, was fascinated. He did not want to leave. He turned and bared his teeth when the professor pulled on his arm. But the professor was firm of voice and firm of hand. He dragged Siggy from the room and into the hall and pushed him ahead.

There was a distant light to their right. The professor steadied himself by running his fingers along the walls on both sides. The plaster was cool, possibly wet. Soon they began to hear voices. Siggy reached up for the professor's hand.

'Last time I lost this much was down at the Clover. No luck that night. Not much better tonight, goddamnit.'

'Are we bitching and moaning here or are we playing cards?'

'Playing cards, Jack.'

'Then shut the fuck up and play cards.'

'Deal.'

The room was filled with smoke and perspiration, the telltale sweat of gamblers. It was no good having a poker face in this town if your underarms couldn't back you up.

Five men sat around a circular table. All but one had removed their jackets. There was a large pile of cash in the centre of the table. Three other men stood by a small bar at the far corner. One was Siggy's agent, Harry Finkelstein. The other two were the muscle they'd met at the front door, Al and Lewis. All three nodded at the professor's entrance. Harry put his hand to his lips to indicate they should keep quiet.

'Give me two, Sam.'

'Lew, get me a drink.'

'Sure thing, Mr Jack.'

'Goddamnit, Irving, don't you ever fucking sweat?'

'Sometimes at tennis, Bud. Never at the table.'

'Little prick.'

'I'll take one.'

Siggy was walking slowly around the table, chattering softly to himself. He climbed the back of a chair and began peering over one of the men's shoulders. The man turned his head to look at Siggy. Siggy kissed him. The man sprang to his feet, holding his fanned cards against his hip.

'What the fuck? Hey, what gives here? This monkey's looking at my cards.'

'What are you talking about, Jack?'

'You know goddamn well what I'm talking about. This monkey's looking at my cards. It's a goddamned card monkey! I've heard about this scam before. Monkeys, chickens, dogs – you name it. Who set this up? Was it you, Sam? Bud? How about you? You need a fucking card monkey now, huh?'

'Jack, do you have any idea how absurd you sound? That's Siggy the Wonder Chimp. He's one of ours.'

'I know he's one of yours, Irving.'

'Oh, Jesus, Jack – come on.'

'Please, sir. Don't antagonise him. Let me look after

him. He could turn on you in a second. Any second! Siggy! Come!'

Siggy ran to the professor's side.

'And who the fuck is this? Get this goddamned monkey out of here. Al, Lew – take care of it.'

'What do you want us to do, Mr Jack?'

'Put a goddamned bullet in it for all I care.'

'Now, Jack, don't be stupid. That monkey is valuable studio property, and I won't have him tampered with in any way. He's contracted for at least another two pictures, and who knows what other opportunities might arise? You might even want us to lend him out one day.'

'What about the other guy?'

'That's Captain Joe. He's the trainer. He's Hungarian.'

'Any objection if the boys work him over a little?'

'None spring to mind. Who let him in, anyway?'

The professor looked at Harry for support, but Harry couldn't help him. He simply looked at the floor. Al and Lew looked at each other. For a second, no one said a word.

'All right, boys, get these two out of here. Take 'em out the back way, understand? Work the Hungarian over. Soften him up a little. Doesn't look like he'll feel it much anyway. Have a little fun. But leave the monkey alone, okay?'

'Yes, sir, Mr Jack.'

Lew took Siggy by the hand and walked him out the door. Al's large hand clasped the professor's shoulder and pushed him after them. His legs were not his own.

The hallway had become a tunnel. He heard Lew's voice just ahead of him, soothing Siggy and urging him on, but he could see only dim shapes in the darkness. He could smell the damp earth around him.

He needed a drink.

A voice whispered in his ear, soft as a lover's lie.

'Sorry, Cap. Believe me, this is going to hurt me a lot more than it's going to hurt you.'

A light was approaching, faster and faster.

Dorian Mode

The Final Diaries of Herman Garfield

Herman W. Garfield. Early thirties, pebble glasses, grey cardigan, suede shoes. If it weren't for his Woody Herman record collection and his extensive knowledge of earthworms, he'd be considered boring.

I met Herman one night when I needed a horn player for a gig in a local restaurant up here on the Coast (yes, I'd really made the big time). I usually did it as a duo with Johnny, a local tenor player who had a style that was a cross between late 60s Stan Getz and early 70s Pol Pot. Johnny was notorious for putting dud musicians in at the last minute and then not answering his phone for a week till you cooled off. But Herman was . . . How can I put it? . . . a 'unique experience'.

Herman could play all right. He was the sort of player who could read fly shit but couldn't improvise a fart after lentil soup. Another problem was that he turned up to the gig in a tuxedo and tails. (Perhaps a little formal for a Chinese restaurant in West Gosford.)

After the first song I could see it was going to be a long night. There's nothing worse than someone who thinks they can improvise but can't. He also had a terrible habit of doing a kind of jig as he soloed. This made him look like Mr Bean's slightly musical brother.

The gig mercifully finished. As we ate our complimentary noodles (oh, there were perks!), we shared a beer together and chatted. I must say, I enjoyed talking to Herman. Behind thick lenses, his eyes darted like two blue fish as he made wild predictions and waxed lyrical about music and art. In hindsight, had I known he was bipolar, I would've been less flippant with him in the months to follow. (No doubt you'll think I'm an unfeeling creep when you read these diaries.)

Anyway, after that gig he called me from time to time. (If you weren't careful he'd trap you for hours about earthworms.) I even visited him once. He lived in a Brontë-esque Victorian mansion that had been converted into boxy flats. It was dark and mouldy and smelt of cabbage. I remember his landlady. Hair pinned above her head into a skyscraper, peering at me through a crack in her chain-secured door as I climbed the staircase.

In a Sophoclean turn of events, the police presented me with his personal effects several months ago. Apparently my card was found among his things. As I opened the brown-paper-and-string parcel, which was tied with Boy Scout fastidiousness, I found Herman. A pair of Coke-bottle specs, a shining clarinet, some Woody Herman records and these diaries.

(I must confess to editing some of the entries.)

22 January

Tonight's the night. I will kill myself.

I leave my 1952 Silver Anniversary Buffet clarinet and my entire Woody Herman record collection, including *Woody – Live at Stockholm* (valued at $550) to colleague and new friend, Dorian Mode. My earthworms, including 'Thor' (*Lumbricus terrestris*), I leave to Sebastian Scholemski at Northern Worms.

These people have been my only friends.

23 January

I am a failure.

I've bungled it AGAIN! I tied the rope around the light fitting, jumped off my reproduction olde worlde VCR cabinet (that I'd just finished paying off), and the entire light fitting detached from the ceiling. I nearly broke my damn neck! (I blame inferior workmanship and a general lack of pride in the building industry.) The cursed thing dangles above me like a boa constrictor as I write, mocking me! To make matters worse, my Landlady – Mrs Warboys – bullied her way in after she heard the noise. She saw the rope, the light fitting, the plaster, and put two and two together. She also saw the damage to the bedroom, where I tried to shoot myself on Thursday and – not realising it was a flare gun – set fire to the drapes.

She is not a happy woman.

27 January

Mrs Warboys presented me with a bill last night. She's told me I am not to kill myself until I pay for the damage (in full!), which she estimates at $2678.50!!! I am, however, insolvent. Must call Dorian about launching my jazz career again. Can't leave this earth a debtor! Left message for him at 11:30 a.m. No reply.

Prediction: Woody Herman will become THE musician of choice for young people by 2005.

1 February

Mrs Warboys has come up with a scheme for me to pay back the debt. She says I am to have *sex* with her!

She says that each time I do this I will reduce the debt, after which I can do with my life as I please. God! I haven't had sex since that terrible episode with Margaret at the Scouts–Guides Ball. (My head still spins at the thought.) My woggle kept getting caught in her orienteering pin. (We'd both had one too many West Coast Coolers.) Akela had to separate us in the end. Horrible.

What to do???

Idea for a movie: Gifted clarinet player kills his landlady in order to avoid sex.

8 February

Dorian Mode hasn't returned my calls. Therefore, I have no further bookings at the Imperial Duck. Have no choice other than to have sex with Mrs Warboys.

Feeling anxious . . .

10 February

Last night is over. THANK GOD!!! Mrs Warboys came to my flat in her fluffy pink dressing gown, dropped it to the floor, lowered a spinnaker of underwear and told me, in the voice of a schoolmistress, to remove my clothes. (However, I must say, for a woman in her early fifties, she has the body of a twenty-year-old.)* She threw herself on my bed, opened her legs and started reading a book on the late Princess Diana, then said: 'Let's get on with the arrangement, Mr Garfield. I'm icing a cake in half an hour.'

As I was engaged in 'sexual relations' with her, she didn't ONCE look up from her book. So to get her back, I started reading the newspaper. (I imagine this is what they mean by 'casual sex'.)

Anyway, I was in the middle of a very interesting article on organic farming when I heard Mrs Warboys say in a deadpan voice, 'I'm coming, Mr Garfield.'

My musical ears detected her breathing grow slightly heavier as she turned the pages of her book. Then she said, 'You may remove yourself, Mr Garfield. You now only owe

---

* Having met Herman's landlady, this is a slight exaggeration. D.M.

$2648.50.' I argued that I should only owe $2578.50! After much heated debate we split the difference.

God, I hate this woman!

Current debt: $2628.50

13 February

Dorian Mode FINALLY called today. Told him I planned to kill myself this month. He said I should read something to cheer myself up. He's suggested Nietzsche. I need some light reading. Will visit the secondhand bookshop tomorrow.

2 March

Have reduced debt considerably and am feeling quite cheerful, so I'm thinking about killing myself again. Mrs Warboys has offered to help after I service the debt (sweet). She is connected to the Internet and says there are websites for help with suicides. She found one today called www.pop-your-cloggs.com.

Current debt: $2078.50

13 March

Someone called today trying to sell me a *Eudrilus Eugeniae*. I said that that kind of earthworm hasn't been allowed into Australia since 1964 and I don't buy black-market worms. Then I heard a giggle on the phone. It was Sebastian. My musician's ears normally pick people using cunning disguises. Anyway, he said the worm farm is making a good profit now (after five years!) and has asked me over on Thursday to help him with some soil shipments (his car's blown AGAIN!). Told him I have to kill myself on Thursday so could we possibly arrange it for Wednesday. He giggled. Why don't people take me *seriously*? Must be the glasses. People say they make me look intellectual.

Idea for a novel: An earthworm farmer is tragically killed when a truckload of soil is dumped on him after hearing about a friend's sudden suicide.

21 March

I think Dorian Mode was being sarcastic when he suggested reading Nietzsche. I don't find his style funny at all. Left another message on his machine. No reply. I'm starting to think Dorian Mode is an Ar*#hole. Why can't people be more like the noble earthworm?

29 March

Mrs Warboys isn't so bad, really. Her insatiable desire for sex is not her fault. I blame technology. You see, Mrs Warboys has a chihuahua named Mr Biggles. She presents

Mr Biggles at dog shows etcetera. She has also recently discovered the internet. She showed me how it all started (poor thing). She typed into what's called a 'Search Engine', the words: 'Dog' and 'Style'. You wouldn't BELIEVE the filth that came up. I turned red. Mrs Warboys and I were instantly forced to have sex. (None of us are immune to its power!) You see, Mrs Warboys has led a sheltered life. She always thought pornography was the study of people living in Third-World countries.

Current debt: $1778.50

10 April

Perhaps I was a little hasty in my condemnation of Dorian Mode. This Nietzsche says, *When stepped on, an earthworm doubles up. That is clever. In that way he lessens the probability of being stepped on again. In the language of morality: humility.*

Exactly!

23 April

Mrs Warboys and I are starting to become good friends. I've even asked her if she would mind not reading while we are having sex. She explained she does this because she finds it hard to relax. This makes sense because I in fact read to get to sleep. (My mind buzzes all night with ideas.) I've also asked her to not tell me so 'dryly' when she is 'coming' (a word she picked up on the Internet i.e. having an or#*sm). We have agreed that, from now on, in order for me to know when she is having an or#*sm, she will hum the Petula Clark classic 'Downtown' (a song played on her honeymoon). I argued for Mozart's Clarinet Concerto but she found the adagio difficult – and she said my correcting her kept 'spoiling the moment'.

Current debt: $1478.50

30 April

Had sex with Mrs Warboys again. She asked me to dress up as a pizza boy (something she'd seen on the internet). I almost climaxed until she screamed: 'Burt Lancaster!' (From now on I've asked her to turn off 'Sale of the Century' while we are having sex.)

Idea for TV Show: Game show all about sex (innuendo etcetera), featuring the music of Woody Herman. Possible working title: Woody's Woody.

Current debt: $1328.50

9 May

Left ANOTHER message for Dorian Mode. No reply.*

---

* I was out of town. Well, I was thinking about going out of town – which is the same thing really.

16 May

Had sex on Mrs Warboys' kitchen floor (something she'd seen on the internet). Mrs Warboys has a nice flat – albeit dark. As a heartfelt tribute to her deceased chihuahuas, she's had them all stuffed. They are scattered around the flat like hairy Egyptian statues. The one in the toilet, Mr Tibbs, is losing his fur so he looks a little scary.

She's also an expert on Lady Diana Spencer. She can tell you where she went to school, her first boyfriend, her shoe size, everything! Another remarkable quality is her psychic powers. (I call it a gift.) She reads tea-leaves! She told me today that I have a lot of 'brown stains' in my life – which is amazing, because that's exactly how I feel!

Idea for a documentary: Psychics of Woy Woy.

Finally seen what *Mr* Warboys looks like (I should say *looked* like – he died in a tragic swimming accident in The Hyde Park Fountain). In some photos he looks like Sean Connery, others Robert Redford. Another, the spitting image of Michael Caine. A very handsome man to say the least. God knows what she sees in me! (Must be the clarinet – sends some women wild with lust.)

Current debt: $1178.50

29 May

Think I'm falling in love with 'X'. If I can just get 'X's chihuahua to stop growling at me when we have sex. Actually considering asking 'X' to marry me!

31 May

Today, I told 'X' (i.e. Mrs Warboys) that I'm in love with her. She seemed angry and asked me not to say it again. Wasn't what I expected.

What to do?

1 June

Mrs Warboys read my tea this morning and says I am 'very leafy' at the moment! This means I am to come into money, apparently. She's said nothing about last night and my declaration of love for her. Although, something odd happened. We had sex today and she started to cry. Didn't know what to do. All I could do was to cradle her like a newborn child.

It was the most intense and loving experience of my life.

12 June

Asked Mrs Warboys to marry me today. And . . . she's accepted!!! Called Dorian Mode and left message asking if he'd be Best Man. He called back to say he'd be delighted. Hope this doesn't offend Sebastian (an older friend) but jazz musicians are kindred spirits.

Prediction: More young men will marry older women by the year 2007.

22 June

To celebrate our engagement, I have decided to treat Mrs Warboys to a big night out! Had planned to take her to Lithgow to see the glow-worms (very romantic), then off to the trout farm. But it's a long way in a Gogomobile. So, since she's predicted I'm to come into money, AND she likes dogs, I've decided to take her to the greyhound racing at West Gosford! Perfect!

27 June

Last night was intense.

We had a delightful à la carte meal at the track in the exclusive *Muzzles* restaurant. After the soup, I gave her the engagement ring that I had been fastidiously paying off. (Genuine diamantés in a nine-carat-gold setting.) I don't know what she thought of it. She has literally drawers full of jewellery at home. (She says they're all fakes.) Anyway, she seemed pleased. I noticed her eyes seemed to sparkle in the artificial candlelight.

After TWO helpings of oysters, Mrs Warboys (tipsy

from the Baileys and wild with desire from the oysters) called me into the men's toilet to have sex with her (something she'd seen on the internet). Mrs Warboys was leaning over the basin, knitting (she was making a new outfit for Mr Biggles), while I was engaged in sexual relations with her from behind, when she said: 'I believe we have a spectator, Mr Garfield'. I looked up as an elderly gentleman, in a beige safari suit, flushed and raced out of the bathroom (without being able to 'go').

As we continued, Mrs Warboys unexpectedly started screaming: 'Yes! Yes! YES!' This got me quite excited until I realised she was listening to her race over the speakers that were piped into the toilets. (She won $167.80.)

We went back and ate our main course with good appetite. I had Lemon Sole. Mrs Warboys had Beef Wellington – a little overcooked we thought. (Oh, now we are formally engaged she has asked me to call her 'Mildred'. Difficult. I've called her Mrs Warboys for some time now.)

It was after dining that the shameful incident occurred.

While collecting our winnings, I presented the bookmaker with the ticket. He said 'Congratulations!' I told him that it wasn't for me but for a 'special lady' in my life. I glanced over at Mrs Warboys. He handed me the cash and said: 'I hope your mother has a nice evening.' I was outraged. I told the man that she was not my MOTHER but my future WIFE! He sniggered and turned his back on me. The rude ba#*ard! I insisted he immediately apologise. Then I heard Mrs Warboys say in a quiet voice: 'No, he's quite right, Mr Garfield.' She gave me back the ring and walked away.

Then the bookmaker fired some vulgar words at me and a scuffle ensued. Security was called and I was punched in the face and ribs and thrown out of the ground. (Must remember to write to my local MP about it!) Before I knew what was happening, she'd vanished.

Knocked on her door this morning but no answer.

1 July

Been knocking on Mrs Warboys' door for days now. No answer. Perhaps she's gone to her sister's. If ONLY I could remember the address!

Feeling anxious.

3 July

Devastated.

I finally crawled through a bathroom window to find Mrs Warboys lying dead. She'd killed herself using information she'd got for me over the internet. Called the authorities and was asked several questions by an indifferent police sergeant eating a packet of jelly babies.

I feel as if my soul has been wrenched from my body.

9 July

Crying for days now. Can't write.

18 July

Too sad to eat.

25 July

The doctor has put me on some temporary medication for depression. Seems to be helping.

2 August

Been looking into my teacup for answers. Sadly, I don't have the gift. Although, I don't recall Mrs Warboys using tea bags.

4 August

What am I meant to learn from all this, for God's Sake???
Nietzsche says *In pain there is as much wisdom as in pleasure*, but he suffered from syphilis.

6 August

Mrs Warboys' sister (who pulled up in a Rolls-Royce) came and took the dog and cleaned out her apartment.

She told me that Mrs Warboys had been suffering from depression for some time and had attempted suicide on several occasions. She also said that Mrs Warboys had never married. She'd simply cut out pictures of movie stars from magazines and placed them in frames.

3 September

Been sitting in Mrs Warboys' apartment every day for a month, now. Each day I watch the motes of dust dance in the sunlight that streams through the curtain-less window. The only thing of her that remains is a dying aspidistra.

Watered the aspidistra.

8 September

Noticed the aspidistra seems to lean towards the kitchen. Wonder what's so important about the kitchen? Must be the moisture.

Think I will kill myself tonight.

Must find someone to water the aspidistra first. Mrs Warboys would want that.

13 September

I've realised that the aspidistra is not leaning towards the kitchen, it's leaning towards the sun!

Is this a sign from Mrs Warboys???

16 September

Have placed the aspidistra directly in the sunlight. It's sprouting new shoots! Mrs Warboys would be most pleased.

20 September

Incredible news! Her prediction came true! I'm a rich man. Turns out Mrs Warboys was a multi-millionaire! Not only did she own her flat but the entire building! (And several others across the state!) Her solicitor informed me that I would never have to work again! Feeling stressed, though. Had planned to kill myself this week but have to put it off to fill out forms and receive the money etcetera.

10 October

Received the money today. Fifteen million! (My God!)

25 October

I have decided people are more like plants than earthworms. Earthworms don't need light. They burrow deep into the earth and live in perpetual darkness. Humans need light. So, before my departure, I've installed skylights in the entire building. It's now a palace of golden sunlight. The tenants seemed most excited. People who have never said 'boo' to me were running around like children, shaking my hand, smiling. Wonderful.

Still missing Mrs Warboys, though. My heart aches to write her name.

14 November

Bought a BMW today. Gave it to Sebastian (with my entire worm collection). He didn't recognise me at first (till I started giggling). You see, I've thrown away my glasses (laser surgery), given my clothes back to the Salvation Army, and bought an entire new wardrobe from a place called Armani (the salesman was most helpful), and have a completely new hairstyle (bit trendy for me but I'm getting used to it).

I know I'll never see him again so, before I left, I hugged him and said, 'People are more interesting than worms, Sebastian.'

I left him with the keys and paperwork. He had a look on his face as if I'd hit him over the head with a frying pan!

25 December: Christmas Day

At sunset, I sprinkled Mrs Warboys' ashes at Terrigal Beach. I leave for Italy tomorrow. I have come to the conclusion that it is wrong to kill yourself. When you die, you are buried and eaten by worms. We are put here on this earth to LIVE – in the light! Not be buried in dark earth. I will spend the rest of my life chasing the summer across the globe. Have started reading more Nietzsche – and Spinoza and Descartes, too. Want to find out more about them. Where they lived. Why they thought the way they did. I want to find out more about people.

Whoever finds this diary I want you to know that Herman Garfield *did* kill himself but was reborn.

I love you Mildred Warboys.

XXX

Prediction: The clarinet will have a major impact on the heavy rock scene in Europe over the next ten years!

Steve Coogan's

Top Ten

1. 'The First Time Ever I Saw Your Face' – Roberta Flack

2. 'All the Time in the World' – Louis Armstrong

3. 'Life on Mars?' – David Bowie

4. 'Anarchy in the UK' – The Sex Pistols

5. 'Shipbuilding' – Elvis Costello

6. 'Kinky Afro' – Happy Mondays

7. 'Casino Royale' – Burt Bacharach

8. 'Love and Affection' – Joan Armatrading

9. 'I Close My Eyes and Count to Ten' – Dusty Springfield

10. 'Ever Fallen in Love (With Someone You Shouldn't Have)?' – Buzzcocks

Max Sharam

Essential Listening for a Big Night Out

I was recently taken out on a date here in Los Angeles, and was picked up in the new Sports Jaguar by a guy that many local women would consider 'a real catch' – independently wealthy, a trust fund baby, only-child and sole heir to the family inheritance, tall, generous, articulate, the list goes on. Personally, I find him obnoxious, seedy, (did I mention bald?), and the tone of his incessant voice grates on my nerves, but he does his homework. I got in the car and there it was: David Bowie's 'Aladdin Sane' coming through his choice Bose sound system. I didn't say a word. I just relaxed back into the sculptured leather seats, relieved at what could have been a cacophonous cocooning. I could be taken anywhere, with anyone, if they play me 'Aladdin Sane' on a judicious sound system.

The guy didn't get laid but I'm sure he got off on the fact that he hit the nail on the head with his musical selection. Some may consider that first base.

The other essential song for the chicks when we hit the

road to go snowboarding is Cake's version of 'I Will Survive'. That song does it for us as a girl-group (as in a group of girls together) – regardless of sexual preferences.

The all-time favourite songs that still really do it for me though – timeless masterpieces – are 'Can We Still Be Friends?' by Todd Rundgren and 'Is This Love?' by Bob Marley. I'm not sure if it's just magical memories/associations or that these song titles both end in question marks, but nonetheless you will always get a reaction out of me when I hear them.

Michael Witheford

Time Gentlemen

'You'll have to go up another step,' said Andy who was in no danger.

Steve, who soon would be, replied, 'Have you seen *Vertigo*?'

'Ooh yeah, Kim Novak. Now was that Jimmy Stew— ?'

'You bastard . . . unscrew!'

Steve teetered on the penultimate rung of a flimsy stepladder. He waved an arm and a leg in the air, struggling for balance, like a kid with comically poor motor skills attempting ballet. Four spidery fingers brushed the bottom of the blown light-globe but a decent purchase was agonisingly elusive.

'. . . or was it Cary Grant?' Andy continued. He looked up. 'You'll have to go up an—'

'Yes, you just said that and I'd rather not. I can see the curve of the Earth already.'

'I've got you,' Andy lied.

'No, you've got my trouser leg. That's not me.'

From the safety of the floor, Andy kept a desultory hold on one of the splayed legs of the ladder. He did have that fistful of denim, too, but it served no real practical purpose, and was of no reassurance to Steve either.

'Ice began to form on Steve's upper slopes,' Andy chuckled quietly to himself.

The distance to the light (which swayed on a cord about a foot below the high Victorian ceiling) wasn't as much a problem as the need for a vertical viewpoint. Steve was forced to peer directly above, losing any perspective of a 'horizon', and his inner-ear equilibrium wasn't designed for these sorts of challenges. Dots danced crazily before his eyes, and the visual periphery around the light-globe merged into an amorphous mass.

After stretching every tendon and cartilage to snapping point without success, Steve sucked down several hard breaths and reluctantly wobbled onto the top step of the ladder. Once more he lifted his head in slow deliberation, as if following the trajectory of a rocket on take-off, until he was eyeballing the ceiling again. His buttocks clenched reflexively in raw terror.

'You want to be careful now,' Andy advised.

Steve would have cast a downward look of disdain if it hadn't meant another perilous bodily adjustment. Instead he panted, 'Right, just catch me if I —'

'Go ass over,' Andy interjected nonchalantly. 'That's what I'm here for.'

'No, you're here because you knew I had beer in the fridge and twenty channels of cable,' Steve muttered under his breath, as though the vibration from his regular voice might precipitate a seismic jolt. 'Oh shit . . . this is scary. Okay, unscrewing, unscrewing. Give us the other bulb.'

Andy looked around. 'It's on the bed. Hang on.'

'I haven't got anything to hang on *to*, you prat!' Steve yelped. 'Don't let go!'

'It's over here,' said Andy, deserting his post.

As he pulled the new light from its box, an unnerving wail chilled his blood. It was the sort of nerve-strafing noise he most feared, and it made him wish he'd stayed at home.

'Oh! . . . Woh! . . . Woh!'

Andy knew what that baleful, funereal complaint meant, and spun around with his arms instantly stretched out in a slips-catching position.

High above – and Andy noticed now just how far it was from the floor to the pressed-metal ceiling – Steve was lurching to and fro, fighting to correct what was clearly a serious imbalance.

'Fuck! Aaaargh! Wohhh!'

Andy had visions of Buster Keaton, Charlie Chaplin and Harold . . . Harold . . . that silent movie bloke who hung off the clock hands twenty storeys up and seemed destined for a messy end as pavement pizza. Andy supposed it wasn't really the time to ask if Steve could provide the bespectacled comedian's surname, since he was in a bit of a situation himself. Andy never thought silent movies were funny and he wasn't especially amused now – the sight of Steve flailing at the air might, in retro-spect, be viewed as classic real-life slapstick, but right now it was a problem. A potential disaster.

Andy watched helplessly as his stricken chum thrust himself first forward into the position of a downhill skier, arms windmilling in a desperate flap, then, in an over-correction, violently back up and beyond the vertical, causing his spine to arc like a spinnaker. This futile adop-tion of two equally catastrophic positions must have been repeated four times at least, as Andy, hoping to calculate which gravitational travesty would finally bring his friend closer to him, shuffled from side to side below.

'Woagh . . . naarg!' cried Steve, clearly unhappy.

When he inevitably lost the battle to regain his compo-sure and crashed to the floor – in the exact spot where Andy wasn't – the noise was tremendous and split into three impacts. First there was the thick, wall-quaking *thud* of Steve landing on his side, then a nanosecond later the resounding *bonk* of his head bouncing off the floor, and finally the *shriek* of the stepladder smashing onto a small table, sending mugs and a teapot to all corners of the room.

'Oh shite. Steve? Can you hear me?' Andy shouted, gently patting Steve's face.

Steve was out cold for about ten seconds.

'Steve, say something, man!'

Andy discerned a faint gurgle. 'Oh, thank Christ you're alive.'

Another gurgle. It sounded to Andy like 'Oo super car' or maybe 'Oops soup can'.

'Speak up, mate, what is it?'

Steve hissed, 'You . . . stupid . . . cu—'

'Wahaay, that's the way!' Andy laughed. 'You're all right then.'

Steve groaned. 'My head really fucking hurts.'

'Yeah, well, that's where you landed,' Andy said helpfully. 'Better get you down the bathroom. See what the damage is.'

Steve gingerly reached out an arm and was pulled roughly to his feet. A tsunami of crashing pain surged through his skull.

'Woagh!' He bent over and gripped his head like a football.

'Remember that bit in *Withnail and I*,' said Andy, 'when Withnail says "I feel like a pig shat in my head"? Is that what it feels like?'

'I might have a fractured skull, you twat!' complained Steve in a voice loud enough to make his head throb even more. 'I might have bloody internal . . . bleeding. Jesus, you might have to drill a hole in my skull.'

'Oh shit, no, I can't do that, man,' Andy grinned, no longer especially concerned about Steve. 'I wouldn't know what size "bit" to use to start with. Could ask the man at the hardware store, I suppose.'

'Wanker,' Steve grumbled as he shook off Andy's arm and made for the bathroom mirror.

'Harold *Lloyd*!' Andy trumpeted triumphantly.

'What?' whispered Steve.

'Nothing.'

Fossicking gingerly through his dark messy hair, Steve located the burgeoning lump, but no blood, no pulped tissue or jutting bone. He winced as he touched the spot and attempted to subjugate the pain by fiercely shutting his eyes. As he did this, something very strange happened . . .

In vivid colour, in full virtual wide-screen, Steve saw Andy in the kitchen drinking a beer and rummaging in the cupboards for food to steal. Steve instantly opened his eyes and stared at the mirror. Andy was standing by the door. Steve looked at him quizzically.

'What?' asked Andy.

'Nothing,' Steve replied after a long pause. He found two Panadol, filled a glass with water and leaned back to swallow the pills, once more closing his eyes. It happened again: another DVD-quality projection against the black screen of his eyelids, this time featuring him handing the telephone receiver over to Andy, who was wearing a palpable (and quite new to Steve) expression of shock. The tablets almost stuck in Steve's gullet.

'Okay,' Steve thought aloud, eyes wide open and barely daring to blink. 'Just a bit of concussion. Nothing to worry about.'

'Bit dizzy, are you?' Andy enquired. 'Fancy a lie-down?'

Steve leaned against the sink for some time before tentatively shutting his eyelids, hoping his brain would have perhaps re-calibrated, and that he'd just experienced an extravagant version of 'seeing stars'. It wasn't to be. This time, instead of darkness, there was Andy again, back in the carnage of the bedroom, gesticulating frenetically about something. Steve shouted 'Aaargh!'

Andy jumped. 'What the fuck's going on?' he cried.

'I'm seeing things,' said Steve.

'What, dead people?' Andy laughed nervously. Steve didn't laugh so Andy coughed politely.

'When I close my eyes,' Steve said, wandering into the kitchen, rubbing his chin, 'I can see —'

And turning around, that's when he became seriously spooked. He saw Andy drinking a beer and rummaging in the cupboards looking for food – again. Clearly this was no ordinary bump on the head.

'. . . I can see into the future,' Steve finally mumbled ruefully as Andy swigged on a Melbourne Bitter and rummaged for finger food.

Andy paused, his stubbie a few inches from his face, and his mouth frozen in an 'O'.

'Oh . . .' he offered, after a pause so pregnant it almost gave birth. 'Look, mate, maybe we should get you checked out. I think you've done yourself a bit of mischief, and —'

'The phone's going to ring and it'll be for you,' Steve murmured.

'Why would anybody ring me here?' Andy asked, and casually quaffed his beer. After a stentorian belch, he continued, 'I mean, I only came round because —'

The phone rang. Steve inhaled noisily and raised his eyebrows as he slipped past Andy and ventured down the hallway.

Andy stood in the kitchen perplexed, still holding his beer as though it were a microphone.

'It's for you,' Steve shouted, after a brief exchange with the caller.

'Jesus,' Andy muttered, shuffling towards Steve and taking the receiver. 'Hello . . . Oh hi . . . No, Steve needed a hand with a globe . . . A light-globe . . . Well, it wasn't an ordinary job . . . Um, I'm not sure. He's hurt his head, so I'm just making sure he's not clairvoyant . . . What? . . . I said concussed, didn't I? . . . Did I? Um, well, look, do you want me to ring you later? Okay . . . Bye.'

Andy hung up, and looked at Steve. 'It's a wind-up.'

'Oh, of course it is,' spat Steve. 'I told Jen I had this total wheeze of a trick to play: at 9.17 p.m I'd dive head-first into the ground from six feet up, and then she should ring at 9.25 to make you think I'd transmogrified into Nostrafuckingdamus. Fuck off!'

Andy rubbed his chin with the neck of his stubbie. 'How long?'

'Eh?'

'How long between what you see happening and when it actually . . . transpires?'

Steve shrugged. 'About three minutes.'

'Try it again.'

Steve closed his eyes. He'd worked through the shock, and was becoming acclimatised to this pre-empting of his experiences. 'We're in your car driving down Bridge Road towards town.'

The fear had also subsided, and now Steve was bristling with annoyance instead. A quiet, unobtrusive chap, he was stalked by small-scale, localised disasters. They trailed around after him. And being slightly vague and easily distracted, he was often asking for it: forgetting food was in the oven until the smoke detector deployed with a panicked squeal, or running a bath and losing himself in a magazine article before being alerted to the sound of waves breaking on the stairs.

Steve was tall and dark, and enigmatically handsome, but lacked confidence with women. He'd been single for a few years now, having almost married a girl he taught with at a local high school. Andy had eventually convinced him she was too straight for his lifestyle, which essentially meant Andy feared losing his drinking buddy. Andy, after all, was shorter, stockier and less likely to inspire admiring glances. He was, however, blessed with indomitable self-belief, and could generally disarm girls if given an opportunity.

'Short people have built-in charisma,' was his dubious mantra often trotted out after the fifth or sixth beer. 'Pacino, Hoffman, De Niro . . . Bonaparte.' But he needed Steve as a tag-team partner, to pique that initial interest from women who might have otherwise given him short shrift.

'So . . . do you know why you can see us in the car, my dear Watson?' Andy whispered mischievously.

Steve shrugged. 'You're taking me to see the men in white coats?'

Andy shook his head piteously. 'We're going to the casino to win an absolute shed-load of cash! Wahaay!'

Andy had rapidly decided that unless Steve began oozing blood from both ears, this extrasensory power would not remain a private medical matter. After all, Steve could scarcely say no, unless he was as mad as cheese.

'We'll get caught,' Steve half-heartedly pleaded.

'Caught!' Andy guffawed. 'This is not cheating, my friend. This is undetectable magic. This is conjuring with no sleight of hand and no rational explanation – no matter how many times they watch the surveillance tapes.'

Andy pushed a reluctant Steve towards the bedroom, and continued to rant. 'You look at the numbers on a roulette table totem pole . . . in your mind's eye that is, and when you coordinate what's happening in real time . . . probably a three-spin lag, we break the Bank of Monte Melbourne.'

'I saw this,' Steve sighed.

'What?' Andy asked.

'You giving me this ear-bashing.'

'Fuck, it's really happening, isn't it?' Andy muttered. 'Well, you also saw us in the motor vehicle so get your shoes changed and let's rock.'

Steve had to privately acknowledge that Andy's was a foolproof plan, and God knows he could do with the money. The mortgage on his small terrace house was a killer. His head hurt, he was confused and he wished he could go to bed, but there was no denying he was in a profoundly exploitable situation. If things stayed this way there'd be no hurry. He could casually bet on a few horses tomorrow and win thousands, but if the lump wasn't going to last forever then maybe his status as soothsayer wouldn't either.

Andy started the car and they headed towards the city.

'Shit,' Andy said, braking at a set of lights on Flinders Street.

'Problem?' Steve asked.

'What if you see something, and we do the opposite,' Andy mused. 'Like, say you see us park on Level 2, and we deliberately park on Level 3. Oh, fuck, this is doing my head in.'

Steve had a think. 'Maybe we should just follow the flow and worry about the actual technicalities of this later.'

'Yes,' nodded Andy. 'Yes, brilliant! In fact, don't close your eyes too much. We can't risk the reward.'

'No, never mind the fact that fucking with the formula might detonate my brain, killing me instantly,' said a disgusted Steve.

Andy wasn't listening. 'Can you just give it a whirl for a tick?'

Steve sighed and shut his eyes. 'Looks like we're parking.'

'Oh hell!'

'It's okay. I don't know where.'

'Good, good. Fine,' said Andy, soaking in his own adrenaline.

The casino was crowded with a prime-time Saturday night crowd as Steve and Andy entered the gaming area. A cataclysm of flashing neon made empty promises of unlikely wealth. Machines beeped and pinged and rattled.

Unhappy-looking people joylessly punched the buttons of poker machines, and small crowds aggregated around blackjack tables.

'We'll have to do this in bits,' Steve said. 'No massively unlikely wins, just extreme good fortune. We don't want to draw attention to ourselves.'

'Yeah, right,' said Andy, eyes darting around, not listening.

Steve closed his eyes, stroking his eyebrows with one hand to appear merely tired.

'Are you okay?' Andy asked.

'Reviewing the situation,' Steve said. 'We're at a table.'

'Which one?'

'The one we're at,' said Steve and began walking through the room. Andy followed.

A few minutes later they nestled into a free spot on a five-dollar roulette table. Steve grabbed one of the pencils and number sheets provided for those who believed the run of spins had some sort of predictability.

'Write these down,' said Steve, handing paper and pencil to Andy and doing the shut-eye bit-of-a-headache thing again. '. . . Thirteen, thirty-six, thirty-four, three, eight, twenty-two.' These were the numbers that the silver ball would soon visit – numbers from the future displayed on an electronic score-pole beside the table. This was the knowledge gamblers are granted in their dreams. Destiny sat in the palm of Steve's hands. Absolute power was there for the taking. Never mind Packer and Murdoch, Gates or Branson. He could give God a run for his money.

The croupier whipped the ball into the slowly rotating wheel. 'Last bets . . . no more bets.' She spread her arms across the table. The ball clanked and bounced before settling.

'Thirty-four black.'

'Right,' said Steve, now fully informed about the result of the next spin. He began shuffling through the pockets of his jacket for a long time. 'Bollocks.'

Andy looked at Steve, who said, 'Forgot my wallet. What have you got?'

Andy fearfully thrust his hands into his jeans, finally locating a note. 'Ten . . . only a bloody ten!'

'That's fine,' said Steve, and dropped the note on the table. After paying the winners and herding the lost chips down a metallic funnel in the table, the croupier looked at the money, then looked at Steve with stiff-necked contempt. 'Cash fives please,' Steve said sheepishly.

'She'll not be looking so smug in a minute,' Andy smiled.

'Would you like to put the chips on number three then?' Steve said. Andy complied.

'Well I never . . . Can you believe that? Who'd have thought?' Andy made a bit of a meal of the win, as the ten dollars returned an instant 350.

The money was soon elongated by several extra zeros, although Steve sensibly ensured that on some bets he and Andy lost big. Working on a three-steps-forward, one- step-back strategy, and being careful to win mostly by placing large bets on either red or black (for a return doubling the outlay) or the 'one chance in three' perimeter area of the table, the pair were soon shepherding a mini-metropolis of chips. To the other players, Andy and Steve appeared to be privy to nothing more than a slightly unusual lucky streak.

They switched tables twice. Andy continued to react with thespian astonishment to each win or loss – behaving as though any outcome was entirely a matter of luck or his own particular 'gut feeling'. Steve plodded on with a few gut feelings of his own; mostly nausea brought on by the atmosphere of the gaming room, the unerring accuracy of his prophecies and the money. The money made him dizzy. Was it his? Could he walk out feeling satisfied about fleecing the casino, even if the *raison d'être* of casinos was to fleece people anyway? What if he needed all the money they could win *times ten* just to somehow find a neuro-specialist who could shut down this cinema of the near-future rolling in perpetuity inside his head?

Andy kept the haul in a slightly floppy plastic cup (used more normally as a coin receptacle by pokies players). When it was full, they exchanged the grey twenty-five-dollar chips for a more glamorous and manageable pile inscribed with a one-hundred-dollar value.

This enabled them to enter the high rollers' room where, as matter of routine, thousands of dollars were sometimes won but mostly lost. The place on first impression was identical to the rest of the gaming locations. The people looked as ugly and porcine, or gaunt and bedraggled, as in any other area of the casino. They were still shabbily dressed and chain-smoking. They still lost. They still seemed a little slacker in posture but otherwise unimpressed if they won. Anyone in a tuxedo would have looked like they were taking the piss.

A couple of blinks by Steve netted the pair more than ten grand. A few carefully choreographed losses to deflect notions of cheating, then one more feasible but extremely lucky 'get' pushed the winnings into six figures.

'That's it,' Steve said. 'Enough.'

'For tonight at least,' Andy replied.

'I see,' complained Steve. 'You'd like me to soothsay for the rest of my life, would you? How would you like it if you were woken every morning by the sight of yourself letting the morning toffee go, or having a slash? Perhaps you'd get confused and piss in the bed. That'd go down a storm with the *laydeez*, eh?'

'I'm sure it's temporary,' Andy assured Steve. 'It'll fade away with the bump and the bruises.'

Steve indicated that he and his friend would like to take their chips and swap them for folding bills. The croupier obliged and congratulated them both, and the woman who was supervising the tables asked Steve if they could take his picture to show how lucky you can be if you stick at the gambling, but Steve declined, citing his shyness. So they walked down to the cashier, with an escort who assured the money people that the win was bona fide. And they were given a massive amount of cash. So much that the cashier had to go out back and open a safe.

Andy was a little rueful about any prospective termination of Steve's condition. He'd gladly have swapped places . . . for a while at least. There were all sorts of avenues to explore. What about, for example –

'The Pub!' Andy had no intention of going home just yet. 'Let's go to the pub. Imagine what you can do with extra pulling power.'

'I'm not in the mood for sexual lab experiments, thank you,' huffed Steve.

'Well, I'll do the experimenting.' Andy decided. 'You just feed me a little information to astound the girls.'

'You're phoning Jen later, yeah?' hissed Steve.

Andy screwed up his face. 'I'm not sure we're that compatible actually.' And saying this he scuffed the carpet with one shoe, doing his best to look like an innocent casualty of a wrathful Cupid.

'What utter, *utter* bollocks,' scoffed Steve.

Steve felt thoroughly nauseated now. The lights, the avarice, the whole thieves-in-the-temple vibe had turned his stomach. His head throbbed too, and instinctively he shut his eyes again to eliminate the flood of flashing lights. His mind's eye continued to alert him to events yet to be. 'Fuck it,' he muttered between gritted teeth, as a vision of him and Andy waiting for a taxi to pass at the casino car park entrance played in his head.

'Come on. Take me home. You've had your fun.'

'But we can do it again tomorrow, all being well?' Andy implored.

'All being well? All being fucking well?' Steve shouted as he strode purposefully towards the exit. Andy had to skip every few steps to keep up, and he also had to attempt a re-phrasing of his last unfortunate comment.

'Well, when I say "well" . . . I mean unwell, I suppose . . . or the same . . . as now, that is.'

Steve was relieved to be out of the stultifying fug of the gaming area. As he and Andy paused, and the foretold taxi duly passed by, it became apparent that the margin between the preview of an event and its occurring was much less than the three minutes he'd become almost accustomed to. It was closer to two minutes, if that. Steve shut his eyes again and a projection of him and Andy in the car, swinging around the exit ramps of the car park, played in his mind's eye. It was only ninety seconds later that this action became reality.

'That's odd.' Steve said to himself, before realising that in fact the odd thing was being able to see into the future in the first place, rather than the convergence of a predicted event with the here and now.

'What's up?' Andy queried.

'Hmm? Oh, nothing,' replied Steve, turning his head away, eyes closed, keen to see if his futurist powers were indeed closing in on real time. His mind prophesied a rolling view, west along City Road towards the bay.

Andy handed a ten-dollar note to the car-park attendant. 'Keep the change,' he said (probably for the first time in his life), then, without having to stop, he took advantage of a green arrow and made a hard right onto City Road. The vista which filled the windscreen was the one Steve had visualised only thirty seconds earlier. Andy hummed a tuneless song, clearly satisfied with the evening so far, while Steve grew increasingly hopeful that his off-kilter brain was recovering.

'Close your eyes and tell me which pub we're off to,' Andy said, smiling broadly. Steve did so, but it felt to him like he hadn't. The initial three-minute gap between what had happened and what was about to happen, had wound back to less than ten seconds. By the time Steve had looked into the future and opened his eyes again, that future lay in wait less than 100 metres up the road.

Steve didn't let on, suggesting the Cricketer's Arms from familiarity rather than the use of ESP. Andy said something then but Steve didn't hear it, because a powerful wave of dizziness had begun to surge through him. His head lolled slackly and his stomach sent a message to the rest of his body claiming he'd already had a hundred beers. Andy heard Steve groan, and saw his head flopping around.

'Shit,' Andy said. 'What's up?'

Steve was about to yell for the car to be pulled over so he could puke, but before he had the opportunity he felt himself become suddenly light, weightless. And with a swift whoosh he was lifted from his seat and out of the car by an osmotic whirligig; a force with no respect for impenetrable barriers. Steve was staring down from an ever-increasing height above the vehicle's roof . . . at City Road . . . at Melbourne. Achieving the physically impossible and defying the laws of physics were no longer classified as surprise events in Steve's life. The thing that was happening to him, and which he'd quietly surrendered to, was like an extreme G-force ride at the carnival, with one added element. Rather than seeing his life flash before his eyes (an indication perhaps that his number was up, and not on the roulette table), Steve found himself flashing past his life. It was as if he was being swung around and up the interior of a giant cylindrical gallery, and on show were hundreds of metres of celluloid; an interactive recording of his recent past.

Initially he saw himself travelling backwards in the car, then walking backwards from the car into the casino and handing back the money, before striding backwards through the gaming area into the high rollers' room and so on. Within a minute Steve was in his house taking his good shoes off, and reversing down the hallway with Andy, who was apparently speaking in tongues. Steve was at once viewing and experiencing this; like the sort of dream you can step back from, or enter, depending on the emotional topography of the subconscious world. But Steve had no choice. He couldn't shake himself awake and away from a potential nightmare. Now Andy's phone conversation with Jen unspooled before his eyes, and next he was in his bathroom dabbing at the bump on his head. Steve noticed that these counterclockwise events were starting to decrease in velocity. Time was not screaming past in a subliminal blur anymore. Time was edging towards the logical, the familiar, but it was still going the wrong way.

By now Steve was able to predict what would happen next. Strolling slowly down towards his bedroom while looking at where he'd been, he bent down (as he knew he would) into a crash of head pain, before softly and gently lying on the floor. Once again there was pain. It arrived, not with the stabbing suddenness of an impact, but in increments, throbbing more and more violently before it suddenly ceased – the signal for Steve to be catapulted onto the top rung of the ladder.

And then he was thrusting forward into the position of a downhill skier . . . again.

Steve's journey was about to end. He guessed it was about to, and he was mostly right. What he didn't realise was that he would have no recollection of any of it; the fall, the powers, the vacuum cylinder which dragged him into a cinematic vortex, or the money; the money that made him ill; the money he was planning on giving away because if he was meant to predict the future, it must have been to participate in a nobler cause than a get-rich-quick scheme.

As soon as Steve's feet touched the next-to-last rung of the ladder, the nausea flooded his body again. For a portion of a second he blacked out, but regaining his senses, and fully utilising the top step as a shin-stop, a brace, a balancing agent, he didn't fall. Down below bloody Andy the pest was saying 'You'll have to go up another step'.

Steve thought about it, but something told him it wasn't a clever idea. Somewhere at the back of his mind he could see himself falling and being hurt.

'Sod it,' Steve said. 'I'll get a bigger ladder.' He began his descent, saying 'Let's just get some beers and watch the game'.

'You're the boss,' said Andy.

Steve picked up a pair of trousers and frisked them, finding nothing. 'Bugger. No money. Have you got any?'

Andy slid a hand into his jean pocket and pulled out a note. 'Only ten,' he said.

Steve rubbed his hands, expectant, pleased. 'Brilliant!' He began to walk towards the hallway.

'Ten dollars is more than enough,' he said.

Sean Condon

Condon Ah Um

Two days earlier Sally and I had returned from a long weekend in the wilds of Vermont where I'd helped remove porcupine quills from a stray dog's mouth, and ever since I'd been feeling a little . . . feeble. Possibly rabid. It was our second last night in New York City and our friends Eric and Maria had big plans for us: drinks at Time, a cruise along the Hudson River in Lower Manhattan, a second round of drinks at Milano's on Houston, a late dinner in the faux-smoke of Pastis, finishing in time to catch the Mingus Big Band at Fez. You don't *see* jazz, you *catch* it – like a virus. There were rumours of an approaching electrical storm that would promise a spectacular show above. There would be music, alcohol, dancing, cigarettes, laughter and lightning. It sounded great and I was looking forward to it, so much so that I'd decided to spend the afternoon resting in preparation for this wild night in the city that never sleeps.

Late in the afternoon I found myself having real trouble

carrying tissues and crossing the room. This wasn't a big room: this was the living room of Eric and Maria's railroad-style apartment in Manhattan's crowded upper east side. (They're called railroad apartments because they're long and thin as railroad cars. And, as hundreds of Manhattanites have no doubt quipped before, because you get railroaded on the rent. Thousands probably – they're very witty, the people of Manhattan.) Eric and Maria were at work (advertising and PR respectively), and Sally was out shopping or researching bagels or something. It was just me, flat on the couch with the remote, and I was getting breathless hopping from station to station. Everything was Rudolph Giuliani: his prostate cancer, his wife-dumping, his expected dropping out of the senate race, and this strange footage of a dog licking his face earlier in the week, which seemed to be on every station all the time. My temperature was climbing and even though I knew it wasn't – that it couldn't be – the other side of the room looked very far away. I let out a small moan: the tissues on my lap were crushing me.

Because I'm embarrassed about discussing medical intimacies with my male friends, and because I thought there was a small chance that I might burst into tears as I related my woes, I telephoned Maria.

'Hey, how are you, Sean?' she asked.

'Terrible!' I croaked quite dramatically. 'I have a high fever, a headache that's lasted since the weekend, incredible fatigue, nausea, dizziness, a sore neck, a sore back, extreme glandular tenderness on my upper-left thigh and there are red spots dotted all over me. Also, I get these incredible internal chills where I can't warm up for a few hours, then I get boiling from all the blankets.'

'What else?'

'Isn't that enough?'

'I'm trying to work out what might be wrong. Is there anything else?'

'Well, I keep wanting to sing "Oh My Papa", but I don't know the words. Except for that line.'

'Okay, here's what I want you to do . . .' What Maria wanted me to do was get a cab to the emergency room at Lenox Hill Hospital at 77th and Lexington. To not wait; to go there immediately.

'But what about tonight? We're, we're supposed to be —' I stammered.

'Go!'

I went.

Films like *Bringing Out the Dead* and television shows such as *Chicago Hope* have given me certain rather vivid expectations of the New York City hospital waiting room. So, as I threw seven dollars at the cab driver ($2.75 fare, plus rage-evading tip), I fully expected to enter a world of blood and vomit, screams and wails, of rushing gurneys and flying stethoscopes wrapped around blurred white coats, of gunshot wounds and stabbings and bloated, panting overdoses. I suppose I simply forgot that I was on the upper east side, rather than Hell's Kitchen – or indeed Chicago. The floor of the small, quiet emergency room was black and white marble – not so much as a drop of plasma on it – and seated around its edges were less than a dozen well-behaved people, none of whom looked in even remote danger of passing out, let alone dying. Many of them were smiling and chatting pleasantly with one another, presumably comparing minor ailments and slight aches. A small wave of pride coursed through me as I realised that I was, by a very long way, the sickest person there.

It had been years since I'd been in a hospital emergency room, and I was unfamiliar with the correct procedure and protocol one was supposed to follow in order to receive treatment. I briefly considered rendering myself unconscious, thereby having it all done for me, but that marble floor looked pretty hard and my head hurt quite a bit already. I looked around. One sign said 'REGISTER HERE'. Another, above a clipboard, said 'Put Your Name Down HERE and WAIT Until Your Name Is Called'. A security guard with a gun stood in front of a locked door to the hospital proper. Inside a small glass booth I saw a triage nurse talking to a tiny old Jamaican woman with big wet eyes behind her bifocals. I put my name down on the clipboard, printing it in clear capital letters, lest somebody call out Shananna Cowdroy and I miss my shot at survival. I wondered if I should REGISTER THERE but the glassed-in registration booths were unmanned. I sat down on a chair in a row by myself and waited for my name to be called, either by a nurse or by some large figure dressed in black carrying a chess set.

I ended up waiting for neither. Not five minutes after I slumped onto the vinyl chair I broke out into a drenching sweat and found myself fearfully short of breath. I also had the strange febrile sensation that Mayor Giuliani was licking my face: for fleeting moments I was *certain* of it. Being a highly self-conscious person it takes a great deal for me to jump a queue full of (allegedly) sick people, but as I leaned over in my chair and saw great drops of perspiration splatting onto the marble floor, then looked up to see a group of women staring in open alarm at me, I decided to forsake my dignity (or was it vanity?) and ask for immediate attention as I truly thought that these might very well be my last moments on earth and that actually dying in a hospital waiting room, while not uncommon, would be an irony of the most profound and tragic form. I staggered, somewhat theatrically I have to admit, over to the triage booth and looked imploringly in at the nurse behind the bullet-proof glass. She nodded to the security guard and I was buzzed in. The Jamaican woman was hastily ushered out of the booth and I slumped (slumping and staggering was pretty much all I was capable of) into her seat, apologising for being so near death and yet so pushy.

'That's all right,' the nurse told me, a little bitterly. 'What's wrong?' I listed my symptoms, ending with my temperature, which I felt to be somewhere around 150. 'Take off your jacket.' I removed my heavy leather coat. 'And your sweater.' Off with the jumper. 'Shirt and boots and socks, too.' I pulled off my shirt and, sitting there in just a thin T-shirt and pants, almost immediately felt better. 'Anything else?' the nurse asked. She was a hatchet-faced woman with hard, dark eyes and a small, very deep scar high on her cheek, just below her left eye, as though she'd had a third eye removed. I couldn't take my eyes off it. I felt like faded paint. 'Any *other* symptoms?'

'I was up in Vermont a few days ago. My hand was in a dog's mouth for a while. I have a very sore neck,' I informed her scar.

'Quick, put this on,' the nurse said, handing me a mask. I slipped the mask over my mouth and ears, as she said in precise US paramedical terms, 'Because of what you just told me I have to ask you to wear that mask at all times. You may have meningitis.'

'Bacterial meningitis?' I asked, the horror in my voice muffled by the thick mask. I knew about bacterial meningitis. Bacterial meningitis is an infection of the fluid in the spinal cord and the fluid that surrounds the brain. It is most commonly caused by one of three types of bacteria: *Haemophilus influenzae* type b; *Neisseria meningitidis*, and *Streptococcus pneumoniae* bacteria. The bacteria often live harmlessly in a person's mouth and throat. In rare instances, however, they can break through the body's immune defences and travel to the fluid surrounding the brain and spinal cord. There they begin to multiply quickly. The thin membrane that covers the brain and spinal cord (the meninges) becomes swollen and inflamed, leading to the classic symptoms of meningitis: high fever, headache, and a stiff neck. Other symptoms can include nausea, vomiting, sensitivity to light, confusion, and sleepiness. Knowing whether meningitis is caused by a virus or a bacterium is important because of differences in the seriousness of the illness and the treatment required. The diagnosis is usually made by growing bacteria from a sample of spinal fluid. The spinal fluid is obtained by a spinal tap, in which a needle is inserted into the lower back and fluid is removed from the spinal canal. Viral meningitis is usually relatively mild: it clears up within a week or two without specific treatment. Bacterial meningitis, however, is much more serious: it can cause severe disease that may result in brain damage, paralysis and even death. Even if it doesn't kill the patient, one in seven survivors is left with a severe handicap, such as deafness or brain injury.

'Do you mean bacterial meningitis?' I asked again.

'Possibly.'

'But that's fatal.' I personally knew a woman who went on holiday with a friend who'd died of it.

'Yes it is. It has a very high mortality rate.'

'Oh God.'

'I don't even want to *tell* you how high.'

'I don't want to know.'

'Well, I'm not gonna tell you.'

'Read my lips.' I pointed to my lips and mouthed the words 'I don't want to know'.

'I can't see what you're saying, sir. The mask.'

I slipped the mask off. She told me to put it back on. I put it back on. 'I don't want to know,' I repeated, muddily but firmly.

'Don't want to know what?'

'How high the mortality rate of bacterial meningitis is.'

'Well, *I'm* not gonna tell you.'

I wondered if mortally terrifying patients was this woman's way of punishing those who stared at her scar too long. Maybe she handed out wills to people who pointed at it. 'Do not resuscitate' orders to people who dared ask her about it. I quit staring and tried to breathe through the heavy cotton, gauze and asbestos mask as she took my temperature and asked for my name. The combination of mask, thermometer and Australian accent caused no end of difficulty here, and a few moments later I left the triage booth known as Sien Conlom.

As I made my way back to my seat to prepare for registration, wearing only half my clothes and a greenish mask, there was a lot less quiet chat and a lot more pointed fingers, widened eyes and agape mouths. I felt like I'd shot the president. I told the dog with Giuliani's face to *stay!* then waited to register, whether as Sien Conlom, Shananna Cowdroy or Sean P Condon, I hadn't decided. It was six-thirty – exactly when I should have been drinking champagne at Time. Or a whisky sour. Yeah, that's what I felt like, a whisky sour. Or maybe just a nap . . .

A short, unpleasant while later a small, muscular Puerto Rican fellow in his early twenties burst into the room, clutching a small towel to his forehead which, judging by the blood seeping through, was bleeding. He was in a state of extreme agitation mixed with a hot-blooded and righteous anger, presumably at not receiving immediate attention. As is often the way with the head-injured, the young fellow kept on pulling the towel away and inspecting it in order to ensure that no brain matter had seeped through the gash. When he wasn't doing that he was leaping out of his chair, huffing a lot, glaring at everybody else in the waiting room for not having any visible signs of mortal damage and banging on the glass of the triage booth. I sorely wanted to point out to him that he hadn't even put his name down on the clipboard, let alone REGISTERED THERE and that he was, therefore, a long, long way from any stitching or bandaging or brain-matter reinsertion, but felt that he might kill me if I did so. And the idea of dying in a hospital emergency room, not even as a result of the very possibly fatal complaint which I came in for, was too much. So I kept quiet and he kept on agitating himself and the air in the small room.

Breathing through the mask was tough and I passed out from carbon dioxide poisoning for a little while during which I had a dream that I was licking Mayor Giuliani's face. When I came to, it was noticeably darker outside and a third patient had joined us, a lanky teen gingerly holding a finger of his left hand in a bag of ice – a break or fracture I presumed. The lad was accompanied by his parents, a classically upper east side twosome – a pleasant-looking mother wearing too much make-up and DKNY sweats, and an unpleasant-looking grey-haired father in a tight, dark suit with matching imperious sneer. He had a long black umbrella hooked over his arm and was obviously pretending that he wasn't there, and that none of us around him were there either. Except me. Clearly tired of standing so close to the angry, bleeding Puerto Rican, the wife pointed towards my row of empty seats, eliciting a firm shake of her husband's head and the following urgent (but quite audible) whisper: 'I don't want to get near the guy in the mask. He could be dangerous.' At first I was outraged, then amused and finally frightened – the truth was I really might have been dangerous.

Some time later I registered and, despite the mask and the glass and the usual difficulties North Americans have in deciphering the Australian accent when it's saying anything other than, 'Gidday', 'Shrimp' or 'Barbie', managed to do so in my customary identity. With one small exception – I was known at Lenox Hill Hospital as Sean *Pay* Condon. Also, my occupation was listed as 'tourist', which, once I began to think about it, gave rise to the forlorn truth that it might in fact be accurate – in New York and anywhere else. The Masked Tourist . . . To my great surprise, at no point was I asked for any insurance details. It had been my understanding (thanks to *ER* etc.) that when America's uninsured became very sick, they died. Only later did I notice yet another sign in the waiting room, this one posted above the registration booths, which explained that it was the hospital's legal obligation to give treatment to anybody who sought it. I was surprised. By now, it was almost eight – river cruise time. I wondered if the others were on the boat or whether they were out buying me flowers, about to walk into the waiting room and shower me with concern. I looked out the small, high window as lightning creased the black sky.

Another friendless and wifeless while passed before my name – pronounced 'sane' – was finally called and, nodding politely and sanely to the security guard, I was taken through the locked doors into the actual emergency room, a place of ramps and curtains and very old people with tubes coming out of their noses lying on stretchers, wheezing and looking frightened. Because of my potential infectiousness I was given a room with a solid glass door, rather than a curtained partition. I was glad about that because it meant I didn't have to listen to the sounds outside; a miserable melange of sobbing, pained cries, and medicinal shouting along the lines of 'Give me a something of something, stat!' I was alone with my fear. I thought about all the things I'd change if I was given a second chance in life. The main one was that I would no longer go to places where viruses are. Also I would ask Rudy Giuliani to stop licking my face.

'So what's goin' awn?' a man with a Brooklyn accent and excellently blow-dried hair asked me, his question tinted with what sounded like genuine concern. His name was Jimmy and he was, according to his ID badge, a physician's assistant. I told Jimmy, with what was genuine ignorance, that I didn't know what was going on but that I'd sure like to find out.

'Well, we're here to help,' he said, then asked me to strip down to my underwear. My underwear, a thigh-hugging boxer/brief combo full of holes and faded patches where once there were racy, coloured stripes, could best be described as . . . broken. Certainly not the starched and snappy pair of Calvins I prefer to be examined in.

'Say ahh,' Jimmy said, looking into my throat. I said, 'Aah.' 'Say umm.' I said, 'Umm.' Jimmy poked around a bit while I winced a lot, then told me that 'we' would have to do some blood tests, urinalysis and order some chest X-rays. Jimmy gave me a plastic thing to pee in and left. While he was gone I peed and, feeling too semi-nude, slipped on one of those backward jackets they have in hospitals to allow patients to maintain plenty of dignity. Films, usually by made Mel Brooks or starring Dom DeLuise, lead us to believe that those jackets are comically difficult to put on because of having to do them up at the back and everything. This was not the case – the jacket quality at Lenox Hill is first-rate. Mine slipped on like a bespoke suit. If it had come with pants I might have swanned around that hospital like I owned the place; I'd find that unctuous lawyer with the broken-finger son and give him a piece of my mind. Then I spilled some urine (my own, thankfully) on my leg, quit swanning around the room and lay back down on the stretcher trying not to die, wondering whether the bar at Milano's was crowded. I'd spent quite a few evenings up the back of old Milano's monopolising the fantastic jukebox they have there and I loved the crummy little joint. I'd probably have me a Tom Collins if I was there. Or maybe an Alka Seltzer . . .

My veins were feeling shy and it took the nurse four attempts in four different spots, finally shoving a needle into the back of my right hand in among all the cartilage and tendons, to draw some blood and then connect me to an IV drip of saline solution. It hurt like hell but luckily the mask suppressed my gasps of pain and the tooth-ground epithets I levelled at the nurse and her ham fists. Just before she left, and because even though I was dying and feverish and nauseous, I was also bored out of my fading mind, I asked the nurse if there might happen to be anything lying around that I could possibly read.

'You could *what*?' she said, squinting at me.

'Read,' I replied.

'*Raid*?! What do you want to raid?'

'No, read – a newspaper or a magazine or something.'

'Oh, reeeaad,' she said, nodding. 'I don't hear so good.'

The nurse said that she'd take a look but she couldn't promise anything. I never saw her again.

The next person I saw was a tall, taciturn orderly whose job it was to wheel me to radiology. Before we left he covered me with a sheet, unhooked the IV from the stand next to the stretcher and laid the bag of nothing-coloured solution on top of my head. Lying down, staring at the ceiling (sections of which, I noticed, had calming floral scenes painted on it for the benefit of the supine) while being trundled around on a gurney with a plastic bag on my head was about as foolish as I'd ever felt. Not that the staff hadn't seen this kind of thing thousands of times before, but it was *my* first time as a bag-head invalid, and I hadn't planned on being one until

I was around seventy. I'm only half that age. It is quite disconcerting to hear what is going on all around you, but not actually see it: it was like being semi-blind. I heard a woman somewhere behind me plaintively calling out 'Rod!' I wondered what was wrong with Rod, whether perhaps Rod was the angry Puerto Rican. Then again, closer this time, 'Rod?' I hoped Rod was still alive.

Suddenly an upside-down face with severely arched eyebrows loomed over me and a hand grabbed my shoulder. 'Oh,' the woman's mouth said. 'I thought you were my boyfriend Rod.' I didn't know what to say. I wasn't her boyfriend Rod. I said nothing.

The orderly told me to stand 'very esstremely' still, with my chest 'very esstremely' close to the screen, then he ran out of the room to a control panel with a viewing window where he pressed a button which made a loud clumping noise that meant my X-ray had been snapped. Why, I wondered, do they have to be out of the room when they take X-rays? If it's so dangerous why am I still in here? It was all over quite quickly and before long I was lying down again, masked, with the IV bag resting on my skull. As we rolled out of radiology I looked to my left and saw, sitting in a neat, posing-for-a-portrait row, the upper east side son-with-a-broken-finger family. As the father's eyes caught mine, I heard him say, with appropriate awe and fear, 'Jesus Christ . . .'

Back in my room, Jimmy the physician's assistant and a doctor were waiting for me. The doctor was a youngish fellow named Andrew. His first question, which he put to

Jimmy with great puzzlement, was 'Why is he wearing a mask?' I explained that the triage nurse had ordered me to; that I might be infectious and deadly.

He smiled and shook his head at Jimmy. 'Nah,' was the doctor's firm diagnosis. 'Tell him to take it off.' Without waiting for Jimmy to repeat the instructions, I gratefully tore the mask off and began gulping air like a man saved from drowning.

The doctor asked Jimmy what was wrong with me. Jimmy explained my symptoms. The doctor told Jimmy that I had a virus, that he wasn't sure what sort – bacterial or viral – but that the test results would help determine its nature, and that I should try to get some rest until the tests were done. Jimmy told me that I had some sort of virus – bacterial or viral – but that test results would . . . Nobody mentioned any spinal taps.

A couple of hours later – during which I had fallen asleep and dreamed that I was licking Rudolph Giuliani's dog's face; during which my wife and two friends had enjoyed what they later described as a 'terrific dinner just one table away from Lauren Bacall and Neil Simon' – a nurse I had never seen before came in and told me that all my test results were negative.

'Is that good or bad?' I asked.

'Oh you kidder!' she said and laughed.

'Seriously, is it good or bad?' I asked again.

'It's good. Why wouldn't it be good?'

'Well, if I was trying to get pregnant, it wouldn't be good,' I offered.

'Oh you kidder!' she said, yanking the IV needle from my hand.

Jimmy came back and gave me a prescription for some wildly expensive antibiotics (Biaxin 500mg/$US125), explaining that if whatever I had was bacterial, the pills would be useless but that if it was viral they'd 'probably get it'. I thanked him for everything he'd done.

'We're here to help,' he said again. And it was true; they were and they did. For free. I was amazed. Sick as hell, but amazed.

I left the hospital and took a cab back to Eric and Maria's. I thought about catching up with them and Sally at Fez, but to be completely honest, Charles Mingus was dead (amyotrophic lateral sclerosis got him in 1979) and I myself felt pretty close to it. I'd had a hell of a night.

The next day Rudolph Giuliani, unaccompanied by any pets, announced that he was dropping out of the senate race due to his having prostate cancer. And even though he was a philanderer and a cad, I silently wished him well, knowing that ahead of him was quite some time in a New York hospital.

Late that night, still quite ill, I had to catch a plane back home to Amsterdam. Because all my symptoms were still in full effect, it was a truly awful flight. I don't even want to tell you *how* awful. So I won't. Read my lips – *I won't.*

Postscript. In May 2001, one year after the above incident, two things happened: my friend Chris Burns, who is a doctor but not the medical kind (he has a PhD in organic chemistry), took three seconds to – accurately, it would turn out – diagnose my condition as Nile River Fever; and I received a bill for US$750 from Lenox Hill Hospital. What *was* I thinking about that whole free medical care business?

Armstrong & Miller's

Essential Listening for a Big Night Out

1. 'Somebody Stole My Thunder' – Georgie Fame
2. 'Temptation' – Heaven 17
3. 'Diamond Dogs' – Beck
4. 'Debaser' – Pixies
5. 'Brown Sugar' – Rolling Stones
6. 'In It for the Money' – Supergrass
7. 'Babies' – Pulp
8. 'Heroes' – David Bowie
9. 'Every Day Is a Winding Road' – Prince
10. 'What'd I Say' – Ray Charles

Nick Robertson

Cocktail

Linda Jaivin

Lucky to Have Them

Darling, you wouldn't believe the day I've had. Flat out. To start with, I broke a nail trying to get the lid off the Beluga. My usual nail technician is on holidays, so I had to chase all over Double Bay to find another one, and then the day spa called to ask if I could get there an hour earlier for my facial, which meant that I had to re-schedule my shiatsu. And of course, there's my hair. As you can imagine, I'm feeling absolutely stretched.

That's right. Colour, cut and blow-dry. The works. I do appreciate your squeezing me in at the last minute. Joh usually does my hair, but Nicole needed him today and you know how insistent those stars can be. Mind you, I reckon she's a trifle overrated. And no one needs to be that thin.

Thank you, I'd adore a coffee. A double skinny decaf mochaccino. Two Sweet 'n Lows. Ta, darling.

Yes, tonight *is* a special occasion. Mother's eightieth. Dear Mother. She's the backbone of the family, always was. A proper matriarch. She worked hard raising us –

Father passed away when I was still quite young – and I think she deserves a lot of credit.

No, we're not having the party at home. I find dinner parties *chez nous* can be just so gruelling. One has to organise the flowers and choose the caterer and hire the waiters, and it's not that easy to find good help these days. Jack is partial to that agency that supplies models, but frankly, I don't see that pert breasts, or taut thighs and buttocks, are any guarantee of a solid professional training. I mean, at Jamie and Sarah's wedding, all the drinks girls were models, and with those short skirts you could practically see up their shazaams, but do you think they knew their martinis from their margaritas? I mean, really. Not that Jack even noticed. He couldn't stop talking about them for days.

Where are we going? Alfred's on the Pier. You know Alfred's, of course. Alfred always looks after us so well, he's a personal friend . . . I suppose it is a funny expression, now that you point it out. But there are friends and then there are personal friends, don't you think?

And then there are rellies, and they're another kettle of fish entirely. Jack's brother Martin is all right, I suppose, even if he can't handle his drink . . . Oh, no, he doesn't get violent or anything, he just tends to nod off between the pudding and the coffee. His head will be lolling on his chest, he'll suddenly jerk it up with a snort, look around, and then his eyes flutter back down and he's out.

I really don't know how Susanne puts up with it. Then

again, she's no paragon. My sister-in-law likes her G&Ts, she does. As Martin drifts off, God help us, she gets more lively. What? Oh, she sings. It's awfully embarrassing. She's no Celine. And Mother encourages her, I don't know why. I do hope she doesn't start acting up at Alfred's. And if she does, I pray for God's sake that she keeps her top on this time. Maybe if Martin bought her nicer clothes, she'd be more inclined to leave them on. It all comes down to class in the end, doesn't it? Either you have it or you don't.

Yes, that's right, 'Pale Ash' for the streaks and 'Bomb-shell' for the rest.

Jack has a sister as well, but we don't talk about her. The less said about Maryanne the better really. You don't want to know, darling . . . no, seriously, you don't. I mean, she does claim she's completely innocent, but I say you don't get yourself into a Thai jail being completely inno-cent, do you? My word. Jack's folks, John and Muriel, won't be able to make it either. They're over in Bangkok trying to find her a lawyer. Which is a bit of a relief, not that I don't adore my in-laws. It's just that what with his Tourette's and her politics, they can be a bit of a trial.

Mother is very good with them. She humours John, cursing right back at him, just to make him feel comfort-able. I was quite shocked the first time. I don't know where Mother picked up such language. But she pretends it doesn't bother her. And she lets Muriel drag her off to her 'women's groups'. Those two gave us all a fright when, coming home from one of their meetings, they insisted on performing a striptease in the lounge. I said, Mother, I really don't think you ought to traipse around trying to be a goddess at your age.

An only child? No, I've got a brother. Oh look, I know I'm supposed to call him my sister now, but Lloyd will always be Lloyd to me. I don't care how many hormones he's been eating, I still can't bring myself to call him 'Lydia'. It feels quite ridiculous. Even if his breasts are bigger than mine now. Honestly. When he told me he was getting the snip, I said for God's sake Lloyd, Lydia, whatever your name is, don't tell Mother, it'll be the end of her. But he did and now they're closer than ever. Go figure. He's bringing a boyfriend tonight. I just hope it's not that dreadful Malcolm McDee . . . oh, you know Malcolm McDee? . . . yes, of course, he's very sweet, I didn't mean . . . it's just those apricot-coloured suits . . . That's true. You're quite the observant one, aren't you? But I'm entitled to wear apricot. It matches my colouring. You'll see when you finish touching it up.

No, my husband doesn't mind my brother. Jack is a very open-minded man. He meets all types in his work. His work? He's in the entertainment business. No, not film. You know the Flamingo Nightclub?

Yes, where that raid took place. Thing is, you can't screen everyone who comes into a club. Jack was furious. He assumed he had a special relationship with the police. God knows he's paid enough for it over the years. But every time they have one of those pesky anti-corruption campaigns it takes a while for things to get back to normal.

Don't get me wrong. Jack's a pillar of the community and has always been a brilliant husband and father. True, there was that dreadful wee misunderstanding with his secretary. I wouldn't want to tell you how much money the little minx extorted for the baby, though Jack swears up and down that it wasn't his. The newspapers didn't make it any easier for us, splashing his picture all over the front page again over that teeny-weeny problem with taxes a few years ago. I mean, he simply forgot. He's a busy man. Things slip his mind from time to time.

It would have been a disgrace if they'd kept him in prison for the full term. I mean, we have two lovely children and they need their father.

My daughter is nineteen this year and an absolute beauty. She looks quite a lot like me when I was her age, if I don't say so myself. Of course, I plucked my eyebrows. A monobrow is just not good style. It wasn't when I was young and it still isn't, unless I've missed something in the latest *Vogue*. You know, I really don't understand why she doesn't take more advantage of her looks. I mean, she dresses like a ragamuffin. We can afford to buy her anything she likes. She could have Cardin, YSL, anything. She even has her own DJ's credit card. But do you think she uses it? No way. She shops in op shops. Yech . . . Yes, I know vintage is all the rage, but why can't she be like Julia Roberts and wear vintage designer? I mean, you wouldn't believe the things she gets around in. To top it off, she won't wear perfume or deodorant, and darling, would you believe, lets the hair grow under her, you know, arms. And on her legs. Really. And the hair on her head, it's like a rat's nest, not that I've ever seen a rat's nest . . . yes, dreadlocks. If I brought her in, could you just comb them out or something? . . . I see. She has to want to. Of course. That'll be the day.

She's invited her boyfriend, Blue, to Mother's party. What kind of name is Blue, I asked. 'Mu-um,' she replied, in that cranky voice, as though it were self-explanatory. He's a deejay, which in my day meant someone who had a radio show. Apparently he's a big deal at those, what do you call them, rage parties. Imagine. He has pink hair. And his clothes, they're even more lairy than hers. I say, if you're going to wear fur, always go for the real thing. And then, of course, there are those earrings all over his face. Why do kids do that to themselves? What worries me is that sooner or later, Trish is going to get her braces stuck on one of them. There'll be tears before bedtime that night. I don't mind telling you that we've spent a fair bit of money on those teeth of hers.

And I've told her that whenever she's ready, she can have her nose fixed. You wouldn't credit the filthy looks she gives me when I say that. You'd think that it was a crime even to think about cosmetic surgery. I mean, I had my nose done when I was her age. I don't mind telling you that I've had a fair bit of work done over the years. The lip-flip wasn't all that successful, and I had to go back a few times, but it's okay now and I'm most pleased with the Botox. Jack says it makes my face look like one of those lovely masks they wear at the carnival in Venice.

He's so sweet. I have to say, Mother was less kind . . . I'd rather not say. She's a dear but she really doesn't understand the pressure I'm under to look good.

But back to Trish. I really don't know what to do about that girl. Peter, my dear friend Eleanor's son, whom Trish has known since she was a little girl and who has a very nice career as a corporate lawyer, is single and has always liked our Trish. Eleanor says he's about to get engaged, but I'm sure all Trish has to do is let him know she's keen and he'd drop the other girl for her in a flash. 'But Mummy,' she squeaks, 'I'm *not* keen. Besides, Peter's boring.' The way she pronounces the word 'boring' makes it sound like some kind of disease. She says, 'Blue is so much more interesting.'

Between you, me and the wall, if Blue was any more interesting he'd be in jail.

In fact, I nearly reported him to the police a month ago. I'm not quite sure how they convinced Mother to do it, but the two of them took her along to a rage, and, well, you'll keep this under your hat, won't you, gave her one of those pills . . . Yes, an 'ecstasy.' Or a 'disco biscuit' as Mother so quaintly phrased it afterwards. As if it were something one had with tea. Can you believe it? No respect. Anything could've happened. How could they know how it would interact with blood-pressure medicine? Anyway, she danced all night – and that can't be good, much less seemly, for a woman her age. Thank God I knew nothing about it, or I'd never have got any beauty sleep that night. The next morning, she called to say she'd had a great time and they'd all just had breakfast, and Trish was going home to Blue's place, could I pick her up? I was very stern with her, I was. I told her, Mother, don't complain to me if your other hip goes now.

We have a son as well. Alan's a smart boy, always did very well in school, could have had any career he wanted. But I do worry about him. We don't see him for months and then we switch on the tellie and, oh dear, he's either raising a banner from the roof of the prime minister's residence about the plight of reffos, or scaling the walls of the nuclear reactor with that group, what do they call themselves, Greensleeves, no, that's not it . . . You're right. Greenpeace. I mean, he could be anything he wants to be. He's got brains, he just needs to start using them.

Is that shade really ash? Yes, I know it'll look lighter when it's dried. It's just that, it looks more, I suppose, champagne than ash. Not that I have anything against champagne. That reminds me of that time I served it at the Greensleeves meeting when they were discussing that French nuclear testing thingamabob. I said, Alan, I just want to make your friends feel welcome here. Funny lot they were, terribly serious and sober for young people. None of them even touched the Veuve.

Next thing you know, they're calling for a boycott of French goods. Alan, I said, I'm *not* giving up my brioche or croissants, I don't care how many little boats they blow up. Well, would you believe, I go into the kitchen only to find Mother chucking the Dijonnaise into the bin. Really,

Mother, I said, but do you think she'd listen? Next thing you know, she's marching out the door together with Alan and that scruffy mob, and they've even given her a placard to hold.

Mother really is so tolerant. I don't know how she manages it. I will give her this. She does stay active. I think that's the key, don't you? Mind you, I'm not too keen on the new boyfriend. He's half her age. Frankly, I suspect he's after her money. Once, after a few cocktails, I think I may have actually said as much. Would you believe it, he just pulls her to him and says, 'Not at all. I'm in it for the sex.'

What did she do? Tsk. She laughed. 'That's all I'm interested in too,' she cackled. Blush? I thought I'd die.

Is that it? It looks divine, thank you, darling. Mmm, the back is nice, too. It's been gorgeous chatting to you. The time just flew. What's your name again? Michael? Lovely. We must have you round some time . . . Yes, thank you. I'll certainly give your regards to my family. They really are a special bunch. I'm lucky to have them, don't you think?

Tyne O'Connell

Larging It in Hollywood

Whatever I wear I always accessorise it with lashings of cleavage, six inch heels and attitude, and if people say stuff to me like: 'Are you sure you should be wearing that?' I immediately erase their name from my address book. First rule of surviving life as a single woman in your forties: never trust anyone who asks you to doubt yourself. I learned that in Hollywood, where I've spent a lot of time over the last few years trying to break into the studio system as a sitcom writer (with medium to no success). This particular trip to LA was different though, I was on a mission to ruin my best friend's engagement party. Like they say in mobster films, it's a dirty job but someone's got to do it.

Mags was not only my best friend but my co-writer on numerous crappy sitcoms and one tragically bad – albeit well-paid – flop of a pilot. We write our scripts by email in our own private chat room, and a few times a year I go to LA and we pitch something to a bunch of studio executives in the hope that they'll realise we are the female equivalent of the Coen Brothers. Every so often we'd make a sale. Okay, so we weren't on the fast track to the Emmys but we were living the dream, baby.

Our comedy connection relied on two things: cocktails and our positive single-girl energy. Single girls like Mags and me (in their early forties), don't get married, they just don't. Sure, we sleep with men, play with men, work with men, laugh with men, gossip about men, but we most definitely do not marry them! That ship has sailed, a decade or more ago. We waved it off at the dock without regret.

Mags was too eccentric for marriage. Hell, after forty any woman is too eccentric for marriage. Along with perfect mattresses, we've found our style and, damn it, we're set in our ways. 'Marriage is like cigarettes, once a lifestyle now a health hazard,' Mags would quip when people (usually married ones) asked about our lack of husbands. But it was as if she'd never said those words now. 'Oh Clara, the engagement party is going to be ginormous. Between Percy and I we have so many friends we've had to hire the Beverly Hilton.'

Percy was Hollywood's most sought-after lifestyle coach, so it was a given that it would be a star-studded affair. Everyone who was anyone in LA had a lifestyle coach – I'd even thought about getting a lifestyle coach myself once but, as Mags pointed out, I'd have to get a life first. We hate that expression 'get a life'. Everyone I know that has 'a life' (i.e. a partner and a regular job) is about as exciting as a party without a cocktail shaker. Besides, I may not have a life but I have the wardrobe for a life, mostly made up of lingerie and shoes admittedly, but impressive none the less once I've packed it all up. I'd blown my first option cheque on a Louis Vuitton suitcase – you know, the one that has all the little drawers. The only problem was that it was hard to find a taxi with a trunk big enough for it. I'd been standing on the kerb at LAX for half an hour waiting for a station wagon.

Finally, my driver arrived and watched impatiently as I hauled my LVT into the back. It's a fact that men stop helping you lift heavy things once you turn forty – just when your bones start thinning. It was around midday and the sun was belting down on us with a ferocity you just don't get in London, even with global warming. I always feel positive and hopeful in this town, people are always shallow enough to pretend they like me and the pretence of affection is enough for me – like most girls my age, my friendship list is already full. Shallow is the new deep. I wish the citizens of London would try and be a bit shallower, actually. Especially the guy upstairs, who still holds a grudge against me because I told his new live-in girlfriend, Cornelia, that he'd once offered me money for sex after she'd quizzed me beadily about our relation-ship on the stairs – well, I was badly hung-over. They've been uncivil to me ever since to the point that I don't regret waking them up last week at 2 a.m. to let me in because I'd left my key in the cloakroom of Claridges (along with my coat). Very Holly Golightly–ish, I thought, but himself and the wretched Cornelia don't agree. The horrible pair have worked themselves up into such a lather about me they've accused me of stealing their mail. Gees, take a diazepam. God I hate couples.

I told the driver to take me to Chateau Marmont as I wound down the window and stretched out. Even in a taxi it always feels like you're in a convertible when you drive through LA; it's the palm trees, stretch limos, valet parking, gorgeous men – all gay, but a girl can ogle. I had been looking forward to this trip with a heightened sense of trepidation since the invite to Mags's engagement party first appeared in my in-tray a month ago, well not literally my *in-tray* because that suggests a desk, and an office, possibly even a fax machine. Okay, so I discovered it on the mat of my Clapham terrace flat along with a stack of computer magazines (the hateful pair upstairs), and bills (me), around ten, just as I'd finished making the first latte of the morning. I'd climbed back into bed and snuggled under my duvet to open it.

In copperplate engraving, Mr and Mrs Huff were requesting the pleasure of my company at a party to celebrate the engagement of their eldest daughter Margaret to Percy Schnapperfraum. Once I'd stopped falling apart with laughter at seeing Percy's surname in print, and finished mopping up the latte I'd spat everywhere, I started to feel guilty. The burden of saving Mags weighed heavily upon my conscience. I couldn't let this happen. Apart from the fact that Percy was about as sexy as a Virgin Atlantic sleepsuit, Mags was an inspiration to single women everywhere. She practises casual sex and means it. While every so often she might insert a new guy in the line-up and lavish special affection on him for a few months, eventually he took his place with the others – on her conveyor belt of booty calls. One of her booty calls was Percy. They'd shagged about six times in as many years and never once a hint that she wanted more. I had even shagged Percy myself once. It was the night I'd discovered Gingertinis and declared I was going to drink nothing but Gingertinis ever again! Significantly neither Percy nor Gingertinis have passed my lips since.

Mags and I laughed so hard during our Percy comparisons that our notes ended up forming a major part of the comedy in our pilot *Girls On Top!* And that had bombed big time. 'About as funny as setting a fart alight!' declared the *Los Angeles Times.*

Ensconced in my suite at the Marmont, I began to marshal my arguments. Once the champagne was flowing tonight and I could get her alone in the loo for a proper girl-to-girl, she would see that marrying Percy was madness.

Refreshed by an afternoon nap and after a few forays into the minibar for Oreos and an invigorating shower, my car arrived to take me to the party. I was wearing an YSL trouser suit without anything underneath, cleavage down to my navel and six-inch heels. I'd only ever been to the Beverly Hilton for Writers Guild Award ceremonies, where needless to say Mags and I were not on the nomination list. We didn't mind, we might be faceless nobodies on paper but in our dreams we were living it large. The doorman winked at me and I smiled back – at forty-something a girl takes flattery where she can and a lewd wink from a five-foot mustachioed Mexican is still a lewd wink.

Mags had asked me to give a short speech, but because I was hoping it wouldn't be necessary I hadn't bothered writing one. My palms felt clammy as Percy greeted me. 'Clara . . . wasn't it?' he offered vaguely.

'Oh come, Percy, don't tell me you've forgotten the best sex of your life?' I tormented and then watched with egotistical glee as he went bright red and sweated in his tux. He was smaller than I remembered, diminished by his receding hairline, which gave his face a ratty look. I almost felt sorry for him.

'Yes, um, that's right,' he stuttered. (Oh no, I did feel sorry for him!) 'Good of you to come, Clara.'

I congratulated him on his engagement like the two-faced bitch that I am and made my way into the heaving crowd. I recognised several well-known celebs, but because there's a myth in this town – perpetuated by agents mostly – that no one drinks, I can't give you their names. I can, however, reveal that the Scientologists (you know who they are) were as sober as ever. That's another thing, Scientologists are *never* single! Grabbing a glass from a passing tray, I made my way through the crowd, craning my head for a glimpse of Mags, occasionally stopping to air kiss (or ass kiss) the people I knew. The orchestra were paying old jazz songs and there were already people dancing (none of them Scientologists). I spotted a group of staff-writers we'd employed on our fated pilot and made my way towards them – and there she was, resplendent in red velvet and diamonds.

Mags threw her arms around me and squeezed so hard

I thought my lungs would pop. I cuddled all the writers as if they were all old friends. Relieved when the fake bonhomie was over, they drifted off, leaving Mags and me alone. I told her how fabulous she looked (true) and how happy I was for her (false).

'I'm so glad you came to be with us on our big night,' she said, wrapping me in another squeeze. She looked so happy, the star of her show. Could I really spoil all this for her? (Yes.)

We both took another glass from a passing waiter even though I hadn't even started my first. 'Why marry him, Mags? Can't you just serial-shag him?' I asked as we made our way through the crowd. She slapped me on the back (Mags can get quite butch after a few drinks). I checked my watch. The speeches were due to kick off in about three hours. I was going to have to work fast if I was going to save my friend.

'Who would have thought, me getting married!' she announced (a bit madly I thought).

'Don't do it, Mags. It's not too late! Move into my room at the Marmont while all the fuss dies down, and then write Percy a heartfelt letter of resignation.'

She giggled. 'I'm so glad you came, Clara, I knew I could rely on you to make me laugh. Let's dance.'

She grabbed my hand and I felt the sharp pressure of her Fuck-Off diamond solitaire ring. 'I'm serious, Mags, is this what you really want?' I shouted in her ear as we started to jive away to a jazzy rendition of 'No Strings'.

I couldn't tell what she was thinking because when

Mags dances she really lets go. Her limbs were flailing about without reference to the beat and she was singing along at the top of her voice.

'You know it's never too late to change your mind. Percy will understand,' I yelled, but it was pointless, she was lost in the music. When it changed to a slow Marlene Dietrich, I asked her if she wanted to go to the loo with me.

We stocked up with two more glasses each.

'You know that feeling you get when you jump off a yacht into the ocean and you fall like a rock?' Mags yelled out from her toilet cubicle.

'And your lungs fill with water?'

'That's how I was feeling when Percy proposed.'

I waited till we were at the basins before I confronted her. 'So, are you saying that Percy makes you feel like a drowning woman?'

'It was like everything was wrong in my life and saying yes was the only thing that made sense.' This was going better than I imagined. The girl *was* having doubts.

Sitting on the handbasins sipping our champagne, I asked her what she meant about everything in her life being wrong. 'I don't understand, I thought we were living the dream, Mags. Independent Women – like Destiny's Child.' I sang a few bars of the song to remind her.

She snorted in derision. 'They're, like, how old? Ten? I'm forty-four, Clara, I want to know there is someone who's always on my team.'

'I'm always on your team, Mags! I can move out here. I'm done with Clapham; the place is riddled with couples and their spawn. I'll move in with you. We'll take this town by storm, baby.' I held my glass up for the anticipated toast.

Mags shook her head. 'You're so sweet, Clara, but that's not what I mean. I'm marrying Percy. I hoped you would be happy for me.'

'Of course I'm happy for you.' Not. 'It's just that you've been shagging him on and off for years. Why the sudden move to marriage?'

'Don't you like him?' She looked stricken.

'I liked him enough to have drunken meaningless sex with him didn't I?' I reminded her. After we finished giggling we swapped industry gossip and discussed our next project. Every few minutes, guests from the party wandered in for a pee or to touch up their make-up. I began to grow frustrated and worried that I would have to give that speech after all.

When we were alone again, Mags turned to me seriously. 'Have you ever been in love, Clara?'

'No, my marriage to Dom was a total sham,' I replied, trying to be breezy but not succeeding. Between twenty-seven and thirty-two, Dom had been the focus of my world. Unfortunately the focus of *his* world was a woman twelve years my senior. I actually lost my man to an older woman. We were almost out of champagne and I could see my chance to talk Mags out of her marriage slipping away. 'Think carefully, Mags. Do you want to nurse him in sickness and pay for his dentures when the bottom falls out of the lifestyle-coaching market?'

Mags rolled her eyes.

'Well, that's what marriage is, sickness, health, richer, poorer, better, worse.'

'Not in LA. We're promising to nurture and allow one another room for growth. Come on, let's get back to the party. Percy will be wondering where I've got to.'

Great, already they were joined at the hip. I put my hand on the door handle but didn't twist. 'Do you love him, Mags?'

'What is love really?' She pushed the door.

I spoke quickly. 'Love is *When Harry Met Sally*. Love is *Sleepless in Seattle*.'

The band was finishing off an Eartha Kitt number, 'I Love Men'. Mags grabbed us refills from a passing tray. 'Look, Clara, Percy is no Tom Hanks, thank God, and I'm no Meg Ryan. Our feelings for one another are more cerebral, more Woody Allen than Nora Ephron.' She looked straight into my eyes, straight into the very heart of my plotting subconscious. 'Clara, are you trying to talk me out of this?'

'No!' (Yes.)

'Are you trying to say you're not happy for me?'

'No! No! No!' (Yes! Yes! Yes!)

'Because I'm marrying Percy, whether you like it or not. Be happy for me, Clara.'

I grinned maniacally. 'I am!' (Not.)

'I've always preferred *Husbands and Wives* to *Sleepless* anyway. I thought you did, too?'

I felt my face redden. She was right. I'd played my last

card and I'd lost. The band started to play 'The Way You Look Tonight' and as Mags took me in her arms for a waltz – we were always great waltzers, Mags and I – I decided to throw in the towel and be happy for my friend. If Percy made her happy I should be happy for her. I *would* be happy for her. Mags pulled me in close and I rested my head on her shoulder.

In the end I did give my speech. Totally unprepared, I decided that plagiarism was the best policy and recited the immortal lyrics of 'Love Is the Sweetest Thing'. I was well into the bit about 'love is the strongest thing, the oldest and yet the latest thing,' before my audience finally cottoned on and I got my laughs. Mind you, they probably would have cheered a sock puppet by that point. It was somewhat delayed due to what was meant to be a quick dash to the loo for a last-minute pee.

'If Mags was happy, I was happy,' I told my reflection. 'Besides, fifty per cent of marriages end in divorce.' I splashed some water on my face and gathered my thoughts but I was interrupted by a throaty cry I'd recognise anywhere.

'Fuck me!' it moaned. 'Oh Steven! Yes! Yes! Yes!'

God love her, if it wasn't Mags, shagging the living daylights out of the champagne boy.

Forty-something women are like that, so are twenty-something and sixty-something women, for that matter. This is a story that never will end. Love really is the sweetest thing.

Deborah Mailman's

Big Night Out

1. 'Pump Up the Jam' – Technotronics
2. 'Lullaby' – The Cure
3. 'Buffalo Stance' – Neneh Cherry
4. 'Silence' – Delirium featuring Sarah McLachlan
5. 'Insomnia' – Faithless
6. 'Unfinished Symphony' – Massive Attack
7. 'Blackfella/Whitefella' – Warumpi Band
8. 'Time Is Now' – Moloko
9. 'Scorchio' – Sasha & Emerson

My choices for essential listening come down to the most-played songs in my collection. My taste in music is pretty eclectic, and any one of these songs guarantees to put me in a good mood for a Big Night Out.

I'll listen to anything from Faithless through to Warumpi Band and The Cure.

Being a 1980s kid I was groovin' on the dance floor of the Mt Isa Irish Club to Black Box, Neneh Cherry and

Prince. 'Pump Up the Jam' by Technotronics is an old-time favourite. It just has a great beat.

Neneh Cherry is hot. When female rappers like her and Salt 'n' Pepa blasted onto the scene, it just made dancing to music that much sexier.

I find it hard to ignore The Cure. They were the band I was listening to when I was studying at uni. I love 'Lullaby', 'Love Song', 'Just Like Heaven', 'Boys Don't Cry'. *Disintegration* is still one of my favourite albums.

Warumpi Band are just amazing. I love that classic country rock, and coming from The Isa, it was the music I grew up on. 'Blackfella/Whitefella' gets me dancing every time. Such a great start to the song. *Big Name No Blankets* is a fantastic album.

I can't get through a night out without listening to club mixes. Faithless, Sash, Basement Jaxx, St Germain, Moloko, Soul Vision, Delirium, Sasha & Emerson . . . I love all that fast dance beat. I just love a good dance.

Nick Hornby's

Top Five Songs for a Big Night Out

(Over thirty-fives only, no trainers)

1. Getting ready:
   'Lowdown' – Boz Scaggs
   Make sure you have speakers in the bathroom. Play
   while you are shaving and/or putting make-up on.
   This late 1970s disco classic will make you feel slinky,
   sexy and slightly cheesy, all at the same time.

2. In the car (designated drivers only, please):
   'Kitty's Back' – Bruce Springsteen
   Learn a few weeks before proposed Big Night Out,
   so that you can get all the vocal inflexions, sing the
   backing vocals, and parp along to the horn riff.
   Energising. When you get out of the car you will feel
   like Leonardo DiCaprio in *Romeo+Juliet*. (This, by
   the way, is a good thing.)

3. On the dance floor:

'Groovejet' – Spiller

On the presumption that you only really have one decent dance in you, due to age, drink, drugs, lack of coordination etc., avoid all older (and, let's face it, funkier) songs. Choose this one, in a hopeless and embarrassing attempt to prove that you're Down With The Kids. They hate it, but to anyone over thirty-five it sounds cool. And modern.

4. Later:

'Your Love Is the Place That I Come From' – Teenage Fanclub

You are drunk, and you have been flirting desperately, shamelessly and comically with someone several years your junior and – it turns out – of a different sexual orientation. Return to your partner and sing this hymn to the joys of domesticity and monogamy. It won't do you much good, unfortunately – indeed, it is very likely to achieve an effect precisely opposite to the one intended – but never mind. You tried.

5. Back home:

'Lay Me Low' – Nick Cave

Presuming that your night out will end in despair, in self-recrimination, self-pity and self-loathing, then how better to end the evening than with a song that imagines the circumstances of one's own funeral? Enjoy.

Andy Quan

On a Night Like This

Pamela Joanne Sutton looked at her life at forty-five and felt a vague dissatisfaction. She had a kind, strong husband named Bill who had his own flooring business ('Billsworld Flooring'), two teenage children – sometimes moody these days but basically good kids – and a tidy, spacious home in Pennant Hills. She was big-boned like all the Sutton women and had no major health problems, not like her neighbour Elsie who had breast cancer last year. She kept herself busy with volunteer work at the local youth centre and occasional reception work for her doctor when the regular office staff were off on holidays.

Still, she had thought about it for a long time and tried to picture the life that she'd like to lead. *Free* – though she did love her family. *Colourful* – though she did try to dress in bright clothing and decorate the house with panache. *Exciting* – well, when was the last time she felt her life was that?

Pamela Sutton looked at her life and asked herself

501

what life she wanted. Who was having the most fun? It was an easy conclusion. It was gay men like her brother Roger and his partner Wayne: men who had beautiful apartments and homes, good jobs and glamorous vacations. They dressed well, kept in good shape and they were so handsome! She had a mental flashback to a time long ago when she'd brought her children Adam and Kylie to the Mardi Gras parade. They'd waved at Roger and Wayne who were marching in the float for the local AIDS service organisation. She'd never seen so many beautiful, glittering faces.

Roger was surprised to get Pamela's request to be taken out for a night on the town, 'at one of your locals'. The two of them were friendly, though slightly distant. He did like the kids, but he didn't see them much. Maybe when they were older he would.

Wayne, on the other hand, was amused. 'We could go to the Imperial. Or the Albury. No, let's take her to the Newtown Hotel. Mitzi McIntosh will be on. She's always good for a laugh.'

And that was the start. From then on, Pamela would go with Roger and Wayne, or even just Wayne by himself since he was more tolerant than Roger, to see drag shows at gay bars in Sydney. In her 'regular' life, she hadn't been getting out much, and these nights made her giggle and glow.

'Whose mother are you, darling?' said Mitzi, leaning forward, a husky voice emerging from a powdered white face, eyelashes from here to eternity, and more make-up on than Pamela had in her whole bathroom cabinet.

Pamela had the eyes of everyone in the bar upon her, and the hot glare of a spotlight. But she didn't care. 'Yours!' she shouted, laughing and spilling her beer.

The first step was drag queens; the next, drugs. They sounded wonderful. Well, not all of them – not the nasty street ones like heroin and crack, and cocaine sounded a bit dangerous too – but ecstasy seemed worth a try. The day after the Millennium celebrations, she'd read an interview with a young policeman working on Bondi Beach. Violence was almost down to nothing that year because young people were taking ecstasy instead of drinking alcohol. People were hugging instead of fight-ing. He was fired soon after for saying something that his superiors couldn't, but the story stuck in Pam's mind. Besides, Roger and Wayne had hinted about it for years. She'd asked how they could possibly stay up all night at their parties. Wayne had winked at her. 'With a little help, Pam. You're such an innocent soul!'

So it was Wayne rather than Roger who had taken the responsibility of giving Pam her next advice. 'Only have a half,' he warned her. 'It will take between half an hour to forty-five minutes to come on. Drink lots of water, but not too much. Eat healthy things afterwards even if you don't feel like it. You don't want your family to suspect anything. And call me if you need to – you have my work number.'

Roger thought she was crazy. Absolutely raving. But Pam had decided she wanted to be somewhere safe and familiar for her first experience, and where better than her own home? It had to be a day when the kids were at school, and not one of her volunteer days. Bill would be working as always, and she made sure it was one of his busy days so he wouldn't surprise her and come home early. She prepared a casserole, salad and jelly as soon as they all left the house, so she wouldn't have to worry about it later. She set the timer on her oven to both start and finish later that afternoon (technology – marvellous!). Then she sat down at the kitchen table and looked at the innocuous-looking shape in her hand. Wayne had divided the pill already, so it was just a half, and it said 'C', which she understood was half of 'CK'. Calvin Klein. She wasn't sure if it was a joke or not. Why would you name a pill? She swallowed it down with a big glass of water.

It took, as warned, about half an hour to take effect, during which time Pam had convinced herself that nothing was going to happen. She tuned in the radio to a channel Kylie listened to, as Wayne had said that she'd probably like music, and then she got out the vacuum cleaner. She'd felt a horrible wave of nausea but had not been able to vomit. *Oh, what have I taken?* Soon her vision became shaky and the furniture more vibrantly coloured. Suddenly, she felt like vacuuming. She grabbed the hose, turned it on and the roar filled her ears. She couldn't hear the stereo so she turned it up loud and then started a cha-cha around her living room, the dust swirling in the sunlight, colours bursting through the windows, the pattern on the rug changing as the vacuum moved over it. Wonderful. *Goodness, what a great way to tidy up!*

When Bill and the kids had arrived home, the house was cleaner than it ever had been, and Pam was fast asleep. Kylie woke her up.

'Mum, did you wear yourself out with the cleaning today?'

Beneath Pam's eyes, patterns were still forming and unforming but she pulled herself up, went down to the ready-made meal, and said that she'd been busy and had maybe overdone it. She was feeling a bit fluish.

'You don't really seem tired,' said Bill, looking at Pam's flushed face.

In Pam's mind: shapes, colours, sounds, relief.

It took Wayne to actually remind her the next day that she'd called him.

'Are you all right, love? You can get a bit down the next day if you don't watch out.'

'I called you?' It slowly came back to her that she'd told Wayne how happy she was for him and Roger *and* how maybe she hadn't paid enough attention to Roger's life *and* that she was having a wonderful afternoon cleaning the house. The pill seemed to work just fine. Her only regret was that she didn't have someone to share it with. She was feeling so much love.

It's upon her now, her big night out. Pam looks back at that first experience with a Cheshire-cat grin. It's still new to her, this *life*, but she's well-prepared. She's made a big fruit salad for tomorrow, and stocked up on fresh fruit. She'll remember to take vitamins after, and she'll take a long nap this afternoon. Even though it's Saturday – usually a day for a roast – she'll make an enormous pasta. Carbohydrates have been recommended for the long night ahead.

'14 000 people?' she'd exclaimed. 'That's like a small town.'

Wayne had explained that the Sleaze Ball is Sydney's second biggest party, a more manageable version of the famous Sydney Gay and Lesbian Mardi Gras, with fewer tourists and more locals. Plus, people weren't exhausted from being in the parade just before. She would be *fine*. They'd stay with her to make sure everything went okay.

Pam thought long and hard about what to wear, and eventually decided to dress like one of the women in the flyer that Wayne and Roger gave her. One woman was a cat, the other a bit like a Playboy bunny wearing rabbit ears like the pair that sassy young woman who almost won 'Big Brother' wore. Pam found an appropriate pair, bought a big pink feather boa from a fabric store nearby (she didn't even know they sold them!) and is now ironing a black sleeveless blouse made of lightweight material. It will breathe in the midst of the crowds, she expects, and it's slimming. The trousers, too. All the Sutton girls are big but Pam figures that she carries it well.

Roger's loaned her a CD, *Groove Armada*, and she thinks she'll go out and buy a copy for herself. Kylie, in the living room, mouths to Adam who's coming through the door: 'Mum's listening to *dance* music!'

506

Pam listens to the beats of the song. She closes her eyes, just a moment, and can feel a spot in the back of her head widening and filling with warmth – a summer bloom in new heat. It's been weeks since her first experience but, if she concentrates on that one anatomical spot, she can feel it again: herself weightless and happy.

At the showground, there's a line-up at the gates and a bag search before they are allowed to enter. A net of energy is upon them: anxiety, excitement, anticipation. Two young men have started early. Their eyes roll and their skin flushes, and they start to sway and dance to music unheard by others. The theme of this year's party is 'Beast' and one of them grasps a mylar dolphin balloon, reaching up and stroking it. Pam has never thought of a dolphin as a beast before.

'Does anyone want to touch my dolphin?'

The replies:

'Keeeerist, let us in.'

'Gimme a ciggy, I'll touch that dolphin.'

'Lookit them, they've taken their e's before they've even got in.'

Pam, Roger and Wayne enter, and Pam comes face to face with a seven-foot drag queen.

'Move along, doll! Have a good Sleaze.'

A comic monologue rolls through a megaphone and over the top of them. She sees man-leopards, woman-snakes, boy-bears and girl-cats, feathers and fins, furs and wings, sequins and sparkles. People of all ages and colours, but mostly gay men. Gay men! Why didn't she spend more time with Roger in the past?

They turn off to the right into the Royal Hall of Industries. The interior is a gothic castle, a huge hippo's mouth gapes at them from the far end of the hall, fluorescent paint gives a fun-fair feel to the painted brick backdrops. Huge gargoyles perch off every pillar, overseeing a crowd of unearthly creatures.

'It's time, isn't it?' she giggles.

'Hang on, Miss.' Wayne heads off to buy some water and leaves Pam with her brother.

'You're ready?'

Roger grabs Pam's hand and slips a magic pill into her palm. She's going all the way this time, no half-pills tonight! Wayne returns and they begin their night. They move onto the dance floor.

It's a great song, whatever the song is. She can't tell when the last one finished and the next one began. In no time at all, she's dancing. *God, I hardly ever go out dancing!* Wayne and Roger decide to take a breather, but keep Pam in sight. She gives them a little wave. The e seems to be having an effect. She recognises a familiar wobble in her stomach and a catch in her breath from the last time. The music is somehow becoming more complex. She doesn't know much about this type of music, whatever it is, but she can hear runs of notes and melodies clearly, the voices and the instruments, the parts and the whole, sharp in different parts of her mind. One melody sends a shot of warmth up her spine, the chorus bounces from ear to ear, over the top of her head, and down her bunny ears.

It's such a friendly crowd! Everyone enjoying themselves, smiling at each other, at her. She's in love, a teenager in love. With everyone! Except it's not so chaste really, she feels damp outside and in. *Let go!* a voice inside her head whispers. She leans over and hugs a sweaty athletic boy next to her (who hugs her back!); she turns to the man next to him and runs her hands down his torso. Has she ever felt bodies like these?

'Wayne, Gawd, Wayne! Pam has just run into the crowd and she's groping the muscle boys.'

Wayne's eyes follow the line of Roger's finger, but he can't quite see her. He'd burst out laughing but thinks it's better not to. 'Oh come on, it's funny. And it *is* Sleaze Ball.'

Roger considers this, leans forward and gives Wayne a peck on the lips. 'Just don't tell anyone she's my sister.' They give each other a good old-fashioned pash.

Pam is moving with agile steps for a big woman. Normally it would be difficult to move through a crowd as packed as this, but now it's somehow easy. She's forgotten her nervousness, and her intention to try and keep track of Wayne and Roger for the night. She's loose! She's free!

La la la la . . . Everyone is singing along. She leans over to a small cute girl wearing a sequined turquoise bikini top. She's not very comfortable with most of the women here, they look too rough. She likes the men better in their tiny shorts. But this girl looks a bit like her daughter. 'Is this a new song?'

'A new song? No, it's really old. It came out last year. Don't you recognise it?'

The music is loud and encompassing but Pam can hear her voice as clear as day.

'It's KYLIE, Kylie Minogue: "On a Night Like This". Great track, huh?' She smiles, little lights at her eyes and teeth and dimples. She gives Pamela a hug. 'Happy Sleaze.' And disappears.

Kylie! Like my daughter.

Pam turns and finds herself nearly underneath a tall man, bouncing up and down, one arm in the air. He seems to be gesturing to someone not too far away who is doing the same thing. They're pointing at each other. He has a wild and giddy expression on his face.

'Mr Logan!'

Owen looks down, still bouncing, and then stops. *It can't be.*

'Don't let me stop you. You look like you're having fun!' Pam shouts because Owen is so tall and she so short. 'More fun than teaching French!' She dances off.

Owen doesn't know the cute shirtless dancer next to him but he has to tell someone. 'The mother of one of my students just went by! I can't believe it.'

'Far out,' replies the boy. 'Far out.'

Pam continues her trajectory: fast, far-ranging and happy. She's explored this hall, and decides to wander around. She sees an exit and heads for it. So many people, it's a village, a small city. This many people, and they all seem as happy as her. The array of costumes and beauty continues around her, the streetlights in between the buildings are no longer static. She glances up and sees Bent Street, a shopping strip. The stores are closed but a restaurant and bar at the bottom of the street are open, also some food vendors. She's been here before and was impressed with the busy Saturday-afternoon feel. Now look at it. And look at us!

She follows a crowd into a dark, round building in time to see an acrobat flying overhead, graceful swings and somersaults in the air on a bar suspended from the roof. Even a simple balancing act, an arm outstretched or the performer hanging upside down, seems the most miraculous of acts. The crowd is in awe, cheering and whistling above the continual music, and Pam just floats in place. Happily.

'Having a good time?' asks a couple – a man and woman in fur pelts, who she thinks are barbarians.

'Wonderful. It's my first big party.'

'You should get out more often. Come to ARQ on Saturdays. It's great.' They leave her there thinking about it.

On to the next building, she knows there's another one: the Hordern Pavilion. It's longer and flatter than the last building, and the stage is much smaller. But all around the hall are giant crazed animals, huge statues made of papier-mâché or styrofoam, she doesn't know which, painted in fluorescent colours. It's like a dream of adventurers in ruins in Egypt or Central America or Atlantis or some funhouse land of beasts. She slides into the huge pulsing crowd and finds herself a spot more lit than the others. It feels just right to be here, she's unsure why. There are parts of her personality that are gone and she feels light. Free of anxiety, hesitation, caution. She's exactly in the moment. Instinctual. She nods and smiles at people, and connects. Really connects. If the connection is strong, they wish each other well, or even give each other a hug or kiss.

Now she's noticing a good-looking man next to her, broad shoulders and all sorts of tiny square muscles up and down his torso, which he swings back and forth, making everything ripple. He seems to want to say something.

'Excuse me. Can you move somewhere else? You're really bringing me down.' He looks at Pam's confused face, raises his eyebrows and scans his eyes up and down her body, just so she understands. He looks up, continuing to dance, hoping he won't have to ask again.

Pamela moves away, off towards an exit. It's the first time that night she feels like she's actually walking. Outside, the sun is coming up and the day is going to be clear and hot. She sits on the sidewalk and sinks into herself. Her feet have started to feel heavy and tight, as if they've grown a few sizes but her shoes have not. Her boa is damp and losing feathers. Her head is in her hands.

'Excuse me but are you okay?'

She looks up and sees a tall, gangly youngster. He couldn't be older than Adam.

'You just look like you're having a bit of a rough time.'

'Oh . . . No . . . I'm fine. A little dizzy maybe.' And saying this she realises that she is. 'I'm tired, but good. How are you?'

'I'm fantastic! This was my first dance party. Ever. It was amazing.'

'Mine, too. I've been to bars, but never to a big party like this one. I've heard there's a nightclub called ARQ which is fun.'

'Wow, you'd go to ARQ?'

'Well, maybe.' Pam's only half-convinced at this stage and to be truthful, she's still smarting. 'You haven't been?'

Jason shrugs and then bursts into small laughter. 'I'm only seventeen.'

'What? How did you get in?'

'A friend at my youth group got me a ticket. This has been the greatest.' His eyes are lit up. His body is still swaying to the music and Pamela imagines a snake sloughing off skin, dancing into an adult body.

'You don't look tired at all. Tell me, Jason. Did you take anything tonight?'

'No . . . Yes . . . Maybe . . . I've been downing energy drinks all night. I'm pretty wired.' A thought hits him. Pam sees it lifting the corners of his mouth and eyes. 'You?'

'I took just one,' she admits, guiltily. 'It was wonderful at first, and for most of the night . . . but I, well, I don't know. Maybe it wasn't such a good idea.' She remembers the nasty boy on the dance floor.

'I think it's great that you're out at your . . .' He doesn't finish. 'Do you, uh, do you have any kids?'

'I guess I do look like a mum. Yep, two. A girl, Kylie, and a boy, Adam. Well, not really a boy anymore. Do your parents know where you are?'

'Oh, no,' Jason shakes his head from side to side. 'I don't get along with my parents.'

'Such a nice young man like you! They . . .' She stops herself.

They sit in silence a moment. Pamela grabs his hand and rests it on her knee.

'I'd love to have a Mum like you.' Jason leans over and kisses Pamela on the cheek, like he's seen other people greeting each other at the party tonight. He looks up and sees two old guys standing in front of them.

'Hi fellows.' Pam grins wearily but happily. 'You've found me. This is my new friend Jason. Jason, this is my brother Roger and his partner Wayne.'

'Wow . . .' Jason stands up and shakes their hands vigorously.

'How's your evening been, Pamela? We were a little worried about you.'

'Oh, I'm just fine. It's been a great night. A bit tired though. And gosh, look at this!' She gestures to the crowds around them, stumbling, wide-eyed and disheveled, costumes sliding away, and skin colour glowing in unusual shades of purple and red. 'Does my skin look like that?'

'A little rosy,' says Wayne, smiling. 'But fine.' He leans over and lifts her by her arms to her feet.

'I'm going to go now!' Jason waves, grinning from ear to ear, and bids them farewell.

'Do you want to come back to our apartment for a last drink?' Wayne asks Pam. He looks more alert than she feels. 'We're going to change our clothes before we go out to The Oxford for a drink.'

Pam really is tired. It's 8 a.m. and she wants her cosy home in Pennant Hills, and to snuggle up in her own clean sheets. When she gets home she'll shower (delicious!) and call Bill to their bed where she'll make passionate love to him. So loud that the kids hear.

'No, I think it's time for me to go home.'

'Okay. We'll walk you out.' Wayne and Roger step to each side of her and lead her away. Roger raises his eyebrows, almost to the point of rolling his eyes, but stops in a bright expression of bemusement. Wayne looks at Pamela, who has nearly closed her eyes as she's leaning on them, and then at Roger, and breaks into belly-laughter – happy vibrations that reach right up to the top of his skull.

Bem Le Hunte

The God of Gatecrashers

This is an honest-to-God true story. A story that I have dined out on for many years since it happened. I put it in writing now and offer it to War Child and to you, in memory of the crazy teenage years that we all enjoyed.

In the days when this story is set, I was intrigued by magic. I planned for a miracle on a daily basis, and miracles seemed to happen, just to entertain me. My magic was to be found in friends, happenings, coincidences and discoveries. But mostly it was in the music. The music of my generation.

Here's how this story goes . . .

My friend Janina and I were at Richmond station, on school holidays, thinking about what we were going to do that night. As usual we had just a few coins in our pockets – not even enough for a train fare. But that was nothing new. Janina and I never had any money, but we didn't let it stop us having a good time. We'd befriended one of the guards at Richmond station, so we never had to produce a fare further than the last stop – Kew Gardens. Going out into the world of unknown ticket collectors was tougher, though a little bit of charm always went a long way – and if that didn't work, trickery would replace it.

So there we were, the night ahead of us, and a feeling that we could create anything we wanted out of it.

As it happened the gig to end all gigs was playing that evening at the Royal Albert Hall. Ronnie Lane, from The Faces, had organised a concert in aid of multiple sclerosis. All his mates were playing. Everyone from Led Zeppelin's Jimmy Page to Eric Clapton – from Charlie Watts and Bill Wyman from The Rolling Stones, to Jeff Beck and Rod Stewart. Tickets were £25 each, which was out of the question. But there was no question about whether or not we should be seeing this gig. As far as we were concerned, we were the people for whom this concert was put on. We were the ones for whom the songs were written, and we were the ones whom the forces would conspire to include in this monumental evening, where all the stars were gathering under one glorious roof – the Royal Albert Hall.

This concert was sold out, I should add, but no matter, we had a great gatecrashing record – the bigger the challenge, the greater fun there was to be had. It was a buzz. We, the destined, setting off to South Kensington station, slipping through with the crowds past the ticket collector. Joining the flow of chatter and excitement as we walked the busy streets towards the Royal Albert Hall, now positively charged for an explosive evening.

I remember – I was wearing a full-length velvet cape of crimson, a gift from my mother who understood my quest for drama and magic. I wrapped it around myself and I said to Janina, 'Now remember – we're invisible.'

Our eyes were peeled towards all exits and entrances. We circled the majestic round concert hall, casting glances towards the various doors as the audience started milling in. We were just like them, we kept thinking – only we didn't have those nice white tickets. What we did have, though, was intention and imagination, and they were enough for us to start fading around the edges. We *were* invisible, I'm sure, or at least led by some God of Gate-crashers, who was waiting for the split second when a dozen eyes would blink, to allow us our free VIP entry.

Now there's something very respectable about a rock concert in an orchestral concert hall. The people drifting towards the doors were definitely the £25-a-ticket variety (which was a lot in those days). Many of them were looking forward to smoking joints and snorting cocaine in their private boxes. Today they were going to watch the old-timers at a gig that was hosted by the future king of England and his new wife, Diana, if you please. It was all long gowns and velvet scarves. Pearls and perfumes. I felt good – like I fitted in – a little rock'n'roll, a little sophisticated. A little posh, a little dirty. Wrapping my velvet cape tighter around myself, I took Janina's hand and we mingled with the crowd, disappearing into their chinks, two rock'n'roll teenagers, guided by instinct, daring and trust.

Our moment of invisibility came in the split second that we always relied on for any such scam of a musical nature. The crowds around one entrance were being held back by a line of around fifteen policemen, all guarding a carpeted stairway. All of these policemen were looking out towards the crowds, while the two of us climbed the stairs purposefully, wrapped in an invisibility cape that we shared.

By the time we made it to the top of the stairs we were breathing heavily, flushed and scrambled. Being invisible can do that to you. When you're getting away with something big-time you're in the moment, and you're relying on that moment to carry you forward. Anything can happen.

Here's what happened to us . . .

At the top of the stairs we turned right into an empty room. On a table against the wall there were bottles of champagne on ice, and champagne glasses that were ready to touch the lips of the royal couple. We'd come early, and caught a moment when nobody was around. I swear the place was utterly empty. We were the royal guests of the moment. For those few seconds, this room had been set up for our eyes only.

Thinking on our feet, we backtracked. FAST. By now we were walking out of the champagne room and through another set of doors. Then – *get this* – we found ourselves staring out at thousands and thousands of faces in the concert hall. Believe it or not, we were in the royal box, as replacements for the prince and princess. Our hearts were beating fast. We were thinking escape strategies but, for that one luxurious moment, also enjoying our royal status. How could this be happening to us? Why hadn't anybody stopped us up till now? Years later I read about how a strange man broke into Buckingham Palace, right into the Queen's bedroom, past all the palace guards, and was entertained with a chat and a sherry. I thought about our few seconds in the royal box and realised that, national security threats aside, these things are most definitely possible!

So there we were, looking out onto the crowds who were taking their £25 seats. If someone had looked up, they would have seen that crimson cape, and two girls, temporarily exalted by the God of Gatecrashers.

'Shit, Bem, we're in the royal box!' Janina announced, and we waited, for a moment, to be caught for treason or fraud. We waited to stare in disbelief from our glorious vantage point, onto our subjects. We waited for a few seconds for our blood to start flowing again. And then we legged it.

Where did we go?

The royal toilets, of course. Yes, even royals have to go and relieve themselves occasionally like the rest of us. And there's nothing glamorous about the royal toilets at the Royal Albert Hall, let me tell you. Nothing whatsoever. Three simple loos in a row, as far as I remember. Not much privacy, if you ask me.

We arrived not a moment too soon. Within seconds we could hear the security alert. Prince Charles and Princess

Diana were on their way. Suddenly the stairwell was buzzing with life – a fanfare of noise announced their imminent arrival. We could hear the voices of security men over walkie-talkies. We couldn't see much from where we were, except toilets, but we imagined the newly weds walking up into their box, blissfully unaware of the impostors that preceded them.

Shit. Deep shit.

Only then, in that moment, did we realise that we were in it up to our elbows. What if we were arrested by MI5? This wasn't a schoolgirl adventure anymore. It was serious. It would be phone calls home, police interrogations, the lot. There were burly men outside, for goodness' sake, turning the empty staircase, the solitary champagne room and the lonely royal box into police headquarters. We could be held prisoner, tried as terrorists. Tortured. Anything.

Needless to say, at this moment we decided to hide. We hadn't lost our confidence that we could pull this off, but we were seriously worried about the consequences of being caught. The only place we could think of to hide was behind the doors. So, there we were, the two of us behind a single door, standing as flat as we could possibly manage.

No sooner had we squeezed behind the doors, when one of those walkie-talkie men came in. I kid you not. We could hear him on the other side of the thin doors as he advised some other security guard that the coast was clear. A little bit casual you may say for someone on a national-security mission, but there you go. Our man on the other side of the door obviously didn't suspect that there could possibly be two teenage girls hiding in the lavs. And why should he?

But just in case, he pushed the doors . . .

As the door opened we held our breath and concentrated on our invisibility – erasing all thoughts, in case they could be detected in the atmosphere.

Then we heard him leave the toilets and we both breathed out – a big sigh of relief.

Ye gods! What had we done to deserve this much support? Someone up there was pitching for us, against all odds.

The next part of the story is a bit of an interlude. We were stuck, you see. I can still remember dancing in Prince Charles' toilets with Janina, listening to Eric Clapton singing 'Lay Down Sally'. The world was happening outside and we were caught between a rock and a very hard place. Between the future king of England and his bodyguards, with the prospect of catching the prince with his pants down in the lavs. Meanwhile, Eric, supremely unaware, played to his crowd of £25 ticket-holders.

Now, the next part of the story you will not believe, and I don't expect you to – you have nothing but my word for this, unless of course you want to go recce behind the scenes of the Royal Albert Hall's royal box, and then you'll know for a fact that this is all true.

Remember, we were teenagers, and totally dismayed that we couldn't join the party. The biggest gathering of rock stars since Woodstock was happening outside and we were stuck in a dunny. What we desperately needed was an exit strategy.

Our deliverance came in the form of a small door that appeared to lead to some sort of a broom cupboard. Janina and I looked inside. It was dark. We climbed into what seemed like an archaic cubby with a huge amount of space and even a small staircase inside – just like something out of *Alice in Wonderland*. By now we were in the bowels of the building – a building with invisible corridors like intestines.

And in that broom cupboard what should we do? Look for a way out, of course, as if the designers of the Royal Albert Hall had our little escapade in mind when they put together the plans.

I was the one to find it – a slim crack of light that appeared at the top of the staircase within the broom cupboard. The rim of light was coming from the top of a piece of hardboard, which was easy enough to push to one side. As soon as I had removed the board we were looking into another room, on the next floor up. Hallelujah, we had escaped! In that minute I knew that we had seats in the auditorium waiting for us. Seats with our names embossed at the rear. We were truly meant to be there. Everything was falling into place too perfectly. There were unseen forces at work here. Otherwise why the spectacular entry? Why the broom cupboard?

Destiny has a great sense of humour. The God of Gatecrashers did not want our entry into this magical kingdom to take place without our fair share of challenges, and we were just about to face our next one. Where should we have landed, but the guards' tea room. Through a hole in the wall next to a filing cabinet, to be precise.

Whichever forces organised this little misadventure must have been laughing as they watched us. There we were, crouched next to the filing cabinet, looking at the sink on the opposite side of the room. Who should come in but a security guard. What should he do but walk straight past us, without looking down, as he took his mug to the sink.

It was another moment of truth. Would we be held up and slung out unceremoniously in shame? Slung in a police van, interrogated and abused? We crouched down, blanked our minds and held our breath. Not a hair moved. The security guard turned. His face was pointed in our direction. His eyes would need to drop only a couple of degrees to see us. But did he stop?

No.

By now you're thinking that I've made this all up, and I wouldn't blame you for such an accusation. 'Bem, you're a great storyteller, but stick with the believable.' I see that in people's faces whenever I tell them this story, even if their lips don't move. But no. The security guard was there and he walked past us like a miracle, without saying a word. Another sign that we were tiptoeing along a precipice, but something somewhere was protecting us from falling off. Ours were the dizzying heights. The feeling of absolute achievement, on planes beyond the metaphysical. So close to the edge we could witness everything, with heightened senses.

Now for some quick thinking. Rod Stewart was strutting his stuff by now, as we walked calmly and purposefully out of the security guards' tea room, down the corridor and through an open door. The door led to a private box, where a couple of guys, of the decadent boarding-school variety, sat in a haze of marijuana that seemed to inhale us. They thought nothing of two girls arriving just as Rod started singing 'Do Ya Think I'm Sexy?'

We muttered something about getting lost and sat down. We were in. And there, in front of us, was the most fabulous line-up you could imagine. Charlie Watts on drums, looking over and smiling at Bill Wyman who played with Jeff Beck on lead guitar, and maybe even Jimmy Page somewhere on the stage, I can't quite recall. Down to the right, several degrees below us, we could see the prince and princess, hardly grooving, but nonetheless nodding occasionally, no doubt tapping toes on red carpets and getting into a royal sort of groove.

'That was us,' I said, as I nudged Janina. We smiled and hugged each other. The greatest rock'n'roll band played just for the two of us, and we danced around the box we'd commandeered, aroused on music, fuelled by our fantastical adventure. *This is the life. This is one story I am going to tell the whole world*, I thought, already imagining the faces of my school friends as I told them this tale.

When all the finales were over and the bands had come and gone and come again, the lights came up. It was the perfect ending. But neither Janina nor I was ready to call it the final climax.

There was no doubt about what we should do. If we couldn't go back to the palace with the royals, we would have to go backstage. It was that logical.

And naturally, if we were going to go backstage we would have to go the same way as the musicians.

Once more, we had to pick our moment. As soon as the crowd started milling out in their velvets and satins, we started to home inwards with the instinct of migratory birds, as high as is humanly possible, with an undisputable knowledge of where we had to be. There was nobody guarding the stage, which by now didn't surprise us. Instead the bouncers concentrated on the exits, making sure that everybody left safely. Everybody, that is, except the two of us, who by now were so charged we were unstoppable. It was painfully simple. In a deliriously tense moment of excitement, fear, desire and anticipation, we climbed up onto the wooden boards with our stomachs in our mouths, and walked straight through to the backstage area.

It was a party all right, and there we were in the thick of it. Janina practising her mysterious look for Jimmy Page and me, in my crimson cape, looking like something out of 'The Battle of Evermore'. We mingled with the rock stars and their guests, too cool to talk to anybody but each other. And then, when we finally realised that we were out past my mother's curfew, we took our leave from that surreal party.

Imagine the sight: two girls wrapped up in a single crimson cape, linking arms, heads held high. They walk out the backstage door, and proudly face the swarms of paparazzi.

Somewhere a camera clicks, and in that moment both of them smile.

Donna Hay's

Recipe to Satisfy Even
the Most Wicked Munchies

There are times in all our lives when Ronald McDonald is the man of our dreams and twoallbeefpattiesspecial-saucelettucecheesepicklesonionsonasesameseedbun is the pinnacle of dining excellence. Those times are generally preceded by a couple of Caprioskas, a half bottle or more of Semillon, some tequila shots for good measure and one last beer for the road. But in an effort to end the night with a little decorum (let's face it, the effect of fluoro lights in Macca's on one's complexion post midnight after Alcoholapaloo does not a pleasant sight make), I've put together a recipe that will satisfy the most wicked munchies. The hangover curing combination of carbohydrate, protein, fat (hooray for fat!) and salt can be made in minutes and, unless you're Old Mother Hubbard, all the ingredients should be lying around in your pantry and fridge. For maximum results, make and eat one before you go to bed, and repeat again when you wake up . . . your body will thank you.

Fried-egg Sandwiches
2 slices bread
Butter
2 eggs
4 slices cheese
Salt and pepper to taste
3 glasses water
2 aspirin

Butter the bread and fold each slice in half. Take a bite from the middle of both slices of bread and eat it, leaving a hole in the middle of the bread slices. Place both slices of bread in a frying pan, buttered side down, and cook over medium heat until golden. Turn bread over and crack an egg into each hole in the bread – try and get all the egg shell in the garbage. Eat two slices of cheese for sustenance, then place the others on top of the egg. When the cheese starts to melt the egg is ready. Eat accompanied by three glasses water and two aspirin ('cause it is too hard to get out of bed in the morning to get them and prevention is better than cure).

Maggie Beer's

Recipe for a Big Night Out

When planning cocktail parties I want to make sure my offerings will not only delight but surprise as well.

My favourite finger food of all – well, of the moment at least – is a delicious morsel on a shell. Of course, you need to be organised and have a wine bucket, or similar, to collect shells as soon as they've been eaten, but that's no more trouble than having a tray for olive pips or toothpicks – and much more interesting.

The real trick is to persuade people to use the shell to slide the scallop into their mouth and not ask for a knife and fork. As scallops differ in size, you might find you need to cut really huge meaty ones in halves or quarters – but do this only after cooking. Here in South Australia I'd use Port Lincoln scallops: they are so sweet and nutty – as long as they haven't been frozen and are barely cooked (just to the stage of turning opaque).

Sea urchin roe is now being harvested in South Australia for the first time. It's long been a delicacy in Japan and France (and probably many more places I haven't travelled to), but here it's still considered anything from odd to incredibly adventurous. For me, it's one of the taste sensations of my life – the sweet intensity of the roe, the slightly metallic taste like that of an oyster, and the deep ochre colour that seduces all by itself give such a finish to the scallop that I'm left wondering whether to actually save any for my guests.

Scallops with Sea Urchin Butter
Makes 24 canapés

24 Port Lincoln scallops – or fewer, if larger
Grated zest of 1 lime
100g unsalted butter
50ml olive oil
Sea salt
Freshly ground black pepper
100ml verjuice
handful of plucked fresh chervil

Sea Urchin Butter
75g softened unsalted butter
Roe from 2 sea urchins or approx. 2 tablespoons
    harvested sea urchin roe
Sea salt
Freshly ground black pepper
1 tablespoon lemon juice

Make the sea urchin butter by combining all the ingredients. Set aside.

Clean scallops by pulling away from shell and cutting out black intestinal tract; reserve the shells. Place scallops in a bowl and add the lime zest, a drizzle of olive oil, sea salt and freshly ground pepper.

In a frying pan, melt the butter with the rest of the olive oil and allow to sizzle until nut-brown. Pan-fry the scallops, in batches, for about 30 seconds each side, just to seal them. (Do not try to cook too many scallops at once – you want to sear, not poach them.)

Add verjuice to the pan and deglaze. Place a scallop on each half-shell, dot with sea urchin butter, and drizzle with the pan juices and verjuice.

Put under a hot grill or into a preheated 220°C oven for about one minute – just until the sea urchin butter begins to melt. Sprinkle with chervil and serve.

Louise Wener

Mr Up-and-down-up-and-down Once

He's got a Rolls-Royce. British racing green with walnut trim and tan leather seats. I've never seen a Rolls-Royce before, not in the flesh. It looks fucking ace. In fact, if you want to know what I think, I'd say it makes our street look the bollocks.

Everyone's been acting a bit crazy since he bought it. My mum's swept the driveway four times since Tuesday and the neighbours have been cleaning their cars with a fury all weekend. Mr Calloway has been at it for hours. He's emptied his ashtrays, wiped down his upholstery with a damp sponge, and he's just about to start on his bonnet with the Turtle Wax. I watch him spread it on. He smears it all over and grinds away at it with his cloth but it doesn't seem to be doing much good. The harder he goes at it the streakier it becomes, and the way he's cursing at his dog and kicking at his tyres makes me think he might be close to giving up.

They all give up in the end. They shrug their shoulders, lay down their wash rags and one by one they sidle up the road – all casual like – to come and pay homage to the Royce.

'Doesn't look *all that*, up close,' says one of them.

'You're right there,' says another.

'It's a bit showy, isn't it?' says his wife.

They know nothing.

By teatime on Sunday the whole street has been by to take a look. Everyone except for Mr Up-and-down-up-and-down. He's a weirdo. He lives in the dirty house at the top of the road and he spends all day pacing up and down the pavement talking to himself and shouting things out. Sometimes he forgets where he is and his wife has to come out and fetch him. He doesn't seem to mind, just so long as no one touches his brown leather suitcase. My friend Arnold says he keeps stray cats in that case. He traps them with tins of sardines, then he takes them home, ties them up by the tail and skins them alive with a six-inch hunting knife.

I'm not sure whether to believe him or not. My mum says Mr Up-and-down-up-and-down has got something called Alzheimer's disease and that there's no need to be afraid of him because pretty soon the poor man will have turned into a cabbage. That's all well and good, but the thing is I'm quite partial to a tinned sardine now and again, and the way I look at it, you can never be too careful.

Here he comes now. Juddering up the road like a clockwork toy. Backwards then forwards, then backwards then forwards, then forwards, then backwards, then stop.

He stops right in front of the Rolls-Royce. He clicks his heels and claps his hands and lowers his nose to the bonnet. And sniffs. I swear, he fucking sniffs it. He runs his crooked nose over the bonnet and slowly down along the metal grill. Pretty soon he's reached the silver statuette with the wings and he's sniffing at it hard, like a dog trying to get underneath a girl's skirt.

I leave him to it. I take a quick trip round the block to stretch my legs and warn any stray cats that Mr Up-and-down-up-and-down is on the loose but when I get back he's exactly where I left him.

It seems to me like he's in some sort of a trance. He's rocking slightly from side to side and his back is bent so far over the bonnet it looks like it might crack in two. I'm not sure what to do next. I watch him a while longer to see whether he'll come to his senses, then I pick up my stick, roll up my sleeves and wander over to give him a bit of a talking to.

'What you doing?' says I. 'What you sniffing at, you bonkers old git?'

He doesn't answer. He stays right where he is. His eyelids flicker like a wonky light-bulb and his hands contract into tight fists. He's breathing heavily, wheezing and puffing and gulping for air, and I notice that his left leg is trembling slightly.

By now I'm thinking that maybe he's had a little bit of a stroke, so I edge forwards and I gives him a kick in the foot. Nothing. I try again. Nothing. I rub my chin and wave my stick around for a while and I'm just thinking about aiming a poke at his bony shin when he turns round and makes a grab for my shirt.

He moves like a bastard. Out of nowhere. He swipes his hand from my collar to my throat and I'm just about to piss myself with the shock, when all of a sudden his hand goes limp and he lets me go.

'You like this car, do you?' he says, fixing me with his milky eyes.

'It's okay,' says I, wondering what it's going to feel like when he skins me.

'It's a Rolls-Royce,' he says, sucking the words like chicken bones. 'A Silver Shadow.'

'Y-yes,' I say, 'a Silver Shadow. V8 engine, top speed of a hundred and twenty miles an hour.'

Mr Up-and-down-up-and-down nods his head. A brief smile flickers across his face like he appreciates what I have to say on the matter and he reaches down for his battered suitcase.

'Do you like sardines?' he says, reaching for the clasp.

'No!' I say. 'Jesus, no I don't. I don't like them one little bit. They're disgusting.'

Mr Up-and-down-up-and-down looks disappointed. He stops fumbling with the clasp, tucks his suitcase under his arm and tick-tocks off down the street without another word. He's a good twenty yards away before I realise that I'm shaking. Before I realise that it's Mr Dobrin that's come and chased him off.

'You all right, lad?' says Mr Dobrin, ruffling my hair with his hand.

'No,' I say, glancing down at my trousers to make sure I haven't wet myself. 'That lunatic was about to skin me. That's what he does, you know. It's true. He steals cats and he skins them alive and his wife puts them in a giant cooking pot for their dinner.'

Mr Dobrin starts to laugh. His face wrinkles like a dirty bedsheet and a warm tear skids over his baggy cheek. He's tickled pink. He wipes his eyes and stamps his feet and in the end he has to bend over and clutch his stomach with both hands he's laughing so damned much.

'Come on,' he says, straightening up and allowing himself a final chuckle. 'How's about I take you for a quick drive.'

'In the Rolls-Royce?' I say, unable to believe my luck.

'Yes,' he says.

And off we go.

This is the nuts. It's like driving around in a cruise ship. The seats are high and wide like my dad's armchair, and the leather's as soft as whipped butter. At first I'm a little bit nervous. I'm sitting deadly still and pushing my knees together nice and tight so I don't break anything, but I soon get the hang of things.

Mr Dobrin lets me have a go on the electric windows. There's a button that makes them open and a button that makes them close, and even though I'm pressing them over and over and flicking the radio on and off like a goon he doesn't seem to mind. He twists a gold ring round his index finger and taps his wallet through the pocket of his slacks. I wonder how much he's got in there. I wonder if it's more than fifty pounds.

Mr Dobrin is the richest man in the whole world. No one knows how he got to be quite so rich but my friend Arnold reckons he must be a bank robber or something like that. I once asked my dad if it was true or not but he didn't seem that bothered about giving me an answer. He shook his head, clicked his teeth and went on with reading his paper. My mum rolled her eyes to the ceiling and went on with making the tea.

'Lemon meringue pie for afters,' she said, stirring some milk into her pan.

'We'll have some custard on it then, will we?' said my dad.

'What about Mr Dobrin being a bank robber?' says I.

'Mind your own beeswax,' said my dad.

I even had a go at asking my sister Carol what she thought but she just flicked her fringe, muttered something about Mr Dobrin being a dirty old man and went on with painting her nails.

We leave the confusion of the suburbs far behind us and head out west towards the city. Soaking up the applause from the street. Carving through the traffic like a fine knife. Mr Dobrin rests his elbow on the open window and warns me to keep my eyes peeled for sexy women. He slows right down when he sees one he likes and he gives a quick toot on his horn if he thinks they've got particularly nice tits.

'You want to get yourself over to Portugal, lad,' he

announces out of nowhere. 'Barrels of tits over there. Brown as berries. Stretched out along the sea-front for as far as the eye can see.'

He smiles at the memory and I nod approvingly like I know what he's getting at. But the furthest I've ever been on my holidays is Torquay. And the only tits I've seen are my mum's.

'How's your sister these days?' says Mr Dobrin after a while.

'She's a moron,' says I, wondering when Mr Dobrin is going to let me have a look at the driving manual. 'She's always eating lettuce instead of chips and sometimes she goes to sleep with curlers in her head.'

Mr Dobrin smiles and wipes his lip. 'A right little stunner your sister,' he says, letting off a low whistle. 'Best-looking girl on the whole street.'

He keeps on about my sister for quite a while after that. What nice legs she's got; what a nice summer dress she was wearing the other day; do I think she has any opinions regarding older men? Do I think she might like to come for a ride in his Rolls-Royce sometime? Have I ever noticed her sunbathing without her bikini top on? Have I ever seen her coming out of the shower without her towel?

I shrug my shoulders.

'Tell you what,' he says, 'how's about you put in a good word for me. I'll let you clean the car if you like. And I'll pay you. How does a fiver a week sound?'

A fiver a week sounds good. A fiver a week sounds very good indeed.

'All right,' says I. 'I'll have a word with her. See what I can do for you.'

'There's a good lad,' says Mr Dobrin, patting me on the head. 'Maybe I'll take her up the West End for a steak dinner. That usually does the trick.'

'What trick?' I say, wondering what he's on about.

'The loosening of the old knicker elastic,' says Mr Dobrin, wiping a patch of grease from his forehead. 'Nothing loosens the old knicker elastic faster than a good steak dinner and a trip up West.'

Mr Dobrin doesn't say very much on the way home. I ask him how many miles he gets to the gallon but he's not too bothered about giving me an answer. I tell him all about Rolls-Royce making Spitfire engines during the Second World War and I ask which model he likes better, the Phantom or the Silver Ghost, but he doesn't seem to have an opinion on the matter.

He says he might part-exchange the Roller for something more sporty in the autumn. A Ferrari or something like that. He asks me what kind of car my dad drives and for some reason he has a good old laugh when I tell him what it is.

I'm in big trouble. It's dark by the time we get home and my mum is watching us from the porch as we pull up outside the house. Her face is set in a deep frown and I can see where she's creased the net curtains from holding them away from the window for so long. I ask Mr Dobrin if he can open the bonnet and give me a quick look at the engine before I have to go inside, but he says he hasn't got time to be bothering with all that. I ask him if I can have a closer look at the Silver Lady on the front, but he tells me that he doesn't want me getting my finger prints all over it and spoiling the shine.

'And don't forget to tell your sister I was asking after her,' he says, winking at me as I get out of the car.

'Don't worry,' I say, closing the door tight behind me. 'I won't.'

My mum gives me a good talking to for staying out late and missing my tea. She wants to know if I've finished my history homework (three reasons why the spinning jenny was important to the Industrial Revolution or some such) and when I tell her that I have, she offers to make me a sandwich so I don't go to bed hungry.

She wants to know what Mr Dobrin had to say for himself and I tell her all about him offering me five pounds a week to clean his car. She asks me if I'm thinking about doing it and I tell her right away that I'm not. My dad says I must have a screw loose but I just shrug my shoulders and get on with my sandwich. I don't mention anything about my sister. And I don't tell my dad that Mr Dobrin thinks he drives a funny car.

The next morning I'm up bright and early and I'm out of the house before anyone has come down for their breakfast. I'm wearing my Bionic Man T-shirt and my quietest plimsolls, and I've got one of my dad's screwdrivers tucked into my jacket pocket. The street is deserted. The sun is only just up and if I'm lucky the postman won't be round for a good hour yet.

I get straight to it. I sprint up the road – being careful not to wake next door's dog – fetch the screwdriver from my pocket and take my position in front of the Rolls-Royce.

At first it won't give at all. The threads must be broken or gummed up with dirt, but after ten minutes of gouging and me hitting it with a bit of a rock, the little statue finally starts to give. Bingo. My heart is big inside my chest and I'm breathing faster than our pet gerbil after it's been for a spin on its wheel, but at last I have it in my hands. The Silver Lady. The emblem. The prize.

I stand up and get my bearings. I take a couple of good, deep breaths, wipe my fingers on the pockets of my jeans and glance over my shoulder to make sure no one has seen me. And then I feel it. A damp hand on my neck and the dig of a leather suitcase in the small of my back.

'Jesus H Christ,' I say, jumping out of my skin and swinging round to see who it is. 'What are you doing, you bonkers sod? What are you doing creeping up on me like that?'

Mr Up-and-down-up-and-down blinks his eyes. He edges backwards towards the kerb and shakes his head from side to side to let me know that he's seen what I've been up to.

'Now listen here,' I say, waving the Silver Lady in his face. 'Don't you be saying anything about me stealing this here statue. Don't you be shouting your mouth off and telling everyone what I've done.'

He shakes his head. He lays his suitcase on the pavement and shuffles forwards, cupping his hands together like a fruit bowl. I know what he's getting at. He wants to hold it. He promises he won't tell who stole it just so long as he gets to hold it for a moment.

'All right then,' says I, trying not to panic, 'but only for a second. One second and then you have to let me have it straight back.'

He nods. His face lights up like a Halloween lantern and he opens his mouth to speak.

'I used to be a car mechanic once,' he says, matter-of-factly.

'Is that right?' I say, keeping my eyes open for the postman.

'Yes,' he says. 'I restored classic cars. Very keen on cars. Very keen. Rolls-Royce. Very nice car. Especially keen on the Phantom and the Wraith. Very nice car the Phantom. Very nice indeed.'

For a split second the traffic jam in his head clears away and he almost seems to know what he's talking about. He rattles off the names of his all-time favourite cars. His favourite models, his favourite engines, their technical specifications and the years they were each manufactured. He goes on like this for some minutes, and just when I think he's going to carry on all day, something distracts him and he reaches down for his suitcase.

'Do you like sardines?' he says quietly.

'Don't mind them,' says I, standing firm.

'I've got lots of sardines in here, you know. More

sardines than I know what to do with.'

And then he opens it.

At first I don't dare to look but after a while I find I can't stop myself. It's not what I was expecting. It's not full of tinned fish or madness or stink or bleached bones, it's full to the brim with spanners. And bits of old cars. Half a smashed-up number plate, a scrap of rusty bumper, a wheel nut cut into crisp half-moons and a bunch of other crap and fluff and mess that must be all he has left from his days as a car mechanic.

He crouches down next to the suitcase and runs his fingers over the little statue. Nice and gentle. Like he's stroking a cat. He lowers his head, sniffs it once more for good measure, then hands it back to me, as good as his word.

'No,' I says, all of a sudden. 'You can keep it if you want. I reckon you like it even more than I do.'

He smiles. A smile so wide and bright and gummy that I've never seen another like it before or since. He stands up to leave. He packs the Silver Lady into his suitcase, fixes the metal clasp with great care and tick-tocks off down the street without another word.

Backwards then forwards, then backwards then forwards, then forwards, then backwards, then stop.

Richard Glover

Cock-a-hoop

'You are not gay unless you get an erection when you think about someone else's penis. It's as simple as that.'

Tim was enjoying himself hugely. He stood in front of me, in the middle of the restaurant kitchen, a look of serious scientific inquiry on his face.

'Imagine my penis, for instance,' he said. 'I'm not offering or anything, but as an example. You've got to fix it in your mind. Right? Have you got it?'

The suggestion was meant kindly, so I squinted my eyes and tried to imagine Tim's penis. We'd been taught to do this at school. Not imagining penises, of course. Using visualisation techniques. You'd mentally place something half a metre from your eyes, and then look at it from different angles, as a way of fixing it in your mind.

I'd used the technique to visualise all sorts of stuff – the periodic table, a couple of speeches from *Hamlet*, the dates of World War I. But I was having more problems with Tim's penis. Especially with him just leaning there, less than a metre off, breathing in his wheezy way.

The thing kept coming in and out of focus, metamorphosing, turning into a sausage, then a slug, then a gherkin. Every time I got the thing fixed for a moment, Tim's face would enter the picture, grinning like a lunatic.

I opened my eyes.

'You're imagining a big one, I hope,' he said. 'Huge and sleek. Half rocket-ship, half fire hose. I've never had a proper erection, you know. It's so big that every time it starts to get hard, I faint from the blood loss.'

Yeah, sure. I'd heard this speech before. Along with: 'It's so big I have to throw it over my shoulder so it doesn't trail on the ground.' And 'It's so big sometimes I just wrap it around and bugger myself as I walk along.'

It was one or the many oddities of Tim that he could be spectacularly vulgar, and yet somehow it would all seem innocent and rather lovable. Girls would smile, the boys would laugh. All over stuff that, if I ever said it, would cause everyone to think me a creepy sleaze.

It was part of the mystery of being Tim. And the mystery of being me.

Tim swung himself up on the stainless-steel benchtop in the middle of the kitchen. The top was piled with cutlery still hot from the dishwasher. I grabbed a handful of knives, cradling the hot metal with one edge of a tea towel, while using the whip-end to buff them, then shot them into a plastic bucket. I had a couple of minutes before I'd have to start the table set-up.

'You could help, you know,' I said to Tim, but he

shook his head with a look of mock-seriousness.

'I'm helping my best friend determine his sexuality,' he said grandly. 'I think that is more important than cleaning knives and forks. Now, if you are going to imagine my cock, you might as well be accurate. I see it as —'

'Actually,' I interrupted, 'I was just trying for a cock – any old cock.'

Tim stood up, and let loose a sigh. 'Well, I think that proves it,' he said. 'If you don't see the glory of my penis, then I'm afraid you are straight.'

I gathered up the plastic bin of knives and pushed the bin of forks towards Tim. Like me, he had just turned twenty-three. After a period of terrible struggle, lasting all of two weeks, he had exited the university and landed a cadetship with the city's main newspaper. I was still in a post-university daze, trying to earn some money while deciding between the rich galaxy of choices available to a directionless young man with a mediocre science degree and bad posture.

I gave Tim a shove, trying to shift him from the bench-top. 'Since we've now decided I'm straight – and thank you for the invaluable assistance of your penis in that task – you can help me set the tables.'

We worked our way through the restaurant. I whacked the cutlery down, while Tim hovered behind me, letting loose a running commentary about how everything in the restaurant was slightly wrong, slightly daggy. According to Tim, we were the last bastion of vertical food – each ingredient carefully stacked on top of the last. 'What does your boss reckon? That each plate is a block of city real estate, and he's got to have vacant space around the high-rise?'

I didn't care. It was a job.

Tim, I should mention, was straight. Resolutely, outrageously – and successfully – so. Perhaps it was his very success that was causing me to doubt my heterosexuality. Maybe I'd rather play a sport in which he was not competing.

We'd known each other for three years, and had quickly fallen into this unequal relationship. I was the Robin to his Batman. The Tonto to his Lone Ranger. Or to be more accurate: the Hi Yo Silver to his Lone Ranger. Tim, always striving for the noticeable idiosyncrasy, refused to get his driver's licence. I'd become his official method of transport: he'd whistle me up whenever he wanted to go anywhere.

He was by far the most charismatic person I knew. A new project every five minutes, a new idea every week, a new set of friends every month. A person who could talk about anything, and not just about TV, beer and music, like the rest of us. He'd charge into a rave about philosophy or theatre, politics or fiction. In his company, just for a while, you could become convinced you were part of some sort of smart set.

I enjoyed arguing with him. On this occasion, as usual, he won the debate: as much as I had flirted with the idea of being gay – mentally and, occasionally, in practice – I didn't have what it took. Alone in a bed, my mind would instantly fill with women. Women like Tim's girlfriend Pippa, whose image jumped unbidden into my mind last thing every night, first thing every morning, and about a dozen times in between.

Or, rather, his ex-girlfriend Pippa. Tim had dispatched her the night before, in his typical sensitive way. That's how we'd ended up talking about my sexuality in the first place. We'd got onto the topic via Pippa. And via Tim's big news.

When he'd first walked into the restaurant, earlier that afternoon, I hadn't seen him for days. I'd been alone in the place, filling the fridge behind the bar. He bounced in, looking like a minor celebrity. With Tim, you never knew what look to expect. A month before he was dressing like a bikie, six months before that like a clubber, all toggles and haphazard seams. This time his dark hair was buzz-cut, and he was wearing a pair of pressed pale moleskins, and a check blue shirt. It was the country-squire look, and, with Tim inside the clothes, somehow it looked funky. Urban cool. I was amazed by the effect. Put me in the same gear and I'd look like the Bowral estate agent: fat and forty.

Tim perched on one of the bar stools, grinning. You could always tell when he had a story. He was excited, but with his lips clamped down, as if he was afraid he'd blurt out the punchline before he was quite ready to milk its dramatic potential.

'I broke up with Pippa,' he said finally, helping himself to a glass of water from the jug I'd placed on the bar.

'That's terrible,' I said, 'she seemed a really great person.'

I straightened up and leaned on the bar, facing Tim. I was ready to be solicitous, but sympathy didn't seem to be what was required. I was there to hear one of Tim's stories. Audience more than friend.

'I'd decided it was time to tell her, so I walked around to her flat. You know where she lives, right? And then I found myself stopping in at the chemist and buying a box of tissues.'

He paused for effect, but I didn't quite get his point. He flashed me a look – you idiot – then explained.

'This was subconscious, right. I'd been walking along, thinking how upset she'd be, and the next thing I'm in the chemist buying a pack of tissues. And only when I'm leaving do I realise I've bought the tissues for Pippa – *because I know she'll want to cry her tiny heart out over me!* Isn't that the most fucked thing you've heard? I'm such a pig, I should be studied scientifically.'

Through all this, Tim had been jiggling his leg and letting out little whoops of what was meant to be self-deprecating laughter. He loved the story. Loved the way it made him look bad. But also good because he was willing to admit everything.

Just for a moment, I couldn't stand looking at him. I turned back to the fridge, packing in more beer. Tim kept talking.

'Since I'd already bought the tissues, I thought I'd just keep the box, and take them home after. So, I get to her flat, tell her we are breaking up, and then all hell breaks loose – she runs into her bedroom and throws herself on the bed, crying. Not normal crying. She's like honking and weeping. It's like some African woman at a funeral. She's *keening*. So, what am I meant to do? I get the tissues, walk in, and I put them on the end of the bed.

And I say, 'Just in case you need them, Pippa.'

I kept on packing the fridge. 'So, what did she say?'

'Nothing. She just stared at me, and straight away stopped crying. So the tissues, I've got to say, worked.'

He got to the punchline, and I felt like punching him. I stood up, walked out of the bar, and into the kitchen. I couldn't get the image out of my head, the image of her lying weeping on the bed. Nor the word: *keening*. Tim was so pleased with it. I bet he'd come up with it at the time. This girl is weeping over him, and he's watching, delighted his vocab is sufficiently extensive in order to supply the perfect descriptive term. Ten points to Tim. Improve Your Word Power with *Reader's Digest* and Tim McHeath. Among this month's words: duplicitous, keening, overbearing and egomaniacal.

Certainly, my mind was feeding on the picture of Pippa crying on the bed, and I was busy thinking the worst of Tim. Maybe he'd done the same with previous girlfriends. Did he vary the size of the box according to how long they'd been together? Or according to how prettily his hair was hanging that week? I could imagine him checking the mirror before he left. If his skin was blotchy, the break-up girl could make do with a handi pack; if he was particularly gorgeous, it would be the family-sized box. 'Actually, I'm so attractive I'd best supply you with tissues, some Sudafed for the blocked sinus, paracetamol for the headache, and sleeping pills for the inevitable period of sleepless grief.'

I got the cutlery out of the dishwasher and dumped it with a clatter onto the benchtop, and started polishing.

A minute or two later Tim wandered in.

It was then – just when I thought I'd had enough of Tim to last forever – that he offered Pippa to me. 'You should go and see her,' he said, 'you two would probably get it on. You are pretty similar. I'll give you her number.'

It was a very Tim thing to say. Offering the rejected girlfriend to the sidekick friend, as if – following her demotion – we were both now on about the same level. It was so bizarre, I didn't know what to say.

And that, I guess, is why I'd made the comment about being gay, which in turn led Tim to ask me to imagine his cock. He was being amusing, I suppose, trying to make me laugh, trying to win back his audience, only minutes after convincing me he was the trashiest person alive.

And, amazingly, I played along, trying to imagine his penis, while he joked around about its size. It was strange that I couldn't imagine it, since I was now pretty certain he was a prick.

I spent the next ten days listing the reasons a phone call would be a big mistake. I didn't write down a list, but in my head I had something that looked like one.

1. I've only met Pippa three times, and always with Tim. Ringing up would be a disaster, as it's quite likely she won't remember who I am.
2. How would I start?
3. By ringing her, I'm endorsing the idea that Pippa is his to bestow.

4. By ringing her, I'm endorsing the idea that I'll do anything Tim tells me to do.

5. She'll hang up on me anyway.

6. If I don't ring, I'll run into her someplace, which would be a lot more dignified.

7. Before I ring, I've got to decide whether or not to leave a message in case there's a message machine, because otherwise I'll leave some stupid embarrassing message and be so mortified that I'll be forced to go around and burn down her house, just so she doesn't get to hear it.

8. What if she already has a new boyfriend?

9. If I did get together with Pippa, I'd never encounter a box of tissues without imagining her on the bed, and without hearing that word. Keening. And thinking of Tim.

10. And, drum roll, the number ten reason: if I did go out with her, I'd be building Tim further into my life, just at the time I've realised Tim is not such a good thing for this particular Tonto.

And so on. Against which there was the single entry on the other side of the ledger: Pippa was this fabulous woman.

So I rang. Did she remember me? She remembered. Did she want to speak to me? She did. Not to brag, but Pippa suggested a drink.

I'll be brief about what happened then, as you'll be able to imagine most of it. Pippa was on the rebound from Tim, and I was in the mood to hear him described in the worst ways. Those few weeks we had a weird kind of fun. It was like meeting someone who shares an obscure hobby – someone who's also interested in French pottery of the 1920s, or British steam trains of the 1890s. We had an esoteric joint interest in bad-mouthing Tim, and we could do it for hours at a stretch.

It didn't take long for Pippa and me to fall into bed, and then for me to move into her flat. I'd made a habit of going out with hippy girls, delicate and wan in a freckly Celtic way. Pippa was the opposite – as tall as me, with big swimmer's shoulders, and strong arms. She was exuberant and outgoing. Sturdy in body and in soul.

She'd met Tim at the newspaper, where she worked as a page designer and sometime artist. She saw him there still, but they rarely talked. Once I'd moved in with Pippa, I kept seeing Tim, but felt less overwhelmed by him. Things seemed to be shifting for both Pippa and me. She was falling into new rhythms, enjoying domesticity, becoming more confident about her work. And I was becoming more confident about myself. Tonto was in a state of successful rebellion.

Then one Saturday, six months on, everything shifted once more. It was early morning, July sunshine slanting into the flat, with Pippa lounging around in my cotton dressing gown. It was tied loosely, and I kept seeing the curve of her breasts as she wandered.

The flat was full of her paintings, and sketches done by friends. Her own work was loud and vivid. She rarely got around to hanging the pictures; they were propped on the floor, leaning against walls, or shoved up on shelves. They looked far better than the carefully hung paintings in my parents' place.

Pippa moved them around, stood back and smiled at the new positioning. And I watched her, as she watched the art. I loved the way she moved, and thought, and joked. And I loved her body. Sometimes it left me quite winded, as if someone was pressing down on my chest and I couldn't breathe.

We were both, I'm sure, beginning to think that this was it. Incredibly, I was someone's *one*. I was Pippa's one. We'd even begun, in a tentative way, to talk about children. Not directly, but by mentioning little kids we'd seen or met. 'Justine and Greg's kid is sooo cute.' It reminded me of the way you talk about sex – generally, and in theory – early on during the night you first do it, as if you just had an intellectual interest in the subject, but no personal plans.

Then, just as Pippa finished blu-tacking one of her own sketches to the wall, she half-turned and spoke.

'I was planning to go and see Tim this arvo.'

'Tim McHeath?'

'Yeah. Of course.'

'How come?'

'He asked me.'

'Yeah? How come?'

'You see him sometimes. I'm allowed. It's no big deal. He looked a bit fed-up, actually.'

For the rest of the morning, I put a fair bit of effort into trying not to say anything. She'd been serious friends with Tim for years, even before they went out together. She had a right to go around for a cup of tea without her nutcase boyfriend getting pathetic.

I even behaved okay as she left, waving her off, telling her to say hello for me, right up to the moment the doors closed. Then I went to pieces. I was convinced she was going to sleep with him. The process by which Tim always made me feel second-rank would be revisited once again.

I still had enough self-insight to realise this was madness speaking, simple insecurity run wild. And more about my relationship with Tim than with Pippa. For a start, it was a Saturday afternoon – not exactly the timing for a mad affair. And Pippa hadn't lied about where she was going. If she was thinking about having sex with Tim, why would she tell me where she was going?

Which is why I decided to look in her jewellery box. It was the place where she kept the little silk bag of condoms she'd take if we were going away for the weekend. There was a little bottle of massage oil in there, and her tiny black vibrator. I wasn't snooping on her; I really wasn't doubting her. I was sick of the doubting voice in my own head. This was a way of lecturing myself, of giving myself a dose of reality. That's what I said to myself, anyway. I'd look in the jewellery box, see the little silk bag safely in position, and instantly be flooded with guilt for my suspicions, and with love for Pippa.

That was the idea, except when I looked, the little bag wasn't there. I searched through the jewellery box again. I emptied it out onto the bed. Then rummaged, desperate, through the contents, then through the rest of her drawers and cupboards. After an hour of looking, and swearing, and searching, I faced the knowledge that she'd taken condoms and a vibrator in order to visit Tim.

And here's a funny thing. I might have had trouble picturing Tim's cock in the restaurant, but I was having no trouble conjuring up a vivid image of it right now.

It was not a pretty scene when Pippa got home. Picture me sitting at the kitchen table, looking up from a novel, ready to ask a few calm questions. Picture me that way if you like. In reality, I was curled in the hallway of the flat, sobbing. The sobbing was partly for her benefit – growing in intensity as I heard her footsteps on the path. But it was still sobbing.

In films about infidelity, the cuckold gets the cuckee to deny everything. And then springs the evidence at her, at which point she breaks down, and is forced to admit both infidelity and fabrication. But I didn't muck around. Blubbing as I was, I didn't have the means to keep any powder dry.

'You fucked Tim. You took the condom bag. I searched your room. Why did you do it?' This all screamed, amid sobs.

Pippa just stood there, a look of deep resignation on her face. 'I took the bag. I don't know why I took it, but

I did. Maybe I felt sorry for him; he's not been with any-one since we broke up. I don't know. But I didn't sleep with him. I shouldn't have taken the bag. It was just an impulse. A stupid idea.'

We argued and talked and cried for days. I can't quite remember how many days now. It seemed to go on for-ever. We'd talk, and then sleep, and then wake in the morning, and it would all start again. It was exhausting and terrible and so, so, sad.

In the end, I believed her. She'd taken the wretched condom bag, but only as a last-minute impulse. She hadn't thought it through. And she certainly hadn't used it. But by then there'd been too many tears. She'd seen me being too weak, too mean, too pathetic. And I'd let Tim into my psyche again.

It's now been five years since I've seen either of them, although I read Tim's pieces in the paper, and see Pippa's artwork, which is now quite startlingly good. And some-times I wonder about the chance of things. Whether we'd still be together if I'd never checked out her jewellery box. Or if she'd lied when she got home, and 'found' the condom bag still in our room. Or, most of all, if I'd had the guts to play for Pippa, and take time off my competi-tion with Tim.

Lisa Armstrong

Absinthe Makes the Heart Grow Fonder

EnemiesReunited.com

'I still don't understand why you're going through with this,' said Richard, watching Sarah stage an SAS-style commander raid on an extensive wardrobe that was roughly the size of the White House.

'Chic or intimidating?' She held a black coat-thing, or it might have been a dress, against herself and sounded cross. Cross but inconclusive – a sign that she didn't know why she was going through with it either.

'You said yourself they were a bunch of sad tossers.'

'I did not,' she retorted indignantly.

'Did so.' She was naked again.

Radio Four droned away in the background. Sarah groaned inwardly. Sometimes, just sometimes, she wished they'd get Tara Palmer Tompkinson on instead of John Humphrys. She'd love to hear her 'Thought for the Day', though she supposed it would be more of a 'Thought-lessness for the Day'. Bound to be more fun than the Reverend All-Inclusive, however.

Richard looked dispassionately but admiringly at Sarah's shapely, neat breasts and her even neater, flat stomach. Sarah's body was just one of her many perfect attributes, as he was quick to appreciate, although somehow it seemed remote from the rest of her. Fondling his way through her quixotic aura, he often had the uneasy feeling that she ought to issue him with a passport when he explored it. Still, viewing it from afar was proving rather enjoyable. Reluctantly he glanced at his watch: 6.55 a.m.

'Sheba wasn't a tosser,' she said. 'Leading light of the sixth form actually. Interestingly beautiful —'

'Is that the same as *jolie-laide*? A.k.a ugly?'

She ignored him. 'And creative. Her parents were in the theatre. I secretly hoped they'd turn out to be lavatory directors or producers of G&Ts in the interval, but they were set-designers. They had this amazing house. All white flaky walls, mottled flagstones and the occasional party with Colin Firth drooping about the place – very *World of Interiors*. The rest of us lived on Barratt housing estates – all Homebase wallpapers and Magnet kitchens, very *Brookside*, I'm afraid. Which one?' She held up two identical trouser suits.

'The black one or the black one, you mean?'

'I mean the Prada single-breasted or the McQueen double-breasted.'

'Ah,' he grimaced in mock gravity. 'Neurotic-chic or Neo-Yuppy. It's a tough call. Tell you what. Let's call the Pentagon – the fate of the free world is obviously at stake.'

A scowl skittered fleetingly across her brow. He suspected it was time to show more concern.

'Whatever she was like, my little tarantula, she couldn't have been as bright as you.'

'Actually, she was highly intellectual. Wore a black armband when John Lennon died.'

'She sounds utterly pretentious.'

'She was ghastly. But so was I.'

'It's a bit Friendsreunited.com isn't it? Didn't have you down for that, I must say. Assumed you thought it was for boring housewives who've spent the last two decades overpopulating the world and underpopulating their brains. You'll be appearing on "Oprah" next,' he said, barely able to keep the mocking distaste out of his voice, which wasn't quite what he'd intended. Emotional intelligence wasn't his forte. The only time he felt real pain was when the stock market plunged.

'Well, maybe that's your trouble,' she said, strapping herself into a pair of shiny high-heeled black boots. 'You assume too much.' She kissed him lightly on the cheek. He hoped she wasn't gearing up for sex – he'd noticed how lately they seemed to require more props to perform than the entire cast of *Lord of the Rings*. Not that he didn't enjoy it, he just had an early start. He couldn't afford to get off-track, even for a moment.

'So, how come you haven't been in touch with her for fifteen years?' he asked, backing out of the room slightly, brandishing his briefcase as if it were some kind of missile defence. Her knight in shining Armani, thought Sarah.

Not quite what she'd envisaged at school.

'Hated each other's guts,' she said, flicking through the rails of black garments again, which to Richard's eye looked as enticing as an attic full of bats.

'Two rival camps. Only hers was camper than mine. She was Highly Artistic. Then for no apparent reason she switched to drama. Total fag hag of course, which is why she was so bloody stylish. Had a coterie of Stella McCartneys in drag all telling her what to wear. She was a bit plump when she first arrived, which was when I quite liked her. Then gradually she got anorexia. After she went to drama school I didn't see her put anything in her mouth apart from several billion Benson and Hedges. Then we lost touch.' She flung the suits on the bed. 'D'you think a dress would be better? Less corporate?'

He smiled, or rather he bared his teeth. Sarah's flashes of self-deprecation were one of her more appealing traits. But then she had everything so perfectly under control these days she could afford the occasional self-lacerating outburst. 'You're asking someone who barely knows the difference between a skirt and a pullover to psychoanalyse a *dress*?'

She padded over to him and kissed him on the cheek, rubbing her bush tantalisingly against his pinstripes. 'Poor Richard,' she grinned, 'you really don't have a clue, do you?'

'We can't all have your finely tuned visual awareness, my little St Martin's flower.' Only half-reluctantly he peeled her arms away from his neck. He wasn't used to her being needy. She was clearly rattled but if he wasn't in the office and on the phone to Tokyo by 7.30 he'd have missed the best of the day's trading.

'Which restaurant did you book for this little display of self-flagellation, by the way?'

'Metro.'

'Perfect. Stylish, but not intimidating to the out-of-towner who wouldn't realise how impossible it is to get a table there. Not too loud, not too quiet. Expensive, but not if you're on expenses . . .'

She shot him a pleading look.

At the front door he felt a small twist of concern. 'She can't be that stylish anymore,' he added encouragingly, 'judging by the paper.'

Even he could tell that a notelet with a rabbit on the front wasn't chic.

'Unless,' he added cheerfully, 'it's postmodern satire.'

It couldn't be postmodern satire, decided Sarah, fingering the notelet later at work and deferring preparations for the next exhibition opening, which consisted mainly of trying to get a bigger than usual discount on champagne from the local branch of Oddbins. Nor was it something she could hang in the gallery as a biting commentary on elitist art, as Richard had wryly suggested. Though come to think of it, it would look quite good next to Kent Darblay's Squashed Trainer, which had a reserve price of £20 000 on it.

She examined the fluffy rabbit for the billionth time. Even if you drank a crate of champagne it definitely wouldn't look like art. Just unfathomably naff. It was also, if she were in the mood for scrupulous honesty – which briefly, she was – the reason why she had agreed to this lunch. She was intrigued by Sheba.

She always had been. Richard was right. The rest of Kingsbury-Newton Upper School were a bunch of sad tossers, but not Sheba. And not her. The one who'd got into St Martin's. The one who'd gone on to really make something of her life. Although she'd always felt Sheba had had the edge – more interesting, more attractive, better name and certainly more popular than she had been. Her parents had been unusually affluent, too. They'd only sent her to Kingsbury-Newton Comp because their socialist principles prevented them from sending her to Roedean – somewhere Sarah would have loved to have gone.

She glanced around at the ferociously chic white gallery. Usually she felt desperately chic working somewhere so uncompromisingly . . . white. But today she felt a pair of Dolce and Gabbana ski goggles ought to be standard issue with the job.

She wanted to see Sheba again, she decided, simply because she was curious. Sheba was so charismatic. And Sarah was now sufficiently mature and self-assured to admit this. She frowned. That wasn't the real truth. The real reason she wanted to see Sheba was because she needed to expunge fifteen years of guilt.

In the back of the taxi she began to chafe at the lunch-time traffic. She didn't want to be late. Not even fashionably.

Not even a sliver of a minute over the hour. It would seem patronising. She caught herself short. That assumed she had reason to patronise Sheba, though she had no reason to suppose that Sheba's life had turned out any less brilliantly than hers. No reason other than a persistent, niggling doubt.

If Sheba's acting career was going according to plan, then why hadn't Sarah heard of her? Her heart began to pound against the breast pocket of her wrap dress. Feeling distinctly nauseous, she wound down the window.

It took forever to grind through the one-way diversion. In frustration, she jumped out, pressed some notes into the driver's hand and ran the last few blocks. On the way she encountered a reeking, mottled tramp splayed out across the pavement. She frowned, crossing the street and wondering if he placed himself so near to an expensive restaurant deliberately. He took a swig from a bottle of something that could have been nail polish remover for all the pleasure it seemed to give him, retched loudly as Sarah swept away from him and strode through the queue of traffic.

She shuddered. Sometimes, in the black of night, when things had been very quiet at the gallery and Richard was being particularly urbane, she felt that not much stood between her and life on the streets. But that was just her neurosis, of course. She would never end up down-and-out. Still, it seemed ironic that Britain didn't seem to have become any kinder and more caring under Tony Blair than it had been under the Tories. Thank God, Richard would say.

To her relief, Will, the maitre d', informed her that her guest wasn't there yet. She took the banquette, the better to spot her when she did arrive – she wanted the full-length overview. She had to know if Sheba's thighs were as dainty as ever.

She sat nervously frisking the menu. She ordered a bottle of still water and asked the waiter to remove the bread. When the water arrived she asked for a bottle of sparkling as well, in case Sheba wanted some, though she was probably on guard against cellulite these days, too. She desperately wanted to go to the loo now, but didn't want to be caught there if Sheba arrived.

She crossed her shiny black Jimmy Choo boots and anchored her nerves by contemplating the still-visible tan on her smooth glossy legs, a memento from a late-winter Caribbean holiday. 'You've come a long way, baby,' a cheesy voice drawled inside her head, as it often did whenever she took stock of her evolution from suburban embarrassment to sleek city-gallery owner. Co-owner, technically speaking, but Cosmo, her partner, was never in the country and, thanks to Richard, she'd put most of the money into it lately.

A shadow crept across the tablecloth. Will announced the arrival of her guest. She heard a tiny but ominous hissing as expensive-but-oh-so-casual Axminster rug met deflating rubber. Then she felt a slight jolt as something collided gently with the table. Sheba had arrived.

'Oh my God, you poor thing,' said Richard, curling up with his laptop. 'A wheelchair. Christ, how did you get through lunch? What the hell did you talk about?'

How typical of Richard, thought Sarah, pouring some more San Pellegrino into her spritzer, to view someone else's tragedy through the somewhat limiting filter of his own sense of inconvenience.

'Oh, you know, compared prosthetics; discussed political correctness in local government planning offices —'

'Scintillating.' His laptop began to emit strange bleeping noises, rather like Richard did when they were having sex. A look of anguish crossed his face and she realised how much he loved his laptop. At least he would never leave her for bigger breasts. Only bigger gigabytes. He tapped furiously on the keyboard and the bleeping stopped, which meant that normal conversation would resume shortly, just as soon as the screen saver was functioning again. Reluctantly he turned it off and picked up the TV listings. He sighed theatrically at all the fluff that had been scheduled for their edification across five channels and seventy cable stations, before flinging them to one side.

'Christ, you'd think the creative powers of our land could come up with something better than "Celebrity Allergies", wouldn't you?'

Sarah wondered if he'd been listening to her at all. She decided to test him out. 'At one point the doctors thought they were going to have to remove her head.'

'Didn't realise there were limbs missing, too,' he said. 'Very Heather Mills. Any minute now *Vogue* will be telling us a missing limb is the new "Mustn't Have". I thought you said she was just paralysed.'

Trust Richard to be demanding even where disabilities were concerned.

'She is.'

'Well, that explains why we've never seen her in anything. Either that or her acting career's been confined to daytime soaps and the odd episode of "Emmerdale".'

There was a pause while he flicked through the remote controls. Jeremy Vine popped up in glorious wide-screen plasma along with the Chancellor of the Exchequer and some bloke from the Federal Bank. State-of-the-art television and seventy-five channels, thought Sarah, and they still ended up watching two bickering economists with about as much visual appeal as a lanced boil. She nuzzled against Richard's chest.

'Not quite what you envisaged, is it?' he said, stroking her hair. 'I mean it's nice to have confirmation that one's outperformed all one's classmates, but to completely trounce them in life's lottery takes the joy out of it a bit, don't you think? It's a bit like being pleased when some shop assistant gives you too much change, only to discover they're blind or something.'

She looked up at him in wonderment. How could someone so completely insensitive be so utterly perceptive at the same time?

In any case, she thought the next day in the gallery, meeting Sheba hadn't been depressing at all. In fact there was something hypnotically life-enhancing about Sheba – an inner peace – that radiated wellbeing.

The trauma Sheba must have suffered would have been almost unimaginable, even if Sarah had possessed any imagination. Yet Sheba told Sarah that she had come to terms with not being able to walk, though she hadn't given up hope of a cure. The doctors all said she ought to recover. She wasn't pinning everything on it though, she said. And if nothing else, losing the use of her legs had forced her to switch careers. There wasn't much work for wheelchair-bound actresses – not that there had been an avalanche of jobs before the accident, she told Sarah wryly but without a shred of self-pity – so she'd taken up illustration, which she loved.

She was very beautiful. But Sarah didn't feel at all jealous. Watching Sheba in her wheelchair, her thin little knees visible through her skirt, she felt she was entitled to her beauty.

And, of course, they hadn't talked about prosthetics or disability allowances during that first lunch, but about love and life. Sarah couldn't remember ever experiencing an encounter that had been so untainted by competitiveness. Not a wisp of envy, not a trace of resentment, not a whisper of superciliousness had clouded their two-and-a-half hours together. Lulled into complicit camaraderie, she'd even had a pudding for the first time in ten years. Why not? She felt weightless – almost as if she had been touched by a celestial being. Not that she could tell any of that to Richard. Or that she and Sheba had made a date for the following week.

'So, how did she end up in a wheelchair?' he asked casually, when they were in bed later and he was sliding his hand between her naked legs.

'Accident in the Himalyas, four years ago,' mumbled Sarah, wondering how their sex life had degenerated into something marginally more boring than 'Thought for the Day'. When she'd first met him he'd been a seemingly endless source of the best sex she'd had since accidentally discovering alternative uses for old bottles of Clinique moisturiser.

'She was trying to find herself. She always was a bit mystical, and fitness-mad.'

'Bloody careless to lose a bit of herself instead.'

'The doctors are very hopeful. She's made amazing progress,' Sarah replied, wishing their physical exchanges these days didn't always feature Richard ambushing her from behind.

'Not in her taste in writing paper,' he panted.

'It was her niece's choice,' began Sarah and then gave up. Suddenly it was no longer important to let Richard know that even a discarded enemy had okay taste; that the only reason Sheba had sent her a picture of a fluffy rabbit in a blue apron was because she'd been having some homeopathic treatment on her right hand that had temporarily put it out of action and she'd had to ask her niece to write the letter for her. Let him think what he liked. But she couldn't resist showing him a photograph the next morning of Sheba and her niece.

They went to see a new print of *All About Eve*. It was Sheba's suggestion. Sarah had been expecting something much worthier – a biting denunciation of a South American dictatorship in the original Aztec, but Sheba said *All About Eve* was her favourite film because she loved the way it portrayed evil. They arranged to meet again the following week when Richard would be away in Frankfurt.

Sarah saw a lot of Sheba that summer. She went round to her flat – the ground floor of a modern block in Maida Vale that was surprisingly quirky and colourful inside, full of Sheba's illustrations and finds from her travels. And often they'd go to a little bar round the corner where they could while away the balmy evenings drinking absinthe, which was Sheba's favourite drink. Sarah thought it very exotic, until the first effects of the pale liquid hit her with the same euphoric, technicolor impact of the ecstasy pills she'd occasionally taken in her twenties.

Much later, when things changed in a way she could never have predicted, when she looked back at the time she spent with Sheba that summer, she realised her memories of those days were much more vivid, more sharply in focus than any other time in her life. Sheba said absinthe was the elixir of artists, of Rimbaud, Hemingway and Van Gogh. It was only afterwards that Sarah realised it was the crutch of delusionists.

'Care in the community, is it?' said Richard, back from Frankfurt and gleefully hunched over his Palm Pilot where he was scrolling through a list of new contacts he'd made there, which was about the closest he came to exhibiting sentimental tendencies.

'Dunno how you can drink that stuff,' he said, wrinkling his nose at her absinthe. 'Maida Vale – very nice. Glad my taxes are going towards paying for all the unemployed to live somewhere smart.'

'She bought the flat with money from her parents. They're dead and Sheba and her sister sold the family home. She's pretty well off, actually. And anyway, she's not unemployed. Seems she inherited her parents' artistic talents. So, when she couldn't act anymore she became an illustrator. Does loads of stuff for magazines and CD covers. She had a bit of a break when her hand was in a bandage, but she's fine now.'

'Sarah?' he said, one evening, tearing his eyes off Jeremy Vine.

'Mmm?'

'Don't get too penitential, will you? Self-sacrifice is very last year.'

The funny thing was that Sarah didn't consider her time with Sheba in the least penitential. It was true she'd agreed to meet Sheba in the first place because of a sense of obligation – a feeling that her run of good luck was up and it was time to make amends. But Sheba had turned out to be good company. She was witty – not in Richard's acerbic, jaded way that entailed mocking everybody but himself – and she was worldly. She could cook brilliantly and she read far more than either Richard or Sarah ever seemed to have time for. She always knew the best exhibitions or films to see and she had so much energy that after the first two or three dates Sarah almost forgot there was anything different about her at all. She stopped noticing that they avoided places without large lifts and ramps – Sheba had got her life so meticulously sorted that there didn't seem to be much missing from it.

And late into the night they talked about being young and jealous: giggling about how much they had hated one another at school, vying with one another to tell stories about how horrible they'd been. Sheba sweetly said that she couldn't imagine Sarah being quite as nasty as she'd been. Sarah had smiled in a noncommittal way and backed off. She wasn't going there.

The one thing Sheba never got around to telling her was why she'd got in touch after all this time. And Sarah didn't broach the subject because she didn't want to have to talk about why she'd agreed to meet after all this time, because she knew it would only lead to her confessing that she had been much, much nastier than Sheba could have imagined.

She became aware that she was changing, becoming gentler, and that her thought processes were becoming less conventional and more quirky, like Sheba's. She stopped agreeing with Richard that Maggie Thatcher was a god and Kilroy Silk a snappy dresser. When a man wearing a fedora and more chunky gold jewellery than the Pope came into the gallery and tried to buy her Starbucks skinny latte, instead of blurting out one of her withering retorts she did her best to let him down delicately.

'If it's already sold, why doesn't it have a sticker on it?' he bleated through a portcullis of gold teeth.

'It's not actually an exhibit. I bought it across the street,' she said tactfully, as if people tried to buy debris off her desk all the time. In a way she supposed they did. She smiled, eyeing his clenched fists nervously.

'But you can have it if you like. It's still warm.' And then suddenly he had beamed back at her, his embarrassment evaporating, like the steam from her latte. And it had felt good – or at least novel – to make someone else feel good.

She didn't tell Richard. She didn't see much of him that summer. He always seemed to be away somewhere, juggling his assets or stripping someone else's. It was a busy time at the bank. Besides, Richard had told her, his sixth sense was screaming that the economy was going to take a dive in the next eighteen months. It was time to keep up with the Dow Joneses he said, and to make hay while the FTSE index shone. Which presumably explained why an important sale she'd been relying on in Geneva had fallen through. Financially this was worse news than she let on, especially to Richard to whom she hadn't revealed just how quiet things had been at the gallery lately. But the real disappointment, as far as Sarah was concerned, was that her abortive trip to Geneva had necessitated her spending five days away from Sheba.

She wished she missed Richard as much as she missed Sheba. But even when he was at home, he seemed somehow absent. It should have made her fonder. She should count her blessings. It didn't seem fair that she had so much when Sheba had so little to look forward to. It wasn't that

Sarah actively wanted children, but she'd always assumed she'd have some sooner or later, just as she assumed she and Richard would get round to marriage, to exchanging their loft for a house with a communal garden and to swapping his sports car for – or at least complementing it with – a four-wheel-drive tank.

But Sheba seemed perfectly contented with her life. She seemed to have lots of friends, though she preferred to see people on her own, which meant she was often busy when Sarah would have liked to see her. But crowds made Sheba feel claustrophobic, so she could never meet in a group. It was her only neurosis, thought Sarah, but justifiable in the circumstances. It lent a certain intensity to their friendship. It was almost as if it existed in a vacuum or a bubble. She wondered how many other bubbles Sheba kept afloat and whether any of them ever bounced into one another.

'A bit enigmatic isn't she, your new project? Do you think she screws men?' asked Richard one Saturday morning, reorganising the list of restaurants on his Palm in order of Michelin stars.

'She can't move her legs, Richard,' said Sarah, eyeing him warily. 'Rather limits screwing possibilities as you so charmingly put it.'

'Heather Mills doesn't have a leg —' he began. He was obsessed. 'And you said Sheba was beautiful.'

'You saw her photo,' said Sarah.

'Did I?' He said vaguely. 'Oh yes. Bit mystical-looking. Liked the look of the niece though.'

★

In the middle of July, Sheba went to America, to a treatment centre that specialised in post-traumatic stress injuries. 'Physiologically there's no reason why she shouldn't make a full recovery,' explained Sarah over the phone to Richard who was on a whirlwind business trip in the Far East. He sounded as if he were on the floor of the Han Seng in the middle of a buying frenzy. 'But for some reason it's come to a standstill.'

'Literally,' he said wryly. 'I take it she *can* stand?'

Sarah wondered why she had ever found Richard's glibness amusing. The man had as much depth as a one-coat manicure. Suddenly the life with Richard that stretched in front of her – a round of perfectly organised dinner parties and on-track promotions – no longer seemed enough.

Eight years ago when she'd met him he'd seemed the answer to her aspirations: droll, urbane and as upwardly mobile as helium. She'd never stopped to ask herself if she loved him.

But Sheba had. Sheba was into all kinds of soul searching. She talked about the meaning of relationships all the time and once she even asked Sarah if she didn't deserve better than Richard.

While Sheba was away in America, Sarah signed up for Italian classes. It had been Sheba's idea. She had suggested they might go to Florence together so that Sarah could take her round the Palazzo Pitti and the Accademia. The last time Sarah had gone to Florence with Richard they hadn't got any further than Gucci and Louis Vuitton.

She began to fantasise about giving up her job and

moving to Tuscany. Perhaps Sheba could come with her . . .

Fantasies of a perfect life together began to consume her. Sarah knew neither of them was gay. And yet for the first time ever that she loved someone other than herself. It would be like *A Room with a View*, she thought. Though obviously the room would have to be on the ground floor.

At the end of August, Sheba got back from America. Sarah raced round to her flat after work and felt the tears running down her cheek when Sheba walked a few steps across the room towards her.

'I'm. Leaving. You.' She heard the words reverberate round the room one by one, like gunshots as she stood gazing at herself in the mirror. Her mouth went dry. This wasn't how she'd planned it. Richard standing there looking pitifully at her, his cases neatly lined up by the door.

'Have you met someone else?' she heard herself asking. As if. The only person Richard was likely to have had an affair with was Jerry, the man in IT who looked after his laptop.

He looked at her pleadingly.

'My God, you have,' she said wonderingly.

'Don't sound so surprised,' he said, dropping his briefcase.

'Well, excuse me, but you've barely had time for a coffee this summer, let alone a full-blown, life-shattering affair.' She turned to look at him accusingly, wishing she'd asked him to do the zip up on her dress before this had happened. She tried to keep calm, to tell herself that her only regret was that she hadn't got in with the desertion speech first. Later, she knew, she'd see that it was all for the best, that it let her off the hook beautifully. But for now she was furious, humiliated. A woman out to scorn.

'So, who's the lucky business associate?' she asked witheringly.

'Sarah,' he began gently.

'Don't Sarah me.' She didn't want his condescension as well as his rejection. 'Whoever she is, I hope she gets more of a rise out of you than I did.'

'What's that supposed to mean?' he asked, suddenly on his guard.

'Oh, come on, you're hardly love's young dream. Can't remember the last time we had sex unaided.'

'It takes two to make a disaster,' he replied coldly.

'And three to turn it into a humiliation. How could you go behind my back? I credited you with more guts than that. God, I have to hand it to you Richard – it can't have been easy finding someone as shallow and selfish as you are, but you clearly left no stone unturned. And at last you've found your cockroach. Should suit you, you being such a creep.'

'I can see why you're hurt.'

She wasn't very hurt, just desperate to hurt him.

'And believe me, I didn't choose for it to happen. But it's a heart over mind kind of situation. She's a much better person than I am. I feel I've entered a new plane.

She's hit me right in the solar plexus, swept me off my feet.'

She must look like a heavyweight boxer in that case, thought Sarah, seeing a straw to clutch at in this painful hour.

'I don't deserve her. I'm sorry if you feel betrayed but I was under the impression you felt as apathetic about this relationship as I do. If it's any consolation I think she's going to make me a much nicer person. And Sarah —' he moved towards her in a gesture of conciliation, 'I think you'll probably be a nicer person without me.'

She wanted to hit him right in his smug solar plexus. 'Richard, I really don't think you've ever impinged on my character one way or another.'

That one hit home. 'You ungrateful cow. You'd still be living in Stoke Newington if it weren't for me.'

She began to laugh. He made Stoke Newington sound like a sexually contracted disease, which in a way, if you fell in love with someone who lived there, she supposed it could be. But in her new state of Higher Consciousness, it seemed to Sarah there were far worse places to live. Tower Hamlets for instance. She decided dignity would be her next approach. Two could play at being on a higher plane, after all.

'I wish you well. And now, if you don't mind,' she said, summoning up all her dignity, 'I'd like to pack. You can keep the apartment.'

She decided not to call Sheba immediately. She would finish packing all her things and then go round there and tell her in person. Sheba was bound to invite her to stay for a while. At least Sarah hoped so. She needed a safe harbour, time to sort herself out as well as work out some kind of rescue package for the gallery. Financially this wasn't the best time to be splitting up.

She heard footsteps and jumped. It was Richard, with a rare glass of one of his vintage burgundies. He looked almost emotional, which Sarah put down to the distress of having to raid his wine collection.

'Peace offering,' he said meekly, surveying the toppling piles of clothing around the room.

She smiled brightly and raised a glass. Typical of Richard not to notice that she'd long ago given up drinking wine in favour of absinthe.

'I don't deserve you, Richard,' she said. 'I used to but not anymore.'

He was about to demur before realising that whatever she meant probably wasn't complimentary.

'It would be nice to be friends,' he said smoothly.

'Who with?' she said innocently. 'Nicole Kidman?'

'You know what I mean. Sarah?' he sat down heavily on the bed.

'Yes.'

'I have to tell you something you're not necessarily going to like. Although once you get used to the idea . . .' He was starting to look clammy round the edges now. He fiddled nervously with his cufflinks. 'That cockroach I've been having an affair with —'

She looked at him blankly. She didn't actually care

which particular office bimbo he'd been shagging. Only that he had had the temerity to finish with her.

He looked at the floor and cleared his throat. 'I promised her I'd tell you —'

Her heart began to palpitate mildly, out of curiosity if nothing else. His hair stuck damply to his forehead. There were sweat circles under his arms. He coughed again, this time so forcefully she thought for a moment he looked as though he was going to be sick.

'It's Sheba.'

The room wobbled in front of her momentarily as though it were in a heat haze.

'Hah bloody hah.'

'No, it's true. We met when you were in Geneva. My fault. I engineered it. Not that I could help it. I fell in love with her the moment you showed me that picture of her. I had to meet her to find out if she was as good a person as she looked. And as you know, she is.'

She waited for him to crack. She wouldn't miss his warped sense of humour. But he looked at her in earnest anticipation. She waited for the scream to come that would pierce this nightmare, but it didn't come. All she felt were the tears coursing down her cheeks. She wanted to yell abuse at him, tell him that it was a good job he was such a wanker because he wouldn't be getting any sex with Sheba. But all she heard was her own pathetic small voice saying that it couldn't be true, even though she suddenly knew that it was.

✳

The waves of hysteria frightened her. Losing Richard, she realised, was a question of dented pride and even more dented finances. But losing Sheba was going to break her heart. It took her all night to pack. At midnight she tossed aside her remaining pride and drove round to Sheba's flat. There was no reply from the buzzer but eventually the porter let her in. As she stumbled across the acres of carpeted lobby, she realised Richard had been following her.

'Dunno why you're bothering,' the porter began. But they both ignored him in what was becoming a farcical race to Sheba's flat.

Sarah could feel Richard's burgundy breath on her neck as she rang the bell. There was no answer. She rang again. An eerie silence ensued. In desperation she kept her hand on the bell. She looked through the fish-eyed security hole and saw her own pupil reflected back at her.

'She's gone,' said the porter flatly.

They looked at him blankly.

'Moved out last week. Sent for the rest of her belongings yesterday.'

'What are you talking about?' Richard said roughly. To Sarah's distress, he extracted a key from his pocket and tried the lock. The heavy door swung open to reveal a scene more devastatingly empty than Sarah's gallery. Except that there weren't even any pictures on the wall. All Sheba's illustrations, every last piece of clutter, all the colour and the warmth and the gentle, glowing table lamps had gone.

Sarah stared accusingly at Richard. He must have got it all wrong. Somehow he'd misread everything horribly and now he'd scared Sheba away. The colour had drained from his face. She noticed for the first time how sallow his skin was.

In disbelief, Richard pushed past the doorman and Sarah followed, walking though the naked rooms like an automaton, her footsteps clattering on the bare floor-boards. The electricity had already been turned off. Only in the kitchen did they find any evidence of recent occupation: a bottle of unopened absinthe and a letter addressed to them both, spotlit by the sickly orange light from a street lamp.

Dear Richard and Sarah, it began, and he couldn't help noticing that there were no fluffy rabbits. This was quality headed writing paper. Smythson, if he weren't mistaken.

You didn't really think it would pan out the way it seemed, did you? Richard, I'd rather spend the rest of my life with a virulent case of hepatitis C than with a self-centred, arrogant, ignorant, insensitive workaholic. But God, it was fun pretending. And Sarah, it was sweet watching you discover a nicer you. The trouble is, I can't ever forget your 'contribution' to my career. Did you really think I had forgiven – or more implausibly still – didn't know that it was you who stole all my artwork?

I assume that was how you got into St Martin's – by

passing my pieces off as yours? I can't think of any other reason why you'd go from being a B-grader to a bursary student. I suppose you assuaged your guilt, if you had any, by telling yourself that the teachers at Kingsbury-Newton High would vouch for me. And they did, but it wasn't enough. You see, I don't think teachers at Kingsbury-Newton carried much clout with St Martin's. And you know me, second best was never going to do – especially after I heard you'd got in. So that's why I went to drama school, the worst decision of my life. I knew it even before I got there. In hindsight I can see that triggered the anorexia. But it turned out that was the least of my problems.

I won't bore you with the details. Suffice to say there's not much worse in life than struggling to be good at something you have no natural talent for – though credit where it's due, I made a pretty convincing cripple, didn't I?

It took a long time for me to track you down and fix this up. You'd think I'd have better things to do, but frankly, I haven't. Life's turned out to be just as empty for me as this flat is – like your lives, I guess. So at least we have something in common. And boy, it's been worth it. I can honestly say I've never met two people quite like you, nor so well suited. Don't try and find me by the way, because you won't. I'm very good at camouflage and disappearing acts – another good thing to have come out of drama school. Your wild-goose chase in Geneva, Sarah – guess who? I suppose I should thank you for that, Sarah.

*In fact I should thank you both for giving me the most
satisfaction I've had in years.*

*I was wrong, Sarah, when I suggested you didn't
deserve Richard. You deserve it all.*

Sheba.

They stood in darkness for what seemed like hours,
although it was probably only minutes. It was Richard
who moved first.

'The bitch. And you're as bad,' he hissed at Sarah
before marching out. It was the first time she'd ever seen
him close to losing control. She waited for the footsteps
to die away, wondering where she would go now. She
stood there for hours, re-reading the letter until the
words swam before her eyes and a sense of hysteria
clutched at her throat. She knew now that nothing could
save her gallery, that after Sheba she would never be able
to trust anyone again. She thought of the tramp outside
the restaurant with his distended nose, crater skin and vile
stench. Eventually the cold got to her and the doorman
called for her to hurry up. She switched off the light and
made for the door, just turning back once to take the bottle of absinthe with her.

David McKay

A Quiet Drink

Jamie Theakston's

Top Ten Worst Songs
of the Year I Turned Sixteen

1. **'Rock Me Amadeus' – Falco**
   For being Austrian – and including the lyric – 'Er war ein Punker'.
2. **'Dancing on the Ceiling' – Lionel Richie**
   Not long after this song was released, Richie's wife attacked him and his lover with a knife. It had nothing to do with his adultery – she was a music critic.
   Horse-faced freak.
3. **'Take My Breath Away' – Berlin**
   For making leather flight jackets with badges on fashionable.
4. **'You Give Love a Bad Name' – Bon Jovi**
   This gave songwriting a bad name.
5. **'Broken Wings' – Mister Mister**
   I find myself losing the will to live when listening to this.
6. **'Stuck With You' – Huey Lewis and the News**
   Don't trust him.

7. **'Greatest Love of All' – Whitney Houston**
   For ruining otherwise immensely enjoyable karaoke
   nights – why cover George Benson songs?
8. **'Glory of Love' – Peter Cetera**
   Who is this?
9. **'Nothing's Gonna Stop Us Now' – Starship**
   This song did.

   Where's the city they built on Rock and Roll
   now, eh?

   It's Luton.
10. **'Addicted to Love' – Robert Palmer**
   Creepy, suited old man who proved good videos
   don't disguise crap songs (see also A-Ha).

   Never forget this man was responsible for the
   Powerstation.

Adam Hills's

Letter from the Hangover Fairy

The following letter was found on the bedside table of Adam Hills, the morning after a particularly big night out. There was no return address or postmark, and although hand-writing tests were undertaken, the results were inconclusive.

Dear Mr Hills,

It has come to my attention that you have been asked to contribute to a book entitled *Big Night Out*. I have therefore chosen you to pass on my message to the world – a message of hope, a message of understanding and perhaps a message of acceptance.

My name is Garry, and I am the Hangover Fairy. (That's right, guys can be fairies.) I have spent my entire life delivering hangovers to those who truly deserve them, and yet I feel I have never received the recognition that I truly deserve.

Oh, you all love the Tooth Fairy – sneaking through the darkness to ferry away redundant molars and replace

589

them with a coin or two. Well, who do you think finances her little fly-by-night operation? Me – that's who. Night after night I rifle through the pockets of drunken revellers, trying to raise the funds to keep Little Miss Dental Care in business, while leaving just enough change so as not to arouse suspicion.

Night after celebratory night it's my lot to fly from bedroom to bedroom, Teflon-coating the insides of mouths, hiding odd socks, and erasing short-term memories. Millions of houses across the globe, 365 nights a year, with no nights off. Did you hear that, Santa? Every freaking night! I have 280 million frequent-flyer points and not a spare day to spend them. Oh, what I'd give for a short-term bout of pro-hibition. Just enough time to spend a few weeks in Tahiti with Tinker Bell . . . but I digress.

The reason I bring all this up (pardon the expression) is that lately the stress has been taking its toll. I'm so besieged by orders that I've begun to make a few mis-takes. I'm receiving complaints from people who have retired early after only two glasses of wine, yet woken up feeling like – as a certain Mr Withnail once said – 'a pig shat in my head'. Interestingly enough, I never receive thank-yous from those who accidentally wake as fresh as daisies after consuming three tequilas, two vodka and cranberries, five pints of Guinness and a Slippery Nipple.

So, here is what I am asking. Firstly, I'd like a little respect – not a lot, just a little. More importantly, I require some basic assistance. The next time you find yourself crawling into bed after a big night out, please follow these instructions:

1. Place at least 1.25 Euros (or the equivalent of your local currency) in loose change under your pillow.
2. Apply a small power drill to each temple for approximately six minutes.
3. Remove one item of food from your refrigerator and place it in the microwave, but do not cook it.
4. If female – hide one earring between your bed and the nearest wall.
5. If male – urinate on a random household appliance.
6. Put yourself to bed – I'll do the rest.

These basic steps will restore the efficiency of my duties, thus ensuring I only deliver hangovers to those that truly deserve them. Who knows – maybe once you've seen the work that goes into delivering a hang-over you'll think twice before bringing one upon yourself? And maybe, just maybe, if you follow the above steps I might see my way clear to letting you off one morning with both a clear head and a clear con-science, after a particularly big night out.

Yours truly,
The Hangover Fairy
(a.k.a Garry)

PS. By the way, Mr Hills, the next time you decide to have a big night out, don't leave a pen and notepad beside your bed. You never know who might use it.

Kathleen Tessaro

A Night to Remember

She opened her eyes.

This was not her room.

She shut them, pressing them together as hard as she could, in case it was a dream.

But it wasn't.

When she opened them again, wincing against the bright sunlight that flooded in the window, it was still not her room.

She tried to sit up, forcing herself up onto her elbows, head pounding. She felt nauseous and shaky.

Slowly, she thought to herself. Gently.

There was the sound of a shower running.

And then the whistling began. Was that the theme to *Hawaii Five-O*?

Shit, she thought, collapsing against the pile of pillows behind her. Please don't say I've fucked a man who whistles in the morning.

She sighed and looked around.

It was a clean room. For a man. Large and bright with the double bed nestled into a generous bay window. And there was a fresh cup of tea on the bedside table next to her. She reached out and pulled it towards her, gratefully taking a sip. It was still hot, very strong, and he'd even thoughtfully piled in a couple of spoonfuls of sugar.

Pulling herself up even further, she wrapped her hands around the mug and tried to focus her mind. Right now the most important thing was to see what, if anything, she could remember about last night.

First there was the pub. They'd gone there after work.

The recruitment company she worked for was large and impersonal, but the people were nice – young, trendy – filling in time between more impressive future engagements. She'd only meant to be there for a few months over the summer until she could find a permanent position in an art gallery or one of the national museums, but somehow the summer melted into the autumn, the autumn into winter, and before she knew it, it was spring. The lull of a regular pay packet had dulled her ambitions and yet she seemed to live constantly in her overdraft. It was boring and predictable and she longed for something exciting to happen.

She concentrated. Had there been someone there, in the pub? One of the guys playing pool?

No, she seemed to recall moving on from there. Just a few of them. To a bar called Castro's in St James.

It had been expensive. And loud. Shots of tequila and Cuban cigars.

She took another sip of her tea and focused harder.

There was an image of her flirting with the bartender, probably a red herring. She always flirted with the bartender; it was the easiest way to get free drinks. But the bar was heaving last night and her efforts got her nowhere. The people she'd come with had wanted to leave, were running out of money, so she'd paid with her credit card.

She scanned the room until she spotted her handbag in a crumpled heap on the floor, next to her knickers, which were wound up in a tight little ball with her tights. Carefully, slowly, she pushed back the duvet cover and swung her legs around.

Creeping out of bed, naked and shivering, she retrieved the handbag, taking deep breaths so as not to be sick. Climbing gingerly back underneath the duvet, she closed her eyes and tried to centre herself, her whole head reeling from the enormity of the effort.

Her wallet was jammed into the top and sagged open, unfastened and empty. Even the change purse was bereft. For a moment she panicked – maybe she'd been the victim of a violent street robbery – it would certainly explain the bruise on her knee. But then she discovered a pile of cash-point receipts – one for £50 at 10.13 p.m. in St James, another one for £20 in Covent Garden, and then a final one for £30 at 1.22 a.m. from a till somewhere on the Kilburn High Road.

How had she ended up in Kilburn, for Christ's sake? Heart pounding, she pressed her hands to her face. Who did she know in Kilburn? Was that where she was now?

Suddenly the shower stopped.

Panic-stricken, she scrambled to locate her compact mirror and flicking it open, surveyed the damage. Her blonde hair was twisted into a kind of architectural shape and her mascara had run, forming two dark shadows underneath her eyes. She hadn't washed her face last night and her skin was red and blotchy. Snapping the mirror shut, she burrowed deep beneath the duvet. Maybe if she was lucky, he'd let her sleep and she could see herself out.

The footsteps moved closer.

Please, please God, don't make him be ginger. Don't make him ginger and fat.

And please, not over forty. I'll never, *ever* drink again as long as he isn't ginger and fat and over forty!

She peered out from under the duvet. He walked into the bedroom, a white towel wrapped around his slender waist.

He was not ginger.

His dark hair was closely cropped and his features classical, even aristocratic. She watched in amazement as he threw the towel casually onto the bed and began to dress. He opened the walnut wardrobe and pulled out a pair of boxer shorts and then a pale-blue shirt. She stared in fascination as he slipped into a fine, navy tailored suit and selected a brilliant gold tie. When at last he had fastened his cufflinks and tied the laces on his polished shoes, he turned and smiled.

No, he was definitely not fat or over forty.

He walked over slowly and sat on the edge of the bed. She pretended to be asleep.

'Amy,' he whispered softly.

That was not her name.

'Amy,' he said again, giving her a gentle shake.

She imitated waking up again, fluttering her eyes and sighing softly.

What *was* his name?

'I see you've had some of your tea,' he laughed.

He was even more enchanting when he smiled.

She giggled, like a naughty child. 'Yes.' She hoped her voice sounded seductive and smooth. 'It was delicious.'

'Well, you'd better get yourself together.' He nodded towards the bedside clock. 'Or you're going to miss your plane.'

Her heart did a somersault. 'Are we going somewhere?'

He looked at her carefully. 'Well, not *we*, but you have a ten thirty flight to LA this morning, don't you?'

Her mind raced.

'Ahh . . . yes . . .'

'And I'll bet British Airways expect you girls to be on time.'

'Oh! Oh, *yes*! Yes, they really want their money's worth!'

Amy the Airline Hostess. How tacky! What had she been thinking of?

'Would you like a shower?'

She nodded her head.

'It's just through there. Clean towels are in the cupboard under the sink.'

Suddenly shy and awkward, she clutched the duvet

around her protectively. The last thing she wanted him to see was that unsightly bruise.

He stood and offered her his dressing gown, hanging on the back of the door. 'I'll go downstairs and make us some toast,' he said.

The perfect gentleman.

She showered, threw up and brushed her teeth using her finger. Then she dressed, un-knotting her knickers from her tights and pulling a comb through her hair.

Alone in the room, she quickly scoured its surfaces for some clue as to his identity – a credit card receipt or a letter – but there was nothing. What was it? James? Jonathan? Geoffrey? How could she be so stupid!

Downstairs, he was waiting for her in the hallway, coat in hand. He handed her two slices of toast, still warm and buttery, wrapped in a paper napkin. 'Listen, I've got to race but I just wanted to say what a really terrific time I had.'

There was that smile again.

He opened the door. 'Want a lift to the station?'

'Kilburn station?' she ventured hesitantly, stepping outside.

'Queens Park is closer.'

'Oh, yes, of course!' She smiled tensely. 'I . . . I was just wondering, you know, if we might ever see each other again?'

He brushed her hair back from her face. 'That's the deal, isn't it? You're going to call me when you're back in town. Don't tell me you've forgotten?'

She laughed hollowly. 'How could I!'

Leaning forward, he brushed his lips against her forehead. 'What I like about you, Amy,' he whispered, 'is you're incredibly genuine and yet so *incredibly* wild!'

She felt herself blush.

A black cab drove up and he pulled the door shut.

'That's me. Are you sure you don't want a lift?'

She shook her head.

Her heart sank as she watched him climb into the back and wave. A moment later it lurched forward and was gone.

She sighed and took a bite of her toast.

Evidently, it had been a night to remember.

Beatie Edney

Story illustrations by Alan Rickman

Don't Let Your Daughter See You on the Stage, Mrs Ferry

Emily was a wilful child; at least that is how her mother, Mrs Ferry, described her.

'Can you do something with this wilful child?' Mrs Ferry asked the nanny, half-smiling, half-exasperated, as she tried to manoeuvre Emily's now rigid arm out of the stiff woollen pullover.

There were always fearful rows about dressing. The garments Emily had herself chosen to wear clearly irritated her mother. True, they were eccentric, but Emily honestly felt she was trying to wear the right thing. In her three-and-three-quarter-year-old mind a ballet tutu underneath a Shetland jumper was entirely appropriate dress for a night out. She desperately wanted to emulate her mother's glamour and as she thought her mother was a princess, something fluffy and covered in sequins seemed the perfect choice.

Emily's perception of her mother's profession wasn't entirely fanciful. Mrs Ferry was often dressed in sequinned gowns, smelling wonderful and rushing home at midnight. From fairy tales Emily had studiously learned that this behaviour was common among princesses. They were always described as beautiful and often fragrant. They wore sparkling dresses and had long, golden hair. In Emily's view her mother fitted all the criteria. Mrs Ferry was certainly beautiful, more so than all the mothers of Emily's friends at nursery. 'Sparkling dresses' appropriately described her sequinned evening gowns. She wore gorgeous perfume and, on the occasions of nights out, Mrs Ferry's personal hairdresser, Francis, would come to the house and spend hours combing her hair into the high-rise concoctions so fashionable in the 1960s. He even magically made Mrs Ferry's hair longer – with the aid of pieces, as he called them. People might not have bowed to Mrs Ferry as they do to royalty, but in public they often stared at her or told her they liked her a lot, so Emily knew she was in some way different and special.

The Dressing Room was Mrs Ferry's very private kingdom and she ruled over it jealously. It was boxed in on three sides by wardrobes with floor-to-ceiling mirrored doors. Emily was expressly forbidden to open the wardrobes, but occasionally she had sneaked naughty glimpses inside. There were silk evening shoes dyed every pastel colour of the rainbow placed in neat rows, and rails of long gowns wrapped in tissue paper. A gold mirror stood on the dressing table. The mirror performed magic. It was in three jointed parts and if Emily angled it the right way, facing the wardrobe mirrors, she could see millions of herself stretching out forever and forever, repeating and repeating, getting smaller and smaller until she disappeared into eternity.

To even enter the domain of the Dressing Room one had to be specifically invited and once inside obey all the local laws or be banished for a very long time. The 'don't touch anything' rule was a particularly difficult one to observe. Everything around smelled so flowery, and delicately begged to be messed with. Emily's little ham fists itched to brush over the pink pompom sitting in the powder box. Her nose twitched to smell the perfumes. She wanted to squash the false eyelashes sitting like delicate spiders in a perspex case. Lipsticks in red and pink waited to be drawn with on the mirror. Scissors were a particular fascination. Emily wanted fantastic hairstyles, like the ones Francis created, so she would attempt a new fringe with the assistance of her mother's nail scissors. It is amazing what a three-and-three-quarter-year-old can do to their hair with some scissors and no comb.

If feeling very brave Emily would steal into the room uninvited, like an illegal immigrant crossing the border. She felt that if she spent enough time in front of the golden mirror improving her regal appearance, then she too would become a princess. Unfortunately, in her own opinion, she fell very short. Well, she was short for a start, even for three-and-three-quarters. What Emily lacked in height she made up for with noise. She had a loud, gruff voice, which one aunt described as a 'mixture of gin and fog'. No one called her pretty or even cute, Emily was instead 'curious'. She had no front teeth. This was partly due to her walking, or rather running, too early. She didn't crawl and then totter and then walk, as was usual with babies. One day she just got up and ran. The day after her milk teeth arrived she promptly took off running down the garden with a toy car in her hand. She inevitably fell, knocking out two new front teeth, and then smiled a gummy gap smile until she was at least eight. Finally there was her hair. She was born late with a black matted mane. During the pregnancy Mrs Ferry had read in a magazine that shaving a baby's head would create beautiful, shining hair. She dutifully shaved her newborn's head. When Emily's hair returned, it was white, and from then on grew upward, straight up – perpendicular. She looked like a startled hedgehog, a bleached-blonde punk way before 1977, way before it was considered fashionable. People would stop her pram in the street and ask her nanny if Emily had had an electric shock.

Emily knew tonight was a special occasion because she had not only been invited into the Dressing Room, but was now actually being dressed there. As Emily's choice of tutu and jumper were firmly discarded on the floor, it was clear she would have to wear exactly what her mother had picked out, with no favourite additions of Barbie tiara, pompoms from her slippers or Batman cape.

She was now sporting a fairly plain red velvet frock with white lace sticking out from the hem. Emily concluded the skirt was almost frou-frou enough, puffed out with a lace petticoat, to pretend that it was Cinderella's crinoline. Her shoes, black patent and buckled, were stiff and squeaky, but she proudly admired her white, crocheted ankle socks, amazingly still clean. Getting ready had taken so long Mrs Ferry was now in a great rush and forgot to say quite how stylish and Barbie-ish Emily looked. She didn't even manage a kiss goodbye before she left the house for her own important engagement.

As Emily was putting on her scratchy tweed coat, her nanny explained she would have to be on her best behaviour.

'This is a really special Christmas treat, your first visit to the theatre. Please don't fidget.'

Emily was a great fidgeter.

Getting out of the taxi into the chilled crispy air, all Emily could see were legs. Lots and lots of legs all shuffling slowly forward. Above the legs almost in the sky were thousands of glinting lights. If she pulled herself up to her highest and looked up as far as she could, Emily just managed to see an enormous sign and on it the letters P-E-T-E-R P-A-N.

Then Emily and the legs were in the biggest room she had ever seen. It was red and gold and huge, glittering and bright. Rows and rows of red velvet seats stretched out in front of her, ending at a big swathe of red velvet curtain. Looking up at the ceiling made her dizzy. It was so far away. Suddenly she felt like a real princess in a real palace. A man, all dressed up like a penguin in black and white, carefully took her hand and led her to a seat in the third front row – Emily counted.

'All the better to see the stage,' Emily's nanny said as they sat down.

The seats flipped down when you sat on the edge. 'What a lovely new game,' Emily giggled, as she tried to flip up and down before her nanny warned, 'Behave.'

There were loud, excited babbles of noise all around and then someone slowly turned off all the lights. As the darkness crept closer, almost in unison the noise faded to a buzz and then a whisper. 'It's like quiet time before bed,' Emily thought.

And swish, the giant red curtain parted to reveal a nursery with three small beds and a large window behind them.

'Can't proberly see,' Emily growled a little too loudly.

'Shush,' said her nanny. Then folding Emily's coat she whispered, 'You can sit on this, it will make you taller. Now listen to the story.'

So Emily listened and she watched. It was like hearing all her favourite bedtime stories without having to imagine what everything looked like. You could see it all happening, and happening as if she was part of it, too. She was captivated and she never wanted the story to end.

By the time the big red curtain closed she had been

introduced to all sorts of interesting people. Tinker Bell the fairy was too small to actually see, but her light danced all over the place. Captain Hook terrified Emily with his curly black hair and on the end of one arm instead of a hand was an enormous hook – his 'iron claw'. Wendy irritated because she was so lucky to be in Never-Never Land bossing the Lost Boys about.

Emily was particularly interested in two new friends, Peter Pan and the crocodile. Peter she adored because he was so naughty, so brave and above all because he could fly, which was something Emily had only ever done in dreams. As soon as Peter flew in to the Darlings' nursery, Emily felt she knew him and had known him for a very long time. Of the crocodile she was less certain. Her eyes were immediately drawn to him when he first appeared, shuffling in a strange, stiff-jointed crawl, his tail creakily swaying from side to side.

'It's as if he were made of wood,' her nanny commented.

It was true he did almost remind Emily of Spotty Dog in *The Woodentops*. She twitched with excitement whenever she saw the crocodile; she could even feel her heart bump. The thrill heightened because she could always hear him about to arrive well before he actually did. A loud tick-tock preceded his every appearance, telling Emily the crocodile was near. Unfortunately it told Captain Hook, too. Emily had never known such a feeling before; it was better than the tingling happiness before opening her Christmas presents, better than waiting for Santa, better even than having her tummy tickled. But she did know it was the feeling that the princess had as she kissed the frog who turned into a prince. Emily wanted the crocodile to have that feeling, too.

Someone turned all the lights on again and the nanny turned to Emily to say, 'It's the interval.'

'Interval' was a new word to Emily and when she tried to repeat it, 'into ball' was what she heard.

'We're going to the dressing room,' said the nanny.

Emily was surprised at this, not one but two visits to *the* Dressing Room in one night. She nearly tripped over her crocheted socks with enthusiasm as the nanny led her through a door next to the huge red curtain.

Behind the curtain it was very dark and very quiet. Emily could see Wendy's house in Never-Never Land. Something was not quite right about it. Up close, the trees didn't look like real trees, more like paintings of trees and all the walls were thin and flimsy. Everything looked sad. Suddenly Emily spotted a green zig-zaggy tail.

'Ver crocodile!' she gasped.

Desperate to kiss and hug him to her heart, Emily ran to fling her arms around his neck. The crocodile didn't move at all. She stroked his tail, but there was no response. It was as if he wasn't there. Emily turned him over to tickle his tummy. The crocodile collapsed in two hollow halves. He was empty inside. Emily had never felt so lonely. Tears prickled her eyes and stung her cheek and a slow sadness ate her up.

Emily couldn't stop crying as her nanny led her down several shabby flights of stairs. Even the fright of seeing

Captain Hook striding towards her didn't end Emily's hiccups. 'He must only be Hook's brother,' she reasoned carefully, as he passed. Although he was dressed in the very same Hook clothes, he had very different hair – no hair at all in fact, and curiously he was carrying a teapot in the hand where his hook should have been.

Emily's sobs quietened to whimpers only when they reached the Dressing Room. She was confused; it wasn't the one at home. Then her tears stopped altogether when Peter Pan answered the door and she cheered up entirely when Peter bent down to hug her.

Then Emily smelt her mother's perfume and felt her mother's hug. Somehow, Emily didn't know precisely when and where, Peter Pan had disappeared and Mrs Ferry was hugging her in exactly the same place.

'Where's Peter?' Emily asked, surprised.

'Darling, I'm Peter,' Mrs Ferry smiled.

Everything was twisted up in Emily's head. 'Yes, I know,' she said, 'but where's Peter?'

'Oh Emily, I'm Peter . . . you know this is what Mummy does. Make believe I'm other people . . .' Mrs Ferry explained.

'Like I do in nursery wivver tea set and the dolls?' Emily asked.

'Yes, that's very good, darling, just like with the dolls.' Mrs Ferry patted her daughter's head and sat down in front of the mirror.

'That mirror isn't magic,' Emily said.

'No, darling, sadly it's very real,' sighed Mrs Ferry,

reaching for her powder compact.

'What's Peter doing now?' questioned Emily.

'Right now Peter is putting on more make-up.'

'Yes, I know you are,' Emily nodded, 'but what's Peter doing right now?'

'Peter,' said Mrs Ferry hopefully, 'is playing chase with Tinker Bell and the Lost Boys.'

'No you're not, you're putting on make-up,' Emily informed her emphatically.

Mrs Ferry was suddenly very tired. 'Emily, darling, Mummy has to go back to work. Go with Nanny and see the rest of the show.'

Emily didn't want to leave. She had thousands more questions to ask Mrs Ferry about Peter Pan, and even more to ask Peter about her mother. How do they both fit into the same body, she wondered?

Back in her third-row seat Emily enjoyed watching the story. She now felt lonely whenever she saw the crocodile, but was not so afraid of Captain Hook. Nothing was quite as thrilling as before the 'into ball'. Except Peter's flying. He would take off effortlessly from the ground, fly around with great panache and land elegantly on tiptoe. He could even perform somersaults in the air. No arm flapping was required. Emily felt a familiar connection to Peter. She was there with him experiencing every moment, especially the adventure where he rescued Tiger Lily from the pirates.

Emily wondered again at how proud she was that Peter was her mother, but just as that proud thought entered her head, she saw Peter had been left alone on a rock to drown. Emily was horrified. And as Peter bravely said 'To die would be an awfully big adventure', all Mrs Ferry's explanations suddenly became clear. In that instant Emily realised that it wasn't Peter, but her treasured mother who was drowning. Emily did the only thing that she could do . . . She stood on her seat and shouted, 'Don't let my mummy die!' . . . There was total silence from the audience, from the stage, no one even breathed . . . Then, as if Emily had commanded it, a huge bird flew down from above somewhere and rescued Peter.

From then on Emily was convinced, with more certainty than she had ever known, that her mother was part of Peter, and he was part of her mother. They both existed separately and together, and they could both therefore fly. If my mother can fly, reasoned Emily, then I must be able to fly, too. She was thrilled.

On the way home Emily resolved to keep her discovery a secret. She didn't want to display her talent until she had some practice and could show off. Before bed, she had a few tries jumping from the bottom of the stairs, but didn't feel quite brave enough.

One icy day out in the park, Emily decided to practise. She assumed it would be easier for her first flight to launch off a swing, and even easier to launch off a swing when it was at its greatest height. Emily needed all the help she could get, being small and without Peter to teach her. She found it hard enough to jump up and down. Emily worked diligently to move the swing higher and higher, thrusting her short legs out under the wooden seat and pulling her arms back on the chain. Higher and higher she went. The chains creaked. The cold air rushed and whooshed around her ears. Her breath panted out in frosty clouds. At the highest point Emily screwed her eyes tight shut, shouted 'I can fly!' and jumped off the seat into the air. She was suspended in stillness for a moment . . . then she started to fall. Emily couldn't see the hard concrete race towards her, towards her soft child's head . . .

After the accident Emily never went into her mother's dressing room again. As her hedgehog hair grew flat and new teeth closed her gappy smile, she soon stopped believing in fairies, magical mirrors and that Mrs Ferry was a princess. She was only absolutely certain about one thing: she would never ever fly. Emily blamed her mother for that.

Jemima Hunt

The Cleaner

On Tuesdays and Thursdays she did the Beaumans' house. Four hours was the arrangement. £7 per hour. She had her own key. Kicking off her shoes, pulling off her socks, she skidded down the hallway in her bare feet. The limestone floor was smooth and cool. The cat was in the living room in a ball on the sofa. She tweaked his ears and ran her fingers down his back before pushing him off. 'Bloody cat hairs,' she said. The cat's name was Liquorice. The soft furnishings were white. She was searching for the remote controls. When she found them, she zapped one at the music centre, the other at the TV. Music and voices barged into the room. Unbuttoning her shirt, she stepped out of her skirt. Housework was best undertaken with as little on as possible. Ideally a bra (plain cotton, no underwire), a pair of boxer shorts lifted from Mr Beauman's top drawer, and rubber gloves. Pink as opposed to yellow. Dragging the vacuum cleaner with both hands, she trudged upstairs, pausing to push the thermostat up to thirty degrees. Heat was her motivator, quickening her actions, clearing her mind. She liked to work up a little sweat. Today she would start at the top of the four-storey house and work down.

Her name was Birdie. She was twenty-nine years old. Her name came from a 40s show tune that her mother used to sing. Kiss me Birdie, make my troubles fly away. The tattoo on her upper-right arm was a present from her older brothers. One day after school when she was eleven years old, they had taken her to a tattoo parlour and sat her in the leather chair. You'll be just like us now, Birdie, they said. One of the gang. Told to shut up and shut her eyes, she had forced herself to imagine that the burning sensation was part of a game. When finally allowed to look, she was presented with Bray Wanderers in inky blue, dotted with pin-heads of blood, daubed across her skin. She was from an Irish family, brought up in County Cork. It was the name of her brothers' football team. You'll have it for eternity, they said. Blinking back tears, terrified at the prospect of her mother's wrath (How could you be so stupid, Birdie?) she had wondered if eternity was a good or bad thing. The truth continued to elude her.

Upstairs in Mr and Mrs Beauman's all-white-attic-conversion bedroom, Birdie opened a window and a top drawer. Mr Beauman had the best selection of boxer shorts of anyone she knew. Any of her clients, that is. Folded in half by Mrs Wong who did the ironing on Mondays and Wednesdays, they were arranged in co-ordinated stacks. Pinstripes to the left. Patterns, Christmas bells, Happy

Birthday, flying pigs to the right. Plain in the middle. One or two were monogrammed. BB for Bertie Beauman. Shaking out a white pair, Birdie put them on. She observed herself in the mirror. Her violet eyes looked permanently surprised, as did her shock of black hair. Cursed with her mother's boxy knees, stocky ankles, her legs lacked definition. But they were strong. Hoisting herself onto Mrs Beauman's exercise bike, she hit SELECT PROGRAM followed by TRAIL BLAZER. She pedalled hard. Then she stopped.

She liked to think of herself as a conscientious worker. Procrastination was a fool's game. Sliding off the bike, she stamped on the vacuum cleaner. It growled into life.

Thrusting the metal pole forwards, dragging it backwards, she skimmed the carpet for cat hairs and dirt. There wasn't much of it. Mrs Beauman, an aromatherapist, demanded that everyone take off their shoes when they entered the house. Guests were asked to wear special socks that she had bought in Japan. The cat was brushed daily. Everything went into cupboards, leaving the surfaces bare. Mr Beauman was a consultant gynaecologist. His doughy face was trimmed with a beard to give him a jawline. Whenever they met, Birdie would stare at his small red hands and wonder where they had been that day. She was training to be a beautician. She went to night school three nights a week and, as long as she passed her dermatology exam, would have her diploma in six months' time. In class the students practised on each other. At home she practised on her boyfriend Harry.

Harry was a saucier at a restaurant in the West End. He had a weakness for ketchup. He ate it with everything, including roast meat. Bald like a gladiator, with powerful arms and a paunch he could no longer hide, Harry's gift was to make her laugh. He was a talented mimic and had a cast of characters, which he performed by rote. Saddam the minicab driver was Birdie's personal favourite.

'Do Saddam,' she would beg, as she steamed his face with the kettle and squeezed his pores.

'Hello, nice lady. You want minicab?' Harry would repeat in a thick foreign accent, as Birdie tinted his eyelashes and plucked untidy hairs. His eyebrows were as slender as question marks. His cheeks shone in the light. The only treatment he had objected to was waxing. One evening she suggested doing his bikini line. 'I don't wear bikinis. I'm not a bloody bird,' he said. So far, this was as close as Birdie had come to beautifying the bodies of strangers.

Whipping the head off the hoover, she ran the metal pole along the skirting boards, hunting for fluff. Fluff balls gathered in the corners of the rooms. The war against fluff balls would never be won. Birdie knew this because she had been cleaning houses since she arrived in London ten years ago. Dust and fluff held the city together. Her job was to hide this fact from those wealthy enough to pretend otherwise. If anyone were to ask her what was the greatest human division, she knew what she would say. It wasn't the gulf between the beautiful and the unbeautiful that split the world in two, but the difference between those who cleaned their own houses and those who didn't.

She had learned to be a woman from her mother. She had learned to be a cleaner from her mother.

Ma was a housekeeper for a family in North Cork with two hundred acres and a twelve-bedroom house. The mortar of the seventeenth-century walls was said to be mixed with the blood of men forced to build them. Ma never complained. Viciously well-organised, she was less than five feet tall with a giant's strength. Her stoicism frightened Birdie. One day, mop in hand, she would drop down dead and that would be that. Take a holiday, Ma, Birdie would plead with her. And do what with myself? she would frown. Birdie blew air into her pink rubber gloves. Shaking a cloud of talcum powder into each, she unrolled them over her wrists and sheathed her arms. The bathroom tiles were sprayed with bathroom cleaner. She sprayed her neck and chest from Mrs Beauman's bottles of Opium, Obsession and Poison. Straddling the bath, one foot in, one foot out, she dripped Cif cream cleanser, lemon scented, down the sides. She turned the shower to full, releasing jets of hot water. She wasn't afraid of getting wet. Rubbing the tiles in a circular motion, she calculated the number of hours left to her of doing this. One hundred and ninety-two. When people asked what she missed most about Ireland, she would tell them the waves. She had been born a mile from the sea. The height of summer was marked by a fishing festival, which was hosted by the local town. From her brothers, she had learned how to spin pollack, catch dogfish, and tell her wrasse from her ling. One year she caught a mackerel.

It had weighed fifteen pounds. They ate it grilled with potatoes from the garden. The insides of fresh potatoes were yellow, not white. They tasted of earth.

It was time to do the stairs.

Birdie had five clients. Today she would visit two. When she had finished at the Beaumans' (she had been with them four years), she would make her way to Mrs Fitzgerald's house a stone's throw down the street. Mrs Fitzgerald, a divorcee, was Mrs Beauman's best friend. Their children were the same age. They shared babysitters, bestsellers, Mediterranean holidays and a cleaner. Birdie's a saint, had been Mrs Beauman's introduction. She will even take your leftovers from the fridge. Untrue. Birdie was not a slob. She once took a mince pie to eat before class.

Mrs Fitzgerald-please-call-me-Liz-and-would-you-mind-awfully-not-deadheading-the-rose? used Birdie once a week. Not often enough, in Birdie's opinion. Mrs Fitzgerald had a house filled with clutter. Pictures were hung next to mirrors stuck with postcards, beneath which crowded pieces of furniture were draped with bits of lace. A diligent cleaner, Birdie had originally taken it upon herself to freshen up the flower arrangements. How was she to know that Mrs Fitzgerald liked her flowers dead? Despite Birdie's best efforts, the house never looked clean. At first she had been depressed by the visible lack of results. Then she reminded herself that dusting and tidying was only a job. That happiness was a habit to be learned if anything at all was to be snatched from the brevity of life. And that she didn't live for cleaning someone else's house the way her mother did.

Coming down backwards, she finished hoovering the Beaumans' stairs. She mopped the kitchen floor. Making herself a grilled cheese sandwich and a cup of tea, she wondered what Harry was having for lunch. He wasn't allowed calls in the kitchen. She imagined him melting butter for a Hollandaise sauce, eating leftover bread from somebody's table. Telling chef jokes. All the kitchen staff had nicknames. Harry was Hog because of his snorting laugh.

The radio was tuned to Radio 4. About to change stations, Birdie found herself caught up in 'Book of the Week'. (Most of the big shore places were closed now and there were hardly any lights except the shadowy, moving glow of a ferryboat across the Sound.) She hadn't read *The Great Gatsby* but had seen the film. It hadn't been difficult to fall in love with the rich man in his big house troubled by his past. She sensed that Mr Beauman was troubled by something. His unhappy scowl was twinned with a faraway expression. He would ask questions about her life: How long did it take you to get here today, Birdie? An hour. How interesting. Not really, Mr Beauman, as though trying to make sense of his own. Rinsing her cup and plate, she replaced them in the cupboard. Returning Mr Beauman's boxer shorts back to his drawer, she knew he would never guess where they had been. If he did, he probably wouldn't mind. Their little secret. Picking up her money left on the letter rack, she closed the door behind her. Outside the darkness was cold and still. Wet leaves and a bonfire choked the air. She went directly to Mrs Fitzgerald's house and passed no one on the way.

'It's only me,' she greeted the barking triggered by the sound of her key in the lock. Pip was a pug who didn't get out enough. Mrs Fitzgerald worked in children's publishing and came home late. Her teenage children would rather do anything than walk the dog. Mrs Fitzgerald bribed them to drag him round the block. Don't bring him back until he's done his business, she would tell them. Birdie patted Pip. She didn't want to like him, he dribbled and chased his tail and shat on the floor, but found his stupidity endearing.

'Poor Pip,' she said.

She hung up her coat. It slipped slowly off the overladen coat rack and onto the floor. She hung it up again. Crumbs crunched beneath the soles of her shoes. Unopened post, ten-per-cent-off-pizza coupons, and last week's newspapers spilled across the floor. She trod over a bicycle, chain dangling, which blocked her path. The house was a tip. Mrs Beauman had a way with words.

'I suppose one's definition of what it is to be house-proud is relative,' she once said, in an attempt to articulate the difference between their two houses. Relative to what, Birdie didn't know. Mrs Fitzgerald was messy and reliably late. A weathered blonde, she wore laddered tights and jewellery that rattled. Rings on every finger, dangly ear-rings and talisman pendants.

A frequent entertainer, she drank a lot of red wine. Organising the empty bottles for recycling was one of Birdie's jobs. Mrs Beauman, by comparison, was a stiff, raven-haired woman who dressed exclusively in black. She drove a Saab, used a Palm Pilot and was the head of the local Neighbourhood Watch. A stickler for detail, she never stopped making lists. The cat had his own supply cupboard. The taps had to shine. The Beaumans' was a skimmed-milk household. Mrs Fitzgerald was strictly full-fat.

Birdie opened the fridge in the knowledge that she would find a half-eaten bar of chocolate somewhere inside. Three o'clock. She needed chocolate and disco to stay alive. A Cadbury's Dairy Milk nestled in the door. Tearing off a chunk, she flicked through Mrs Fitzgerald's CDs, stopping when she came to Earth, Wind and Fire. She pressed PLAY. Voices soared, as did her spirits. Cradling the pug like a baby, the broom wedged beneath her arm, Birdie proceeded upstairs.

To be fair, her own flat was less than tidy most of the time. Harry refused to do housework. It was women's work he said. And, just as he was too tired most nights to prepare anything but beans on toast, so she was usually too exhausted to clean. Swinging wide the door to Mrs Fitzgerald's bedroom, Birdie dropped the pug on the floor and drew a deep sigh. This was the worst she had seen it yet. The room looked as though it had been burgled. How she was supposed to hoover the carpet when it was hidden from view, she didn't know. Inching through the mayhem, she picked up damp towels, odd socks, missing shoes. Reaching for whatever came next, she stopped. Her hand froze. If this was a police hunt, she would wave her arms and shout in order to alert her fellow searchers to the fact they had found what they were looking for. Instead she stood very still and quietly swore.

'Oh. For fuck's sake.'

Bertie Beauman's boxer shorts lay crumpled beneath her feet. They weren't a pair she knew but they were a colour he wore. Mandarin. Then she spotted a tie that she had seen around his throat. Navy blue, it lay like a scribble on the floor. BB. She picked up both and tossed them on the bed. She wondered what to do. Cleaners were invisible. They vanished like dust with the sweep of a brush. It wasn't her business to interfere and she knew what her mother would say. No one likes nosy parkers. She didn't know how she would look any of them in the face. Disgusted by the knowledge of an affair she would rather know nothing about, Birdie furiously vacuumed the room. She felt as though she were somehow to blame. Did she like Mr Beauman?

Did it matter? Not really. Men cheated. Women obliged their indiscretions to ensure their marriages survived. When her mother discovered that Birdie's father had a woman in Dingle Bay she said it was God's work, and that he had a tender heart. Then he left her. Birdie hadn't seen her father since she was six. She heard the door slam.

'Hey Birdie. It's Tom,' he shouted up the stairs.

Birdie stuffed Mr Beauman's boxers and tie into her pockets. Tom was fourteen. Pretty like his mother, focused like his father, a composer who came round from time to time, he went to football practice every day. Then he came home, tormented the pug and ate for an hour. Birdie kept going. The sink in the bathroom was blocked

and they were out of bleach. Rinsing the toilet with net-
tle shampoo, she started on the landing carpet.

Mrs Fitzgerald's vacuum cleaner was an old-fashioned,
stand-up model. The suction was failing. Emitting fiery
fumes, it coughed and spluttered. Birdie switched it off and
on. It groaned and died. That was it. She had had enough.

'I'm not feeling well,' she told Tom who was eating
toast in the kitchen.

'Bad luck,' he said.

He was watching TV and had jam around his mouth.

'Tell your ma I'll be back next week. Though I can
come sooner if she wants.'

'You didn't go into my room, did you?' he scowled.

'I didn't bring my gasmask.' Birdie shoved her arms
into her coat.

Tom switched channels.

'What time's *The Weakest Link*?' he said.

'Do you want to give Pip some food?' she said.

The pug was yapping. She said goodbye. She walked
fast. Letting herself back into the Beaumans' house, she
was met by a wall of tropical heat. She had forgotten to
turn down the thermostat.

'Birdie?'

Mr Beauman stuck his head out from behind the
kitchen door.

'Oh, Mr Beauman. You gave me such a shock.'

'Did you forget something?' he looked perplexed.

Sticking her hands in her pockets she produced the
offending articles and waved them like flags.

'I think you did,' she said.

His frown was succeeded by a hiccup. A gasp. A reddening of the face. He coughed into his fist. Depositing the boxer shorts and tie on the chair beside the door, Birdie turned to go.

'Will you be needing me next week?' she said.

'Yes. Of course,' he finally managed to speak. 'A raise perhaps . . . ?'

Birdie shook her stubborn head.

'You can keep your guilt money, thank you, Mr Beauman,' she said.

She left him to drown in the silence that followed. Outside on the street, she tied her scarf tighter and hid beneath her hat. She would ask Harry to cook for her tonight. Spaghetti carbonara. The creaminess of the sauce, the buttery pasta laced with salty bites of pancetta was like hot love. She would flavour with nutmeg and help him whisk the eggs.

Tim Ferguson

Inner-self Portrait

623

Richard Stubbs

The Demon Drink

From the time you have your first drink to the final shot you have before the nurse covers your face with a pillow at the old folks' home, alcohol is going to play a big part in many of the major events in your life.

As I sit here and think back, I realise that alcohol has been present at all my big ones: first dates, brushes with the law, eternal friendship, making a spectacle of myself, confessing love, conceiving children . . . well, the list goes on and you get the idea.

I think of this as scientific research into the effects of alcohol and I am constantly trying to manage it appropriately . . . Your Worship.

See, right there we hit one of the big problems with alcohol: it has no sliding scale. You would expect it to affect you gradually in ways you'd notice – and it does if you're watching someone else drinking.

If you're the one getting pissed you don't notice the stages: sober; relaxed; had a couple; look out – I'm tipsy;

hey, the lampshade's on my head; I'm dancing, I'm dancing – Bon Scott (whose last words apparently were 'Jeez
I'm pissed – but I'm right to drive!'). As far as you, the
drinker, is concerned it's sober, sober, sober, one more
sip – blind.

It's amazing how fast you seem to go from okay to
having lost the power of speech. This moment usually
occurs just before someone cute comes over to the bar to
say hello. Up until that moment you have been okay
because alcohol is like that – it doesn't really affect you
unless you try to move or talk.

So, you have the fatal sip, the cute person comes up
and says hi and you answer 'Seezasingsongtum?' The
thing is you're just as surprised as they are. You're quietly
having a chuckle to yourself, glancing around the room
thinking Wow, someone's pissed. Only *you* are that pissed
someone, so actually you haven't quietly chuckled, you've
laughed out loud at nothing and then clunked your teeth
on the glass as you go for another casual sip.

All this tends to provoke a response along the lines of
'Oh, you're drunk', and an accompanying look of disgust.
As they spin on their heel you riposte with a brilliant *bon mot*
that, due to your pissed state, is less than effective because
you've forgotten to put the consonants in. 'Eoiaeiouoo!'
you yell as the glass falls from your nerveless fingers.

Let us draw a veil over this scene for a moment and
reflect that sometimes (particularly as a young single lad)
you coldly and deliberately set out to get into this state
because you think it's good.

I've lost count of the number of times I've had conversations along the lines of: 'How was last night?'

'We had the best night. You missed out. We got blind. I couldn't walk; I couldn't talk; I chucked – it was tops! When the cops read back my statement I just grabbed the pen and signed it saying "Yep, a top night!" '

Now, it could just be that this reflects the scum I call friends, but I don't think so.

I know I am as guilty of this as anyone, and I can still recall when I said calmly and determinedly to three of my mates: 'I've never done it. Everyone talks about it, but I've never done it and I think it's about time I did.' Little did I realise that with those words I would set in motion a train of events which was to deeply affect four young lives.

I suppose the first question to be asked is, Why go on a pub crawl in the first place? Well, I think it's because I'd never done it and it seemed like such a large aspect of the young-male group culture that I felt I was denying myself a part of my heritage.

I gathered together my team: Trevor, another first-timer but as eager as I was to make the attempt; Simon, quietly spoken, but with a steely determination that said he would be there at the finish; and Rob, a hardened veteran from the bush and boarding school – we'd be looking to his leadership in the latter stages.

We made our plans, arranged for our pick-up and set off into the warm Saturday evening. We had agreed on Chapel Street in Melbourne for the big attempt since it was close to all our homes, and we decided on two pots in each bar between Toorak Road and Dandenong Road. Little did we realise that there were eleven bars along our route.

Given that we started late, this meant that a run rate of a pot every six or seven minutes for over two hours was needed for victory and, of course, no time for dinner. Salt and vinegar chips would have to see us through – the friend of all pissed blokes on the move.

After a short debate, we chose to include a wine bar and began the evening with two warm white wines and orange juice (my, how refreshing). A piano tinkled and we sat languidly in the genteel atmosphere. We casually finished our drinks and sauntered over to the South Yarra Arms and our first beers.

The pubs started to roll past us. Our early pre-match nerves were well behind us and, by the fourth pub, everyone felt remarkably congenial. The last rays of the sun were slanting warmly onto our table, and there was not a problem in the world that wasn't dealt with.

The Middle East, Ireland, good uses for politicians and even Australia's economy were put to rights. If only we'd had a tape recorder, because oddly I can recall nothing of it now.

The next few pubs fell behind us and we were soon into double figures with our pots. We all agreed at this stage that we'd never known such decent blokes as ourselves. Further, if only our mongrel bosses would appreciate our talents more, we could realise our full potential.

A couple of us got a bit teary-eyed at this and we all swore eternal brotherhood. We left the pub with our back pockets sloshing and headed to the next bar.

Another wine bar loomed up, and now putting down two warm pots of white wine wasn't so easy.

At the next pub we met a friend of ours who was out on a first date. He sighted us first and desperately tried to hide (as a joke, I think) but we joined both him and his young lady for the two pots.

We also recounted the story of how he'd got full and danced naked down Toorak Road – everyone laughed a lot at this story, except him, but then he always was a bit morose. Actually, I haven't heard from him since that night.

A dramatic moment occurred when Simon was suddenly sick as we weaved to the next pub. Not as hideous as it sounds: he just stopped, was quickly ill, and kept walking. We didn't feel we should mention it to him but we were all impressed. His father was an Anzac and I felt quietly that this must have been passed on to the son.

Trevor and I were visibly flagging when Rob began stepping up the pace. The sound of his empty pot being slammed onto the bar boomed and echoed through my head. 'Next,' he bellowed, and we finished up and struggled out.

We'd lost all semblance of order now and were desperate as we headed for the next few bars and the finishing line. Finally, almost right on closing time, we fell into the Railway Hotel. Cheers from our friends who enjoy a good mindless activity greeted us as my vision became unreliable.

My last recollection was dancing with some old lady as 'Tie a Yellow Ribbon' was played on the organ.

I awoke in daylight, staring at the bathroom ceiling. Every light in the house was on. Every door was open, and being a Victorian-style house, passers-by could see through the length of it to my unconscious form.

The lino floor seemed tilted at an odd angle, my bladder was the size of a football and I knew that if I moved I'd be sick. I also realised, as I lay sweating, that if I didn't move my bladder would cave in from the pressure. Hobson's choice.

I moved, I was sick. My body never lies to me in moments of great stress. When the wreckage of the Four got together again, some days later, we agreed it had been the most senseless waste of human life we'd ever heard of.

Rob felt we'd gone just one pub too far and wanted to try again. Two of us held him while the third one put the boot in.

Jamie Oliver's

Hangover Breakfast

When me and Jules got married two years ago I was the first of my close mates to get married, and they are animals when it comes to things like stag nights, so I knew they'd have got something really horrible planned.

Before the big night out I worked on some hangover cures in anticipation. My chef mate Ashley in Australia had a really bizarre one that he came across when he was cooking in Denmark. If any of the chefs were feeling bad after a night out, apparently they used to put a bag of risotto rice against a warm oven, then lean their head on the bag for ten minutes – weird!

A spicy Bloody Mary is the classic, but personally I always have kedgeree when I'm feeling rough – that's what we do at our house on New Year's morning. I reckon it's the cumin that's the secret, because it is supposed to be good for upset stomachs. One of my mates, Johnny Boy Hamilton, had a really, really bad hangover travelling in Morocco, and this geezer gave him a handful of cumin seeds to chew on. He was feeling so ill he would have tried anything, and within fifteen minutes he felt as right as rain! Personally, I think I prefer kedgeree . . .

Hangover Kedgeree

For a few mates feeling a bit rough – or just for a brunch/lunch – you need to boil a couple of eggs for ten minutes, then leave them in cold water until you need them. Cook about 180g of basmati rice in salted water and drain well, refresh under the cold tap, then drain it again and put it in the fridge until you need it. Then put around 700g of undyed smoked haddock fillets into a frying pan with a little water and a couple of bay leaves. Bring to the boil, cover and simmer for about five minutes until the fish is cooked, then take the pan off the heat, cool it slightly and flake the haddock into chunks.

Peel the eggs and cut them into quarters, then melt about 115g of butter in a pan over a gentle heat and add a chopped onion and a chopped garlic clove. Soften without colouring for about five minutes, then add two teaspoons of ground coriander and a teaspoon of ground cumin, and cook for another couple of minutes. Add the juice of a lemon, the fish and the rice, and gently heat through. Finally add the eggs and two good handfuls of roughly chopped coriander. Stir in gently to keep the eggs intact. Put into a warm serving dish and serve with another lemon, cut into wedges.

That'll help cure any hangover!

PS Another hangover cure is a bloody good shag with a cold flannel on your neck and sweat it out . . .

Boy George &
Dragana G. Brown's

Very Good Hangover Cure

Umeboshi Bancha Tea (ume-sho-bancha)

¼–½ umeboshi
½ tsp shoyu
Hot bancha (kukicha) tea

Make bancha tea first by boiling 1 tbsp of bancha twigs in 1 litre of water for five minutes. In a teacup put the umeboshi then shoyu and then pour the hot bancha tea. Drink while warm.

This drink is very good for a hangover (tested on numerous occasions!). What is even better is if you eat an umeboshi plum and suck the stone before your big night out. Umeboshi is a Japanese plum, which when pickled has a very strong taste. It is an acquired taste – you either love it or can't stand it!

(Adapted from *Karma Cookbook* by Boy George and Dragana G. Brown (Carroll & Brown, 2001).)

Gordon Ramsay's

Ultimate Hangover Cure

Hot and Sour Tiger Prawn Soup

My cure for a Big Night Out? Put a tiger in your tank –
tiger prawn that is, in the shape of this very tasty Thai-
style clear soup with lots of interesting solids floating
around, which should help your eyes focus next day.

2 tbsp sunflower oil
2 stems fresh lemon grass, chopped
1 large clove garlic, chopped
1 large fresh red chilli, roughly chopped
1 large fresh green chilli, roughly chopped
2 tsp chopped pickled ginger (sushi ginger)
   or chopped root ginger
2 tsp soft brown sugar
1 tbsp chopped fresh coriander leaves
1 litre fresh chicken stock
1 lime – grated zest and juice

250g fresh shelled tiger prawns
12 asparagus tips
4 tbsp peas
6 large leaves fresh basil (try Thai basil, if possible)
Sea salt and freshly ground black pepper

Serves 4

Heat the oil in a large saucepan and gently sauté the lemon grass, garlic, two chillies and ginger for five minutes.

Add the sugar, stock, lime zest and juice. Bring to the boil, then simmer for five minutes.

Allow to stand five minutes, then strain off the liquor. Discard the solids and return the liquor to the saucepan.

Reheat the liquor until simmering, then drop in the prawns and cook for about two minutes until they turn pink. Then add the asparagus and peas. Simmer for another two to three minutes. Finally, check the seasoning and tear the basil leaves into the soup so they wilt instantly. Serve the soup.

Jenny Eclair

Modern Misdemeanours of Cock and Calories/Whatever Gets You Through the Day

Breakfast

Sylvia Redfern had let herself go, there was no denying it. When Sylvia bent over, her behind was broader than the fridge she was delving into. Stanley watched in disgust, he felt like giving her a good boot up the backside. Let's face it, he thought, she'd be happy enough, face down in yesterday's left over shepherd's pie. She'd nuzzle her way out, making little slurping noises with her fleshy pink tongue, swallowing greedily like . . . Stanley felt the edges of the card in his trouser pocket instantly stiffening Jolene, he visualised the illustration on the front of the card, a monochrome cartoon blonde in a plunging neckline, promising 'frolicking good fun' and a phone number that Stanley knew off by heart. Lunchtime, at lunchtime he would see Jolene, it would be his fourth visit. She liked him, Stanley was sure of it, obviously he was a customer but there was a look of welcome in her eyes. 'Stan The Man' she called him.

Sylvia let off. 'Whoops,' she retorted cheerfully. 'That's enchiladas for you. Refried beans, Stan, they don't half give me wind.'

Sylvia emerged from the fridge, swigging from a pint of milk in one hand, lard and bacon grasped in her other meaty fist. Stanley pushed away his bowl of high-fibre cereal, healthy – but all of a sudden like chewing on wads of old pubes.

Sylvia sat opposite him, idly ripping into a loaf of bread, absent-mindedly rolling balls of dough round her gums. 'Like an old cow,' thought Stanley. 'My wife, the Friesian cow.'

Blue smoke rose from the frying pan. Sylvia heaved herself up and started lobbing rashers into the hot fat, dancing backwards as the bacon spat like frying adders. 'Almost burnt my tit,' she laughed.

Sylvia, like many fat women, was nimble on her feet. They were surprisingly small, a dainty size four, tiny by comparison to her massively swollen ankles. 'Like trotters,' thought Stan. 'My wife, half cow, half pig.'

There was fluidity about Sylvia, with the smallest of movements her bulk would wobble almost rhythmically, as if she were dancing. Sylvia wielded a spatula with all the aplomb of a massive drum majorette, breasts quivering, belly undulating. Stan thought about those islands in the South Pacific where women were only considered beautiful if they were obese. How much would his wife be worth to a Tongan prince? Sylvia was buttering bread now, plastering four slices thickly. Stan squeezed past her; he really needed to floss his teeth.

While Sylvia devoured her bacon sandwich, ketchup and grease trickling warmly into the crevasse of her cleavage, Lorna was lighting her first Peter Stuyvesant of the day. Lorna was not a morning girl, neither was she a girl for that matter. Nudging forty, Lorna had turned into the type of woman who was 'better viewed from a distance'. She knew this herself. She knew that from behind in stretch denim, she could pass for twenty-five; she was trim, she had a good arse and even better legs! It was just that when she turned around, only the most myopic could fail to see that she was an ageing peroxide blonde with long yellow teeth and a tide of pinky orange foundation that ended abruptly just under her chin.

Lorna coughed and spat in the sink, her boys would be here soon, students. She coughed and spat again. Every Monday and every Thursday they arrived on racing bikes; one had dreadlocks, the other a silver ring though his eyebrow. Sylvia paid them forty quid a week to put her cards up in phone boxes all the way from Tottenham Court Road, up through Camden, back down through Kings Cross before ending up locally down the Caledonian Road. She sniffed a pint of milk, thought better of it and opened a packet of crisps – prawn cocktail were her weakness. She was wearing a faded purple candlewick dressing gown; beneath it gleamed a bright turquoise satin bra-and-knicker set. Lorna's undies were divided into 'work' and 'not work'. She was – if nothing else, she reminded herself – a 'professional', right down to her suspenders. Lorna allowed herself a laugh, which turned into a cough, which turned into a gob full of yellow phlegm. The new undies, brand name 'Contessa', were a marvellous colour-match with the veins that bulged from behind her scrawny knees.

Elizabeth was not laughing, she didn't have time, she only had time to argue. Simon had let her down again! He wasn't fulfilling his side of the bargain; he wasn't living up to expectations. Why the hell did she have to do every bloody thing?

Her husband was a disappointment, he was looking seedy too. Simon was losing his hair and he had dandruff. Elizabeth had a thick head of hair. Losing one's hair was a sign of moral weakness. That was Simon's trouble, he was a lazy, stupid slob, he needed a good shake did Simon.

You could tell Elizabeth was angry by the way she walked, tight-buttocked and determined through the rush-hour traffic. A thirty-something brunette in a no-nonsense high street version of a more expensive red suit, gradually coming to the conclusion that she had married beneath herself. Elizabeth had a life plan and that plan did not involve living in a one-bedroom basement flat in Chalk Farm for very long.

Meanwhile, back in the one-bedroom flat in Chalk Farm, Simon was feeling sorry for himself, he was hungry and he was unloved, food was his only comfort, well that and . . . Simon rolled over in the bed, noticing with horror the fresh harvest of sandy hair that had parted company from his scalp the previous night. It was all over the pillow. Christ, at this rate he'd be bald by the weekend. Elizabeth would go mad! He was redundant, receding and constantly ravenous. He padded the few steps into the kitchen, opened a tin of rice pudding and retired back under the duvet with the tin of creamy cold rice and a spoon.

As Simon fed himself as tenderly as a mother would a baby, he reflected that life, hair loss and his wife were bitches, his wife being the prize bitch, and what's more he couldn't get it up anymore, not with Elizabeth that was for sure. It was a good job that he had one secret pleasure left in his miserable existence. Simon checked his dormant penis lying in an exhausted heap, like a baby dormouse nesting in his pubes. 'All right, mate,' he said. 'We'll soon have you up and about, you see if we don't.'

Lunch

Lorna shut the door, time for the puzzle in 'Take a Break', a quick cuppa soup and a fag before 'the next one'. Through the living-room wall she could hear her friend Shelley finishing off her Thursday regular. It was comforting, the idle tap of the cane, the muffled cries. At first it had made Lorna laugh out loud. She didn't offer that kind of service, nothing kinky, just the usual, and there was plenty of call for it. According to Lorna, all that 'fancy stuff' was like foreign food, not everyone had a taste for it. She'd attempted it once – 'a little discipline', tied this fella up, blindfolded him and then, well, she hadn't really known what to do next. She'd ended up tickling the end of his 'you know what' with a feather duster. Lorna put Stanley's fifty quid in an empty video box. He was no trouble that Stan, whimperingly grateful, 'Oh Jolene, Oh Jolene.' Jolene bollocks, she'd nicked the name off a tub of crème bleach that Shelley used to obliterate the suspicion of a 'tash' that shadowed her upper lip.

Lorna laughed and sucked an extra-strong mint, partly to get rid of the taste of prophylactic and partly because fresh breath was an important consideration in this game, she was after all a pro.

Elizabeth did not take lunch. She was at her busiest between twelve and three, that's when she had to be at her most diligent, that's when they all came sneaking in, the snivelling thieves. Schoolgirls who'd spent their dinner money on fags and found themselves penniless and peckish come dinnertime. Old ladies silly enough to waste their pensions on scratch cards but savvy enough to know they still had to eat. A lot of Elizabeth's clients were walking clichés but it was surprising who had to be kept an eye on – respectable middle-aged women were the worst. Those magistrates' wives with their smart hairdos and matching accessories, shoving frozen dinners down their tights, blaming it on their hormones. Elizabeth was sick of all the feeble excuses, the sudden crumbling of the cocky schoolgirl, 'Don't tell me mam, she'll kill me.' The watery tears of the pensioners, boo-hoo, boo-hoo. They couldn't half turn on the waterworks, literally. One old dear had pissed her drawers when Elizabeth's crimson-clawed hand had clutched her shoulder. She knew what she'd done; the evidence was tucked unpaid for in the waistband of her little-old-lady tweed skirt, a tin of processed peas and a pound of stewing steak!

Depression was the commonest excuse. Funny, Elizabeth pondered, how depression manifested itself in the inability to perform everyday common courtesies, like getting your purse out at the checkout and paying for goods taken from shelves in the supermarket. Elizabeth had no sympathy for any of them; the menopausal, the poor, the plain daft, they were all the same to her, petty little criminals.

Today, Elizabeth played bloodhound to a whispy-haired man in his sixties; she was convinced that he was sliding contraband up the sleeves of his mac. She tailed him, silent on her rubber heels. Three steps beyond the automatic doors, she pounced! Elizabeth was a rangy girl, she covered a lot of ground very fast plus she had the bonus of a long right arm, very useful in this job. She grasped his greasy collar and like a six-year-old caught scrumping apples in a pre-war orchard, the man was dragged by the scruff of his neck, back into the store.

Firmly ensconced in a small windowless room, with obligatory security guard in attendance, Elizabeth searched her stunned prey. Two pairs of ladies' tights fell from his macintosh sleeves, one tan, one 'barely black'.

'Pockets,' Elizabeth barked and the man obliged, turning out tampons, kirby grips and a pot of vaseline. 'For my wife,' he stuttered.

Elizabeth sneered, 'Yeah, right,' wife indeed. 'Pull the other one.' The adrenaline rush was subsiding, Elizabeth felt bored and depressed. The police could deal with him now, the sicko pervert. For an instant, without wanting to, Elizabeth imagined him, paunchy in the nylon tights, inserting lubricated tampons up his rectum. Jesus!

Simon walked as fast as he could without resorting to salbutamol, a plastic bag dangled from his wrist and with every step it knocked against his knee and twisted, tightening around his wrist till his hand went white and his fingers turned into blue-tipped bangers. He began to puff, leaning against a wall, he drew on his inhaler, sweat rings under his arms the size of watermelons. As long as he didn't peg out now, not now, later it wouldn't matter. The plastic bag gaped on the pavement; a trove of carbohydrates and dairy products began to roll into the gutter. With difficulty and a slight pain in his chest, Simon retrieved the goodies and trotted down the road. It wasn't easy; it's hard to run when you are laden down with the contents of the local deli, have chronic asthma and an enormous stiffy.

His face mottled grey, pink and purple, Simon pressed the third bell on the right-hand side of a battered white door, Flat C. Two long rings, followed by a series of short, more urgent jabs, come on. Breathing heavily, he pressed his face up against the glass panel, waiting for the blurred bulk that would lumber down the communal stairs and let him in. She was coming, the door swung open and there she was, all dimples and curls, a vast Shirley Temple in peach velour. She winked, grinned and turned. Simon followed her up the stairs, eyes fixed on her shuddering thighs, the visible line of her outsize knickers, her left arm heaving herself up the stairs quivered like blancmange. At the top of the stairs, she paused, allowing him to squeeze past her into the flat. Face to face for a moment he felt the hardness of the doorframe against his buttocks in stark contrast to the sandbags of her flesh pressed against his stomach and thighs.

Simon was a small man, his thinning scalp was level with her lowest chin. He was quite happy to stay there, wedged in the doorway forever, but she squeezed him through and shoved the door shut with her massive arse. Simon stood on the rug and waited till she pushed him back onto the burgundy leatherette sofa and began to kiss him.

'Pressies,' she slurped into his ear. 'Has mister got his ickle baby pressies?'

'Only if baby's a good girl and gets into beddy byes,' replied Simon.

She hauled herself off the settee, her skirt riding up over acres of white thigh, and disappeared giggling into the bedroom. He gave her a couple of minutes, crossed his legs and thought of thin women, his wife, anything to stop him coming right there and then. Slowly he counted to a hundred, then he checked his jacket pocket for a tin opener and feeling like Burt Reynolds, only a bit more masculine, he entered the bedroom.

She was ready for him, the plastic sheet was in place, she lay naked and enormous on the bed, breasts the size of fully grown Labradors hanging by her sides. She was shivering, her eyes tightly shut, they never spoke at this point. In the silence, Simon reached into the plastic bag and removed a tin, the opener bit into it and his hands shook as he turned the key. Once the can was open, he placed it on the mantelpiece and proceeded to open several more. Tins, jars, wax-paper packages, polystyrene cartons, Simon lined them all up like tombola prizes. When the bag was finally empty he removed his clothes.

Every last stitch. As soon as Simon had ripped the socks from his feet he started to throw food at her. Hummus slapped against her calf, baked beans tangled in her hair, cream cheese and maraschino cherries adorned the Everest of her left breast, while taramasalata and pimento stuffed olives decorated the Matterhorn of her right breast. She writhed in pleasure; her hand went to her belly and massaged a lake of Greek yoghurt into a dollop of chocolate spread. He flicked tinned raspberries at her and bid her turn over, the bedsprings were the only thing complaining. She rolled over and he plastered her backside with pastrami and cheese from a tube. As he wrote his name in Primula on her shoulder, like a tattoo, she reached round and grabbed him, pulling him down onto the plastic and together they rolled around in a billion-calorie heaven.

Supper

Stanley didn't go straight home after work; his post-Jolene afternoon stint at the library had been uneventful. When wasn't it? In the past twenty years there had only been three 'incidents' and two of those had been women in advanced stages of pregnancy going into labour. The third had involved a mad person wandering in and attempting to climb the book shelves insisting he was Sherpa Tenzing and 'Where the hell was Edmund Hillary?' Strange but not inconceivable, considering the library was a mere three-minute march from the biggest psychiatric hospital in London.

After two pints of lager in his local, Stanley braced himself for another evening with his twenty-stone wife who was partial to eating pilchard sandwiches while watching the soaps.

As he let himself in, he heard her bellow, 'That you, Stan, I'm just washing the sheets, be with you in a minute.' And she started to sing, very loudly.

Elizabeth took off her good red work suit and changed into navy leggings and a clean T-shirt. Simon was reading the *Evening Standard* and circling jobs he wouldn't get with a red biro.

'Trout,' she snapped. Perk of the job, at the end of the day the management of the supermarket where she spent her days prowling would show their appreciation by offering staff-discounted dented tins, squashed fruit and stale Danish pastries. Today she'd nabbed a couple of broken-tailed trout with bleeding sides and cloudy eyes.

'Er, not hungry,' her husband replied.

Elizabeth ignored him and slapped the fish under the grill. Had she bothered to look, she of the hawk eyes – able to spot a toddler with a smuggled handful of Pick and Mix at a hundred paces – she might have noticed he had a baked bean lodged in his ear.

Patrick Neate

A Big Night Out

This was almost the best bit of the whole night: the anticipation. No. That was wrong. Because the anticipation would never be better than the night itself. Not this night anyway.

Best night of the year. Everyone said so.

'Right you are,' they nodded. 'Right you are.'

He'd pretend to flirt with The Pippa-potamus. He'd pretend to be drunker than he was and lay his cheek on her tit that lolled into a roll, and look up at her with those puppy-dog eyes that the girls just loved. 'Best night of the year, Pip!' he'd say and she'd giggle and blush so hard it would wine-stain her neck and her goosepimpled arms.

'Best night of the year, lads!' He'd raise his glass to Tricky, Stubbs, Dave and Sad Roger. They'd sink their pints in unison and then Stubbs would burp out the first three bars of Jingle Bells.

He'd offer his hand to Tony Cockerill (Tripod Tony,

Tony the Cock, the Cock-Meister, his only equal) and he'd say, 'Best night of the year, Tone!' And Tony would have to pull his mitt from between Theresa's clammy thighs to shake his hand. 'Right you are, my son!'

Christmas Eve? Down The Cobblers on the High Street? Best night of the year. Always had been. Ever since they were teenagers and he played up front – the target man – for the First XI and they won the Sussex Schools and he scored the winner and he had his picture in the local rag and everything. It had been some Christmas Eve that year and the same every year since. Everyone would be there.

Bone (as in 'hard on' or as in 'idle', depending on who you listened to) checked his reflection one more time, narrowed his eyes, and lit another Benny straight from the last. He turned up his music to drown out *Songs of Praise* on his mum's telly downstairs.

'Everybody dance now!' blared the speakers. C&C Music Factory. Wicked. A classic.

He pulled on his cigarette and checked his watch. He'd be heading out soon. Not yet. But soon. He had a thought and he rummaged in the box of tapes that sat beneath the stereo. A while back, he'd been a bit of a DJ and, though he didn't get the chance anymore, he still had the mix tapes to prove it. He found the one he was looking for; the one with 'Rhythm Is a Dancer' as track one on side A. Everyone would go mad when he stuck it on down the pub. Blinding tune. A classic.

All the girls knew they could rely on him to bring the

entertainment. They loved it. And he mentally ran through their faces like he was checking off items on a shopping list: Kelly-Anne with the blow-job lips, Spanish Isabella (stroppy tart), Geeta, Theresa, Tammy 'n' Ina, Amber with the been-to-bed eyes, Stace with the jugs to die for and Joanne who scrubbed up nice with a bit of slap. And the Pippa-potamus, but she didn't really count. He ordered them chronologically by Christmas Eve encounters and realised with some satisfaction that he'd worked his way through the lot of them (except Pippa, of course).

No probs, he thought. Time for round two.

Kelly-Anne was none too shabby a place to start. He wondered if she'd be there. Now he thought about it, he remembered Tony telling him that Kelly-Anne had worn comfortable shoes all along and was seeing some black bird from Manchester. 'She's only a bleeding dyke,' the Cock-Meister had said but Bone hadn't believed him and assumed he must have taken a knock-back. Now he thought about it, he realised that she had moved up North. How long ago was it? God. Must have been a couple of years. Now he thought about it, he realised he hadn't seen her since; not even last Christmas Eve.

Bone quickly checked his list. Spanish Isabella was off limits since she'd married that Rajiv guy who managed the Esso, and besides she'd dropped a sprog, and besides she was a stroppy tart. And Geeta? Last time he'd seen her she'd been suited and booted on the 8.14 fast train to London Waterloo and that was a good few months ago.

Bone was starting to worry and he pulled deep on his

Benny. 'It's all gone pear-shaped,' he said aloud. And that only made him think of Theresa because he'd never fancied her anyway. As for Tammy 'n' Ina, what was it Tony had said? 'One for the price of two, my son. One for the price of two.' Something like that. Tony was well funny.

Amber would be up for it. Amber was always up for it. Trouble was, Tricky had made an honest woman of her last summer. Bone shook his head. He couldn't believe he'd even considered it. So that took him all the way to Stace; tits like Pamela Anderson and a face like David Hasselhoff. 'So keep your eye on the prize,' Tony would say. 'Keep your eye on the prize.' None too shabby.

Bone sang along while he was pulling on his trainers. 'Rhythm is a dancer, it's a yada yada . . .' All these years and he'd never learned the words. He checked his watch. It was three minutes later than the last time he'd looked. He picked up the phone and belled Tricky; number one on the speed dial.

'Wotcha. What time are you heading down?'

'Who's this?'

'Who's this? Who do you think it is? It's Bone, you silly tart!'

'Oh. Wotcha, mate. Happy Christmas.'

'Joyous Noël to you, too, Tricks. So what time are you heading down?'

'Heading down?'

'The Cobblers.'

There was a pause. He could hear Tricky lighting a cigarette and the sound prompted him to do the same.

He burned his fingers on the match and the phone slipped from his ear and he missed Tricky's reply.

'What's that?' Bone said.

'Actually, mate, I think we're gonna have a quiet one.'

Bone laughed: 'Yeah, right. So what time you gonna be there?'

'No. Seriously. Amb's in the shower and we're both knackered. We only got in about twenty minutes ago.'

'Got in from where?'

'Work.'

'Right.' Bone pulled on his cigarette. Rhythm is a dancer. It's a yada yada. He turned the volume down. 'Come on, mate. It's Christmas Eve, you pussy. Everyone'll be there.'

'Like who?'

'Like who? Like everyone! Tony, Stubbs . . .'

'I thought Tony was heading to the West End. Said he'd scored a couple of grams and was gonna have it large.'

'A couple of grams?'

'That's what he said.'

Bone thought about this for a moment. 'Nah, mate. Tony'll be there. Miss out on Christmas Eve at The Cobblers? You're having a laugh. So, are you gonna come down or what?'

Tricky exhaled heavily. Or it might have been a sigh. 'Tell you what,' he said. 'We'll see you down there, yeah? A bit later on.'

'Nice one, son. Everyone'll be there.'

Bone looked at his watch again. The trouble was timing. Get there too early and he'd be pissed by nine; too late and they wouldn't get a table. He might even miss out on Stace.

He considered calling the Cock-Meister; ask him why he was winding Tricky up like that. Head up to London on Christmas Eve? You're joking. He decided not to bother. He'd see him in an hour.

Bone rewound the tape, clicked it out of the stereo and stuffed it in the pocket of his jeans. He tied back his hair and put on his bomber jacket. He checked his watch and licked his lips. He shouted 'Bye Mum!' as he headed out. 'We all like figgy pudding,' sang the telly.

The High Street was quiet – not a soul – and dark apart from the various pub windows that burned like fireplaces. The Red Rover? That was strictly pensioners. The Crown? All the old slags would be in there with their pink lipstick and rouge. The Gatwick Express? Nobody went there. Never had done. No one went there when it was called The Coach and Horses and no one was fooled by the change of name, blue strip lights and cocktail umbrellas. Anyone who was anyone went to The Cobblers, just up from Cod's Own (best chippy in England) and opposite Rajiv's Esso (fags and Ginsters' sandwiches twenty-four hours a day).

As he ducked through the heavy door, Bone thought, London? You can keep it. And he noted with a smile the sign that said 'Strictly Over 21s'. He'd been drinking in here since he was fifteen. More than a decade.

The Cobblers was already rammed and Bone dropped his shoulder beneath juggled pints and shimmied his way to the bar. He stood on tiptoes to have a look around but he didn't see a single face he knew. Missed all the tables, he thought. Everyone had better hurry up.

He bought a Stella, chased it with a Bells just to sharpen himself and headed towards the back of the pub. He sparked a Benny and checked out the talent. Young crowd in tonight.

'Bone! Hey Bone!'

Someone was tugging at his jacket. He spun round and found himself looking down on a circle of Beckham cuts and Atomic Kittens. He frowned at the flushed face smiling up at him, took in the earring, downy goatee and pack of Marlboro Mediums and tried to figure out who the hell it was. Jamie Cockerill? It was only the Cock-Meister's little brother and his mates and they'd only got the best table in the whole bleeding place. Christ on a bike!

'Wotcha, son.' Bone dragged on his fag and narrowed his eyes slightly which gave him, he thought, a practised kind of cool.

'One of Tony's friends,' Jamie was explaining to the table. And then to Bone, 'What are you doing here, man?'

Bone exhaled: 'Just meeting a few people.'

'Yeah? Thought you'd have gone up West with Tony.'

'Up West?'

'Yeah.' Jamie turned back to his friends' eager faces.

'Bought some Charlie Chase and went into Town with Stubbs and them. Some Garage night, know what I'm saying? Nutter my brother. Absolute nutter.'

'Twice As Nice?' asked a kitten.

'Yeah. That's it. Twice As Nice. Boo! Know what I mean? Booooo!'

Bone was staring at Jamie. Apart from the fact that Tony had gone to London, Bone hadn't understood a word he'd said. He fingered the tape in his pocket and looked around the table. The Twice As Nice kitten was eyeing him. She was sitting bolt upright; bleached blonde with a tight white crop top that said 'Bitch' in pink across her perky tits. She had a ring in her bellybutton. She couldn't have been much past sixteen.

'You wanna sit down?' she asked.

Sure. Why not?

Jamie introduced him to the blokes (Wotcha, mate? All right, man. All right, mate? All right, man. All right, man? All right, man) and Bone introduced himself to the Twice As Nice Bitch kitten. She kissed him on both cheeks. 'Angel,' she said.

The table was brassic (typical kids) but Bone was feeling flush – forty quid off his mum and his dole money on top – so he bought them a couple of rounds. Or rather Jamie went to get them while he talked to Angel.

'I like your hair,' she said.

'Thanks.'

'Very old school.'

Bone laughed. 'That's me. Old school.'

655

'You didn't wanna go to Twice As Nice?'

'And miss out on Christmas Eve in The Cobblers? No chance. Best night of the year.'

'This place is a shithole.' She was glaring at him.

'The Cobblers?'

'This place. This whole shitty town. I'm getting out of here as soon as I can.'

'Me too,' Bone said. 'I know what you mean. A shithole. You know what I mean?'

The table coughed up enough for round three (or was it four?) and Bone headed to the bar himself for round four (or was it five?). It was getting on for half ten and he hadn't seen everyone. In fact, he hadn't seen anyone. No one. But he hadn't been looking.

Then he glimpsed a familiar face at a table by the door. It was the Pippa-potamus. Only something had changed. She was still big but she wasn't enormous any more and she looked, Bone thought, like a balloon two weeks after the party. She also had a nose ring and her hair was its natural brown (he'd never seen that) and knotted into crusty dreadlocks. And she was sitting with some black geezer who wore a sports jacket and a pristine white shirt, like a contestant from 'Blind Date'.

'Pip?'

She turned around and her cheeks rosied. It was the Pippa-potamus all right. She looked embarrassed.

'Bone?' she said. 'God. I didn't expect to see anyone in here. Who did you come with?'

'No one.'

'Where is everyone?'

Bone shrugged and that seemed to reassure her. 'So, what are you up to?' he asked.

'I work in town,' she said. 'For the Refugee Council.'

'Yeah?'

'It's a charity.'

'Yeah?'

'What about you?'

Bone wanted a Benny but he'd left them with Angel. 'You know me,' he said.

'Right,' the Pippa-potamus nodded. And then, 'Sorry. This is my fiancé. We're staying at my mum and dad's. Tunde, this is Bone. Bone, this is Tunde.'

Tunde smiled broadly and shook Bone's hand. 'From Nigeria.'

'Yeah?'

The Pippa-potamus couldn't stop blushing. 'He's part of the campaign against Shell.'

'Yeah?'

'Against Shell,' Tunde nodded.

'There's an Esso over the road,' Bone said.

He couldn't wait to get back to Angel and he made his excuses and said, 'Nice to meet you.' And, 'Good luck and that.'

By chucking-out time, they were all hammered. Bone was pissed but coping. They couldn't take their beers, these kids. He snogged Angel in the corner and her tongue tasted of Baileys-sweetened cigarettes. He closed his eyes and raised a hand to her chest. He played with what he thought was her nipple before realising it was the corner of the embossed 'B' of 'Bitch'. He tried to slip his hand inside her top but she wasn't having it and, besides, the landlord had turned on all the lights.

He walked out of the pub with his arm around Jamie's shoulders. Angel went ahead of them and, by the time they hit fresh air, she was throwing up in the bin outside the garage. Bone thought it was a good job he'd already caught his freebie.

Jamie was looking up at the sky. It was starting to drizzle. 'Twice As Nice,' he mumbled. 'Safe, man. Safe.'

Bone gave him a squeeze. 'Best night of the year,' he said, to everyone and anyone and no one in particular.

On his way home, Bone bought twenty Bennies from the Esso. 'How's Isabella?' he asked. 'Okay, thanks,' Rajiv said but didn't seem to recognise him. He picked up a bag of chips from Cod's Own and skirted the old slags piling out of The Crown, drunk and flirty. Some people, he thought. Bit sad.

He'd finished his chips by the time he reached his front door. None too shabby they were, too. His mum had already gone to bed so he went to the fridge and cracked open one of the beers she'd bought special for tomorrow. In the lounge he found his Christmas stocking hanging above the gas fire. He squeezed the satsuma in the toe and headed upstairs. Best night of the year.

Bob Geldof's

Five Favourite Places to Be at 11 a.m.

1. Picasso on the King's Road – because it's not Starbucks and because the girls from Storm Model Agency down the road pass by on a frequent basis.

2. Southeran's of Sackville Street secondhand bookstore, because it's a balm to enter the civilised world mid-morning.

3. Any remote beach with the possibility of one other human sighted as a speck somewhere down the beach.

4. Battersea Park on an autumn morning.

5. On a Sunday, in Rome, en route from Vicolo della Campana to the Pantheon, contemplating an excellent lunch with six mad Romans.

Notes on the Contributors

Jessica Adams is the author of three novels, *Single White E-Mail*, *Tom, Dick and Debbie Harry* and *I'm A Believer* (Pan Macmillan). She has also written two astrology books and is the astrologer for *Vogue* and *Sunday Life*. Her forthcoming titles include *21st Century Goddess* (Allen & Unwin) and *Fantasy Futures* (Penguin). Jessica lives between Bellingen, Australia and Brighton, England, and is often found in her pyjamas drinking tea. She is patron of War Child UK and a trustee of War Child Australia. For more information please visit jessicaadams.com.

Maggie Alderson was born in London, brought up in Staffordshire and educated at the University of St Andrews. She has worked on nine glossy magazines – as editor on four of them – and two newspapers, in Australia and Britain. Her first novel, *Pants on Fire*, was a bestseller in Australia and the UK and she is currently writing her second, *Mad About the Boy*, which will be published in November, 2002. Her fashion column, 'Style Notes', appears every Saturday in the *Good Weekend* magazine in the *Sydney Morning Herald* and the *Age*.

Alexander Armstrong and Ben Miller first appeared on *Saturday Live* in 1996. Since then they have enjoyed huge success with their own Channel Four show as well as a burgeoning office supply business.

As the least athletic pupil at her school it was perhaps inevitable that **Lisa Armstrong** should begin her writing career on *Fitness* magazine. Luckily this didn't entail anything more energetic than exercising her typing skills and answering the telephones for *Penthouse Magazine*, which was in the next-door office (the staff there were always out on long lunches – something the editorial department on *Fitness* clearly couldn't be seen to indulge in). She followed this inauspicious start with stints on *Elle*, before moving to *Vogue*, the *Independent*, and finally *The Times* as a fashion editor. Her first novel, *Front Row*, set in the fashion world, was published in 1998. This was followed by *Dead Stylish*. She is currently working on her third novel. She is married to an architect. They live in London with their two daughters.

Glen Baxter was born in Leeds, England. He taught at the Victoria and Albert Museum, and Goldsmiths College, London. He has exhibited his work in Paris, Tokyo, Sydney, London, New York and San Francisco, and has had a tapestry commissioned by the French government. His published books include *The Impending Gleam*, *Atlas*, *Glen Baxter, His Life: The Years of Struggle*, *The Billiard Table Murders*, *Blizzards of Tweed*. Currently his work appears in the *Independent on Sunday* and *Le Monde*.

After leaving school at fourteen, **Maggie Beer** worked and travelled overseas before settling in South Australia's Barossa Valley in 1973 with her husband, Colin. The establishment of the Pheasant Farm Restaurant was the start of a career that now spans farming, export, food production and food writing. Maggie has written three books drawing on her own philosophy of quality produce and the pleasures of the table – *Maggie's Farm*, *Maggie's Orchard* and the recently published *Maggie's Table* – devoted to her love of food and the Barossa. In 1999, Maggie and Stephanie Alexander wrote *Stephanie Alexander and Maggie Beer's Tuscan Cookbook*, chronicling their Italian cooking school experiences. As both a cook and a grapegrower Maggie made her first commercial vintage of verjuice in 1984; it is now available worldwide, as is her book *Cooking with Verjuice* published by Penguin in Australia and Grubstreet in the UK.

Dragana G. Brown is a private macrobiotic cook and teacher. She found that her switch to a macrobiotic diet in the late 1980s freed her from almost twenty years of nagging stomach problems and even improved her emotional wellbeing. Since then she has become something of an evangelist, introducing friends and family to a healthy diet by plying them with delicious food. She is married to the bestselling feng shui author, Simon G. Brown, and credits his literary success to her cooking.

Lauren Burns came to the attention of millions of Australian and international viewers at the Sydney 2000 Olympic Games as a talented competitor in the Korean sport of tae kwon do. One of only three Australian female individual gold medallists, Lauren has since emerged as one of the most successful Olympians from the Games. She now spends most of her time on the public speaking circuit and conducting active motivational seminars. Lauren also studies naturopathy part-time, is writing a book about her journey, and is the ambassador for World Vision's 'Destroy a minefield – rebuild lives' campaign, which she passionately promotes in an effort to raise funds to rid Cambodia of landmines.

Candace Bushnell is the author of the international bestseller *Sex and the City* which spawned the award-winning HBO television series. Her second novel, *Four Blondes*, was also an international bestseller. She lives in New York and is currently working on her third novel, *Trading Up*.

Theresa Byrnes is an Australian painter and writer and has exhibited annually since 1985 in Sydney, Melbourne, Rome (Art/Science Fusion Project 2001), New York (1998–2001), The Museum Of New Art, Detroit

(2001–2002) and the Embassy of Australia in Washington DC (2002). In 1996 she founded the Theresa Byrnes Foundation Inc., which funded a research fellowship at The Children's Hospital at Westmead in 1998 to further gene-transfer therapy. Awarded a Young Australian of the Year award in 1998, she published her autobiography, *The Divine Mistake*, in 1999 (Pan Macmillan). Currently living in New York, she paints, directs art videos, has opened TBG (her own East Village gallery), and is writing a stage production and her next book. Her email address is theresabyrnes@freethemedia.org

Julian Clary was born in Teddington, England, in 1959 and studied drama at Goldsmiths College, London. After a brief stint working as a singing telegram – around which time he acquired his beloved Fanny the Wonderdog – he appeared on the cabaret circuit, calling himself 'Gillian Pie-Face'. Eventually he achieved cult status on TV as 'The Joan Collins Fan Club'. He is a regular on television and tours frequently.

Joan Collins is one of the most recognisable people on the planet – a versatile actress, a bestselling author, an accomplished producer, a successful entrepreneur and a devoted mother. Born in London, she studied at RADA before making several films with the Rank Organisation. She was then signed by 20th Century Fox, and went to Hollywood where she made, among others, *Land of the Pharaohs*, *Sea Wife* with Richard Burton, *Rally Round* *the Flag, Boys!* with Paul Newman, *The Virgin Queen* with Bette Davis, and *The Girl in the Red Velvet Swing*. Winner of a Golden Globe, a People's Choice Award and countless others, Joan has appeared in more than fifty-five feature films, twenty-five TV programs, such as *Star Trek* and *Mission Impossible*, and many theatrical plays. She is internationally renowned for her TV role of Alexis Carrington Colby in *Dynasty*, has published four novels and five lifestyle books, is a tireless worker for charities worldwide and in 1997 was honoured by the Queen with an OBE.

Sean Condon is the author of three travel novels (all published by Lonely Planet Journeys) and the novel *Film* (Allen & Unwin). He lives in Amsterdam. His email address is powdermaker@hotmail.com

Steve Coogan trained as an actor at Manchester Polytechnic School of Theatre, and started out on the stand-up comedy circuit while still at college. He was spotted by a television talent scout and appeared as an impressionist on shows like *First Exposure* and *A Word in Your Era*. He also provided a selection of voices for *Spitting Image* and was involved with the BBC radio show 'On The Hour', where he created the character Alan Partridge. This character took off to such an extent that he was given his own radio slot, the spoof chat show 'Knowing Me, Knowing You with Alan Partridge' and both shows transferred to TV with huge critical and audience acclaim. He also brought us characters like Paul and Pauline Calf. He won the coveted Perrier Award at the Edinburgh Festival in 1992, went on a sell-out tour of the UK in 1998 and was named the Variety Club Showbusiness Personality of the Year in 1999. He now lives in London and Brighton but returned to Manchester in 2001 to film two movies, *The Parole Officer* and *24 Hour Party People*.

Kaz Cooke is an author and cartoonist. Her latest books include *Up the Duff: The real guide to pregnancy*, *The Baby Book: A fun scrapbook for the first five years*, and two books for children, *The Terrible Underpants*, and its sequel, *Wanda-Linda Goes Beserk*. She's now working on one called *Kid Wrangling: Caring for the 0–5s* and, after that, hopes to write nothing but sophisticated, witty novels about single women having sex with firemen and drinking cocktails (not necessarily in that order). These will also be novels in which no character gets gastro, leaves their creche fruit at home or accidentally teaches their toddler to say 'buggerit, buggerit, buggerit'.

Tracey Cox is one of the world's foremost writers on sex and relationships, and is also a TV presenter. Her numerous television appearances include the series *Would Like to Meet*, a dating program with a difference on BBC2. Tracey was born in the UK but spent many years in Australia where she edited *Cosmopolitan* magazine and had a weekly radio show on Sydney's 2DAY-FM. She has a degree in psychology, is the web sexpert for handbag.com and contributes regularly to leading magazines across the globe. Her books *Hot Sex: How to Do It* and *Hot Relationships: How to Have One* are international bestsellers. She lives in Richmond, England.

Paul Donnellon graduated from Dun Laoghaire College of Art and Design, Ireland, and moved to London to work on the Raymond Briggs film *When the Wind Blows* in the 1980s. Paul worked as a freelance animator for various studios, eventually moving into directing live action and animation videos and commercials. He has a reputation as a talented traditional 2D and 3D animator with an exceptionally versatile style. His recent work includes promos for UK band Orbital, R&B artist Bilal Oliver and online games for the *Guardian*'s learn.co.uk site. He was behind Kate Winslet's promo for her single 'What If?'. Previous directing credits include Pink Floyd's *Time* 70mm concert film, Wet Wet Wet, The Cocteau Twins and Talvin Singh's *OK* video.

Jill Dupleix is one of Australia's most exciting food writers and the author of several bestselling cookbooks, including *New Food*, *Take Three*, and *Favourite Food*. She moved to London in 2000 to take up the position of *The Times* Cook in *The Times* Weekend, and has just released a new cookbook called *Simple Food* (Hardie Grant) which, she says, is for people like her who love to cook – but not when they could be eating and drinking.

Former Queensland and Australia lock **John Eales** is not only the second-most capped Wallaby ever, he is also the most capped Wallaby captain. Regarded as the most out-standing forward in world rugby, he participated in two successful World Cup campaigns; captained the Wallabies in memorable victories including the 1999 World Cup; led Australia through four successive years of Bledisloe Cup wins and two successful seasons of Tri-Nations fixtures; and led the Wallabies to the first-ever defeat of the British and Irish Lions. Since his retirement from rugby in September 2001, he has developed the brand John Eales 5 as well as becoming an executive of the BT Financial Group, an Ambassador of the Australian Rugby Union and a spokesman for VISA International's campaign in support of their sponsorship of the 2003 Rugby World Cup.

Nick Earls is the author of the novels *Zigzag Street*, *Bachelor Kisses*, *Perfect Skin* and *World of Chickens*. *Zigzag Street* won a Betty Trask Award in the UK in 1998 and is currently being developed into a feature film. *Bachelor Kisses* is being adapted for television. He has also written two award-winning young adult novels, both of which have been adapted for theatre. London's *Mirror* has called him 'the first Aussie to make me laugh out loud since Jason Donovan'. He lives in Brisbane, and is the Chair of War Child in Australia.

Jenny Eclair is a stand-up comic, novelist and actress, but only because she has a pathological need for attention. Still the only woman to win the Perrier Award (ha-ha), Eclair has been delivering gusset humour for over two decades, so it's possibly time she grew up. Other career highlights include the publication of her first novel, *Camberwell Beauty*, in 2000, appearing in *The Vagina Monologues* in the West End, and regularly losing (badly) on Radio Four's 'Just a Minute'. A writer of plays, radio sit-coms, newspaper articles and filthy jokes, Eclair is currently ploughing through her second novel. She lives in London with her partner St Geof and their girl child, Phoebe.

Beatie Edney is an actress living and working in London. She has appeared in many films, including *Highlander*, *In the Name of the Father*, *Mister Johnson* and *A Handful of Dust*. On television she starred as Louise in the sitcom *Dressing for Breakfast*. Among her many other TV credits are *Prime Suspect – The Lost Child*, *The Dark Angel*, *Inspector Morse*, *Lost Empires* and most recently, *Uncle Silas* (with Albert Finney), and *A Touch of Frost*. In theatre she has worked in the London West End and on Broadway. She was in the original casts of *Les Liaisons Dangereuses*, *Dead Funny* and *Tango at the End of Winter*. This is her first short story.

Imogen Edwards-Jones is an award-winning journalist and broadcaster. During her ten years in journalism she has written for almost every newspaper and magazine in the UK with columns in the *Independent*, *The Times*, and *Arena*. Her television career includes *This Week Only*, as well as *This Morning*, where she pronounced on fashion, and participated in a more surreal moment where she had her lips injected with collagen on *The Word*. A fluent Russian speaker, she was made an honorary Cossack while researching her first book, *The Taming of Eagles, Exploring the New Russia* (Weidenfeld & Nicolson). She is the author of *My Canapé Hell* (Flame), a satire on the celebrity circuit, and *Shagpile* (Flame), a story of swinging in 1970s Solihull. She is working on her third, *The Wendy House* (Flame), to be published in 2003. She is married and lives in West London.

Barbara Else is one of New Zealand's bestselling writers. She has published four novels and two books for children. Her first novel, *The Warrior Queen*, was short-listed for the Montana New Zealand Book Awards. Her other novels are *Gingerbread Husbands*, *Eating Peacocks*, and *Three Pretty Widows*. She has had work performed on stage and radio. In 1999 she was Victoria University of Wellington Writer in Residence. Barbara is also co-director of TFS, a NZ literary agency and manuscript assessment service, and works as a mentor for developing writers. Her website is www.elseware.co.nz

Tim Ferguson mastered in art at L'Ecole Florent in Limoges, France. He has exhibited works in London, Paris, Boston and Sydney. He currently works as a TV comic, writer and producer. His favourite pastime is tae kwon do which he teaches in his home town of Melbourne.

Jasper Fforde was born in London in 1961 and educated at Dartington Hall school, South Devon. Forgoing further education in lieu of a childhood dream to work in the film industry, he started as an office runner in 1981 and in the following nineteen years worked on twenty-eight features, numerous shorts and over 500 commercials. When Hodder published his first novel, *The Eyre Affair*, in 2001, Jasper had already been writing as a hobby for ten years and completed six books. *The Eyre Affair* was published by Penguin Putnam in the USA in January 2002 and the second in the series, *Lost in a Good Book*, is due to be published this summer in the UK. He no longer works in the film industry and commits all his energies to writing. He lives in Wales and has a passion for aviation.

Bob Geldof, founder of the chart-topping band Boomtown Rats, is most famous for the bestselling single 'Do They Know It's Christmas?' and for organising the Live Aid concert in 1985, which raised millions of pounds for relief of the Ethiopian famine. Most recently, he has been involved with the Drop The Debt campaign, networking at government level to persuade superpower nations to write off the debts of many Third World countries so they may build a new future. He founded Planet 24 (the TV company which made *The Big Breakfast* among others) and continues to make music, most recently with an album entitled *Sex, Age and Death*. Bob is a devoted father to four daughters.

Boy George had a string of hits with his band Culture Club in the early 1980s and now pursues a highly successful career as a DJ and producer. He has written all the songs for his musical *Taboo*, currently showing in London's West End. Once a junk food addict, he turned to a healthy diet in 1988 and the following year began to take lessons in macrobiotic cooking from Dragana G. Brown. He found immediate health benefits in his diet, notably an improvement in his asthma, which had plagued him since he was a teenager.

Richard Glover presents the 'Drive' program on 702 ABC Sydney. He is the author of five comedy books including *The P–Plate Parent* and *The Joy of Blokes* (co-written with Angela Webber), *Laughing Stock*, *Grin and Bear It*, and most recently the bestseller *In Bed with Jocasta*. Richard's writing for the stage includes *Lonestar Lemon*, which has toured nationally with Genevieve Lemon, and *A Christmas Story*, which premiered at the Opera House Drama Theatre in December 1998, with Richard Wherrett directing. A frequent guest on television, his weekly humour column has appeared in the *Sydney Morning Herald* since 1985.

Libbi Gorr is a writer/performer/producer, who splashes about on film, radio and television with joyful abandon. Based in Australia, her television work in the Elle McFeast portfolio has a wide distribution in both Europe and the USA. Currently, Libbi is working on a live show.

Clare Grogan was born in Scotland in 1962. She was discovered by director Bill Forsyth when she was waitressing in a Glasgow restaurant. She shot to fame at nineteen as Susan in the hit film *Gregory's Girl*. Clare went on to become the lead singer of the successful pop group *Altered Images*. When the band split up in 1984, Clare returned to her acting career. As well as her theatre work she has since starred in another Bill Forsyth film, *Comfort and Joy*, and appeared in popular television series such as *Taggart*, *Blott on the Landscape*, *EastEnders*, *Father Ted* and the Cult TV series *Red Dwarf*. She recently got to go-go dance in a cage for her role in the play *Gangster No. 1*. Clare is currently working as a presenter on VH-1 Europe and on Sky Movies and lives in London with her husband, record producer Stephen Lironi.

Titania Hardie is a genuine third-generation white witch, the UK's biggest name in mind, body, spirit publishing and one of the top authors of white magic books. She has a degree in psychology and has trained in numerous fields under the broader heading of parapsychology. She has studied psychological astrology and horary psychology. She also has an Open University degree in English literature and starts a master's degree in 2002. Since her first book, *Hocus-Pocus: Titania's Book of Spells*, was published in 1996, 'the witch', as she is fondly known, has produced at least one new title every year. Her books include *Titania's Book of Love Potions*, a range of *Spell Cards* and *Hubble Bubble: Titania's Book of Magic*

Feasts. All her books continue to be in demand, many of them bestsellers. She lives in Somerset.

After obtaining a Business Studies degree at Sheffield University, **Ben Hatch** made his first attempt at writing a book on a government enterprise allowance scheme. Ben wrote three pages in a garret room in Sheffield over a period of three months and came home in disgrace. A series of sackings followed, including: postman, recruitment consultant, bank teller, barman, video shopman, telesales person (twice), lawnmower salesman and McDonald's chicken sandwich station monitor. Ben then took the opportunity to retrain as a journalist. After five years of reporting/TV reviewing at *The Bucks Herald*, the *Northampton Chronicle & Echo* and the *Leicester Mercury*, Ben began writing full-time. He has written two novels – *The Lawnmower Celebrity* (one of Radio Four's books of the year – 2000) and *The International Gooseberry*.

Donna Hay, at just thirty-two, has one of the most impressive CVs in the world of cookbook publishing. Best known previously for the series of four cookbooks she produced for *marie claire* (*marie claire* cooking, *marie claire* dining, *marie claire* food fast and *marie claire* flavours – published internationally as *the new cook*, *new entertaining*, *new food fast* and *flavours*, respectively), Donna spent the year 2001 breaking more new and very exciting ground. Extending her influence, popularity and reputation for recipes and food styling with an accessible but always fresh and original approach even further, she published the immediately widely acclaimed cookbook *off the shelf* with HarperCollins Publishers, launched her own magazine title with News Magazines, and started publishing weekly food columns for News Limited Sunday newspapers nationally in Australia.

Anthony Stewart Head lives in Somerset with his partner, Sarah, two daughters and endless animals. Best known for his role as Watcher to Sarah Michelle Gellar's Buffy, Anthony works extensively both in the UK and US. As a Piscean this dual role comes easily and he enjoys the opportunities offered on both sides of the Atlantic. After six years based primarily in America, Anthony is now concentrating on his career in England. His recent work includes a new series called *Manchild* for the BBC, in which he co-stars with Nigel Havers, Don Warrington and Ray Burdis while still appearing as a guest star in *Buffy the Vampire Slayer*.

John Hegley was born in Islington, London, in 1953. Before the beckoning of show biz he was a bus conductor, social security clerk, and worked with children excluded from school as a carer/educator/gaoler. His first formal performance as a writer/performer was in Doggs Troup, London (Children's Theatre) in 1978. His first notable media exposure was on John Peel sessions (Radio One) with Popticians – 1983/4: songs about spectacles and the misery of human existence. He was nominated for the

Edinburgh Festival Perrier Award in 1989. His first book, *Glad to Wear Glasses*, was published by André Deutsch in 1990. Since then he has been published by Methuen – verse/prose/drawings/drama/photographs of potatoes – his most recent publication being *Dog*. Three series of 'Hearing with Hegley' have been broadcast on Radio Four from 1997–2000. In 2000 he was awarded an Honorary Arts Doctorate from Luton University. His most notable live engagement was a poetry performance at Medellin, Columbia women's prison, 2000. He was on tour in 2001 and performing at the Lyric, Hammersmith, early this year. His dog ran away in 1985.

Adam Hills is one of Australia's most talented and widely respected comedians. He has won universal acclaim and rave reviews throughout Australia, the UK, Ireland and Europe. After making his first live appearance at Sydney's Comedy Store in 1989, Adam hit the international scene at the 1999 Edinburgh Fringe with his solo show 'My Own Little World', which received a five-star review in *The Scotsman*. He repeated this performance in 2000 with 'Goody Two Shoes' which went on to sell out the entire season. His most recent show, 'Go You Big Red Fire Engine', was nominated for the Perrier Award at the Edinburgh Fringe, 2001. His TV appearances include *The Stand Up Show* (BBC1), *Edinburgh Comedy* (BBC2) and *Live at the Jongleur's* (UK Gold). He has hosted his own radio show in Australia, appeared on BBC Radio Four's 'Loose Ends' and is a regular guest on BBC

Radio Scotland's 'Fred MacAulay Show'. He has appeared at comedy festivals and top clubs all over the world.

James Holland was born in Salisbury, England, in 1970. He studied history at Durham University and subsequently worked for several London publishing houses. He now writes full-time. He has published two novels, *One Thing Leads to Another* and *An Almost Perfect Moon* (HarperCollins), and is currently working on a novel set during the Battle of Britain and also a book of non-fiction about the Siege of Malta in the Second World War. He is married and lives in Wiltshire.

Nick Hornby was born in 1957 and is the bestselling author of *High Fidelity*, *Fever Pitch*, *About a Boy* (all three of which have been made into films) and *How to be Good*, and is the editor of two anthologies, *My Favourite Year* and *Speaking with the Angel*. He is the pop music critic for *The New Yorker* and in 1999 was awarded the E. M. Forster Award by the American Academy of Arts and Letters. He lives and works in Highbury, north London.

Andrew Humphreys lives in Sydney. He is thirty-two years old. His first novel, *The Weight of the Sun*, was published by Allen and Unwin in 2001. He is currently working on a collection of short stories and a second novel, which features characters that appear in his contribution to this collection.

Jemima Hunt is the author of *Notes From Utopia* and *The Late Arrival* (Flame). Born in London, she was partly brought up in America. In 1993 she moved to New York. Starting out as a waitress, she ended up as an editor on *Harper's Bazaar*. She has since returned to the UK and divides her time between London and Devon. She writes for *Harpers & Queen* and the *Observer* and is currently at work on her third novel.

With a career spanning twenty-four extraordinary years, **INXS** are undoubtedly one of the world's great bands. With more than twenty-five million records sold, countless awards and platinum certifications, they are arguably Australia's most successful rock export. Their ten-million selling album *Kick* spawned their first US number-one single 'Need You Tonight' and kicked off a run of six consecutive US top ten singles. Other career highlights include the 1991 Wembley Stadium concert before 75 000 fans captured on the 'Live Baby Live' video and album. Since the death of Michael Hutchence in November 1997, the band have performed with various 'guest' vocalists and continue to be in demand for individual projects.

Linda Jaivin is the author of the novels *Eat Me*; *Rock n Roll Babes from Outer Space*; *Miles Walker, You're Dead* and *Dead Sexy*, and the collection of essays *Confessions of an S&M Virgin*. Her most recent book is about China and is called *The Monkey and the Dragon*. She lives in Sydney.

David James is a footballer who has performed at the very highest level of his profession for over ten years. A goalkeeper, David currently plays for West Ham United in the English Premiership Division, and numbers Liverpool, Aston Villa and Watford among his previous clubs. His status as an England international reflects his standing as a player, although it is his off-field pursuits that mark David out as unique amongst his peers. His skills as a fine artist, an accomplished cellist and a professional model reflect his diverse range of interests and his willingness to look beyond the confines of his sport.

Anna Johnson was born in London and her journalistic career started in Australia with *Stiletto* magazine in Sydney at the age of nineteen. She went on to serve as Fine Arts editor at *Interior Design* magazine, an art critic for the *Sydney Morning Herald*, Radio National and ABC TV and a freelance writer for publications including *Vogue* Australia, *Vogue* UK, *Harper's Bazaar* Australia, the *Evening Standard*, Conde Nast *Traveler*, *Vanity Fair* and *Elle*. There have been arty glamour gigs working for BBC Scotland, being a presenter on SBS TV and, most recently, on Foxtel's *By Design*. Currently she divides her time between New York and Sydney. Her first book was *Three Black Skirts*, published in Australia and America.

Since she was first published in 1995 **Marian Keyes** has become a publishing phenomenon. Her six novels, *Watermelon, Lucy Sullivan is Getting Married, Rachel's Holiday,*

Last Chance Saloon, *Sushi for Beginners* and *Angels* have become international bestsellers and have sold almost six million copies worldwide. She is published in several languages, the most exotic of which are Japanese and Hebrew. Her collection of journalism, *Under the Duvet*, was published in 2001. She lives in Dublin with her husband and is addicted to handbags, shoes and white Magnums.

Adèle Lang is best known as the author of *What Katya Did Next*, which recently entered the *New York Times* bestseller list under the new title *Confessions of a Sociopathic Social Climber*. She is also co-author of *How to Spot a Bastard by His Star Sign* and author of *The Best Book of Girls Behaving Badly . . . Ever!* Naturally, she bears no resemblance to any of her fictitious female characters (including the one featured in *Big Night Out*).

Lauren Laverne was born in a front bedroom in Sunderland, UK, in 1978. She attended convent school, where her chief concerns were avoiding PE and exactly how much lip gloss could be applied before incurring Nun-wrath. She took up with two like-minded reprobates, enlisted her brother, formed a band at a party and accidentally got signed to EMI records. The band, Kenickie, enjoyed the pop low-life and had many adventures involving nightclubs and 24-hour garages. Two albums and several *Top of the Pops* appearances later, Laverne was once more making empty boasts about her abilities at a party which she subsequently had to back up. This led to her current TV and radio career. She lives in Cheam, London, and enjoys quilling. Okay, that last bit was a lie.

Helen Lederer began her career as a stand-up comic in the early 1980s, surviving the Comedy Store and culminating in a sell-out show at the Edinburgh Festival. Probably best known for her performance as Catriona in BBC TV's *Absolutely Fabulous*, she has also appeared in many other shows including *Harry Enfield's Television Programme, One Foot in the Grave, Happy Families, Girls on Top* and *Casualty*. She wrote and performed her own material for *Naked Video* for BBC2, 'Life with Lederer' for Radio Four and currently contributes a regular column for 'Woman's Hour'. She is about to embark on writing her second series of 'All Change' for Radio Four – about the lot of a woman ageing disgracefully. She writes for the *Telegraph* and apart from contributing to *She* magazine, the *Mail On Sunday* and the *Independent*, she also wrote *Single Minding* (Hodder and Stoughton) and is hoping to soon complete her first television sitcom for the BBC. This will be after her stint in the *The Vagina Monologues* in London's West End and finishing her comic novel for Penguin. She occasionally re-visits the world of stand-up to keep herself hungry and sharp – but from an older perspective.

Bem Le Hunte is half-Indian and half-English. She studied Anthropology at Cambridge and has worked as a writer since graduating. Her debut novel, *The Seduction* *of Silence*, is a story involving five generations of Indian women, and is a tale of love, spirituality and daring set in the foothills of the Himalayas and the swinging London of the 1960s. The novel is an international bestseller and was shortlisted for the Commonwealth Writer's Prize. Having recently received an Asialink scholarship and the New South Wales Literary fellowship, Bem is now living in Sydney and working on her second novel.

Kathy Lette first achieved *succès de scandale* as a teenager with the novel *Puberty Blues*. After several years as a singer in a rock band and a newspaper columnist in Sydney and New York (collected in her book *Hit and Ms*), she worked as a television sitcom writer for Columbia Pictures in Los Angeles. Her other novels, *Girls' Night Out*, *The Llama Parlour*, *Foetal Attraction*, *Mad Cows*, *Altar Ego* and *Nip 'n' Tuck* have all become international bestsellers. Kathy's plays include *Grommits*, *Wet Dreams*, *Perfect Mismatch* and *I'm so Happy for You, Really I Am*. She lives in London with her husband and two children.

Paul Livingston is currently a bi-weekly contributor to the *Australian Weekend* magazine with 'The Flacco Files', an illustrated commentary on the state of being which also appears in book form published by Allen & Unwin. Paul's acting credits include *Babe: Pig in the City*, *Mr Accident*, *Dark City*, *Children of the Revolution* and *The Navigator* (AFI nomination best supporting actor). His novel *The Dirt Bath* was published in 1998 by

Penguin. In 1996 Paul was the joint winner of the Sidney Myer Performing Arts Award for outstanding achievement in the performing arts in Australia. In 2001 his play *Emma's Nose* completed a successful season at the Belvoir Street Theatre in Sydney. As Flacco, Paul has toured extensively in Australia and internationally with regular appearances at festivals in Edinburgh and Montreal. Flacco's many television credits include *Good News Week*, *GNW Nite Lite*, *Sandman and Flacco Special* for the Ten network, *Good News Weekend*, *The Big Gig*, *Daas Kapital* for the ABC, and he was a regular on the Triple J Breakfast program from 1994–97.

Gay Longworth was born in 1970 and lives in London with her husband, theatre producer Adam Spiegel. After graduating from university (Durham/Birmingham) she trained as a physical oil trader, the sinister side of which steered her towards writing her first novel, *Bimba* (Pan). *Bimba* was published in 1998 and *Wicked Peace* (Pan) followed two years later. *Dead Alone*, the first in a series of Jessie Driver novels, was published by HarperCollins in September 2002. She is currently working on the second.

Allegra McEvedy's cooking background is international. Her experience, despite only being thirty, is extensive. She has worked in numerous restaurants throughout the world including River Cafe (London), Tribeca Grill (New York) and Rubicon (San Francisco). As of 2002, she is the chef in residence at the ICA on the Mall in London. She catered for an exclusive Democratic Party fundraiser while in New York. Her book *The Good Cook* was published by Hodder and Stoughton in 2000. Allegra's TV credits include presenting the show *The Food File* for Channel Four, *Good Morning America* for CNBC, *Football Fever* BBC, *Big Breakfast* Channel Four and she has a six-part TV series in development. Allegra also writes columns in the weekly *Evening Standard*'s *ES* Magazine and the monthly magazine *Living Etc*. She is based in West London.

David McKay has a diverse involvement in both fine arts and the film industry. His distinctive paintings have been exhibited in Australia and internationally as well as being a permanent part of private and commercial collections all over the world. David's unique style was quickly recognised by the arbiters of Australian popular culture, Mambo, and they have continued to use his evolving designs and illustrations for almost two decades. Concurrent to his career as a painter, David has an ongoing active role in television advertising and film production and is currently working as a director and as a production designer. His short film, *Hoppin' Mad*, has won numerous awards at both local and international film festivals. In collaboration with his sister, Kirsten, and writer Anna Johnson, David created an acclaimed cookbook/CD package for Random House, *The Cosmic Feast*, and went on to produce a sell-out limited edition series of prints from the original book illustrations. Born in the Year of the Pig on a Virgo/Libra cusp, David resides in Redfern, Sydney, with his blue heeler, Betty.

A member of the Go-Betweens, **Grant McLennan** also has a successful solo career. The Go-Betweens moved to London from Australia in the early 1980s and achieved considerable commercial success and widespread critical acclaim, becoming one of the greatest indie bands of all time. They are included in Nick Hornby's music anthology and their latest CD was released in 2001.

Muriel MacLeod was born and educated in the Western Isles of Scotland. As well as being an artist, she is a writer and film producer. When not producing films, Muriel spends her time on her other creative interests, a regular weekly illustration featured in *The Times Education Supplement*, and she has just written her first novel. She is presently working on a screenplay about the history of the Western Isles, a fascinating history of the island so close to her heart. She has two children and has been living in London since the 1960s, with regular visits back to her homeland.

Gil McNeil is the author of *The Only Boy for Me*, and co-editor with Sarah Brown of the anthology *Magic*, which raises funds for the National Council for One Parent Families' Magic Million Appeal. She is a consultant at Brunswick Arts, a public relations company specialising in arts and cultural projects within the Brunswick Group, and she works with Sarah Brown on a non-profit venture, PiggyBankKids, which organises a range of voluntary projects for charities to support their fundraising efforts. She is currently working on her second novel, and lives in Kent, England, with her son.

In recent years, **Deborah Mailman** has become somewhat of an Australian household name. With acting experience spreading across all mediums, she has been acclaimed for her roles in theatre, TV, and in film. Most recently, Deb has been seen as the loveable Kelly in *The Secret Life of Us*, the role for which she received a Logie Award in 2002 for Most Outstanding Actress. The immense success of the film *Radiance*, in which Deb played the character Nona, won her an AFI award for Best Actress in 1998. Late in 2002 she will perform in the one-person play she co-devised *The 7 Stages of Grieving*.

Dorian Mode was born in 1966 – the day Arthur W. Falstaf revolutionised the culinary world by inventing the fork-and-spoon-in-one, known as the 'Spork'. He is a jazz musician and author of the comic novel *A Café in Venice*, published by Penguin. He has penned a screenplay currently in pre-production and has written features for several publications ranging from the *Sydney Morning Herald*'s 'Spectrum' to *Inside Sport*. He lives on the New South Wales Central Coast with his wife and two children, and he enjoys fishing and playing snooker with anyone born between 24 July and 23 August.

Karen Moline is the author of the million-dollar bestselling novels *Belladonna* (LittleBrown/Warner) and *Lunch* (Pan Macmillan), a film critic for BBC World Service Radio, a former 'Two on One' film columnist at the online magazine www.nerve.com, and interviewer for *The Big Breakfast* on Channel Four. She is also a freelance entertainment journalist who has written about Hollywood and pop culture for dozens of magazines and newspapers in the US, UK and Australia, including *Tatler*, *Vogue*, *Harper's Bazaar*, *W*, *Elle*, *Premiere*, *Company*, *New York*, *The Financial Times*, and the London *Evening Standard*. She lives in Manhattan, where she's writing her next novel, *Game Over, You Win*.

Sacha Molitorisz was born in 1969 in Munich, Germany, where his first words were 'Ein Bier, bitte.' He arrived in Australia in 1973, aged four, just in time to see the unveiling of the Sydney Opera House. Sadly, the unveiling of Sacha proved less of a critical hit. With his Lederhosen and humourlessness, he found few friends. Fortunately, however, after studying Arts (English lit) and Law (even more fiction) at UNSW, he discovered writing, through which he not only landed a job at the *Sydney Morning Herald* but also learned to create imaginary friends. By a bizarre stroke of luck, his wife, Jo, is real.

Reg Mombassa, a.k.a. Chris O'Doherty, was born in 1951 in Auckland, New Zealand. Attended National Art School, Sydney, 1975–77. Began exhibiting at Watters's Gallery, East Sydney, 1975. Has worked as a freelance graphic artist for Mambo since 1986. Member of rock bands Mental As Anything since 1976 and Dog Trumpet since 1990. Designed the stages, inflatables and athletes' shirts for the Sydney 2000 Olympic Games Closing Ceremony.

Julia Morris found her in-road to the entertainment industry as a singer and choreographer with Club Med villages all around the world. She returned to Australia to pursue stand-up comedy where she became resident MC and Manager at Sydney's Original Comedy Store. She has appeared in a number of shows on Australian television including her own series *Great Aussie Bloopers* and in 1997 Julia presented 'The Morris Report' for *In Melbourne Tonight*, allowing her to interview such celebrities as George Clooney, Boy George and Bananarama. Her show at the Edinburgh Festival 2001, 'Edinburgh or Bust', won her the Herald Angel award for excellence in live performance. She now lives in London and tours regularly.

Since she burst on the scene in 1990, after being spotted by Storm MD Sarah Doukas, it was obvious that **Kate Moss** was special. During the past decade she has transcended the traditional conventions of modelling by becoming a style icon. Never a follower and always a leader, she continues to beguile both the fashion industry and her army of fans in the public arena.

Tara Moss was born and raised in Canada, and currently resides in Australia as a dual citizen. She has been travelling the world as a top fashion model since the age of fourteen, and has been writing fiction since she was ten. Her first full-length novel, *Fetish*, is a bestseller and was shortlisted for the Ned Kelly Award for Best First Novel. Her second novel, *Split*, has just been released in Australia where it already shares the nationwide top ten fiction bestseller list with the likes of John Grisham, Stephen King, James Patterson, Jeffrey Deaver and J. R. R. Tolkien. You can visit Tara at www.taramoss.com.au

Patrick Neate lives and works in London, often at the same time. He is the author of two novels published by Penguin: *Musungu Jim and the Great Chief Tuloko* which won a Betty Trask Award in 2001, and his most recent *Twelve Bar Blues* which won the Whitbread Novel Award in 2002. His forthcoming novel, *The London Pigeon Wars*, is to be published in 2003 and Bloomsbury will soon be publishing his non-fiction book about the global dominance of hip-hop. It doesn't have a title yet but when it does it's sure to be funky.

Tyne O'Connell's five novels have been translated into French, German, Czech, Slovak and Estonian. Born in Australia, Tyne was educated by Catholic nuns in the arts of deportment, elocution and how to seat people at embassy dinners. After a decade travelling the globe playing poker and backgammon, she moved to Mayfair, London. She has sold two pilot scripts to Hollywood and written articles for *Ms* Magazine USA, *Elle* UK, *Vogue*

Australia, *She* Magazine, *Journal* UK, and *marie claire* Australia. Tyne feels equally at home in the deserts of Africa or the jungles of Asia as she does in the designer stores of Bond Street – as long as there's a poker game in the offing. Her website address is www.tyneoconnell.com

Jamie Oliver is famous as The Naked Chef with a successful TV series, cookbooks and CDs.

Anthea Paul is the author of the bestselling books *Girlosophy – A Soul Survival Kit* and *Girlosophy 2: The Love Survival Kit*. She is the CEO of GIRLOSOPHY, the soul-survival company and www.girlosophy.com. She has worked internationally as a stylist, trend forecaster, photo editor, ski patroller, creative director and art director, and has lived in New York, London and Los Angeles. Currently Anthea is working on a joint project, *21st Century Goddess*, with co-authors Jessica Adams and Jelena Glisic, as well as producing and writing the two new books for the award-winning Girlosophy series. She also contributes to various magazines. Along with her writing commitments she is designing and developing a line of surfboards, and sponsoring a group of young women surfers based in the Margaret River region to help them achieve their goals in the sport. Anthea lives and works on the northern beaches in Sydney, Australia.

Andiee Paviour lives in Sydney with her partner, their twins, a tiny dog and a disdainful cat. She is the movie reviewer for *Who Weekly* magazine and when not sitting in the dark, runs around a lot with various pre-teen children in tow. Andiee has written for *Mode, Cleo, Cosmopolitan, Harper's Bazaar* and *Elle*. With Lindsay Simpson she was co-author of *More Than One: Twins and Multiples and How to Survive Them* (Simon & Schuster), and author of *Unchain My Heart: Memoirs of a Modern Wife and Mother* (Pan Macmillan). Andiee's first novel, *The Would-Be Wife* (Penguin) was published in 2001. She is currently working on her second.

Andy Quan is the author of the short fiction collection *Calendar Boy* (Penguin/New Star Books) as well as a book of poetry *Slant* (Nightwood Editions). Canadian-born, he lives and works in Sydney and is a board member of the Sydney Gay and Lesbian Mardi Gras. Catch him at www.andyquan.com

Scottish by birth, **Gordon Ramsay** was brought up in England. While playing football for Oxford United he was spotted by a Glasgow Rangers scout. After completing trials he was signed by Glasgow Rangers at the age of fifteen. Three years later he gave up professional football and went back to college to complete an HND course in hotel management. He moved to London and joined Marco Pierre White at Harvey's. After a couple of years he moved to Le Gavroche to work alongside Albert Roux. This was followed by three years working in France. In 1993 he became part owner of Aubergine in London, where he won many accolades including two Michelin stars. He has had four cookery books published and has appeared numerous times on TV, including Channnel Four's *Boiling Point* and *Faking It* and BBC's *Friends for Dinner*. In 1998, aged thirty-one, he set up his restaurant, Gordon Ramsay, which has gone on to win three Michelin stars and was recently voted second best restaurant in the world by the industry. Gordon opened Petrus with his partner Marcus Wareing in 1999, and Amaryllis in Scotland in 2001, which won its first Michelin star in January 2002, and in October 2001 he opened Gordon Ramsay at Claridge's which has received extraordinary critical acclaim. Later this year Gordon will take over the kitchens of the Connaught in London.

Rebbecca Ray is the author of *A Certain Age* (Penguin) and has a second novel coming out soon. She lives in London.

After leaving St Martins University, England, in 1993, **Nick Robertson** worked as an artist for three years, developing his work and graphic approach. His company, Wordsalad, was set up in 1996 and has worked across a wide range of areas including all areas of print design from books and CDs to large-scale corporate branding, editorial and publicity design, animation and new media. Nick has worked with individual artists such as Brian Eno and Peter Ackroyd and with Peter Gabriel's Real World Records. He has also done a series of animated installation exhibitions at the ICA, Sadlers Wells, Mass and The Big Chill festival, and was recently showcased on a Channel Four documentary for his visual collaborations with musicians. He regularly receives private commissions and lectures in design at various universities throughout the country.

Max Sharam was raised on a large property in Victoria. After graduating from performing arts college, Max took her guitar to Europe, where she sang, wrote and performed her own compositions in many clubs. She performed in several musicals, plays and television programs around Europe before heading to Japan where she spent a year studying Taiko drums and fronting a band in Hiroshima. After returning to Australia, Max signed with Warner Music. Her debut EP, *Coma*, hit the top-ten nationally, and her follow-up album, *A Million-Year Girl*, was also very successful, receiving strong critical acclaim and eight Aria nominations. In 2001 she staged her one-woman show, *Mad'moselle Max*, at the Melbourne International Comedy Festival. Max is now living in Los Angeles where she is slowly producing her second album, and directing a documentary. In her spare time she loves to draw and drink.

Born in Glasgow, actor **John Gordon Sinclair** came to fame when he took the lead role in the film *Gregory's Girl* (1980). He had already starred in *That Sinking Feeling* (1979) and followed both up in Bill Forsyth's third hit *Local Hero* (1983). Subsequently, he has appeared in several TV sitcoms, including *An Actor's Life for Me* (1985), *Nelson's Column* (1994) and *Loved by You* (1997). In 1995, Sinclair won an Olivier Award for his stage performance in *She Loves Me*. Further film success has come with Terry Jones' comedy *Erik the Viking* (1989) and the wartime drama *The Brylcreem Boys* (1997). A re-partnering with Bill Forsyth gave rise to *Gregory's Two Girls* (1999).

David Smiedt was born in Johannesburg, lives in Sydney and chafes in humid climates. He is the author of *Boom-Boom: 100 Years of Australian Comedy* (Hodder), *Delivering The Male* (Penguin) and has also written pieces for numerous anthologies. His work has appeared in magazines including *Elle*, *Cosmopolitan*, *marie claire*, *New Woman*, *Architectural Review* and *Men's Health*. He has few other accomplishments of note.

Adam Spencer started out studying Arts/Law and ended up studying for a PhD in Pure Mathematics. He is a debating champion and a Belvoir Street Theatresports veteran. Adam presents the Breakfast Show on Triple J radio and the science programs *Quantum* and *FAQ* on ABC television, and has appeared regularly on the TV comedy programs *Good News Week* and *O'Loughlin on Saturday Night*. He enjoys wrestling with the *Times* cryptic crossword every day and has supported Manchester United for over twenty years (no bandwagon-hopping here). He has a friend who is a very good cook.

Natasha Stott Despoja was born in Adelaide in 1969, and received her political grounding at Adelaide University, graduating in 1991. In 1995 she was appointed to the

Senate to represent the Australian Democrats and at the age of twenty-six was the youngest woman to enter Federal Parliament. She was (subsequently) elected in 1996. In 1997, Senator Stott Despoja became Deputy Leader of the Democrats and, in April 2001, Leader of the Democrats – the youngest person of any Party to hold such a position. Senator Stott Despoja has made a significant contribution to a wide range of policy debates from higher education to biotechnology and is committed to Australia becoming a republic.

Richard Stubbs, one of Australia's finest stand-up comedians is a potent force in Australia's radio, television and live stand-up markets. His TV credits include that of writer, interviewer, co-host, host, actor and comedian on many of Australia's top comedy and variety shows, including hosting 120 *Tonight Live* shows aired on Channel Seven nationally. He is one of the mainstays on broadcast radio and has been entertaining successfully over the past sixteen years. Richard's first published book was on the shelves in 1998 titled *Still Life – Thoughts of a Man Hurriedly Going Nowhere* and he is set to begin on *Son of Still Life* in the near future as readers eagerly (and his publisher angrily) await the promised hilarious sequel.

Kathleen Tessaro was born in Pittsburgh, studied drama at Carnegie-Mellon University and emigrated to London sixteen years ago. After ten years working as an actress in films, television, and theatre, she left the profession and spent several years with the English National Opera, while training in the evenings as a drama teacher and voice coach at the Guildhall School of Music and Drama. During this time, she met author and fellow expatriate Jill Robinson, who encouraged her to start writing. Working on short stories during her lunch hour, she soon became a regular member of the Wimpole Street Writers Workshop, a collection of women authors who meet in Jill's home every week. Her first novel, *Elegance*, is due to be published in May 2003 by HarperCollins. She met her husband, classical musician James Rhodes, while queuing for a drink at a performance of *Rigoletto*. They were married last year and live in North London.

Jamie Theakston is one of the UK's highest-profile radio and TV presenters. Born in 1970, he first started his show biz career working on GLR Radio as a sports reporter before moving on to BBC2's *O-Zone* in 1995. He has co-hosted BBC1's Saturday-morning epic *Live and Kicking* and Channel Four's *The Priory*, and presented *Top of the Pops*. He also co-hosts *A Question of Pop* for the BBC as well as his newest show *Holiday – You Call the Shots*. He also presents the 'Jamie Theakston Cricket Show' on Radio Five Live throughout the summer and has his own radio show on Saturday morning on Radio One. He recently played the role of Serge in *Art* in the West End and hosted the BBC's coverage of the Golden Jubilee music concert in the grounds of Buckingham Palace.

Scarlett Thomas was born in London in 1972. She is the author of *Bright Young Things* (Flame, 2001) and *Going Out* (Fourth Estate, 2002). She has written articles and short stories for publications including the *Guardian*, *Butterfly*, the *Stealth Corporation* and *Black Book*. In 2000 she contributed to the controversial anthology *All Hail the New Puritans*. The *Independent on Sunday* recently included her in a list of the twenty best young writers in the UK. She is currently working on her next novel, and reviewing books for the *Literary Review* and the *Independent on Sunday*.

Emma Tom lives in Sydney. By day, she writes a column for *The Weekend Australian* and by night she works on novels. Her third book, *Evidence*, was published by HarperCollins in August.

Louise Wener grew up in suburban Essex and went to Manchester University where she formed her first band. Well known as the lead singer and songwriter of platinum-selling group Sleeper, she currently lives in North London where she writes full-time. Her debut novel, *Goodnight Steve McQueen*, was published by Hodder and Stoughton in August 2002.

Claudia Winkleman was born in 1972. She studied History of Art at Cambridge University and then worked as a fashion editor for *Tatler*. She presents *Holiday* on BBC1 and *Fanorama* on E4 and she went around the world for a BBC special. She is a travel writer for various newspapers and magazines.

Michael Witheford was a music journalist and member of several criminally underrated Australian bands in the 1990s. Feeling increasingly out of touch with 'the kids' and not too keen on getting tattoos either, he retired and drew on the years of heartache to write his first novel, *Buzzed*, which was published by Penguin in 2002. His mother enjoyed it very much but thought all the swearing was unnecessary. Michael lives in Melbourne and describes his short story for this anthology as a 'parable . . . or a fable' because he can never remember which one's which.